BRING
IT

SEELEY JAMES

Published by
Machined Media
12402 N 68th St
Scottsdale, AZ 85254

BRING IT, Sabel Origins #2
Copyright © 2014, 2015, 2018 Seeley James
Original publication, v1.0 April, 2014
This version is v3.30, 14-September, 2017
Formatting: Andrew Montooth
Cover Design: Damonza
Digital ISBN: 978-0-9886996-9-4
Print ISBN: 978-0-9886996-3-2

ACKNOWLEDGMENTS

My heartfelt thanks to the beta readers and supporters who made this book the best book possible. Alphabetically: Melissa "Iceterrors" Capo-Murray, Alun Humphreys, Ken Newland, Jeannine Chatterton-Papineau, LoriAnn Shisk, Gloria Smith, Gail Weiss, and Sue Whitney.

- Amazing Editor: Mary Maddox, horror and dark fantasy novelist, and author of the Daemon World Series http://marymaddox.com
- Extraordinary Editor and Idea man: Lance Charnes, author of the highly acclaimed *Doha 12, SOUTH,* and *THE COLLLECTION.* http://wombatgroup.com
- Medical Advisor: Louis Kirby, famed neurologist and author of *Shadow of Eden.* http://louiskirby.com
- Romantic Ideas Editor: Pam Safinuk

A special thanks to my wife whose support, despite being reluctant to say the least, has been above and beyond the call of duty. Last but not least, my children, Nicole, Amelia, and Christopher, ranging from age sixteen to forty-three, who have kept my imagination fresh and full of ideas.

SABEL SECURITY SERIES

SABEL SECURITY #1, ELEMENT 42

When he goes off his meds, legendary veteran Jacob Stearne can hear the voice of Mercury, winged messenger of the Roman gods. Is it insanity or divine guidance? He must keep it together to help his boss Pia Sabel stop Big Pharma from culling the population.

SABEL SECURITY #2, DEATH AND DARK MONEY

Mercury appears in the flesh to guide Jacob and Pia as they try to stop foreign billions flowing into American elections.

SABEL SECURITY #3, DEATH AND THE DAMNED

Jacob Stearn wrestles with his sanity while Pia Sabel wrestles with billionaires smuggling terrorists into the country. Is Mercury helping or hurting their mission?

COMING OCT-2017:
SABEL SECURITY #4, DEATH AND TREASON

A dying man gives Pia clues to Russian plans to dismantle American democracy. She and Jacob will face the most emotionally traumatic series of events in their lives. Lucky, they can rely on Mercury's heavenly assistance. Probably.

SABEL ORIGINS

Ever wonder what Pia and Jacob were like when Jacob was still on his meds and no one knew about Mercury? Read Origins.

SABEL ORIGIN #1, THE GENEVA DECISION

Athlete Pia Sabel must learn fast when she's forced to take over her father's security company.

SABEL ORIGIN #2, BRING IT!

Jacob Stearn must rescue the boss when she takes on an enhanced interrogation operation working with pedophiles.

For Amelia & Chris

CHAPTER 1

PIA SABEL TRAILED FIVE YARDS behind Agent Marty, her head of security, as sunlight stabbed between the leaves overhead and the oppressive weight of Washington's summer pressed in. For the last three days, everything in her life had focused on those who hurled the javelins of power and those impaled on their spikes. In her twenty-five years, she'd grown accustomed to winning, from Buenos Aires to London to Beijing, and had long ago lost patience with anyone or anything that distracted her from her goal. Yet she was walking toward just such a distraction.

Agent Tania followed two yards behind. "You think they're really going to press charges?"

Pia glanced over her shoulder. "They can't. The State Department doesn't have the authority, or the evidence, or any enforcement charter."

"Then what the hell does State do?"

"Make sure US corporations get foreign contracts, make sure our spies have somewhere to hide, and make sure US travelers stay out of trouble."

"Foreign contracts? Is that how we won the Algerian deal?"

"The Secretary helped us land that one. That's the only reason I'm taking this ridiculous meeting."

They walked up the slight incline in silence. Marty reached the corner, checked both ways and made a hand signal, all clear, and disappeared to the right.

"But the letter said something about crimes against humanity," Tania said.

"You were there; you know we did the right thing."

"What you rich, white girls don't understand is guilty and innocent don't mean shit in court."

"You and Marty have Sabel Security lawyers at your disposal. But you won't need them, it's a bluff."

"Why do you care about that boy anyway?"

Pia turned around with a withering glare, bit her lip to stop herself from saying anything angry, and turned back.

"OK, sorry," Tania said. "I'm no psychologist but even I know this obsession with Mullaitivu is beyond your tortured-childhood thing."

Pia turned the corner. Ahead of her, Marty's head swiveled right and left, up and down, taking in every window and door in the forsaken neighborhood.

A bright glare reflected off a car's windshield, spearing her eyes. It took her back to that night and the blinding flash. The boy's eyes pleaded for help. He was inches from her outstretched hand when the tall Arab snatched him away. Bullets strafed the ground between them, denying her forward path. Then Tania blew up the gas tank on the resort's bus, the blinding flash, and the ensuing chaos changed everything. Her chance evaporated, the bad guys got away, and here she was, back in DC, waiting to hear some load of crap from a bureaucrat.

"OK, change of subject then." Tania turned the corner and hustled to keep pace with Pia's long strides. "Why'd we leave the limo way back there and walk five blocks? It's hotter'n hell today."

Pia kept walking.

"This would be a good time for one of your annoying little positive thinking speeches," Tania said. "Something like, 'heat is a state of mind,' or, 'people pay for this at the spa'. You got any pearls like that?"

Positive thinking was just what she needed. The Assistant Secretary of State, Donald Patterson, demanded she meet him in Carver Langston. The Major advised her to make a friend, not an enemy, of the man. Looking at the positive side, the State Department could be a powerful ally. But the tone of Patterson's email was far from positive. He riddled it with threats. And Pia never made friends with people who use threats.

Ten yards ahead of her, Marty picked a path through small wire tables scattered on the sidewalk and ducked inside a café. The scent of frying food covered the sidewalk like a layer of grease. In three seconds he popped back out and gave her a barely perceptible nod toward a table with two chairs near the curb. He took a seat near the café's door, his back to the brickwork.

Pia scraped back her assigned chair, positioned it facing the street, exactly opposite the table's other chair, and sat. They were uncomfortable chairs meant to keep patrons from overstaying their welcome. Indicative of the neighborhood as a whole.

Tania yanked a chair from the next table over, clattered it down next to Pia, and plopped in sideways, also facing the street. Tania's curly black hair sparkled as she shook it in the sunlight. Her dark skin was custom-made for late summer and contrasted well against her yellow polo shirt. With a quick scan, Tania measured the buildings, windows, and rooftops. She glanced over her shoulder. "Think they have a waiter?"

"You're not sitting with me."

"The hell I'm not. I dragged your ass off the bottom of the Atlantic. I sit where I want." Tania leaned back and laughed. "Besides, everyone knows you're in a mood. The Major told me to make sure you don't shoot anybody."

Not worth the argument.

Marty said, "Shooting someone might be necessary in this part of town. Three times the murder rate of the rest of the city. I'll say it again: *I don't like it.* Picking this hood is totally off for a government official, especially an O-6."

"I'm sure he has a reason," Pia said.

Pia took another look around. Air conditioners hung onto windowsills for dear life. Bad wiring looped from rooftops to telephone poles. Satellite dishes leaned out of the occasional window. Toys, worn and faded and broken, lay scattered in small, gritty yards. Across the street, the whole block had been converted to small businesses: a dry cleaner's that advertised self-serve washing machines, a dollar store that looked overpriced, a pawnshop armored with heavy steel bars, and a liquor store with a Bud Light sign that flickered behind dark glass. Powerball was up to forty-eight million. Two men in trench coats talked in the liquor store's doorway.

Pia pulled out her phone and called her assistant. "Send my

maintenance crew down here, and have them clean up a four-block radius. And bring some toys too. First thing in the morning. Yes, keep it anonymous."

Pia clicked off.

Tania said, "Why do everything anonymously?"

"Don't want to ruin my reputation."

A skinny guy with a scrawny goatee, wearing black pants and a white apron popped out the café door and smiled. Before he could say a word, Pia ordered three diet sodas.

She guessed the men at the liquor store were Mediterranean, originating somewhere between Israel and Greece: Crete, Syria, Lebanon, Cyprus. Albania, maybe? No way to narrow it down without getting a better look, but they were definitely out of place for the neighborhood.

"You going to marry Mark?" Tania asked. "He's a hottie."

"Shh. I need to focus."

"Just stating the facts." Tania settled back in her chair to keep watch.

Pia was in no mood for Tania's small talk. All she could think about was that one boy, out of all the others, his eyes wouldn't leave her alone.

The men in trench coats caught Pia's eye again. They were talking to someone inside, and not nicely either. She could tell by the way the backs of their heads moved—up and back while talking, down and forward afterward. It was contemptuous body language: exposing the throat as an invitation for the other party to strike—*Go ahead, take a shot*—and then lowering the chin when finished as a sign of domination—*Couldn't do it, could ya?* The men were using hand gestures too, but their hands disappeared from the sunlight into the inky blackness of the liquor store. After a last vehement gesture by the guy in the gray trench coat, they turned and walked down the sidewalk. Their faces pinched in hard, red anger.

Pia's mind rolled back to Patterson and the power he wielded. Was he acting like the men in trench coats across the street, rearing his head back, testing her resolve? Logically, she should give in. Do whatever he asked. Let him win, then move on. Even her father had said so. But she didn't like it. In the twenty years she'd spent playing soccer around the

4

world, giving up was never an option.

Patterson could help her if she could get him to understand the problem.

"What's the plan then?" Tania asked.

Pia sighed. "I don't have one. I don't even know what they want."

"Well, why're you watching those guys over there instead of thinking one up? You're good at thinking up plans."

"Then let me think."

"Don't worry about the guys across the street. Marty and I are tracking them. They're not a threat to us, but if that changes, we'll handle it."

"I know, but I might take them down just for practice," Pia said.

Tania crossed her arms and looked away.

When Pia couldn't solve a problem by thinking about it, she could usually solve a problem by not. She refocused her attention on the men across the street, a good mental distraction.

The trench coats went into the pawnshop. Loud voices greeted them. Hailed as if they were friends returned from a journey. This time they didn't stand in the doorway. They were sucked inside with a hearty welcome. The door closed.

The waiter came out carrying a tray with three Styrofoam cups. He set them down, one at a time, in front of Pia. As he moved the third and final cup from the tray to the table, she looked at him until his eyes met hers. The waiter hesitated, half-stooped over, glanced at Tania, then over his shoulder at Marty. The cup in his hand moved directly to Tania. He pulled two straws out of his apron and tossed them on the table. Pia thanked him. He nodded, picked up the third cup, and delivered it to Marty with a straw. Then he disappeared.

A few minutes later, the trench coats left the pawnshop. A fat man followed them outside. They stood on the sidewalk chatting and laughing for a few minutes. As they talked, the fat man nodded several times with his head bowed, then looked up and spoke. The trench coats liked what the fat man said and extended their hands for a shake. The fat man spread his hands wide, smiled, grabbed the gray trench coat's hand, and pulled him into a half hug and added a back pat. He repeated the familiar gesture for the man in the dark trench coat. The threesome parted. The men in trench coats turned and walked toward the dollar store, and the fat man went back to his pawnshop.

They infuriated Pia.

Tania stood suddenly. "There he is. Only suit on the street. Gotta be him, right?"

A block away, a man in a suit stood at a shop window, checking his reflection. He looked official and out of place and had government shoes. He appeared satisfied with his reflection and resumed his march up the sidewalk toward them. Pia noticed he kept his pace controlled, his steps precise, and his gaze leveled at her.

"You ever see him before?" Tania asked.

"No."

"But that's him, right? Looks like a navy guy, walks like a navy guy—gotta be a navy guy. So, you think he's going to arrest us?"

CHAPTER 2

DONALD F. PATTERSON, ASSISTANT SECRETARY of State, Bureau of Political-Military Affairs, exited the Stadium-Armory Metro stop at Nineteenth Street SE. He marched up the sidewalk with the same pride he had once felt on his destroyer's bridge. His mission reminded him of looking down the Strait of Hormuz to see the might of the United States Navy stretched out behind him. Destroyer after destroyer, sailing in tight formation, sending a clear message to Iran: *we dictate policy in these waters.* He was about to dictate policy again.

He took off his jacket, hooked it over his shoulder on a finger, and kept moving.

It was Patterson's good fortune to get the assignment. His boss had told him to report to the Under Secretary for Civilian Security and Human Rights for a special assignment, and there it was, like a gift: bring in Pia Sabel.

Something that should have been done years ago.

Rich kids are the scourge of any democracy. They never serve in the military, never work their way through college, never struggle in life. Yet they throw their money around in politics and causes, and people trip over themselves to lap up every dollar.

Pia Sabel's philanthropy may have endeared her to the masses long before she brought home a World Cup and Olympic gold, but Patterson knew her real story. It was high time someone brought her to justice. She'd had far too many privileges granted, too many sins forgiven. Someone had to make the arrogant young woman understand the consequences of her actions. She was not above the law—no matter how much money she had. No one can run amok in a third-world country, upend American operations, and walk away.

She had to be stopped.

And Donald F. Patterson was the right man to stop her.

Patterson had scripted his plan. He'd given it careful consideration, thought through Pia's possible responses, dreamed up her potential flanking maneuvers, and crafted solutions for those contingencies. He had this meeting covered from every conceivable angle. Just for practice, he ran through the script in his head and decided that it was perfect. When he was done, she'd never mention Snare Drum again. He nearly shivered with excitement despite the late summer heat.

Patterson made a crisp crossing at the intersection and continued marching north, toward C Street. According to his calculations, it was just under a mile to his destination—fifteen minutes from the Stadium-Armory Metro stop to the meeting. Altogether, he would be nine minutes late: late enough to signal his importance but not enough for her to cancel. Timing designed to make her understand who was in charge of this meeting.

He stopped at the light on Benning Road. There were no cars in sight. He waited. Two blocks to go. He felt a trickle of sweat run down his back. In uniform, he never let the sweat show. He could stand in sweltering equatorial heat, and the sweat would be contained in his T-shirt, roll down his back, down his leg, and pool into his shoes. He was confident in the knowledge that it would never stain his armpits.

But Patterson wasn't wearing the uniform he'd proudly worn for twenty years. He wore a summer-weight Brooks Brothers suit, highly recommended by his boss. Washington was a Brooks Brothers kind of town: not too fancy, not too cheap, not too fashionable, crisp and good-looking. But would it show sweat? He had no idea. He found a reflecting window on the next block, slipped his jacket back on, and checked his reflection.

As he looked for signs of perspiration, he fumed about the situation Pia Sabel had created. A Colonel was dead, an entire village was on a rampage, and Sri Lanka's Mullaitivu district was in upheaval—all thanks to her. Diplomatic outrage had been heaped on the American embassy in Kotte. The outrage bubbled back to Washington, to the Under Secretary. Then it landed on his desk.

He wasn't afraid of her.

Today she would answer to Donald F. Patterson.

Satisfied with his appearance, he turned and resumed his march.

Then he saw them: Sabel security agents. They were indeed professionals. Two assets were deployed for maximum coverage: one covering the southern approach, the other on the north. Right in the middle sat Pia Sabel—staring him down.

He maintained eye contact while assessing the others in his peripheral vision. The multiracial woman had spotted him first. She recalibrated her position, separating from her boss and her counterpart, making any attempt to shoot them exponentially more difficult. Not that he planned to shoot anyone. Her move was not a reaction to any threat he might pose. It was movement by instinct.

From his research, he knew the woman's name: Tania Cooper, a decorated veteran sniper with two Purple Hearts, courtesy of the Taliban before going to college and returning as a fast-track officer. Her service record had only one blemish, a sealed court martial that resulted in a demotion from captain to warrant officer. She left the Rangers days later and joined Sabel Security. Intelligence placed her in Sri Lanka at the time of last week's incident. The other agent was harder to identify. He was average build and average height, had a tight haircut, and was white with no distinguishing features. Most likely Agent Marty Browning, chief of personal security for Pia Sabel. Neither of them was a threat to Patterson. He had nothing to fear from bodyguards. There would be no violence. She must have brought a show of force just to intimidate him. But it wouldn't work.

Pia Sabel was a lot taller than he'd imagined. He knew she was a world-class athlete and knew she cross-trained and worked out like a fanatic, but that hadn't prepared him for seeing her in person. She had an extraordinary presence. She wasn't beautiful like Miss America, but a type of beauty emanated from her. Her countenance rippled with tension, as if a tremendous potential energy lay hidden just beneath the surface.

Like a tiger.

What struck Patterson most was the intensity in her eyes. Gray-green, they focused on him with unrelenting precision. She was measuring him, taking in the way he marched, the way he swung his arms, the way he shifted his weight with each step. She was calculating the length of his stride, the balance of his heel, the amount of bend in his knee.

Like a tiger.

Patterson took a deep breath and steeled himself. He twisted his neck, working out any kinks. Everything was going to be fine. He had decades of military experience, years of command, years of success. She was nothing more than an orphan fortunate enough to have been adopted by a grad student who became a billionaire. Anyone could succeed with that kind of luck.

She wore a snug, gray Under Armour tank top and tight yoga pants with running shoes. That surprised him. He'd expected a business suit— something more professional, something that indicated she was the owner of Sabel Security, not some kid on her way to the gym, even if her father had given her the company for a birthday present.

Patterson lifted his chin and marched straight toward her. He had a job to do. He'd planned his conversation from start to finish. He'd practiced it too. He was ready. He rewound the script to the beginning. First, he would establish dominance by placing himself directly in front of her, in her space. He grabbed the wire chair at her table and tugged it.

CHAPTER 3

PIA SABEL TURNED SLIGHTLY TO her right, giving her leg room to work. Patterson yanked the chair four inches off the ground, swung it through the air, and repositioned it closer to her. It was a power trip—an aggressive and presumptive placement away from the table so that nothing would stand between them. The man dropped the chair as dramatically as possible and stepped around it to sit down. He never broke eye contact. Neither did she.

All those years in soccer had taught her how to aim a powerful kick without ever looking down. Her body knew exactly where her leg and foot were—and where they needed to be in three milliseconds.

She kicked hard and fast. Her foot moved between his knees so quickly he had no time for defense. The sole of her running shoe connected with the leg of his chair. The chair skittered backward until one of the legs found a crack in the sidewalk, caught it, and flipped end over end with a series of loud clanks. In the same instant, she grabbed his tie. His butt was behind him, halfway to the now-missing chair. His backbone was forty-five degrees from standing.

For a split second they stared into each other's eyes.

Pia said, "You have a mother?"

"Of course I have—"

"Did she raise you to sit at a woman's table without asking permission?"

"Uh, no."

"No ... what?"

"No, ma'am." He turned red and missed a beat. "May I join you? Ma'am?"

Pia let go of his tie. "Were you going to ask me out on a date?"

His chin snapped back an inch. "No. Certainly—"

She pointed to the far side of her table, directly across from her. "Then put the chair back where it was. Now show me your identification."

Patterson picked up the chair, glanced at Marty and Tania, and brought it back to the table. He fit the chair in the narrow space between the table and the curb. She watched him make the calculations she'd already worked out. If he scooted back an inch, one leg of the chair would drop off the curb and send him tumbling backward into the street. He glanced her way like a condemned man and sat. He put a business card on the table between them.

"Did I ask for a business card?" she said.

He fumbled into his jacket, retrieved his State Department ID badge, and carefully placed it in her outstretched hand. He said, "I need to see your identification as well."

"No, you don't."

Pia examined his three-by-five badge. *Donald F. Patterson, Assistant Secretary of State, Bureau of Political-Military Affairs.* His title barely fit on the card and was followed by a departmental heading and division code. Instead of returning it, she placed the badge on the table between them.

"The President has a Secretary of State," Pia said, "who has two Deputy Secretaries and six Under Secretaries. You are the Assistant Secretary to the Under Secretary, four levels below the Secretary. Did it strike you as odd when they asked you to deal with me?"

"I asked to see your identification."

She tapped her fingernail on his badge. "Did you ask yourself why?"

Patterson said, "It is illegal for an American citizen to break the laws of a foreign government. That reciprocating concept exists between all civilized governments, forming the basis for extradition. You have been—"

"Did they make you feel special when they sent you, Patterson? Like you were on a high-profile mission that would change things?"

A flicker in his eyes, a pause in his verbal assault for a fraction of a second.

Then he tipped his head forward and forged ahead. He said, "The government of the United States of America will not stand idly by while a citizen acts as a self-appointed vigilante and executes an official of a foreign government. The State Department has restricted your passport and will—"

"Your handling of the naval standoff in Somalia was brilliant. You brought home American citizens and sent several pirate boats to the bottom of the sea without killing anyone. That's the career of a hero. Then, back when Obama was president, there was a four-year blank in your service record: no commendations, no command, no reprimands, no assignments. Usually that means, CIA duty. Now you're the Assistant Secretary, lackey to a political appointee. What happened, Patterson?"

Another pause in his verbal march.

He said, "You are required to turn you passport over to me—"

Pia slammed her palm on the table. "Get real. I have attorneys on call. I checked with them. Political-Military Affairs doesn't handle passports. There's a legal process involved, and you're not part of it. Now quit bluffing, and talk like an adult."

"You're right," Patterson said with a smirk, "normally I'm not part of that loop. But since I am meeting with you and I represent the State Department, I *will* be confiscating it. You will have a chance to exhaust your legal process later."

"While you search your pockets for the court order authorizing your *confiscation*, Patterson, tell me what your boss expects to happen."

His gaze stayed locked on her. "We can and will have the Justice Department issue a warrant to have you brought in. The charges in Sri Lanka are not something you can—"

"Let's pretend you get some kind of warrant. What happens next?"

"You come with me to answer charges," Patterson said. "After some court proceedings, you will be sent to Sri Lanka to stand trial. The government of Sri Lanka demands that you answer for the death of Colonel Nakdali, not to mention the village riots, the orphanage arson, and the destruction of the military compound. I have been assigned to ensure that you answer those charges."

Patterson punctuated his statement by leaning back.

"Extradition is a law enforcement matter," Pia said. "Why is the State Department involved?"

Patterson blinked and leaned forward. "We're trying to spare you any embarrassing headlines."

"Wrong."

He frowned. "Like it or not, that's what we're doing."

"Why you, Patterson? You moved from navy to State a couple months ago? Why did they pick a former navy captain with no legal or law enforcement experience to bring me in?"

"Your arrogance is overwhelming." Patterson stared hard as he spoke. "I'm as ranking an official as you deserve. We could have sent out a police officer. You're not that special."

"My father has a political philosophy," Pia said. "He believes Republicans cost twice as much as Democrats but stay bought twice as long. In the end, they cost the same. Last year, he was the largest contributor to both parties."

"Cynicism won't save you."

"I'm not my father. I don't give anything to either party. But that doesn't mean they don't want my money. Take a look at this picture." She pointed to her phone and slid it across the table. "Recognize the guy next to me waving the Fourth of July flags? Right—Secretary of State Highsmith after a few beers. He was hitting me up for Super PAC money."

Patterson glanced at the phone. His eyes widened, then narrowed. "Your problems have nothing to do with campaign donations. Your insinuation makes me sick."

"They are who they are, and they do what they do. Beats a monarchy any day. But, you know what makes me sick?"

"That you're going to answer for criminal charges in a foreign country?"

"They picked you because you execute orders without question—just as you did in the navy. They know you want to be a *great* Assistant Secretary so you can move up to Under Secretary—and they're pushing that button."

Pia leaned back in her seat and glanced across the street and back at

Patterson. She said, "My team blew up a wall and incapacitated twelve guards, but Colonel Nakdali was alive when I left. And the orphanage—was not an orphanage."

"Tell that to the authorities in Sri Lanka."

"I did. I told them before I went to Mullaitivu. I had a conference call with some bureaucrats who kept telling me I was wrong about the Colonel—even after they admitted they'd never heard of him. I wasn't wrong."

"You'll get your day in court."

"I keep asking myself," she said, "why would a decorated navy captain move to the State Department?"

"This isn't about me. You have to answer for the crimes—"

"Wrong. It is about you, Patterson. When you ask yourself why they picked you, you'll understand that." Pia let her words sink in. "Let me guess why you made the move to State. You wanted to make a difference in the world, so you joined the navy. But our enemy is a bunch of rats hiding in the mountains of Afghanistan and Pakistan, five hundred miles from the sea. Terrorists don't have navies. There will never be a battle like Leyte Gulf in your future—not even a Falklands War on the horizon. You moved because you wanted to make a difference."

Patterson's eye twitched.

It could have twitched because she nailed him. But he might have been impressed that she knew Leyte Gulf was the largest sea battle in history based on the tonnage of ships sunk. It was the kind of trivia she looked for in her pre-meeting research.

"We're not so different," Pia said. "I want to make a difference too. It's easier than you'd think. You just have to keep your eyes open and look for the right opportunities."

She pointed across the street, where the two men in trench coats were emerging from the dollar store. Patterson's gaze followed her finger. The men were yelling obscenities over their shoulders into the open door. A woman inside was yelling back. The obscenities were in a language Pia couldn't identify, but the inflection required no translation. The man in the gray trench coat stabbed a finger at someone deeper in the store and yelled even louder.

"Tell me," Pia asked, "why did you choose this neighborhood? So no one from Capitol Hill would see you? It's either here or Anacostia, right?"

Patterson nodded.

"Did you know that was going on?" she asked and pointed across the street.

"What do you mean? What's going on?" He turned to look.

Pia recounted the trench coats' movements and their arguments with the shopkeepers. She pointed them out again as they went inside the dry cleaner's. She asked, "What do you think they're doing?"

"I don't know," he said.

"I do. It's easy to see when you think about it. It's the trench coats on a hot summer day. That's not right." Pia shoved her chair back, nodded at Assistant Secretary Donald F. Patterson, and walked away.

CHAPTER 4

PATTERSON CLENCHED HIS FIST AND almost pounded the table with it. Instead he checked himself and ended up looking like an epileptic having a seizure. He wanted to grab her, yank her back, sit her down, and give her a stern talking to. Never had he seen such impudence, such wanton disregard for authority, such plain rudeness. Being raised by a single dad who was focused on his business had certainly left a vacuum in Pia Sabel's manners.

What bothered him most was the picture of the secretary with Pia. Patterson hadn't considered that kind of connection. He should have. He needed to mitigate his risk, create another way to shift blame if something went wrong. Since the Under Secretary believed himself to be in control of the operation, Ms. Sabel's connections would be the Under Secretary's problem. All Patterson had to worry about was whether he should report now or later that she'd left the negotiations.

He pulled out his phone, looked at it, and turned it over in his palm. How much did the Under Secretary need to know?

As he unlocked his phone to dial, he felt a firm hand squeeze his shoulder. At the same time, Agent Tania Cooper stepped into his line of sight. The hand would be from Marty, standing behind him. Tania would deliver the message while Marty took control without presenting a target. These guys were good.

"No calls, Mr. Patterson," Tania said.

"What are you talking about? I can call anyone—" Patterson felt the hand on his shoulder dig into his muscle precisely where a bundle of nerves wound through the collarbone. His arm went numb. The padding in his suit's shoulder offered no defense against Marty's grip. He winced.

Marty reached over and grabbed Patterson's phone while maintaining painful pressure on his shoulder. Patterson had no choice but to let go and watch it disappear behind him. The fingers digging into him relaxed. While his anger raged beneath the surface, he knew that only a cool head would prevail.

"Thanks for your cooperation," Tania said.

"Where did your boss go?"

Tania turned and looked across the street. "She hates witnessing crimes. Probably over there kicking some ass. That's her thing."

"Oh, I see," Patterson said, nodding his head. "It's some kind of setup or you two would be over there, keeping her safe."

"No setup. Check it out if you want. I'm not going over there because she'd be pissed if I got knifed or something. Nothing she can't handle on her own. But go on, see for yourself."

"If there's a crime in progress, why not call the police?"

"In this neighborhood?"

Patterson said, "You're in a lot of trouble. You know that, right?"

"I'm not. Those guys in the trench coats are."

"I don't mean here. I mean in Sri Lanka. We know you were there. If you come in and make a statement, I'm sure the prosecutors will cut you a deal."

"You hear that, Marty?" she said. "He must not know what went down in Mullaitivu."

"I know Colonel Nakdali is dead."

"If you'd been with us, you'd have killed him yourself."

"So you admit it then. You killed him."

"Nope. Ms. Sabel wouldn't let us. She's kinda anti-killing—a goodie-goodie type. But you expect that from a civilian who never served in the wars. Still believes in peace and love. If she'd been a veteran, she'd a killed him right off."

"I read your service record," Patterson said. "You were the victim of an IED, weren't you? Burned the flesh off your legs. Did that bother you? Did it set you off on a rampage? Murdering Muslims like Nakdali wherever you find them? Is that why you killed the only authority in Mullaitivu?"

Her eyes flashed with anger. "I told you, Ms. Sabel wouldn't let us kill anybody. But if you'd seen what Nakdali was—"

Her eyes flicked up and behind him. Marty had given her the sign to stop talking. She straightened up and said nothing more.

CHAPTER 5

LEAVING HER BAG BEHIND, PIA crossed the street, her long legs taking it in a few strides. She had only one focus: cleaning up the neighborhood. She would deal with Patterson later. She passed a beat-up motorcycle leaning against a bike rack and pulled open the dry cleaner's door. A cowbell hanging from the crossbar banged on the glass. She stepped into a small, dim space that smelled of laundry, warm and soft. Decades earlier the walls had been painted pale blue. The scuffs and scratches of customers carrying their loads covered every surface, dating the place in wear and tear. Even the calendar on the wall was on last March.

Two men in trench coats stood at a warped counter, their backs to her. Pia was taller than the average American male, and these two were shorter. The gray trench coat was barely five-nine, his darker associate an inch shorter. She labeled them Graycoat and Darkman.

A short, plump woman stood behind the counter. Her half glasses dangled from a chain onto her ample bosom. Her eyes were swollen, her cheeks streaked with tears, her posture weary. Three paces behind her, a man stood between the rows of plastic-covered clothes on wire hangers. His thin arms hung at his side while the sleeves of his T-shirt trembled.

Darkman glanced over his shoulder while Graycoat turned halfway to face her. The woman behind the counter gave her a startled look.

"May I help you?" the woman said.

"Oh, no, please," Pia said and gestured to the trench coats. "They were here first."

Graycoat stepped back, smiled a thin smile, and waved a hand toward the counter. *Go ahead.* Pia smiled politely back at him and stepped behind Darkman. She stopped in an awkward position. Her left leg was directly behind Darkman's right side, uncomfortably close. Darkman craned over his shoulder for a glance but quickly resumed staring at the plump woman.

"I forgot my ticket, but I remember the number," Pia said. She kept her eyes locked on the woman. The woman picked up a pad and pen. "It's C-A-1-1-9, um, eleven."

The woman wrote it down and looked at her pad, then back at Pia. She frowned. Pia nodded. They stared at each other for a moment. Slowly, the woman's eyes widened, she scribbled something more on the pad and handed it to the man behind her. He read the pad, turned, and walked down the aisle between the clothes.

"Where you guys from?" Pia asked Graycoat.

His eyes narrowed. His hand slipped inside his coat, moving for something.

He was on to her.

Now was her best chance if she intended to keep the element of surprise.

In an instant, she snapped her left knee into the bottom of Darkman's butt. An unsportsmanlike foul sure to earn a red card even in an English soccer match, it was a momentarily debilitating injury. The pain shot him upright and a little backward. Pia slipped her left arm around his neck, clasped her left hand with her right, and leveraged her right elbow into his back. The tension she applied was life threatening, a fact the man's face transmitted to his surprised friend.

She twisted to the right, holding him in front of her.

"It's called the LA choke hold," Pia said to Graycoat. "The LA Police Department banned it years ago because too many suspects died in custody. So let's make this quick. Drop the gun."

Graycoat made no attempt to hide his rage. His face turned crimson, and his lips pulled back to show gnashing teeth. He tugged harder in his coat.

Pia tossed Darkman's body across her hip. His scrambling legs tried to find solid ground but kicked Graycoat instead. The sawed-off double-barrel shotgun he was attempting to raise went off with a deafening bang, having not made it past forty-five degrees. Wood flooring splintered in the corner.

The woman behind the counter shrieked like an actress auditioning for a horror flick.

In the split second it took her adversaries to regroup, Pia kicked Graycoat in the side of the knee. His leg bent sideways and tendons snapped. Howling, he fell.

She maneuvered Darkman closer to the counter and banged her left knee into his butt—this time the other cheek. His knees weakened, and she threw her body weight high on his shoulders, driving his head into the counter. Grabbing a fistful of hair, she pounded his head a second and third time and let go. As his comatose form fell to the floor, she reached in and found his weapon.

Unfortunately, Darkman carried only a child's aluminum bat. The shotgun was still in Graycoat's hands.

Not the equalizer she'd hoped for.

Graycoat swung his gun.

Standing at an odd angle, she swung the bat underhand and knocked the barrel upward. It fired into the ceiling.

The plump woman shrieked again—this time with more feeling.

Pia smacked the underside of Graycoat's chin with the bat. He snarled and brought the gun barrel up a notch, as if she wouldn't notice. She jabbed the bat hard into his windpipe.

She heard footsteps behind the counter and ignored them.

"Two barrels," she said, panting away adrenaline, "two shots fired—you're empty. Drop it, and I won't have to split your skull open."

His eyes were wild with rage, but he kept the gun.

She shook her head, squatted next to him with the bat readied to strike another blow, and said, "Know the difference between a regular athlete and an Olympian?"

He glared at her.

She heard the sound behind the counter again. Not good.

She swung again, and the shotgun skittered across the floor.

Movement in her peripheral vision drew her eyes up. A man in a tan barn jacket reached over the counter with a pistol in his hand. With another swing of the bat, she caught a piece of his wrist before he could aim. The gun flew out of his hand into the air. He thrashed for it with both hands and managed to catch it.

Graycoat saw an opportunity and punched her in the jaw, sending her sprawling backward on her rear end.

As she crabbed to a better position, the two men came at her.

Barnjacket tried to jump the counter. It was wider than he'd thought, and he fell to his knees. He scrambled upright.

Graycoat leapt to his feet only to have his injured knee betray him. He fell and rolled in agony.

Pia got to her feet first but lost the bat in her rush. She kicked Barnjacket in the face, grabbed his gun hand, and spun around. She tried to remember her training for this situation. It didn't come to her, so she bit his wrist as hard as she could. He yelled and countered with a stinging blow to the back of her head. She wheeled around, trying to snap his elbow, but he yanked his arm back and freed himself.

He still had the gun.

Pia faced Barnjacket and threw a left jab that he blocked like an expert. She could win a fistfight with a man only if he were untrained. This was the wrong man to fight. He had some skills.

So she drove her forehead into the bridge of his nose instead.

The gunman staggered backward, dazed but not enough to count him out. To her right, Graycoat ignored his broken knee and swung the shotgun like a bat. Pia dropped her knees fast, keeping her balance, and let the gun swing over her head. It caught the top of her skull with a glancing blow. Blood oozed from the gash. It wasn't serious, but it stung nonetheless.

Barnjacket stepped back to avoid the follow-through of his comrade's errant swing and tripped over Darkman's prone body.

Rising on her powerful legs, Pia planted a shovel punch in Graycoat's belly. Twisting her torso, she pounded Graycoat's head with her forearm and wrenched the shotgun out of his hand. She swung it and caught Barnjacket's wrist.

Again, he lost his pistol. This time, it clattered out of reach. He dove for it.

Pia swung the shotgun back into Graycoat's face, the wooden stock splintering across his cheek, leaving an ugly streak of blood behind. He staggered back a step, grabbing his face as his knee buckled again, and forced himself to stay upright.

Pia spun around and pressed the shotgun barrel into Barnjacket's back.

He froze, giving her just enough time to smack him in the back of his head but not enough time to stop Graycoat from yelling something in Arabic—no doubt something about the shotgun being empty. She tried to get a new grip on the shotgun to bash Barnjacket again when he rolled over and aimed his pistol at her.

"Freeze!" Tania's voice shouted from the doorway.

Startled, he fired two poorly aimed shots in her direction: the first through the window and the second over Tania's ducking body. She rolled and crashed into the counter, her gun trapped beneath her.

Pia leapt on Barnjacket, trying to beat him with the shotgun while landing her knees on his arms. The gun hit the floor as his body rolled underneath her in a wrestling move.

Wrestling was a sport she had no chance of winning. It was all weight and upper body. He could reverse their positions in a second if she didn't do something fast.

She jumped up, splitting her feet apart. At the same time, he tried to roll her over but grabbed air instead. The move gave her just enough time to jump a second time, landing her left foot on his wrist and her right on his face. She could keep him immobilized only as long as she didn't move. He stopped struggling for a split second while he thought about his next move.

Pia could feel the limping Graycoat coming up behind her. She needed a next move too.

"Freeze!" Tania shouted again. She scrambled to her feet and kicked Graycoat hard in the groin from behind.

Pia planted her feet, grabbed Graycoat, and used his momentum to throw him on top of his pistol-packing friend.

The bang was muffled.

Pia grabbed the bat off the floor and pulled it back, intending to swing at the first opportunity. But Graycoat wasn't moving. Neither was his friend.

Slowly and quietly, Graycoat rose on his hands.

Beneath him, blood gushed out of Barnjacket's head and spilled across the floor in a grotesque, expanding puddle. Barnjacket's right hand pointed at his temple where the bullet entered. The opposite side was missing a fist-sized chunk of skull.

The collision had pushed the gun into the perfect position for an unintentional suicide.

The woman behind the counter began an endless and horrific shriek.

Pia turned to the trembling man. "Call an ambulance."

He nodded rapidly and grabbed the phone.

"Should I dart him?" Tania asked, leaning over Pia's shoulder.

"Not yet."

Graycoat knelt over his dead associate. He looked up at Pia. She readied the bat for another strike.

He shook his head and held up his blood-stained palms, his eyes heavy with tears. There was an unmistakable resemblance in facial features between the two, a squared chin and thick brow. Barnjacket was a few years younger.

Graycoat's body slumped. His fight was over.

Pia gave him a moment to grieve.

Tania patted him down and put plasticuffs on him.

Pia nodded at Darkman, who was slowly regaining consciousness. She said to Graycoat, "Outside—carry him."

Pia moved behind them, hoping to conceal the fact that she was shaking with excess adrenaline and abject fear. Her knees quivered, and her hands could barely hold onto the bat. She pressed it to her leg and took a deep breath. She took another deep breath more slowly and a third even slower. Tania put a hand on her shoulder and squeezed. Calming down was always hard for her.

Graycoat hobbled over, Tania draped the other man's arm around him, and he staggered to the door.

As he passed her, Pia said, "Sorry about your brother."

"No good for us in America." He stopped and looked over his shoulder. "Omar was meant for education, not this."

His candor surprised her. She said, "Shame."

He nodded, took a last look at the body in the corner, and shuffled out the door.

CHAPTER 6

STEPPING INTO THE DAYLIGHT, THE shotgun tucked under one arm, the aluminum bat in the other, Pia marched the two trench coats outside. She'd seen enough concussions to know Darkman would be incoherent for hours—a classic grade IIIb concussion on the American Academy of Neurology's scale. She'd seen plenty of knee injuries and knew Graycoat would limp for weeks. And Omar? She could have resolved the confrontation several different ways, but an outburst of violence was the least expected and therefore her best option.

Would the police see it that way?

What bothered her was their strategy. Two guys in the front, shaking down a small business, she expected. But a third man in the back?

Marty crossed the street and double-checked the restraints while Tania kept a gun on the men.

The waiter brought a damp towel from the café and gave it to Pia with shaking hands. She pressed it to her head and nodded thanks. He turned and left without a word.

Patterson stood on the far curb looking both angry and uncertain. She waved him over. Halfway across the street, he hesitated for a split second when he saw her captives.

She tugged on Graycoat's arm. "What's your name?"

He looked over his shoulder at her with feeble eyes and said nothing. Marty pushed him to a seated position on the sidewalk. Graycoat winced in pain and pulled his associate next to him.

"Where you guys from?" she asked.

He didn't reply.

"How do you know Patterson?" she asked.

He didn't reply.

She squatted next to him. "I'm not the one who pulled the trigger. Omar made that decision. Tell me, how do you know Patterson?"

"I don't," he said. His eyes darted left and right.

Patterson approached and stopped three yards away. The two made eye contact.

"Where did you see him last?" she asked.

Darkman leaned over and threw up, saving his associate from answering.

"What have you done to these civilians?" Patterson said with a scowl and an indignant wave of his arm.

"Who are they, Patterson?"

For just a second, Assistant Secretary Donald F. Patterson looked ill. Then he straightened up and tugged the hem of his jacket down. "What have you done?"

"We'll leave that to the police."

"Praise Jesus in heaven!" A voice boomed from behind them. "You did it! You did it! You answered our prayers!"

Pia turned to see the woman from the dry cleaner's jump down the stoop and cross to her, the trembling man following in her wake. Pia let the woman give her a hug and lost her breath from the force of the embrace. Just when Pia began to see stars, the woman let go and took the damp towel out of Pia's hands. She pulled Pia's head down to her level, examined the wound, and dabbed at it.

"You're not a dream," the woman said. "You're real. Praise Jesus! Oh, how we prayed for salvation. Thank you Lord!"

Around them, others came out of their stores, hesitating in their doorways and staring at the captured men. Onlookers formed circles across the street.

"I'm Raissa. Pleased to meet you," the lady from the dry cleaner's said. She turned to the other store owners and shouted, "She did what none of you would do. She took down the Syrians. You should've seen her! One of them shot himself."

Her announcement was met with an odd silence.

Raissa turned back to Pia. "That's a nasty cut. You'll need stitches."

"A butterfly suture will do fine."

"I have one," the trembling man said and disappeared.

"Where did you learn to fight like that?" Raissa said.

"Started boxing when I was fifteen. It comes in handy now and then."

The trembling man returned and did his best to get the suture to stay in place. Pia thanked him.

Pia looked around at the small crowd scattered in clumps around the block. All eyes were turned up the street. She followed their collective gaze and saw an older SUV rolling toward them. Inside, three silhouettes were visible through blacked-out windows.

Agent Marty moved to the left, Tania to the right. Both drew their pistols.

The SUV angled across the street a hundred yards away.

The passenger window came down, exposing an indistinct face behind sunglasses and a hat. The man held a phone to his ear. The window behind him dropped, revealing only shadows. One could imagine a rifle held in the dim interior.

Tania stepped into the line between the SUV and Pia, planted her feet, and raised her gun, aiming directly in the second window.

The dark glass closed up, and the SUV turned around, driving over the curb, and rolling away slower than it had arrived.

"Permission to chase them down," Tania said.

"Trap," Marty said.

Tania nodded and holstered her gun.

"More of your friends, Patterson?" Pia asked.

The woman from the dollar store rushed out to them. "Was that Hamoud?"

Pia looked a question at her. Raissa introduced the rail-thin middle-aged woman as Louisa, owner of the dollar store.

"Goatee, short guy?" Louisa said. "He's their leader. Nasty little piece of—"

"Syrian mafia," the trembling man said. "We didn't have the payment today."

Patterson stepped close to Raissa. "Did you witness her assault these men?"

"Assault? *Assault?* Who do you think you—" Raissa's voice boomed until Louisa put an arm across her chest to brush her back.

"These men been coming around here for a month or more," Louisa said. "Them and their little boss, Hamoud. Don't know where they came from, but they took over. Killed a couple crackheads, kicked out some of those gangbangers, and took over."

Pia checked Patterson's reaction. He kept his eyes fixed on Louisa, his face blank.

With a roar, the SUV reappeared, barreling down the street toward them. The window came down, and a gun barrel poked out. Tania drew her gun and aimed at the gunman. Marty did the same, stepping to the curb and aiming at the driver. Both held their fire to avoid collateral damage.

Everyone fled. Patterson flattened on the sidewalk. So did Graycoat.

Pia ran to the motorcycle parked in front of the dry cleaner's.

No keys.

The trembling man leaned out the door, trying to stay narrow next to the wall. "Come inside, quick."

"I need the keys. Yours?"

He tossed her a small key and slipped back.

The first shot hit Darkman's chest. A chunk of flesh and bone and blood popped out his back. The second shot creased Graycoat's hair and ricocheted off the sidewalk. The third went high, into an upper-story window, as the shooter ducked to avoid Tania's aim. The SUV sped up and swerved down the street.

Everything Pia knew about motorcycles came from watching TV. That was the extent of her experience. She stepped on a peg, twisted the gas, and eased the clutch. The bike shot forward.

She stopped it, walked it a few clumsy steps to get the front wheel pointed in the right direction, and felt Tania jump on behind her. She twisted the gas and released the clutch again. They streaked over the curb into the street, wobbled left and right, and flew past a stunned Marty.

"Hey, you OK with this thing?" Tania shouted.

"Fine. Just like a bicycle."

"No, it's—"

"Just do the shooting."

The engine screamed as the rpms rose, begging for an upshift that Pia had no idea how to do. The tight confines of the street kept the SUV's speed down, allowing her to keep pace and even catch up.

As Pia closed in on the SUV, it hit the brakes. Smoke poured from all four tires as it drifted around a corner, nearly rolling in the process. Slamming on her brakes, Pia almost passed the cross street before swaying to a stop and turning. Accelerating, she once again nearly lost control.

Tania said, "Hey, let me drive."

"Who's going to shoot?"

"You can shoot a lot better than you drive."

"You're the sniper."

"I can't see over your shoulder."

Pia dropped her body close to the tank.

"STOP! STOP!" Tania screamed.

The SUV's back window opened upward, and a gun barrel aimed at them. Pia squeezed the brakes. Both tires melted into the pavement. She fought the front fork as it shuddered and vibrated in her hands. The bike slowed and leaned right. Tania leapt off, tucked in her arms, and rolled down the street. Pia stuck out a foot hoping to right the bike only to have it slide out from under her instead. Her right foot stung from the impact.

The SUV slid around another turn and disappeared.

Pia was left standing in the middle of the street watching the bike slide into a telephone pole a few yards away. She limped back to Tania and offered a hand.

Tania sat up on her elbows. "Next time, I drive."

CHAPTER 7

WHEN THEY ARRIVED BACK AT the scene, an ambulance and two squad cars were angled across the street. An officer was stringing up yellow crime scene tape while an emergency tech shook his head over Darkman. Several knots of onlookers gathered on the sidewalks, watching from a safe distance.

Two uniformed policemen and a plainclothes detective were taking statements. The detective questioned Patterson. A group of shop owners argued while waiting their turn. Pia approached the group.

"Don't deny it, Douglas. You were helping them," Louisa said. She raised a fist and began to charge at the fat pawnshop owner. "You useless piece of—"

Pia grabbed her arm and spun her around as the man flinched. "Hey, calm down. Everyone deserves a chance to explain himself."

Pia turned to Douglas and waited.

He looked her up and down, curled his lip in disgust, and turned to Louisa. "What're you doing sucking up to this white girl anyway? Just cause some bitch comes in from the burbs wanting to be the next Abe Lincoln doesn't mean you gotta kiss her ass. We got problems we gotta solve for ourselves."

"Oh really, Douglas? You're Mister Big Shot now?" Louisa said. "What was your plan then?"

"I was working on it. I had some things going on the inside. Say, why you wanna let a white woman run you around? She's just another one like them."

"Fool, don't you know who she is?"

"Hell yes. She's that rich bitch from Potomac." Douglas looked back and forth between Raissa and Louisa. "Don't matter. She'll just cause trouble, get it half done, we'll never see her again. We'll be stuck with the Syrians."

"What have they been doing?" Pia asked.

Raissa told her about the extortion ring headed by Hamoud and his countrymen. After they'd kicked out the gangbangers and drug dealers, they demanded protection money. The police were always reluctant to come to Carver Langston. City resources went to Georgetown and Capitol Hill first and Carver Langston last. When the business owners complained about ever-increasing prices for protection, the Syrians stepped up the violence.

"Did today's level of violence seem unusual?" Pia asked.

"Oh yeah," Raissa said. "They were looking for trouble."

Pia said, "How many of them are there?"

"I've counted thirty or more of them damned Arabs," Douglas said.

The detective called for Pia Sabel next. She excused herself from the locals and gave her statement.

Halfway through, the detective stopped her. "Why did you jump them?"

"They were wearing trench coats."

"What're you, the fashion police?"

"The only reason someone wears an overcoat in hot weather is to hide something."

"Every cop knows that. Where'd you learn it?"

"My dad started Sabel Security with Secret Service agents. They taught me how to read faces, clothing, and posture."

The detective tapped his pen against his chin.

"When I was ten," she explained, "an extortionist threatened to assassinate me if my father didn't send him money. Dad didn't like the threat, so he used the ransom money to start Sabel Security instead."

The detective's eyebrows rose. "Tough being rich, huh?"

She didn't answer.

After a beat he said, "OK, so you saw a couple guys in trench coats. Why not call the police?"

"You know the Homeland Security campaign 'If you see something, say something?' I think it should be 'If you see something, do something.'"

He eyed her for a moment. "Lots of ordinary civilians get killed thinking like that."

"I'm no ordinary civilian."

"Uh huh. You didn't think they were shoplifting?"

"In a dry cleaner's?"

He tapped his pen on his chin again and pursed his lips.

"That," she said, "and long coats are used for hiding guns. Shoplifters would use something lighter."

"Yeah, you do know your stuff."

The detective went back to the timeline and had her tell him the story three times. He checked it against Raissa's statement and cleared up details. Then he gave her a business card, turned her loose, and called up the next witness.

Patterson stepped to Pia. "We're not done. You need to come with me—"

"Damn right, we're not done. You have some explaining to do."

"Wait. You don't think I'm connected to this."

She grabbed Patterson's arm and dragged him to the back of a patrol car. Graycoat sat in the open door, handcuffed and shackled. She said, "What's your name?"

He stared straight ahead.

She said, "The people who sent you failed to tell you anything about me. That little omission cost Omar his life. You don't owe them anything." She softened her tone. "So, what's your name?"

He looked up at her and thought for a moment. He said, "You asked me what made an Olympian different. What is it?"

Pia recalled the question. "Reaction time. We have quicker reactions than other people. If you throw a punch, I'll get hit you first."

He nodded, then looked at Patterson and frowned. He sighed and leaned forward and rubbed his damaged knee. "Hamdi Dakka."

She leaned in, caught the man's gaze, and pointed at Patterson. "Where was the last place you saw this man?"

Hamdi looked at Patterson again, and his face tightened. "No more. I'm through with Snare Drum."

Patterson's face moved back as if dodging a slap.

Pia said, "Where did you see him before, Mr. Dakka?"

"Beirut."

"What were you doing at the time?"

"Applying for political asylum."

Pia stood and pushed Patterson back five yards. He didn't resist.

"I made a mistake," she said. "Earlier I asked why you picked this neighborhood, but I answered for you. Lawyers call that leading the witness. So this time answer me—why did you set the meeting in Carver Langston?"

Patterson looked away, took a breath, then tried to meet her eyes but failed.

"Did you know?" she said. "Or did someone set you up?"

He started to answer; his head shifted a millimeter to the side indicating a negative. But he stopped himself.

"Ever wonder why I accepted the meeting with you?" Pia asked.

Patterson looked at her, curious.

"Normally I'd send a couple lawyers to a meeting like this," she said. "But Agent Marty did the background on you and told me you were a decorated veteran. I believe in veterans, Patterson. Seven out of ten Sabel Security agents are veterans. I met with you because I thought you'd help me. So tell me who's pulling your strings."

"No one's pulling my strings."

"Either you're in on it, or you were played."

Patterson looked at the ground again.

"You figured it out," Pia said, "when you recognized Dakka. They were here to kill me. We both know it."

Patterson took a half step back. Pia stepped in.

"Look," Patterson said, "I have no idea what you're talking about. You have no reason to believe—"

"Why did you set the meeting in Carver Langston?"

"It was recommended to me."

"By whom?"

He shook his head and turned away. "You should, uh, come to the State Department to answer charges in the death of Colonel—"

"We knocked out twelve of nineteen guards before we blew the wall.

It was three in the morning. They didn't know what hit them, and they started throwing grenades. The civilians, if you can call them that, scrambled. People were running everywhere, bombs going off, a real war zone. I found the boy we tracked from Mumbai. He was shivering with fear. He was nine years old, kidnapped, abused, and in the middle of a firefight. He needed someone to save him, take him back to his family.

"But the remaining guards were closing in on my position. We were separated because I don't speak Hindi; I couldn't tell him to stay with me. A tall man with a beard picked him up and carried him to the docks. They were loading speedboats with everything they could carry, including some of the children from the—what did you call it?—*orphanage*?"

"You saw him? Close enough to remember?" Patterson said.

"Yes, and I'm going to find that boy."

"I meant the tall man."

Pia stopped for a moment. "After what I just told you, that's what you want to know?"

She stared at him and waited for an answer.

Patterson went pale, beads of sweat broke out on his forehead. After a moment he said, "You still have to answer for killing Colonel Nakdali."

"Five speedboats and one seaplane got away. We mopped up, liberated twelve children, and hunted down Nakdali. We found him cowering in the jungle. At first light, we brought in the local tribal elders. They were so shocked they couldn't decide if he should be flayed alive or boiled to death. They sent for elders from several other villages. I wouldn't let them kill him, but I couldn't stay there forever. I had to find the boy and the tall man. Nakdali was alive and in their hands when we left."

"As I said before, tell it to the Sri Lankans."

She asked, "What were your orders today?"

"To bring you in."

"From a neighborhood where you turned loose a bunch of Syrian thugs with orders to kill me? Was that the price of their asylum?"

"The State Department isn't the CIA, you know. We don't kill people."

"How do the clandestine services—the CIA, DCS, NSA—get around the globe then, Patterson? Which department do they rely on to move them from country to country?"

"You have no reason to believe ... You're just paranoid. Those men weren't here to kill you."

"Hamoud sent three guys to collect for a protection racket? And three more to kill their own? I'm no expert, but that sounds excessive." She leaned into his personal space. "What did Dakka mean when he said he's out of Snare Drum, Patterson?"

Patterson's head snapped around to look at her, then turned away again.

"Whether you like it or not, you're going to answer for Colonel Nakdali's death. Whatever you're implying—"

"I'm not implying. Every six minutes, a child is kidnapped in India. I was in Mumbai on business. I saw a child snatched off the street, the boy I found in Mullaitivu. The Mumbai police followed the trail to a ship that left for Sri Lanka. The police filed a complaint with the Sri Lankan embassy. The two governments disagreed on where the ship went and what cargo it carried—bureaucratic standoff. So I went there on my own. It took me three days to find him."

Pia pushed Patterson back a step.

"I found him, just before I lost him again. He was in a closely guarded compound with a twelve-foot wall around the outside. In the middle was a bunkhouse for children ages six to twelve. There were ten cabanas on the beach. We crashed the party, but the guests fled before we could secure the compound. Who left that night, Patterson? Who got away? Where did they go?"

Patterson's gaze broke off. He looked around at the crowd.

"Five miles north of Pulmoddai," she said, "and ten miles south of Alampil, in the middle of nowhere, there's a long stretch of white sand. Check the satellite maps if you don't believe me."

"Nothing for me to believe," he said. "You should come in and answer the charges. Officially."

"I'm going to find that boy first—and the tall man." She pushed him again. "Just tell me, Patterson, who am I fighting? Nakdali's allies? The Syrian mob? Or the State Department?"

CHAPTER 8

ONE THING EVERY GOOD OFFICER knows is when to retreat. Patterson had been a good officer. It was time to find some answers and work on an alternate plan—somewhere else.

Patterson shouldered through the crowd and found Agent Marty. "Give me my phone."

Marty tossed it.

Patterson caught it and checked it. "What was this call?"

"We checked out your system. We like to know which encryption you use so we can help the FBI get a warrant."

Patterson shook his head. "I gave her a chance to come in quietly, but you still have your chance. You want to do the right thing?"

"I was there," Marty said. "I did the right thing."

"Morality is subjective. Anyone can bend it to their will and throw it around. The question is, did you act legally? Institutions decide legality, not individuals. They've been empowered by the people to decide what punishments are meted out and which tactics are allowable. You have no such mandate."

Agent Marty turned his back.

Patterson felt his muscles tense, and blood rushed to his head. He fought the urge to beat the crap out of the impudent agent. It was time to leave, time to find another solution to the problem.

Something made his skin crawl. He glanced over his shoulder to see Pia Sabel staring at him from fifteen yards away. The sun's heat sank into his coat, and her glare burned into his eyes. His blood pressure rose. If he stood there another second, he would explode.

He walked away.

What about her version of events? She had no proof, no evidence, nothing to make anyone believe her. Yet it was a convincing story. He almost believed her. She had a credible and compelling manner. Is that how she'd gotten away with so much in her short life? Just because she had an intimidating stare and spoke with authority, people believed anything she said?

If she told her story, people would believe her. He would have to deal with that reality.

He had to do something.

Assistant Secretary Donald F. Patterson crossed the street, passed through a group of onlookers, and continued down the sidewalk. He could feel her eyes on him every step of the way. Slipping through a knot of people near the café should have freed him from her accusing stare, yet he could still feel those eyes watching him.

Like a tiger.

He hadn't understood the question she asked at the beginning. But it was clear now. He knew why they chose him for the mission. The Under Secretary was afraid of her.

As he neared the corner, he glanced over his shoulder and saw her still staring at him. His back tingled with terrified anticipation as he half expected her to leap the distance between them and sink her claws into his collarbone a second before her canines snapped his neck.

He quickened his pace.

Down the block, he took a right on Nineteenth Street. The Stadium-Armory Metro stop was less than a mile away. He pulled out his phone and called his boss.

Under Secretary Jordan Evans picked up his call on the sixth ring.

"Deciding whether to take my call, Jordan?" Patterson said.

"No, I … What do you need?"

"I need to know why the Syrians were there."

"I don't know what you're—"

"Like hell. Six weeks ago I went to Beirut at the request of your friend, Under Secretary McCarty. Today, I ran another errand for him, and those same Syrians showed up."

"Well, uh, Don, you'll have to ask him yourself."

"Which Under Secretary do I work for? You, isn't it?"

"Yes. Yes, and, uh, that's true. But I don't know anything about his mission. It's a need to know—"

"You recommended me for a special mission," Patterson fought to keep his voice even, "and you're telling me you don't know anything about it? How did you decide to recommend me?"

"Now, Don, just calm down a minute," Evans said and forced a bad laugh. "I don't know what you're worked up about. I mean, well, heck, Don, I don't recall how your name came up. We Under Secretaries talk in terms of resources and capabilities. He might have asked for you. He was looking for someone reliable, someone who knew how to follow orders."

"He asked for me? McCarty came to State just a few weeks ago. How would he know my name?"

"Uh, well, I don't know." Evans paused. "You should talk to him. I find direct communication is always best."

"Didn't you work with him before you came to State?"

"Well, yes, that's true. And you did too indirectly, right? Last year, if I recall correctly. Anyway, I can't discuss that with you."

"Why did he ask for me?" Patterson said.

"Because you have a good record. Anyone else would have been a nonstarter. His target would meet with you out of respect for veterans in general and your record in particular."

"You recommended me for the Beirut job."

"You were in Turkey, practically there already. It made sense."

"Why didn't you volunteer for the mission today?"

"Uh—you really should talk to McCarty. I have to go now. Good day."

Patterson stopped marching toward the Metro stop, stared at his phone, and said, "Weasel."

He dialed Under Secretary for Civilian Security and Human Rights, Bill McCarty. McCarty picked up on the first ring and said, "I told you—Evans is a moron."

Patterson resumed his march, carefully scanning up and down the street. A middle-aged woman pushed a shopping cart full of plastic bags on the opposite sidewalk. The sun tried to glint off dingy chrome on parked cars. One car stood out from the ten-year-old Nissans and Chevys: a late-model Crown Victoria, navy blue with dark windows.

"Why were the Syrians there?" Patterson asked.

"You had a simple mission: bring her in. You relied on a ridiculous bluff. You failed."

"And the Syrians succeeded?"

"No need to argue."

"You should've told me. I would've taken a different approach."

"Need to know, Patterson." McCarty sighed. His breath sounded wet and fat. "And I need to know you're going to solve the Sabel problem."

"I'm not going to kill her on the street. I never signed on—"

"It's common knowledge that she sticks her nose into every crime she sees. She beat up some armed robbers in Adams Morgan a year ago and broke up a banking conspiracy in Geneva last spring. Someday, she's going to take on the wrong guy and end up with a bullet in her brain."

"I'm the one who brought the Syrians in. They're connected to me."

"Then you'd better get to work."

Patterson stopped walking, pulled the phone from his ear, squeezed the metal case, and looked into the sky. He shut his eyes and bit his lip. With a sigh and a whispered curse, he put the phone to his ear again. He said, "You set me up."

"I gave you a mission. You jumped at it. Ah, so eager to please, so ready for a pat on the head."

"Well, I'm done. As you said, I failed."

"Failure is when you quit." McCarty chuckled. "It turns out her survival was a good thing. A certain senator sent a request for information to the CIA. The senator's a great admirer of Ms. Sabel and an old family friend. He helped Alan Sabel land all the satellite communication contracts that kick-started his fortune a couple decades ago. He wants all the CIA's information about Abdul Nakdali's travels for the past two years plus any and all connections to the US government."

"I don't understand why that's—"

"Don't be coy with me, Mr. Patterson. You know what it means. I need to know how much Ms. Sabel knows and who she's been talking to.

I need to know right now—tonight."

Patterson's fist clenched. He glanced at the Crown Vic. "I need a Plan B."

"You *are* Plan B. Now get moving." McCarty clicked off.

The Crown Vic turned out of its parking space and pulled alongside him. The driver's darkened window dropped, revealing a middle-aged muscleman in a dark suit and sunglasses. He leaned back and grinned like a Halloween pumpkin. "Need a ride?"

CHAPTER 9

I LIFTED HER LIGHT-BROWN LEG, pushed it gently off my stomach, and took another look at her. Even with drool under her mouth, she was gorgeous. She muttered Spanish in her sleep and rolled away from me into the blade of sunlight stabbing between the curtains.

The buzzer rang again.

My head hurt.

Tossing back the sheet, I sat up and squinted through one eye at the clock. Two and change. Afternoon? Ouch. With one deep breath, I pushed off, staggered into the kitchen of my Capitol Hill one-bedroom, and slapped the intercom button. "Yeah."

The voice sobered me like a dive into a frozen lake. "Jacob, buzz me in."

Holy shit.

Pia Sabel.

I was in a world of trouble.

As soon as I buzzed the outer door for her, I dashed into the bathroom. It took three cold splashes in the face to work up the courage for a glance in the mirror. Last shave: three days ago. Two-inch slash at my hairline: scabbed over and ugly. Eyes: bloodshot. Hair: short for simplicity and still a mess. I yanked the butterfly suture off my forehead and squirted a stream of Visine at each eye. I shook out four aspirin and four Advil, chewed them up, and sent them to work with a handful of water. One more splash into my hair and a quick comb, and I looked vaguely hominid.

Close enough.

I shoved a toothbrush in my mouth and squeezed in some paste. Working the brush hard, I checked my wardrobe.

Buck naked might be the way I'd like to answer the door for Ms. Sabel, but it was probably a bad career move. Getting fired from Sabel Security would mean never seeing her again. Suicide was a better option. Not that I had a chance in hell of winning her, but a man can live for decades on hope alone.

I ran back to the bedroom where Bianca rolled up on an elbow.

"Sweetie," I whispered, "very important guests coming up. Stay right here, and don't make a sound. If you hear gunfire, don't call the police. Just wait a couple minutes after they leave. Then sneak out really quietly. 'K?"

"That was funny the first time."

"Still. Silent mode." I put a finger across my lips.

She rolled her eyes and rubbed her temples.

I put on jeans, commando for now, and a wrinkled T-shirt. I shut the bedroom door just as I heard a knock on the front.

"Good morning," I said.

Agent Tania Cooper, an exotic beauty, stood in my doorway looking me over with condemning eyes. Guess my quick splash-n-clean failed. Judging me was hypocrisy in her case—I'd carried Tania from dance floor to cab more than once during our brief-but-memorable relationship. She pushed past me, eyeballed the tiny living room, did a quick look in the kitchen, and came back.

Pia Sabel stayed out on the landing, a glowing earbud in her ear and a phone in her hand, looking like the goddess of women's soccer. She nodded at me, gave me a be-with-you-in-a-second gesture, and turned away.

Tania touched my elbow and said, "Police up your tongue, soldier. Who's in the bedroom?"

"Nothing but memories of you, babe."

"Shove it, Agent Jacob. Who is she?"

"Bianca Dominguez, NSA analyst, Central America Desk. Unarmed."

Tania shook her head in disgust and took a position, back to the wall, bedroom on her left, front door on her right. She gave Ms. Sabel a nod.

Ms. Sabel walked in like sunshine from behind a cloud. She was wearing her version of gym clothes: snug microfiber spandex that clung to every curve, rib, and muscle. Dressed like that, she fired my imagination in a way I hoped didn't show.

She finished her call, clicked off, and slipped her phone in the outside pocket of a waistpack she'd slung from her shoulder. It was an unusual bag, carried in an unusual way, and she was dressed in an unusual manner for the owner of a billion-dollar business. But then, she was an unusual woman.

She stared at me. Her gray-green eyes zapped me from head to toe in a nanosecond. She didn't mentally undress a man—she dissected him, instantly assessing his strengths, weaknesses, and current condition. Given her curled upper lip, I wasn't registering a high score.

"You were supposed to be back on active duty this morning," she said. "I understand you called in sick."

"Touch of something, ma'am," I said and did my best to maintain eye contact.

She stared a hole through me.

The Major once warned me that honesty was the *only* policy at Sabel Security. Even a white lie could end a career, and besides, she deserved the truth. I said, "An old friend called last night and wanted to reminisce, so we met for a drink."

A smirk crossed her face, and I remembered how much women love to hate—and hate to love—a player. Even so, she left an awkward silence.

Compelled to fill the void, I said, "She presented an opportunity, and I pressed it immediately."

It was a direct quote from Ms. Sabel herself. Of course, she had been referring to her goal against Brazil in the Olympics, but it worked. She acknowledged it with a barely perceptible smile. I went deeper into my bag of job-saving tricks and rubbed my hip where two bullets had shattered the bone during Ms. Sabel's first operation as head of the company. I literally took a bullet for her—and was not above milking it.

Her phone buzzed, and she glanced at it without a second thought. She turned away for privacy but ended up holding the screen right where I could see it. Mark Fitzroy, her boyfriend, if my sources were trustworthy, was giving her a hard time about not answering his texts.

She thumbed out a quick response: *Later. Busy now.* How could she date someone so self-absorbed when she had so many options? When she faced me again, I had the grin of a daydreamer, and she raised an eyebrow.

"I need you," she said without knowing how that phrase made my heart stop. "Are you fit for duty?"

"Ready, ma'am," I said and saluted.

Three months into the job, and she still hadn't worked out how to react to employees like me who saluted in their sleep. A touch of a smile started at the corners of her mouth, but she reined it in.

"Do you still have contacts in the DIA?" she asked.

I'd spent a couple years putting my Pashto and Arabic skills to use in the Defense Intelligence Agency with the hope of avoiding yet another Purple Heart.

"Yes, ma'am. We keep two colonels and three majors on the list for the Redskins and Capitals tickets. They owe me."

"Good. Agent Marty already sent you all the information we need researched. If you're not too busy," she nodded at the bedroom door, "we need you to read it, research everything, analyze it, and get back to me. I need to know who we're up against and what kind of resources we'll need to find Nakdali's other installations."

Nakdali's Mullaitivu installation was not a pretty fight. Ms. Sabel had pursued criminals into their territory with too small a team and too little intelligence. She was making a habit of acting on impulse, which was not something soldiers like from their officers. Now it sounded as though she were doing it again—running off to save the world without regard for safety. And she was starting right there in my shabby apartment. The skeptic in me, the one who looked forward to a long life, needed more information, so I waited.

"Someone at the State Department set me up to be killed."

My eyebrows went up. "Because of Mullaitivu?"

"Are there other reasons to want me dead?" she asked with a smile.

I searched for a way to pull my foot out of my mouth.

"Yes," she said, "that *is* what I need to confirm."

The bedroom door opened, and Bianca tried to step out in a T-shirt that didn't cover as much as she thought. Before she took her first step into the room, Tania shoved a Glock 33 up her nose. Bianca let out a clipped screech, and her Latina face turned whiter than an English royal's.

Ms. Sabel stared at her a moment, then nodded to Tania, who backed off.

Bianca took a moment to compose herself and said, "Sorry, I don't suppose you remember me. I was captain of the soccer team at Bethesda High when you were a freshman at Saint Muriel's. I, uh, um."

Ms. Sabel made no sign of recognition, which took the drive out of Bianca's little speech. But my plucky girl *du jour* took a breath and pressed on, talking fast. "Two seconds after kickoff, my defender popped the ball into the air. When it came down, you volleyed it straight into the net from thirty yards out. It was amazing. I ... um," Bianca blushed like a celebrity-obsessed stalker meeting her crush for the first time, "have followed your career ever since."

A slow smile spread across Ms. Sabel's face, and she snapped her fingers. "Oh, yeah. You tried the same volley in the second half, right?"

Bianca nodded with a happy-to-be-remembered grin. "Yes, but you leapt up and headed it before I connected. My leg smashed into you. It was like kicking a rock."

I tried to visualize the matchup. Ms. Sabel stood a head taller than Bianca and was a lot more serious about her fitness.

"Grab your things," Ms. Sabel said. "I'll have my driver take you home. We can catch up." She jerked a thumb at me. "Your boyfriend is going to be busy."

A few seconds later, with Bianca chatting like a sorority sister, the three women in my life were gone. An ex, a current, and a daydream. The good news was, my daydream turned to me when she needed something important.

That fact alone gave me reason to live.

CHAPTER 10

I BOOTED MY LAPTOP, POPPED a Provigil, and made a PBJ. The information Agent Marty sent was sketchy and disconnected: a former destroyer captain turned Assistant Secretary of State, an urgent meeting request where the State Department thought Ms. Sabel would surrender her rights, three Syrian thugs with redacted dossiers, and a reference to Ms. Sabel's adventures in Mullaitivu. Who or what tied them together? And since when did State get this deep into an extradition?

If Marty had outlined the facts without mentioning the Department of State, I would've said this reeked of another CIA operation gone rogue. But seeing *State* all over the place gave me pause. Weren't they the good guys?

Marty had sketched a little background about Sri Lanka's Mullaitivu district for me in an email. The place was a forgotten backwater populated by poor fishermen with no local industry or infrastructure. The people of Mullaitivu had suffered for thirty years under the Tamil Tigers, who used the remote district as a base for their terrorist war. After the tsunami hit in 2004, things hit rock bottom, and even the Tamils gave up.

One hopeless day, ex-Colonel Abdul Nakdali materialized. He was a private security contractor from parts unknown who built a compound on the beach. He used imported labor, snubbing the locals and defying the Sri Lankan government. His compound featured armed guards who gave trespassers one warning shot.

How did the Syrians tie in? Sri Lanka and Syria are separated by five thousand miles, Sri Lanka is largely Buddhist, and the Syrians in DC were five thousand miles in the other direction.

But Ms. Sabel had a reputation for seeing connections where anyone else would see nothing more than a nutcase conspiracy. Looking at the threads she was weaving into a tapestry, I was leaning toward the conspiracy theory. The fact that she wanted me to tap our DIA buddies meant even she knew it was far-fetched. But if Pia Sabel wanted me to connect JFK's assassination to the discovery of the Higgs boson, I'd get 'er done.

Once a person leaves the intelligence community, that person's access is cut off forever. But my friends would look up little bits for me once in a while. As long as I spread my questions around, asking a single question from each friend, I could find out all kinds of things. For the next half hour, I called everyone I knew, posed the questions as best I could without mentioning Ms. Sabel herself, and had six people digging into the background of the players. I stuck to the staff—people on my level—keeping the officers in reserve in case of roadblocks.

Just as I was dialing my seventh contact, the Major called.

Major Jonelle Jackson ran Sabel Security while Ms. Sabel traveled the world toppling dictatorships and crashing child-prostitution resorts like the one in Mullaitivu. Without introduction, the Major said, "Jacob, are you taking your meds?"

"Yes."

"Have you been taking them all week, no voices?"

"Yes." I hung out the last letter long enough to let it carry my annoyance.

She didn't care.

"Pia's panic alarm went off not too far from your apartment—on the corner of Twenty-First and I NE. Agent Tania was with her and is not responding. Agent Marty was two blocks away, went to investigate, and also stopped responding. Assume they were ambushed. I want you there immediately—eyes only. Do not engage. Help is on the way, but when they get there, this is your op. You run it."

"On it." I clicked off, grabbed my earbud and Glock, and threw on a running outfit. I slipped my gun into the concealed holster on my running pack.

On the drive, I wondered why Major Jackson put me in charge. Was it my charm and good looks? Or my exemplary service in the army? Since none of those things existed in real life, I decided she knew how I felt about the boss and expected me to die for her.

All in.

Two miles down the hill, I slowed my Jetta to a crawl and rolled through Carver Langston. Nothing looked out of place. A derelict staggered down the sidewalk on one side, and a pair of old ladies traded gossip on the other. The apartment buildings were in bad shape with peeling paint, sagging doors, and boarded windows. After searching four blocks, trying to be inconspicuous, I parked and began a jog down the street.

I could run a 10K race in forty minutes, but I ran at half that pace, trying to look like a tired marathoner training in the wrong part of town. I let my eyes wander over every building, car, tree, and citizen.

You'd need an army to take down Pia Sabel and two veterans like Tania and Marty. Either the bad guys had cleared out in a grab and go, or they had an apartment nearby. Three of ours and six to ten of theirs would leave a trail no matter which way they'd done it. Since the GPS on Ms. Sabel's phone put her on the corner a block away when she pressed the panic button, something went down within fifty yards of me. Yet nothing looked out of place.

I turned onto I Street and jogged toward Twentieth.

Two-story red brick apartments lined the block shoulder to shoulder. The featureless cubes made me depressed just looking at them—nothing remotely artistic in sight, no planters in the window sills, nothing painted a different color, no individuality expressed anywhere. A badly paved alleyway led around back. The derelict I'd seen earlier had staggered a block over, and the gossips were still in place.

A ten-year-old Mercedes, excessively waxed to conceal its age, rolled slowly down the street booming bass out the open windows. Three young black men eyeballed me as they cruised by.

A few strides later, the Major's voice came over my earbud. "You're passing the site now. She pressed her panic button somewhere within ten yards of you."

My eyes scanned the area. A chain-link fence surrounded a scrap of half-dead grass. From the fence to the street lay three feet of sidewalk, two feet of dirt, and a chipped curb. No skid marks, no signs of scuffles in the dirt, no people on the street, no faces in the windows. A curtain moved on the upper floor apartment across the street, leaving a dark, narrow triangle. A glint of shiny glass caught my eye at the base of a tree. I stopped to tie my running shoe.

Not far from me, I heard boys arguing in hushed tones. Unable to place their direction or distance, I checked what caught my eye: several glass shards lay in the dirt between the sidewalk and the road. Gorilla Glass, the kind used in smartphones.

Three feet away, a brass shell casing. One of ours. I could tell by the brass crimp marks that gingerly held the dart in place. I looked around but saw only the one casing. I finished tying my shoe, started running again, and pressed my earbud. "No signs of struggle but found a piece of a phone and one of our shell casings."

"A single shot fired?" the Major said. "Not good."

"Had to be a small crowd attacking them."

"Any open parking spaces where you saw the glass?"

"Yes." I did another sweep of the area before my feet carried me too far away. "Wide-open curb. You think they pulled up and jumped out? Tania would have had a gun out in a split-second."

"No. I think they walked into a trap."

"You mean, the way Ms. Sabel helps people?"

"Exactly. Someone says, 'My cat's in a tree,' and she's three branches up before you can tell her it's not safe. Missing persons requires twenty-four hours, so we need to find her ourselves. Keep looking. Your backup is ten minutes away."

We clicked off without voicing our mutual fear: that we'd find her body.

I rounded the corner on Nineteenth Street and jogged halfway to Maryland Avenue, where I spotted an alley. The voices of boys floated my way again, and I followed the sound down the trash-strewn lane. Keeping my back to the wall and dodging between dumpsters and cars, I came up behind them unseen.

Three middle-school boys huddled over a box. One was taller and skinnier than the other two and spoke the least. The other two were average, with one being a little chubbier. I picked out the leader by his body language; he was more muscular and flexed a lot. They argued over the value of whatever was in the box.

I clicked on my earbud so the Major could hear me.

With two quick steps, I was on them. I shoved my gun in the leader's ear, headlocked the chubby one, and stared down the tall kid. They froze.

I said, "What's in the box?"

Without hesitation, the tall kid said, "The white lady's phone."

My headlock victim tried to tell the tall kid to shut up, but I squeezed him harder. While the leader was jumpy about having a gun in his face, the tall kid was calm and unmoved. He never took his eyes off me.

"Listen up, boys," I said. "I'm going to offer you a reward for information about the white lady. You guys good with rewards?"

"Rewards are cool," the leader said. "You don't gotta jump us or nothing, man."

"Sorry." I lowered the gun and released the headlock. "I'm looking for the white lady. How'd you end up with her phone?"

"Maybe we took it," the chubby one said.

"No way. She'd have torn you apart and spared her two bodyguards the trouble. You don't have to pretend you're tough. Just tell me what went down."

"Group of people come down the street," the tall boy said, "talking and making plans when all of a sudden the van opens up, and everybody gets quiet. We couldn't see much, but the white lady got in the van— then bang, and they was gone."

The sequence of events struck me as odd. He didn't have white middle-class eloquence, but there was purpose in the way he spoke. I rolled his words around in my head for a moment: *Got in the van—then bang, and they was gone.* Ms. Sabel got in the van, then there was the bang of the gun, and then they left. If Tania pulled the trigger, she would have done it before Pia was shoved into the van.

I said, "Making plans?"

"Yeah, she and Sister Raissa, all them crazy Jesus people, talking about what they gonna do to the Syrians. They was pointing and talking."

"Who was in the van?"

"Couldn't see nothing."

"How'd you get the phone?"

"After they all left. It was on the ground. But it's broke. They smashed it. Didn't need to do that. Perfectly good phone."

Watching the reactions of the other two, it sounded plausible.

"You didn't catch the license plates?"

"Taped," he said, meaning electrical tape had been used to make an *E* into an 8 or a 4 into an *A*.

Two blocks after nabbing their victim, they would have opened the back doors, reached over, and pulled the tape. They wouldn't even need to stop. It was a standard bad-guy trick that Tania would have spotted. A Sabel agent doesn't walk past a car with electrical tape on the plates. That meant they weren't ambushed. So what happened?

Marty's original report included only three locals and three Syrians, two of them dead, so there must have been others.

"What do you mean about them leaving? Did they all get in the van?"

"No, just the white lady. When the van left, Sister Raissa and the others started crying. They carried themselves over to Raissa's place."

His words struck me again: *carried themselves.* "The light-colored lady—she got shot, and they carried her?"

"That's right."

"What's the reward?" the leader asked.

"So far, he's earned twenty bucks. What do you have?"

"I got something worth more than twenty."

"Let's hear it."

"Let's see it."

I pulled a twenty out of my wallet, gave it to the tall boy, and enjoyed his smile for a second. I flashed the open wallet with three more twenties and two fifties in it. The leader smiled.

"For the fifty," he said. "I know where the spotter is."

I pulled a twenty and said, "This is for the info. The fifty is to take me to him and set up a distraction."

The chubby kid said, "What do I get?"

In unison the rest of us said, "Nothing."

The leader nodded to seal the deal, then lifted his nose toward a flight of stairs going up the back side of a building nearby. It was the same apartment with the triangle of open curtain. The spotter's nest. The window on the back side was a piece of plywood that had been there at least a year. Smoke stains curled out of the frame and up the wall. An abandoned building chosen for the view.

I pulled out all my cash, set it on the ground, and put the box with Ms. Sabel's phone on top. "We're going up there. You open the door, call him, or play a prank on him that brings him out, and then you run. If I live long enough, you circle back and take me to Sister Raissa; then tell the boys in the Mercedes to meet me at the café later. You do those three things, and all this money is yours to split up."

They grinned, eyes on the cash.

The chubby kid turned and climbed into a dumpster. After a couple seconds, he tossed a brown paper bag over the top and started climbing out. The tall kid took the bag, ran two yards over, and scooped something into it.

The leader took the bag, nodded to me, and climbed the stairs like a thief in the night. I followed him, matching his stealth.

At the top of the stairs, he twisted the knob. Locked. I stepped to the side and peered through a hole in the blacked-out window. Pulling a plastic jimmy from his jacket, he slid it into the jamb and worked it a few seconds until the latch snapped open. He pushed the door open a foot, pulled out a lighter, and set the bag on fire. When the flame got to a size he liked, he tossed it to the right, ten feet into the apartment's kitchen, and laughed out loud like the prankster he was.

He gave me a thumbs-up and ran noisily down the stairs.

There was something likable about these junior hoodlums. I hadn't seen the dog-shit-on-fire trick since I was their age.

CHAPTER 11

TEN SECONDS WENT BY BEFORE a medium-sized Syrian-looking guy came into view. He ran down the short hall and stepped into the tiny kitchen. His eyes were fixed on the flaming bag, which he proceeded to stamp out with a large, black boot. After three stomps, he realized his predicament, lifted his shoe, and looked at the sole.

He never saw me enter the room, but he felt my gun's muzzle when I touched it to his neck. He went rigid as I stepped to face him.

"Where's the woman?" I asked in a quiet voice.

He answered me with an Arabic insult. I tossed a few back at him, including calling him the son of a whore in the same Levantine dialect he used—the dialect of Bashar al-Assad, Syria's dictator. I slammed my knee into his groin. As he doubled over, I swept his legs out from under him, slammed him to the floor, and bashed his head into the linoleum several times. When I considered him docile enough, I put my gun to his nose and patted him down.

Not a nice guy. His pockets held a collapsible baton, a Sig Sauer P229, a hunting knife, and a garrote. A handheld radio, a Motorola business model, went straight into my pocket. I tossed his other toys across the room and propped him against the wall.

"Where is she?"

He sneered at me. I stood up and kicked him in the face. His nose bled, and he smiled. He was a tough guy—either a long-term gangster or a veteran of Assad's secret police. Questioning him would be unproductive.

I heard the wheeze of a wounded man in the other room. I'd not secured the place, and my victim still looked dangerous.

So I shot him.

Sabel Security darts look and act like regular bullets except that they're a lot quieter and less accurate. Instead of a chunk of lead at the front, the casing holds a small cylinder filled with a nonlethal dose of Inland Taipan snake venom and a heavy sedative. The cartridge is interchangeable with a regular bullet but holds less gunpowder due to the longer payload. The venom puts the target into a state of paralysis, so he can see and hear, but his primary motor cortex is disconnected. He can't move for about ten minutes. By the time that wears off, the sedative will have put him to sleep. Good for two to four hours of incapacitated bad guy. The only drawback: unintentional death. Some people have a violent reaction to the poison. For that reason, all Sabel Security agents are required to carry antivenom injectors, which are administered to prevent accidental death and the nasty lawsuits that follow.

He slumped over.

I patted my runner's pack. All Sabel Security agents carry antivenom injectors except anyone who may have flown out of his house in a desperate rage.

Oh well.

I hoped he was going to live. I needed to interrogate him when he came around.

I heard movement in the front room and moved silently into the hallway. I crouched and spun around the wall. Agent Marty lay on the bare floorboards with a nasty gash on his forehead and a bruise high on his cheek. Just beyond him, a metal folding chair sat four feet from the window. Two strips of paper were taped up to look like a curtain.

It would take more than one guy to beat Marty, so I secured the apartment before attending to him. One bedroom and closet, empty. One filthy bathroom, empty. One kitchen with a breakfast nook, equally empty, not counting the incapacitated Syrian. I checked outside the door. The boys were gone; no one was watching. I closed the door, slapped the Syrian with plasticuffs, just in case he was immune to the sedative, and went back to Marty.

A small-caliber bullet hole wheezed in his chest with each breath. His head showed signs of a serious concussion from a pistol whipping. Not life-threatening, but serious wounds nonetheless.

The Major called the police and ambulance while I looked the place over. The setup was obvious: our Syrian was the spotter who radioed instructions to the men in the van. After the takedown, he waited for Ms. Sabel's backup to arrive. He probably lured Marty by fluttering the curtains—the same trick he tried on me. When I didn't run straight for him, he probably figured me for a real jogger and relaxed. Marty would have been in bodyguard mode, pissed and running around with his gun drawn. He would have jumped at the curtain. I would have too.

Agents Miguel, Carmen, and Tony arrived a minute before the ambulance. Carmen, a former medic, took over on Marty and had him talking in no time. Unfortunately, he wasn't sure which city he was in, much less what happened to Ms. Sabel.

I let Miguel deal with the police and sent Agent Tony back to the café to retrace Ms. Sabel's steps, while I ducked out to look for my boys. As soon as I hit the bottom of the rickety stairs, the tall, skinny kid materialized. He led me to Sister Raissa's apartment in a slightly nicer building at the end of I Street and left me on my own.

Inside I could hear voices raised in anger.

When I knocked, the voices stopped in unison. There was some shuffling before a voice came through the door. "Who is it?"

"Jacob Stearne, Sabel Security. I'm here to help."

An argument in forced whispers broke out and carried on for thirty seconds before someone hushed everyone else. The voice said, "How are you with God?"

Not the usual through-the-door question.

Honesty is the only policy.

"I was facedown in a drainage ditch in Hindu Kush with three hundred Taliban raining lead on my squad. I swore to God if he got me out of there alive, I'd believe the rest of my life."

"And you made good on that promise?"

After a breath, I said, "No ... but I'm working on it."

The door opened, and a black woman with glasses hanging on a chain around her neck stepped out. She wrapped her arms around me. "Ain't none of us as good as we should be. Knowing that is a good start."

She introduced herself as Raissa and led me into a small room with five people. One of the people was Tania, out cold on the couch. I knelt by Tania's side and checked her pulse while Raissa introduced Louisa, Douglas, and Jamal. Louisa owned the dollar store; Douglas ran the pawnshop; and Jamal was Raissa's lesser half. He trembled a lot and said little.

I instinctively reached for my missing antivenom injector and grimaced.

Louisa was a fine-looking woman who turned her face to hide her smile when I winked at her. I kept my eyes on hers, and she lifted her shoulder to hide her spreading grin. Mature women have a sensuous confidence and realistic expectations, while younger ladies have annoying neuroses and schemes. Forced to choose, I'd take the mature woman any day. When this op was over, I'd come back and call on Louisa.

They all started talking at once.

"They shot her," Raissa said.

"They have my daughter," Douglas said.

"She gonna be OK?" Jamal said, pointing to Tania.

"We should call an ambulance," Louisa said. "I don't see blood, but she's hurt."

The dart left a mark on her neck just below her ear. I stood and held up my hands to stop their jabbering. "She's going to be fine. I take it they shot her with her own gun?"

"Yes," Raissa said.

"Did anyone tell them it had darts, not bullets?"

"Darts? No."

"Then they intended to kill her."

The three of them nodded, their eyes locked on mine like sad puppy dogs.

"It was an accident," Louisa said. "They thought they'd killed her. They freaked and ran."

"What happened?"

"Ms. Sabel offered herself in place of his daughter," Louisa said.

"They took my daughter," Douglas said again.

This time it sank in. "They double-crossed you at the exchange?"

They nodded in unison. Raissa said, "It was her idea. Pia said she was the one they wanted. After all, it started when she took their guys out." Her eyes rose to the ceiling. "That was something. You shoulda seen it. Like some kinda avenging angel or something, she showed up and kicked their asses." She hung her head. "Uh, not that I condone violence, mind you—"

"Did they release the girl?"

"No. They're supposed to call here and tell us where to find her."

"Have you called the FBI?"

"They said we needed proof she'd been kidnapped."

"Wouldn't need proof if we was in Georgetown," Douglas said.

A loud rapping on the door silenced all of us. I drew my weapon and took a position to the side of it. I pressed my hand to the peephole to block the light. No one started shooting, so I took a look. When I saw who it was, I opened it.

Five foot five, slender with her hair pulled into a tight bun at the nape of her neck, Major Jonelle Jackson had the presence of a giant. She always had a serious look that came from a lifetime of life-and-death decisions. When she strode into the room, Raissa and her friends fell into a silent semicircle around her. Greeting each of them with a slight nod and a reverential look, Major Jackson gave them a dual first impression: that she respected them and that they'd better tell her the truth.

We went through a timeline of events. To get back at Ms. Sabel for beating the crap out of their thugs, leaving two dead, the Syrian mobsters snatched Douglas's eight-year-old daughter. Ms. Sabel found out about it when she returned from my place and immediately offered to trade herself for the child. With Tania advising against it, they went straight to the van on Twenty-First Street. The deal went sideways. Three Syrians jumped Tania, shot her with her own gun, and took off.

"What about Raya?" Douglas asked, his face drained.

With a glance, the Major told me to keep quiet. She didn't need to; I knew damn well the chances of the girl being alive right now were slim and dwindling fast.

After a moment of silence, I said, "They took Ms. Sabel's phone and smashed it. Did they take her bag too?"

"No," Raissa said. "She just got in the van like she knew what she was doing."

That was good news. The Major nodded at me. There was no need to tell them Ms. Sabel carried a concealed Glock 33 and a reserve phone in her waistpack. She had a hundred purses, backpacks, and waistpacks all fitted with secret holsters. Either luck or stupidity stopped the thugs from dumping her bag. The gun in it was light enough to make the pack look normal, but anyone who grabbed it would know it was too heavy for makeup and money alone. The good news: no one expected a former athlete to carry a piece.

I checked my watch: twenty minutes had passed. The Syrians could have taken her anywhere.

Douglas's phone rang. He nodded to us after checking the caller ID and took the call on speakerphone.

"Daddy, I don't like your friend," a little girl said. She paused between sentences. "His breath smells, and he told me you were supposed to meet us here. Where are you? When are you coming?"

"I'll be right there, honey. Where are you?"

She hesitated, and someone spoke in the background. She said, "At the zoo—the gorilla cages. I don't like gorillas. Come get—"

"I'm coming, honey." Douglas kept talking as he ran out the front door. Louisa followed, offering to drive.

They weren't asking for help, no doubt expecting me to be a liability, but I had to participate. It was our only lead. I had to nab a Syrian during the exchange.

I checked my stolen radio. It was on, volume up, but there was no suspicious chatter. Did the Syrians know I'd captured a radio? I set it to cycle through the various channels, trying to find which one they were using. All I had to do was listen for Arabic. There had to be a second guy who would have seen me and laid low. I expected to hear him warning his pals over the unit, but so far, nothing. Why have expensive radios and not use them?

CHAPTER 12

I PICKED UP AGENT TONY and flew across town. Washington was laid out a hundred years before the automobile with picturesque traffic circles for promenading in your horse-and-buggy. Those same circles turned into demolition derbies at anything over five miles per hour. Cars complicated traffic to the point where even natives used satellite maps to find the elusive Northwest Passage.

Tony ran nav and comm while I concentrated on getting there before Douglas. Tony reported that the Major had pulled all available agents into the Carver Langston neighborhood. Until we had Ms. Sabel back, it would be the safest part of town.

As I threaded my way around Mount Vernon Square, Tony found the zoo's service entrance off Beach Drive on the map. We might have to jump a fence or two, but I was confident I could get there before Louisa and get a look at who was holding the girl. I needed a talker, since I lost my patience with the last guy, and the radio was still strangely silent.

Tony worked his former colleagues at the FBI to aim manpower at the child abduction. His persistence helped to move the colossal bureaucracy faster than an ordinary citizen might, but in the end, he could get only a rookie named Verges. Agent Verges couldn't mobilize in time for the zoo, but he promised to coordinate security on-site with local police. With any luck, Tony and I might not die in the crossfire.

Flying around Thomas Circle, I noticed a motorcycle gaining on us. He'd been a few cars back before I'd ducked a bus in a risky maneuver near Mount Vernon Square. He wasn't tailing us; he was trying to catch us. I floored my Jetta and took the rest of Thomas Circle on two wheels.

Tony managed to follow my glances in the mirror and found the biker. He pulled out his Glock and dropped the magazine. I could see the decision written across his face. Sabel darts would never penetrate the biker's leather; the needle could penetrate little more than a shirt. If he switched to Parabellums, he'd have to hit a moving target from a moving platform without missing.

Unlike movie bullets, a real bullet will go through sheet metal, drywall, glass, and anything else short of concrete until it killed someone. The afternoon streets were crowded with pedestrians and drivers heading home. Bullets were not an option. Tony cursed and slammed his magazine of darts back in.

The biker shot past the car behind us and followed me around Scott Circle, riding my right rear fender. I tried scraping him off by driving over the curb when we left the circle. He swerved around a street light and two pedestrians and was back on me in a beat. We flew up Mass Ave and, having gained a little open space, I floored it, drove into the oncoming lane, passed two cabs, and pulled back in. I hit fifty miles per hour as I pressed the yellow light and crossed Seventeenth Street, three car lengths ahead of him.

All lanes were parked for the light at Eighteenth Street, where a cab pulled up and pinned me behind a UPS truck. The biker blew through the light at Seventeenth and squeezed into oncoming traffic to come alongside me. I was trapped. He smashed my side window with a glass-breaking hammer, tossed in a brick, and spun a U-turn.

It wasn't a brick.

Tony bailed out right, and I bailed left. We slammed our doors and took three steps before the device exploded inside. A thousand chunks of safety glass hit me hard, shredding my shirt and peppering my back. The glass did its job and absorbed a lot of the impact, but my back still hurt as if a spurned woman had clawed it. Tony was behind the UPS truck before the explosion and fired three darts at the biker.

One dart managed to catch the man's ankle. He went limp at the controls, left his lane, snagged a parking meter at speed, and tumbled onto the sidewalk in a heap. We ran over to him as police cars swarmed out of thin air. We trained our guns on the biker and approached his crumpled body. His position looked bad, like he was broken somewhere he shouldn't be. It could be the snake venom, but my bet was on a broken back from bouncing off a concrete planter. I wouldn't get much intel out of this guy either.

Tony checked the Syrian's pulse and nodded—*still alive*—then shrugged—*but not good*. He patted the biker's pockets and pulled out a phone and a wallet. He snapped a picture of the driver's license and the wallet's contents and put it all back. He dialed our special number from the biker's phone to capture his information. In sixty seconds, the biker's phone would have downloaded an app that spewed its contents back to Sabel headquarters for analysis. Anything short of DOD encryption would be hacked in an hour. With any luck, we'd have our first damn clue.

I holstered my gun and bit my lip. There were so many things wrong with the afternoon's events that I had trouble finding a focal point. Several problems fought for mindshare: The little girl was still missing. Ms. Sabel's meeting request from Patterson had a true sense of urgency. I'd told no one where we were going, yet the Syrians found us. And Marty's notes said it appeared that Patterson's goal was to have Ms. Sabel go somewhere with him. A guy who walked to the meeting wanted her to, what, give him a lift to her own hanging? Tacky.

For the police arriving on the scene, my smoking Jetta was the first priority.

I stood on the sidewalk watching them.

Tony stepped to my side.

People in nearby cars pointed us out to the cops.

While we waited for the police to make a move, I called the Major to warn her. But she'd already escaped a similar attack, and so had Miguel. That prioritized my list for me. I'd have to deal with Raya's abduction as soon as the police were done taking our statements. I clicked off.

Across the street, the toughest-looking officer turned to us and bellowed, "Freeze! Hands in the air! Face on the ground, now!"

We complied.

CHAPTER 13

AN HOUR LATER, THE LOCAL police turned us over to Agent Verges of the FBI. I learned a few things during our questioning. First, the FBI wouldn't call the event a terrorist attack because it looked as though we were the only targets. When Tony complained to his former boss, he was told to prove Sabel Security's mettle by finding a shred of evidence. Nice. Second, there were no Syrian men with an African-American child at the zoo. No such combination showed up on the video recordings for the entire day, and all children were accompanied. Third, Hamdi Dakka, the Syrian Pia Sabel had subdued, had claimed diplomatic immunity and been released.

The last part shocked me. Diplomatic immunity was defined as a three-tiered program by the Vienna Convention on Diplomatic Relations in 1961. Diplomats have full immunity all the time. Administrative and technical staff have immunity from criminal prosecution but have civil immunity only in the course of their official duties. Service staff have immunity only for official acts. For Hamdi to be out already meant he had convinced someone he was part of the Syrian Embassy. So why had he been applying for asylum in Beirut?

My line of thinking came around to how much the Syrians knew about us. They'd attacked us successfully twice and unsuccessfully three more times. They'd lost the all-important element of surprise, which should have cancelled the IED attack on me, but they went ahead anyway. And the radio was still quiet.

"Maybe they're after us," Tony said, meaning the company as a whole. "We have operations all over North Africa protecting oil companies against al-Qaeda. They could be trying to distract us while there's an attack underway in Algeria."

"If they were from any other country," I said, "I'd think about that, but Syria is unlikely. The revolution's kept everyone busy the last couple years."

"You're thinking the diplomatic immunity means they're al-Assad's people. Look at it from all the angles you can think of. They could be al-Assad's people fleeing while the fleeing's good. Or maybe they're revolutionaries tired of the war."

That thought made me ill because it was just crazy enough to be possible: The State Department finds a group of poor refugees applying for asylum and brings them in as diplomats representing the revolutionaries. These Arab Spring revolutions don't always go the way the US government would like, and having a puppet diplomatic corps in place could help control the situation. State's hand-picked ambassadors would have connections the new Syrian government would need and would become de facto diplomats. The only problem for State would be the interim. What does it do with a crowd of puppets when Syria already has an embassy in Washington?

I ran that scenario past Tony.

"Turn them loose in Carver Langston," he said, "and let 'em make a living as best they can. Everyone knows the North Koreans deal drugs smuggled in diplomatic pouches to finance their embassies around the world. Why not let Syrian thugs run wild in the ghetto until the government figures out if they have any value?"

"No way," I said. "State would never get involved with that kind of deal."

Tony laughed. "You're such a boy scout."

I watched the remnants of my car being shoveled onto a flatbed to be dumped somewhere.

Tony's idea made sense, but the implications for Ms. Sabel made my stomach turn. She was in the hands of criminals who had nothing to fear from the law. And someone at the State Department set it up. Was it Patterson? If he were leading the op, would he be dumb enough to meet Ms. Sabel in public? Or had someone set him up?

What did Sabel Security do to get on State's bad side? And why was State involved anyway? The FBI should handle Sri Lanka's extradition request. Yet, we could barely get the FBI interested in helping us on the kidnapping.

Headquarters made progress on the biker's phone. Three messages in Arabic and several phone numbers were retrieved. Now that an FBI agent was involved for the kidnapping, Tony and I translated the messages for him. Nothing important came out of it—just things like, *Nadim, call me. It's Yasser.* We ended up with three first names and twelve phone numbers. The biker was in intensive care and hadn't been identified. His driver's license belonged to a Mexican national living in Rockville.

Our FBI agent was ready to turn us loose.

Just before he said anything, I had an epiphany. I knew why my stolen Motorola was silent.

"Hey, Verges," I said and dug the Syrian's radio out of my pocket. "Sorry, I forgot to give this to you earlier. I took it off one of the bad guys."

The agent took it, scowled at me, dropped it in an evidence bag, and trotted away.

Tony stared at me, dumbfounded. I said, "The biker wasn't behind us for the first mile. Nothing was coming in, not even a construction crew, because it's a one-way, talk-only beacon."

He nodded. "That changes the whole scenario for the zoo excursion."

"Yes, it sure does."

I never doubted that the Major would set me up with a ride, but we had something more than a car waiting for us just a few yards away.

Cousin Elmer and his teenage sidekick leaned against two exotic cars in the Omani Embassy's turning circle. Cousin Elmer was the dim-but-dedicated cousin of our billionaire founder, Alan Sabel, and the curator of his collection of cars and limousines. He handed me a bag from Hugo Boss stuffed with new clothes and keys to a Lamborghini Aventador Roadster. "Mr. Sabel says if you bring Pia home before dinner, you can keep the car."

He turned and started for the Maserati.

"What if I fail?" I asked.

Over his shoulder he said, "He's a practitioner of the Mayan rituals."

Tony touched the door handle, and the scissor door flipped skyward, almost hitting him in the face. "No pressure."

I slid into the driver's seat and found a sticky note from Cousin Elmer on the starter button. It read, *I'll do anything to help. Please bring her back.* I looked up and watched him pull into traffic with that same stone face he had when the guys at the estate ridiculed him. Ms. Sabel was probably the only person on earth who'd said a kind word to the man. I caught his glance as he sped away and gave him a small salute.

The drive back to our temporary headquarters in Carver Langston was difficult. Neither of us wanted to put the top up on the convertible in the futile hope that some ladies would see us driving it. Word is, Lamborghinis have a special kind of high-tech paint that makes single women stick to them like a magnet. That remote possibility forced us to shout over each other and the traffic noise on our competing calls.

Some of my friends at the DIA had bits of information for me.

The first report said twenty-seven Syrians were given special asylum visas and flown from Beirut to Andrews Air Force Base. Naturally, the trail grew cold from Andrews, where a State Department representative had signed for them. Any request for further information would raise a flag and get my friend in trouble, which was not something she was willing to do for me. Anymore.

The second report said the Syrians' paperwork had been approved by the Under Secretary for Civilian Security and Human Rights. I asked my friend if she could find any similar scenarios out of the region, and she promised to get back to me. Her enthusiasm caught my ear. I'd have to look at my calendar for an open Friday night when this was all over.

The third report was the most interesting. Bill McCarty, Under Secretary for Civilian Security and Human Rights, had been at the CIA and was grilled by senators in a closed-door session. Rumor was that the CIA had caught him red-handed abusing the Patriot Act, engaging in covert operations that targeted US citizens residing in the country.

That was an abuse the Obama administration never got caught doing. The new administration had their own interpretation of the Patriot Act. In the space of five days after the senate hearing, the president nominated McCarty for the Under Secretary job, and the Senate rushed through his confirmation. Bang—he was a State Department man, and the CIA problem evaporated. My friend at the DIA thought maybe, just maybe, illegal wiretaps had senators from both parties by the gonads, and the job at State was a blackmail settlement. Her opinions often reflected the redacted portions of documents. I owed her a favor.

She suggested L'Enfant Café, a nice little wine bar in Adams Morgan.

I tried to remember her. Bridgette, a petite, bobbed blonde with freckles—maybe? I'd need more than that to pick her out of a crowd—which is why I always linked phone numbers to pictures in my address book.

"I'm driving one of Mr. Sabel's Lamborghinis," I said. "Text me. I'll make a reservation."

She giggled.

I clicked off and thought about the timeline. Three days after blackmailing the Senate and moving to State, McCarty approved the Syrians for asylum. Several days later, a clean-cut former Navy captain met with Ms. Sabel, and she ran afoul of the same Syrians. Asylum was McCarty's domain, and Patterson was as far from it as one could get. Patterson worked the other end of State, making sure military bases didn't upset local governments more than usual and that jihadis never ran off with a loose nuke. How had those two paths crossed? And what would either of them need with a platoon of Syrians?

Arabs sucking up to the US intelligence community was no big deal. All an Arab needed to say was, "My brother joined al-Qaeda. I can get you inside information." But those types were a dime a dozen and were brought in under a cloud of suspicion on an individual basis, not in clumps of twenty-seven.

Whether the Syrians were political refugees or the ambassadors of an unformed government, where were their families—their wives, mothers, and fathers? Twenty-seven men on one plane. No women. No children. Not even a cat.

Tony's unsettling concept was making me paranoid.

Then there was Mullaitivu. Ms. Sabel and her team exposed Nakdali, and days later we were knee-deep in Syrians. I could guess those things were related, but guesses like that often obscured the truth. And there were too many problems: I didn't see Asian pedophiles mixing with Syrian thugs, revolutionary or not. I didn't see pedophilia being protected by political appointees at the State Department, even if they were former CIA guys. And Ms. Sabel was on to something, so killing her would bring an investigation. Patterson's meeting centered on Mullaitivu. Was that a ruse? Was there some other reason State wanted Ms. Sabel's head on a platter?

It wasn't her fault we lost the 2011 Women's World Cup.

I shared my intel with Tony. "You ever hear of McCarty when you were the FBI's liaison to the CIA?"

"Oh, yeah," Tony said. "Not a pretty memory. I was brand-new, straight out of Quantico a month after the 9/11 attacks. Because I spoke Farsi and Arabic, I was water boy for a seasoned agent named Ali Soufan."

"The guy who contradicted the CIA's use of enhanced interrogations?"

"The same."

"Not a very patriotic guy. We needed that information."

"You know what people don't get?" Tony asked. He turned in his seat, glaring at me. "The FBI interrogates hostile witnesses thousands of times every day. We've extracted information from all kinds of people— religious zealots, drug kingpins, mobsters, terrorists, the criminally insane. I'm talking about people who don't want to give it up. We've been doing it successfully for a hundred years. Through world wars and the Cold War, terrorism and saboteurs, we know how to get the truth out of people.

"The CIA is in a different line of work. Spooks talk targets into giving them information in exchange for money or sex or citizenship. It has a history of buying information, like the Bay of Pigs, the Shah of Iran, Saddam Hussein's WMDs, and the Chinese Embassy in Kosovo. At the opening of the War on Terror, the CIA didn't do interrogations. It had no idea how to get information out of a terrorist who didn't want to give it to them. You would think it'd turn to a guy like Ali Soufan, who'd been working over al-Qaeda for years and getting results. You'd think the CIA would go to him and say, 'Help us out here,' but guess what it did?"

"Well, they didn't ask me."

"The CIA pulled in a contract psychologist who came up with an interrogation plan." Tony's voice rose about twenty decibels. "That guy had never been involved in real interrogations and had nothing behind his theories. The CIA decided to ignore a hundred years of successful technique, and a team who'd taken down several al-Qaeda guys already, just so it could experiment on prisoners.

"In the end, all the actionable information we got from the terrorists was taken by the FBI's team. Mr. Soufan was doing great: getting real information, getting in deep. So what does the CIA do? The CIA squeezed him out. It wanted to torture those guys despite the endless proof that torture is illegal and unproductive."

"I thought we found bin Laden from information extracted through torture."

"Hollywood misconception," Tony said, spittle flying out of his mouth as his volume rose. "The name of the driver was extracted years before the CIA workers even realized they had it. It was only after they stopped torturing people that they started to understand what information was real and what was made-up. Hell, the CIA worked those terrorists over for years, long after any knowledge they might've had was outdated. And y'know why those terrorists are still in Guantanamo? Because we tortured them using techniques are illegal in any court in the world. Those guys can't be tried in anywhere.

"For a hundred years, the FBI's been perfecting interrogations. A hundred years! But no, a contract psychologist who never once conducted an interrogation has a great idea. Let's go with that and kick the FBI out of the war zone." Tony slammed his fist on the dashboard. "Stupidest goddamn decision in the history of intelligence gathering."

"Whoa. Easy there, Tony. I'm on your side." Tony and I were pals, traveling and partying together since we met at Sabel's initiation seminar. I'd never seen him so heated up about anything.

CHAPTER 14

I PULLED TO THE CURB in front of Café Carver, the Major's new headquarters. Sabel agents swarmed in to check out my ride. Tony climbed out and took a bow. I eyeballed all of them until they went back to their job: watching the street. I knew the Sabel family would replace my Jetta, and the Lamborghini was one of three, but the thought of an IED landing in the front seat of an automotive work of art was an unthinkable sin. I posted one of our junior agents at the front fender.

Major Jonelle Jackson had excelled in a male-dominated army partly because she didn't command her troops, then or now, by bellowing like a man. She issued visual orders. I stormed down the sidewalk, making a beeline for Douglas, when she put her hand up like a traffic cop.

Stop.

"Before you go anywhere," the Major said, "tell me about the connection between State and these Syrians."

I told her what I'd learned from my friend Bridgette at the DIA. She thought about it while I watched Douglas. He was sitting in a metal chair at an outdoor table, talking with Raissa, Agent Carmen, and Agent Verges. The fact that Verges beat me to the café meant I'd been doing more cruising in the Lambo than I'd intended.

"It doesn't make sense," the Major said. "Patterson brought her here. But he had to know the connection to the Syrians would come to light."

"Patterson didn't know. Someone above him offered him a chance to prove himself, and he jumped at it."

"We need to know who's calling the shots. Making assumptions won't give us actionable intel."

She was right. Whether Patterson was pawn, rook, or bishop didn't matter. The top priority was getting Ms. Sabel back before the Syrians took her someplace and killed her. I needed a live Syrian who would talk, and I needed him fast.

"Patterson was a destroyer captain," I said. "People like him don't do covert operations. He wouldn't know how to handle a group like this, and he wouldn't have learned at State. He hasn't been there long enough."

"Even so, I want you to find Patterson and take him apart."

The old Mercedes with twenty coats of wax stopped in the street. The three occupants got out, tossing hard looks through their dark sunglasses. I waved them over. The leader was the spitting image of the tall, skinny kid. His posse stood behind him and folded their arms. He slouched and said, "Who the fuck are you?"

I gave him a formal introduction, including the Major. He told us to call him Ishmael. "You and I have a problem with Syrians and—"

"Damn straight. They shot Rashad."

"—I need your help."

He winced when he realized what I'd said. "Why I should help you?"

"I'll make the Syrians go away," I said.

He stared for a long time, reading my eyes, then looked at the Major. He took a deep breath and checked out the eight agents roaming the block. "And I'm supposed to believe you're gonna take them out, move on, and leave me alone?"

"I don't care what you believe," the Major said. "We're at war with these guys. After we clean up, we clear out. We're not here to change your life one way or the other."

He soaked up her words for a beat, then nodded and pointed at her. "I like you. You're straight up. What d'y'all need?"

"This is a long shot," I said. "Do you know where I can find Hamoud, a short guy with a goatee?"

"You for real? If I coulda found that slimy Arab, he'd be dead a month."

"OK," I said. "Second option: I need a Syrian, preferably one of the outcasts."

"You can't catch one?"

"They see me coming, they draw guns and start shooting."

He looked hurt. "They don't see me as a threat?"

"Not today. Today, I'm their number-one problem."

The fat guy behind him tapped him on the shoulder and whispered something in his ear. He nodded and said, "You gave some kids fifty bucks. What's in it for us?"

"First, you give your brother his fifty bucks back. Then bring me a Syrian, and I'll give you two hundred."

"Each," he said and gestured at his companions.

The Major fisted her hips and stuck her chin out. "Three hundred for each babbling Syrian. Split it anyway you want. No babble, no money."

He smiled and put out his fist. The Major bumped it. I bumped it. He and his posse turned and left.

The Major said, "You figured they've been watching the herd for the last couple weeks, looking to cull the weak, so they're ahead of us."

"That's right."

"Pretty smart—for a man."

Best compliment I would ever get from the Major.

In the three years I'd known her, I'd never heard her talk much. Her power came from saying little and meaning a lot. Yet early on, I had the impression that beneath the icy surface was an ocean of hardship. While I lay in the hospital recovering from the Cameroon mission, I researched her background. She was forged in the crucible of LA's Crenshaw neighborhood when large, organized drug gangs ruled territories measured in square miles. Her younger brother died at age ten in a drive-by shooting, and her mother ceased to exist in official records by the time the Major was twelve. Community leaders recommended her to West Point, where she was a star.

Her service career was stellar too. Had she been male, earning the same combat citations as her peers, she would have been a general—maybe with multiple stars. But right at the height of her career, when she was up for an important position in the Pentagon, she went to work for Alan Sabel.

I said, "I want to question Douglas."

She nodded her permission.

I assessed him as I approached. In my experience, a grown man won't cry unless his daughter turned sixteen or he lost a brother in combat. Douglas had never been to war and his daughter was young. He was a man who didn't cry because he hadn't learned how. The fact that he wasn't crying about his kidnapped daughter wasn't what bothered me.

It was geometry.

I reached across the table, grabbed his shirt, hauled him to standing, and dragged him around Carmen to face me.

"Why did they dart Tania, Douglas?"

His eyes blew open big as saucers, and his head shook slowly from side to side.

"Hey!" Agent Verges stood to challenge me.

Carmen, who knew me well, didn't move. Raissa gasped.

"Tell me the truth, Douglas. You walked to the van with Tania and Ms. Sabel. You were expecting to trade Ms. Sabel for your daughter. The Syrians slid open the van door. Then what happened?"

Douglas's eyes searched mine and found no sympathy. His breathing was heavy with fear. He said, "She pulled a gun. They grabbed it and done took it away. Shot her with it, too."

"No, Douglas. I want the truth. You walked up to the van. Who was in front?"

"Ms. Tania. She said for security."

"And where were you?"

Douglas's eyes darted sideways. He squirmed in his shirt trying to get away.

"Where were you when the van opened?" I asked.

Raissa answered for him. "He was behind Ms. Sabel and me."

"You were expecting to retrieve your daughter from kidnappers, and there was a triangle of three women in front of you? Why weren't you at the front of the triangle, Douglas? Why weren't you pushing your way past everyone else?"

"But I thought ... Ms. Tania said ... I—"

"Knew your daughter wasn't there," I said.

He went limp. I let go.

He collapsed on the ground, then levered himself up on his elbows. "You don't understand. They got her. They gonna kill her."

"The trouble with lying the first time is getting everyone to believe you the second."

"You gotta believe me. They got her. They said they'd kill her."

"Where, Douglas? Where do they have her?"

"I don't know." He turned his face away.

"That's your second lie," I said. "One more, and I'm leaving you to the Syrians."

"I'm telling you—I don't know."

I squatted, grabbed his ear, and pulled him close. "Zoo security said you turned around pretty quickly. You knew she wasn't at the gorilla cage. Obviously, the Syrians made you believe they'd kill your girl if you didn't give them Ms. Sabel, but you're not dumb enough to take their word for it. You had to know where she'd be and how you'd get her afterward. Without that information, you never would've given up my boss."

"They gonna kill her," he said.

That part was probably true. His daughter's life hung in the balance of our actions, but the path to saving her lay in standing up, not giving in. As the concept began to seep in that the Syrians would kill his little girl anyway, Douglas broke down. His tears began to flow.

Raissa came close and sat next to Douglas. She took his hand and stroked his head. She said, "You gotta tell them what you know. I saw that woman in action, and I'm telling you, she is a servant of the Lord, Douglas. You gotta believe in what these people can do. You gotta tell them where she is."

Douglas looked at me with swollen, tear-streaked eyes. "Don't know about all that religious stuff. They told me, come alone after the cops leave, or they gonna cut her. But can you do it? You swear to God you can bring her back alive?"

I was with him on the religious stuff. I already had an open tab with whatever deity has the Grim Reaper's leash, and I didn't want to run it up so high that I'd have to join a monastery. "I can do my best, and that's a better chance than they'll give her. Right now, they have no reason to release her. She could testify against—"

"Whoa!" our FBI man said. "Hold it right there. Kidnapping is FBI territory, not a place for mercenaries or vigilantes or whatever you are. No. You stand down. I'll handle—"

I rose and stepped close to his face. Tony stepped in behind him, and Carmen took the left. Five feet away, Agent Miguel stared at him.

"You're right," I said. "Get on the phone, and rally your team. Have them meet you right here."

Verges stared hard for five seconds, then glanced away.

I grabbed Douglas by the collar and dragged him to his feet. I pushed him into the street while Miguel, who stood six-four and weighed 220, took over the nose to nose with Agent Verges.

CHAPTER 15

CARMEN AND TONY FELL IN behind me. A block up the street, Carmen borrowed a garden hose from a front yard and looped it over her shoulders. Tony found a pile of bricks, shoved one in each pocket, and carried several more. Douglas looked confused at their actions. I didn't bother to explain anything; I just kept pushing him to show us the Syrian lair.

"That one," he said when we stopped at a corner.

A cube-shaped brick apartment house stood at the end of the street. Douglas said the Syrians had his daughter on the second floor, corner apartment. The rest of the building was abandoned.

"OK, Douglas," I said. "You stay right here until you hear gunshots. Then you come running as fast as you can. Do not look at anyone. Do not duck or hide or get scared. You run to the door, pick up your girl, run around the side of the building, then run down the street. Do *not* look back. No matter what happens to me or my team, no matter what you see or hear, your priority is to get her to safety. We clear?"

He nodded without looking at me.

I grabbed him by the shoulders and turned him to look at me. His frightened eyes rose to meet mine.

"Dougy, this is for her. One mad dash up to the building. One mad dash down the street. No matter how scared you are. No matter how dangerous it is. Can you do this?"

He swallowed, clamped his jaw tight, and straightened up as tall as he could get. "Yes. Yes, I can."

"Now tell me—how many are in there?"

"Two."

"Any of them hanging out in other apartments?"

"No. A meth lab blew up in there, musta been a year ago. Stairs was concrete, same as the landing, but the floors was wood. That was the only one still has a floor."

"Any names?"

"Hussein was the one I spoke to. I don't know the others."

I patted his shoulders and turned away.

My friends' faces were tight, set on the fight ahead of us. The risks were understood, and we knew we would win. We just had to stay chill and execute the plan.

We took the long way around, coming at the building from the opposite corner. No one was on the roof, no one patrolled outside the property, and only one man was posted on the ground floor. As we pointed out our separate paths to each other, the ground floor guy stepped outside.

He cupped his hands around his face and lit a cigarette. I darted him from far beyond the dart's effective range and yet managed to tag him. He slipped to the ground, sitting upright with his back against the door, propping it open.

I'd like to claim it was my excellent marksmanship, but there's no denying it—sometimes I get lucky.

We took it as a good sign.

At that distance, the gunshot was no louder than a slammed door, but the missing man would draw attention sooner or later. We went into action. Carmen flew straight to the fire escape at the back. Tony ran to the side of the building. I went for the back door and stopped with my back to the brick.

Carmen scampered to the top and onto the roof in a flash. She found a good position and reported over our earbuds. Tony stepped out in front and threw his bricks—one into each corner of a window, knocking the sharp edges out of the way. Carmen was over the side, dangling by her garden hose. When the last brick went through, she followed it. By then, I was already on the landing. I knocked politely.

A burst of three rounds answered my knock. Disciplined shots—an amateur under attack from the window would have emptied half the magazine. That meant Douglas was wrong, there were more than two guys in this deal. I reached across and knocked again.

In Levantine Arabic, I said, "Hussein, let me in. Hussein."

Another blast. This time, half his magazine shredded the door. His pattern started in the middle of the door and went across the handle, through the jamb, and continued through the paper-thin walls. Most people will stand on the knob side to avoid getting shot through the door. I always stand on the far side. It's an illogical spot because of the longer reach and, therefore, less likely to become a target. It worked.

I cried out in a howl of pain that would have won me an Academy Award if Tarantino had been filming it. I followed up in Arabic, "Hussein, I'm hit! You shot me!"

Light flashes under the door indicated someone close inside. I slammed my foot into it, and it splintered out of the lock and bashed him hard in the face. He recoiled and tried to bring his Colt SMG up to fire. I reached around the frame and fired three darts. He fell.

Carmen stepped into the tiny hall behind him, her gun leveled at me. She lowered it.

"Damn it, Jacob," she said. "You wanted one of them awake."

"You already darted the other guy?"

"Other two. They still had their backs to the window, dodging bricks when I came in. They had sawed-off shotguns. What was I going to do?" She turned and ran down the hall. "C'mon, I found the girl."

A surprised girl with wide eyes tracked our every move. She sat in a chair with a coloring book and crayons. We moved in slowly, Carmen saying gentle words as Douglas came charging up the stairs. The reunion was quick. Raya tossed her crayons aside and flew off the chair into Douglas's arms. At least the man cared about something. With his daughter clinging to him, Douglas looked at me, speechless.

"I told you to take her and run. I meant it. This is not a secure location."

"Thank you," he said.

I squeezed his shoulder. "You're welcome. But I can't trust you. I need you out of here."

He nodded and ran.

We secured the Syrians and left them for the FBI.

Carmen returned the borrowed garden hose while Tony and I combed the apartment—bare wood floors, water-damaged drywall, dirty windows, and a layer of dust on the floor. One folding chair, one plastic lawn chair, a wad of bubble wrap, and a padded bill folder from Visa were the only loose items in the building. Inside the folder was a waiter's pad with a sandwich order written on it and *Sabel, no later than 3:00 p.m.* in Arabic. Both parts looked like the same handwriting.

My watch read four thirty.

I called the Major. "That goateed waiter at the café—have Miguel try some Arabic on him. If he answers, hold onto him."

She turned to someone and made it happen before asking me for details. After some background discussions, she came back on. "Turns out he owns the place."

When I filled her in on the pad, she agreed, my handwriting analysis implicated him. Not a smoking gun, but definitely a sign the café owner had not yet chosen sides. Part of me understood him. If we lost the war, the Syrian retribution would be terrible.

By the time I got to the café, Miguel already had the guy in tears. As I thought, the café owner was under the same pressure as the others and had done whatever the Syrians had asked of him.

He told us that after Ms. Sabel walked away from Patterson's meeting and headed into the dry cleaner, Hamoud arrived at the café's back door and stayed until he had watched the drive-by shooting. The café owner took a cold compress to Ms. Sabel with the idea of warning her, but he chickened out at the last minute and said nothing. He swore his allegiance to us and admired the number of armed security people we'd brought. But as far as I was concerned, he was just another spineless guy in the hood.

I had more respect for Ishmael and his crew.

Hamoud had to be one cold SOB to kill his own men. There had to be something driving the Syrians we had yet to understand. Since they had diplomatic immunity, Hamoud feared what his people would tell Sabel agents more than what they would tell the police. We don't have the Bill of Rights hanging over our heads; we can question people all we want.

The Major and I speculated on the cryptic note about Ms. Sabel.

"The Syrians were planning to hand her off by three," the Major said. "They took her a little after two thirty, so they handed her off twenty minutes from here."

"You could barely make the Beltway in twenty."

"You could make the State Department building."

"True." I contemplated that idea for a minute. Obvious, but secure. Still, it would take one seriously rogue secretary to do something that dicey. "I think that's unlikely. I'm thinking suburban—a safe house. A Silver Spring condo? No privacy. A farm in Prince George's county? Too far. Oxon Hill?"

"Suitland would make sense," the Major said. "Anonymous neighborhoods and lots of forest off the parkway there. Plenty of places for a transfer."

But we were both wrong.

Agent Carter called in from headquarters, and the Major patched him in.

"Ms. Sabel's secondary phone just came on. We had a lock on it for a few seconds. Then it went dark again. Last position was three hundred feet above the runway at Andrews Air Force Base, heading southeast at 110 knots, climbing and gaining speed."

CHAPTER 16

THE VAN CAREENED AROUND THE corner at high speed, leaning dangerously close to the rollover point. Pia Sabel's three Syrian captors snapped looks left, right, front, and back with furrowed brows.

"You should be worried," Pia said. "You just shot someone in broad daylight and left three witnesses."

The driver looked at her in the mirror. Then the front passenger gave her a quick, angry stare. But none of them spoke. The front passenger was a little older, had a hint of gray in his beard.

She twisted slightly and pressed her back against the waistpack they'd forgotten to take from her during their frantic getaway. Turning and pointing quickly, she indicated a street they'd just passed. "Was that a cop? He had his lights on."

The driver looked over his shoulder first, then the others. The driver turned his head forward in time to swerve around a slower car before diving back across the lane to catch the access ramp. He accelerated onto the parkway as fast as the old van would go.

"You may have fixed the license plate, but you're going to wreck the car if you don't slow down."

"Silence, woman," the driver said.

She put out her palms and shrugged. "So we all die—what's the big deal?"

The man in the passenger seat berated his companions in Arabic for several minutes. Her captors kept looking out the windows, searching for signs of the SWAT team they were sure would descend on them at any moment. The leader stopped talking as the van slowed on a sweeping exit ramp. Through the windshield, over the driver's shoulder, Pia caught a brief glimpse of a large gate next to a brick building. The van swayed and creaked to a stop.

All she could see was an open, treeless space in front of them. A uniformed man came to the driver's window, and the driver gave him papers. The leader stared at Pia. She gave him a contemptuous smile. The side door creaked open, and a uniformed soldier with a dog poked his head in. The dog gave a few sniffs, and the soldier pulled back and slammed the door closed.

Then the door slid back open. The soldier with the dog stared at Pia.

"Excuse me, ma'am, but are you that, um, soccer lady?"

The leader looked at the driver, who tensed, but said nothing.

"Pia Sabel. Nice to meet you," she said. She gave the soldier a small wave and a smile.

"My sister's a huge fan," he said. "She's center D at Arkansas State."

"I'll bet she could block my shots."

He leaned back with a big grin, glanced quickly at Pia's traveling companions, then blushed. "Oh, sorry. Didn't mean to hold you people up."

"No problem. If you have something to write on, I'll give you a note to send her."

His face lit up. "Really?" He patted his pockets, then held up a finger. "Hold on a sec." He disappeared into the guard building for a moment, then raced back out with a Joint Base Andrews postcard and pen in his outstretched hands.

Pia took them and wrote, "Your brother says you're good. Next time you're in town—bring it." She added her phone number and signed the card with a smiley face underneath. When she handed it back to the young SP, he thanked her continuously.

While the soldier spoke, the man sitting next to Pia leaned over and slammed the side door closed. The gate opened, and the van moved through.

After driving most of a mile, Pia saw a large, fat airplane with a bulbous nose and two propellers on each wing, alone on the tarmac. She'd seen the same type of airplane many times in her travels. One of her pilots had flown them in the military and spoke of it fondly: short takeoff, heavy lifting, indestructible. It was a C-130, if she recalled correctly. They were used for cargo, hurricane research, forest fires, and a host of other things. A large ramp led into the back of the plane, but nothing was moving.

The guy in the passenger seat continued berating his men. Their heads drooped.

Pia unbuckled her seat belt without a sound and held it in place long enough to let the slack release unnoticed. She pulled her waistpack around, rehearsed her movements in her mind, and prepared for the right moment.

The van slowed to a stop two hundred yards short of the plane.

"Should we kill the stupid people now or later?" Pia said.

The Syrians stopped talking. A little confusion and curiosity registered in their faces. The driver's eyes met Pia's in the rearview mirror. She pulled the Glock out of her waistpack's hidden holster, pressed it to the thigh of the man next to her, and pulled the trigger. The front passenger jumped at the noise. He spun around, looking like an angry bear, and tried to leap on her. He forgot his seat belt.

Her second dart hit him in the neck.

The driver fumbled out of his belt and reached for something in his pants pocket. Before he could get it, Pia had her Glock pressed to his neck.

He froze.

"You're just the delivery boy," she said. "I have no problem letting you live."

He relaxed a little, and Pia asked, "Did you release the girl?"

He looked over his shoulder and frowned.

"Don't play dumb. I traded my freedom for the release of Douglas's little girl. How do I know you've released her?"

He shrugged.

"You just drive the van. I get it. So tell me, what happens next?"

The driver didn't speak.

"I know you speak English," she said. "You looked at me in the mirror. Your friends weren't so quick. So I'm going to ask you one more time: In your orders to bring me here, what happens next?"

"We give you to Caldwell," he said with a light accent.

"Here?"

He nodded toward the plane. "Yes."

"I'm going for a ride?"

"Yes."

"When?"

"Few minutes. We're early."

"Who is Caldwell?"

"I don't know."

"What does he look like?"

The driver shrugged.

"The little girl?" she asked.

"They never took her. How do you say—eh, hoax."

Pia dropped back in her seat and thought for a moment. "You fooled Douglas? And me? I don't like that." She leaned up close to him and pointed at the plane. "Are you coming with me?"

He shook his head no.

"I'll save my questions for Caldwell then."

She pulled the trigger.

Pia propped up the three men to look as though they were resting, then rifled through the driver's pockets until she found the paper he'd shown at the gate. It read, "Department of State, Under Secretary William H. McCarty." It gave a tarmac location and permission for six people to go there in accordance with Project Snare Drum. Nothing else.

She folded the paper and stuck it in her waistpack. She retrieved her darts and shoved them into an empty soda can, then cracked the front windows to give the sleeping Syrians some air and climbed out. Heat shimmied off the tarmac, and the sun beat through her. She adjusted her ponytail and looked around.

Everything was still, quiet, and hot.

Pia leaned against the van and watched two fighter jets land and taxi from one of the runways. Joint Base Andrews, formerly known as Andrews Air Force Base, was busy protecting the nation's capital, the Pentagon, and hundreds of vital government sites.

Decision time. Her plan had been to find the trafficked children and liberate them. She was convinced there was a connection between the

Syrians and the children. It was a simple plan: let the Syrians take her to their hideout, and Tania and Marty would raid the place. But that plan was trashed. Tania wasn't coming, and Marty hadn't picked up. Worse, an air force base never entered her mind for a location, much less a flight somewhere. Should she risk the plane trip to who knows where? Or grab the Syrians she had and question them? How long would that take?

She couldn't bear the thought of what those children were going through right then, much less letting it go on for another day. She thought of the boy being dragged away by the tall man.

It couldn't wait.

If she recalled correctly, the C-130 was about half as fast as her jet. No matter where her captors took her, a team of Sabel agents could land minutes later. The plane would take her one step closer to where the children were held. Not too bad of a risk if she could free the boy and the others. If the tall man were there, she could wrap the whole thing up.

What's life without a little risk?

She checked the time and thumped the tarmac with the toe of her shoe.

A car appeared from behind the C-130, drove in her direction, accelerating to a rate of speed higher than reasonable. Two silhouettes sat in the front, none in the back. One had bulky shoulders, and the other looked average.

Showtime.

Pia stepped away from the rear of the van and slung her waistpack over her shoulder. It crossed her mind to buckle it around her waist as designed, in case she had to run, but this way her gun was easier to reach.

The Crown Vic angled as it approached, swerved to Pia's left, and stopped.

The driver opened the door, planted his feet on the ground, and hoisted himself up using the door frame as an aid. He was a large man with overbuilt muscles, and he rose to a height a few inches taller than Pia. He had a fighter's nose: broken repeatedly and never set properly. His ears and browridge were deformed by violence. His eyes were bloodshot with leathery bags underneath. His neck was thicker than most people's thighs. Other than the effort required to get him up and standing, he moved like someone fifty pounds lighter.

The passenger remained inside, obscured by shadow.

"What the hell happened here?" the driver said, striding toward the van at a rapid clip.

"Hi, I'm Pia Sabel, and you are?"

"About to beat the shit out of you if you don't tell me what happened to my guys."

"I'll just call you Pinhead then."

"Fuck you." He strode toward the van, letting his sport coat flap open to show off the holster on his belt.

"Did your mother teach you that kind of language, Mr. Caldwell?"

He stopped in his tracks and turned around, reaching for his weapon.

She put her hands in the air, palms out, and mouthed, "Oh my! He has a gun."

He huffed and turned to look in the van. He ripped the door open, and the front passenger fell out as far as the seat belt would allow. Caldwell felt for a pulse, then pushed the man back in and closed the door. Trotting around to the driver's side, she heard him repeat the procedure. He stepped back into view at the front. "What'd you do?"

She put a finger to her lips. "Shh, you'll wake him up."

"Don't give me that. What happened to them?"

"Do you drug test your thugs, Mr. Caldwell?"

He stormed toward her. "How'd you know my name?"

"You're listed on this authorization paper." She held up the document she'd removed from the driver. "Signed by Under Secretary William H. McCarty. It says you're authorized to fly at your convenience with guests of your choice. Is that me? Am I your *guest*, Mr. Caldwell?"

He snorted.

She shifted her stance, crossed her arms, and asked, "Where'd you play football?"

"Arizona Cardinals."

"Oh, never made it to the pros then?"

Behind her, Caldwell's passenger laughed.

"How'd you know I played?"

"Bad knees, head trauma, steroid muscles, not too bright—not hard to figure out."

Caldwell glanced around the area. "Put your hands out."

"Make me."

He strode to her, his face growing redder with each step.

The passenger door opened, and a familiar voice called from behind her, "Just a precaution, Ms. Sabel. A formality."

Without turning, she said, "Shut up, Patterson."

Caldwell slowed and glared at his companion. "You screwed up the operation, Patterson. She was supposed to be delivered in chains." He turned to Pia. "You're getting shackled, one way or the other. Now put your hands out."

"You'll have to clear that with the guard at the gate."

She tossed her chin over her shoulder and Caldwell's eyes followed her. Reading her adversary's face told her that her soldier watched them with binoculars.

"You think you're smart?" Caldwell said. "Fine. He can't save you where you're going."

She pushed off the van and started walking ahead of them. "Is this your little airplane? I'd have taken us there in my jet if you'd asked nicely."

Caldwell scoffed.

She ran ahead a good distance, then stopped and looked at Patterson. "Are we going to meet Hamoud and watch him shoot one of his own men again?"

CHAPTER 17

"NICE WORK," PATTERSON SAID. "SHE outmaneuvered you in ninety seconds."

"You think so, asshole?" Caldwell said. "Wait til we get to my house." He walked a few strides in silence. "You need to get something straight here: You don't out rank me, we're peers. I work for McCarty. I don't know who you work for."

"I work for…," Patterson gritted his teeth, "McCarty too."

"And he gets his orders straight from TGW. So quit pulling your bullshit rank on me."

Patterson kept his eyes aimed forward, trying hard to let the man's insubordination slide for now. He was an appointee while Caldwell was an employee, a distinction he would have to ignore for the time being.

After a few strides, Caldwell said, "She said Hamoud shot one of his own men. I heard he got them both."

"He missed the second one."

"That's not good."

"Shooting them was idiotic. Broad daylight, plenty of witnesses—whose harebrained idea was that?"

"McCarty makes those calls, not me. I'm in charge of site security. Today I got a last-minute call to put my interrogation expertise to use. But I get it. You blew the job, so McCarty brought me in to fix things. I have no problem beating the shit out of a girl until she breaks."

"Whoa, we're not beating her up. No. That would be a bad—"

"Look, Patterson, I have years of experience from Guantánamo. I know what I'm doing. I do the interrogation, and you call it when we're done. You don't have to like me, but don't worry, I get results. Results matter. In the meantime, you need to grow some balls." Caldwell pointed ahead. "Besides, she's got one tight ass. Y'know what I'm saying?"

"Nobody cares what you guys did with a bunch of cab drivers from Tora Bora. Pia Sabel is a high-profile citizen. If something happens to her, a whole world of shit rains down on Snare Drum and anybody near it."

"TGW's in a big hurry to find out if Sabel compromised the program. This is my op, so we're doing it my way. That's why they picked me for this part."

Patterson tensed as they walked. "All I'm telling you is, respect her."

"Scared of her, Patterson?" Caldwell said. "TGW doesn't think she's such a big deal."

Patterson went quiet for a moment. "How do you know? Did you talk to him? Do you even know who he is?"

"No. And neither do you. We're not need-to-know people."

"Who does know TGW's identity, McCarty?"

"I'm sure he has his guesses." Caldwell gave Patterson a sideways glance as they walked. "You think about the wrong things, Patterson. We have a job to do. We're going to do it. End of discussion."

"Aren't you going to restrain her?"

"Why? Look at her. She's going like a lamb to the slaughter."

Patterson walked up the cargo ramp into the belly of the plane and squeezed past two shoulder-high pallets. The pilots were giving Pia a tour of the flight deck. He couldn't suppress a sneer. Low-priced contractors enamored with a minor celebrity.

The loadmaster closed the side door and pointed Patterson to a row of nylon web seats attached to the fuselage.

Near the flight deck door, Caldwell took off his jacket and tie, folded them neatly, and put them in a stowage bin. He looked back at Patterson. "Relax. It's going to be eighty-five when we land."

Patterson nodded and stowed his coat and tie.

They sat, leaving an empty seat between them. Caldwell leaned over. "Do you have some specifics you need to know?"

Patterson thought for a long moment before he answered. "I need to know if the guest list has been compromised."

"Guest list?"

"Yes."

"That's cute. Are you trying to protect somebody's identity, or discover it?"

Patterson stared straight ahead.

"OK," Caldwell said, "so there were people there. She saw them. We want to know if she can identify them. Hell, that's easy. You take 'em to international waters, fly about a thousand feet over the waves, lower the cargo ramp, and start asking questions." Caldwell laughed. "Works better if you have two. You toss one of them out to make sure the second one knows you're serious."

Patterson took a deep breath and walked to the rear of the plane. The loadmaster nodded at him, raised the ramp, and sealed the plane.

Patterson pulled out his phone. He texted: *Who vetted Caldwell?*

The answer came back almost instantly. *He's vetted. Why?*

Patterson texted: He's dangerous and uncontrollable.

Known issue. Anything else?

TGW's identity may be compromised. Who is supposed to know?

Only you.

CHAPTER 18

PIA THANKED HER HOSTS FOR the tour and took a seat across the fuselage from Patterson. Like all military planes, this one smelled of hard work: scratched aluminum with a dash of grease, the ozone from warm electronics, and a hint of sweat.

Caldwell scowled, crossed over, and sat next to Pia.

Up close, he smelled of a bad hangover.

"I like to stay close to my guests," Caldwell said. "In case they need something. Do you need anything? A beverage perhaps?"

Pia looked him over slowly and shook her head.

"Where're we going?" she asked. "Somewhere special?"

"Yeah, Disneyland."

The engines fired up one at a time until Pia could barely hear herself think. Then they revved up another notch, and the plane rolled across the tarmac. It made a sweeping turn and accelerated down the runway.

Pia reached into her waistpack, found her reserve phone, and turned it on. She saw texts from the Major, Agent Jacob, Dad, and several others. A string of them came from Mark, each increasingly demanding. She sighed and moved on. She estimated about thirty seconds online would give her crew her location. She counted the seconds in her head and turned the phone off.

Caldwell leaned in close. "No reception at altitude, and no service where we're going. You can try all you want."

She fake smiled at him and put her phone away.

He fake smiled back. "Give me the bag."

"No."

His arms whipped out from behind him, a loop of rope in each hand. He landed one loop around her neck, and after a quick tug, she was choking. Her hands reflexively pulled on the nylon noose before she realized he had the second noose wrapped around her wrists. He rose, lifted one eyebrow with a mocking look, and tugged hard.

She couldn't breathe.

In another flash of movement, he had the rope around her shoulders and back, more of it winding her arms against her torso. She kicked at him, only to find another noose waiting for her feet. He gave another tug and dropped several rope ends on the floor.

"There," he said. "You're not free to move about the cabin, and I don't have to worry about you the rest of the trip."

He loosened the noose around her neck just enough for her to breathe.

She started to scream and got half a syllable out.

He quickly pulled the rope tight again. "Ah, ah, ah," he said. "No talking during the in-flight movie."

She stopped trying to scream, and he loosened the noose.

Across the way, the loadmaster stared with his mouth hanging open, his face as white as a sheet. Pia pleaded with her eyes, but he looked away. She turned to Patterson next, but he was trying hard to read a magazine.

Caldwell took her bag without looking in it and tossed it to the loadmaster, who dropped it on the floor and kicked it under his seat. Caldwell pushed some bags that looked like parachutes across several seats, making a relatively flat surface. He patted it, gave it a satisfied look, and lay down for a nap.

Pia worked her wrists against the ropes and tried her fingers on the knots, but everything she did earned a snap of the rope from Caldwell. After six tries, she stopped. Thinking would be better than struggling.

Thirty minutes into the flight, Pia caught the loadmaster's eye and did her best to pantomime a question about the flight's length. After figuring it out, he indicated four hours on his fingers. From the few windows available, she'd caught an occasional glimpse of ocean and noted that the sun was on the right of the plane. They were going south and a little east. She scanned a map in her head but could visualize only the Bahamas. The Bahamas were closer than four hours, even in a turboprop.

Her jet full of agents wouldn't know where to go until she landed.

Taking the trip might have been a mistake.

Another thirty minutes later, when Caldwell's snoring reached a crescendo and Patterson was nodding off against the fuselage, she tried working the ropes again. The loadmaster watched her carefully but didn't say anything. Just as she was about to pull one hand out, Caldwell snorted, sat up, and tugged hard.

Pia choked and gagged.

She waited two more hours, leaving about an hour of flight time. Then she announced loudly enough to wake Caldwell and Patterson both, "I need to use the toilet."

She pointed with her chin at the inelegant open commode attached to the forward bulkhead.

Caldwell blinked and nodded. He let out a little slack for the ropes.

Patterson looked up with one eye from his resting position and watched them.

"I'll need my purse," Pia said, pointing to her waistpack under the loadmaster.

Caldwell sneered and motioned for the loadmaster to hand it to him first.

"Actually, I just need a tampon out of it."

Caldwell and the loadmaster froze. Patterson reclosed his eye and shifted his position as if snuggling against the fuselage.

Caldwell said, "Give it to her."

The loadmaster tossed her waistpack. She trapped it against her chest with her bound hands.

She stepped to the toilet and made a production out of pulling the plastic privacy curtains around her. Not full length, the curtains left her feet and ankles exposed. "Could you untie one hand?"

"No," Caldwell said. "Make do."

"You afraid I might jump?" She nodded toward the window.

He laughed. "Figure it out."

She closed the curtain and put her pack in her teeth. With some effort, she retrieved her gun, dropped the pack on the floor, and wiggled her knees to look like squirming. She sighed and said, "Yoga pants are really tight. Could you help me?"

Caldwell threw back the curtains with both hands and a big grin.

Pia darted him.

He fell like a dropped piano.

She aimed at Patterson and eyeballed the loadmaster.

The loadmaster sat with his elbows on his knees, his mouth hanging open, and holding an e-reader. Not a threat.

She shook off her ropes, stepped to Patterson, and took a seat next to him.

"I was hoping you'd turn into a good guy, Patterson. But here you are, working with a foulmouthed gangster. What's up with that?"

"He's not a gangster."

She stared.

Patterson squirmed. "He's new at State. I met him just before takeoff."

"Why is he here?"

"I have no idea."

"He thinks he's responsible for me. You told me you're as ranking an official as I deserve, so you must be in charge. That means you should know more about him, doesn't it?"

"I'm not on the need-to-know list."

"Why did your Syrians try to kill me?"

His eyes rose to meet hers but dropped again. "Not my Syrians."

"You helped them get asylum."

He took a deep breath. "I was in Turkey. Someone asked me to check them out."

"Who are they then?" she asked.

He didn't answer.

She asked, "Did you fail to check them out, Patterson?"

His mouth opened, as if to say something, but he shut it without a word coming out. He gripped his knees, his gaze still on the floor. "I'm not on the need-to-know list."

"You sure don't need to know much."

He rubbed his face with his hands. "Where did you learn to fight?"

"I find boxing to be therapeutic. You wouldn't believe how much stress you can relieve by beating the crap out of someone who's trying to kill you."

He winced and bit the inside of his lip.

"I thought you'd take me somewhere closer to home, outside the beltway or West Virginia—maybe as far as Fort Benning." She waved at the pallets. "Guess I was wrong. Where're we going, Patterson?"

He shook his head.

Pia said, "What are your orders?"

"Make sure you stay alive."

She pulled the trigger.

He slumped.

"Thanks," she said, "but I'll take care of myself."

Training her weapon on the young loadmaster, she moved next to him.

He dropped his e-reader but didn't reach for it. With his hands on his knees, he looked at her with wide eyes. "This is a pressurized flight, ma'am. Uh. A bullet in the fuselage could—"

"Where are we going?" she asked.

"I don't know," he said.

She waited.

His knees bounced up and down, his feet vibrating with the rhythm of his nerves.

"It's an island," he said, "but I don't know what it's called. We're just a contract crew. We carry stuff and some passengers."

"Big or small?"

"The island? Tiny. The landing strip is a stretch of rock on the beach."

"No military base?"

"Not to land in. Guess there's one somewhere around there."

"Tell me about the island."

"I dunno. We come in at dusk. There're no lights, no towns, no people. We land; an old truck comes with a couple guys; we off-load the pallets and passengers; then we leave."

"Straight back to DC?"

"No, ma'am." He gulped and stared out the window on the far side. "Refuel in Florida. I'm not supposed to be telling you this."

"You're doing the right thing. Just one more thing: How often do you make this trip?"

"Whenever they tell us. Sometimes once or twice a week, sometimes not for a couple weeks." He leaned forward and ran his shaking fingers through his hair. "Why did you kill them?"

"They're not dead," she said and explained Sabel darts. "I'm the good guy."

He shook his head and turned a shade of green. "I don't know about that stuff. I don't know what's going on or who you are or anything. I mean, why did you do that?"

"Ever see Caldwell before?"

"Yeah."

"Think he's a good guy?"

"No."

"Trust your instincts then." She shot him in the thigh. "Sorry, my friend, but for now, you'll just have to trust mine."

She found a bungee cord and hooked it around the loadmaster to keep him upright in his seat. Reluctantly, she did the same for Caldwell and Patterson, then gave all three of them an injection of antivenom.

She untied a corner of the tarp on one pallet and checked it out. There were white cardboard boxes with nothing on them but a seal from a warehouse. Peeling back the tarp a little farther, she pulled open a box filled with toothpaste. The next was OxiClean. Another had deodorant and condoms. A larger box contained brand-new 16GB thumb drives and 500GB USB hard drives. She stared at them for a long time, trying to imagine where the drives fit in. The second pallet had many different types of boxes. Canned food filled the first three, and cereal filled the next two. Pia took a deep breath and pushed everything back in place.

The pallet had that industrial look to it, as if someone were stocking the shelves of a warehouse. She glanced at the three darted men. She was looking at a supply flight for a much larger operation than she had anticipated.

Pia checked her magazine: three darts left.

She rose and headed for the forward bulkhead.

Just outside the door, an unmarked box filled with toys caught her eye. Deeper in it were wet wipes and military MREs. Tilting the box to see all the outside corners, she found a label. This one was from Amazon and had a shipping label to S. Kowalski and a street address in Reston, Virginia.

She climbed the ladder to the flight deck. The small space was insulated from the cargo bay. The copilot looked over his shoulder, curious, as she stepped quickly toward him. Her dart was deafening.

The pilot spun around, directly into her muzzle. A name strip above his pocket read "S. Kowalski." She pulled off his headphones with her free hand and explained the darts.

"So, you have a choice," she said. "You can sleep through the rest of the flight, or you can do what I tell you."

"You're hijacking—"

"Yeah, I have lawyers on retainer who tell me not to do this kind of thing. Just keep your hands on the yoke, and tell me which option you'd like."

He glanced at her, color coming slowly back to his cheeks. His eyes returned to the horizon. "What do you think you're doing?"

"I intend to have a look at Caldwell's little getaway. Ever been there?"

"No."

"What kind of people does he bring with him?"

"I'm not answering questions. You have to turn yourself in. Give me your weapon." He started to push his way out of his seat.

Pia pushed the barrel in his face. "Don't stand up, or you're going out for the next four hours. One of my pilots can walk me through how to land this thing."

He dropped back into his seat. "Not where we're going, they can't."

"Then I'll leave it on autopilot and parachute in. Maybe you'll wake up before you run out of fuel."

He was quiet for a moment and repositioned himself in the chair. "What's this all about?"

"I think Caldwell is doing something offshore because he'd get life in prison if he did it on American soil. And you're helping him."

"I follow my orders and fly whatever he puts on board. What goes on—"

"You already know there's something wrong with this place, Kowalski."

"What do you mean?"

"The box of toys," she said. "Who runs Snare Drum? Caldwell? Patterson? Someone else?"

He looked up at her, scowling.

Pia hopped into the empty flight engineer's chair, above and slightly behind the pilot. "Did they bring the children on this plane, Kowalski?"

He turned away and looked at some instruments.

"Did it look right to you?" she asked.

He sighed and stared out the window for a long time. "They were drugged. They staggered on board and slept the whole way."

"How long ago?"

"Last time? Few days ago. There was another flight two or three weeks before that."

"You didn't question them?"

"I'm not allowed to."

Pia nodded. "You just fly drugged kids from Washington to wherever, no questions."

"Not Washington. We picked them up in the Azores." He took a long time before speaking again. "I have kids of my own. The way these kids looked—it made me sick. I challenged the handlers about the children's safety. They threatened to kill me if I asked too many questions. So, I reported it."

"Who did you report it to?"

"Under Secretary McCarty."

Pia nodded and thought for a moment. Then she said, "The last bunch of kids, they came from Sri Lanka?"

"I have no idea."

"And some of them escaped?"

CHAPTER 19

FROM A FEW MILES OUT, Isla de la Mona looked like a cake on a table. A thin, green line topped white cliffs rising from a deep blue ocean. Kowalski said the island was an uninhabited nature preserve presided over by the barrio of Mayagüez, Puerto Rico. There was a small navy reserve on the western coast, a tiny version of Guantánamo that had been abandoned for decades. The southeastern side had an old lighthouse, and farther south was an abandoned fishing hut with a dock. The island was roughly seven miles long and four across, with a coastal road that circled the perimeter.

The pilot pointed out a dim line of Puerto Rico forty miles off their left horizon. On the right, another forty miles, lay the Dominican Republic. The northern and eastern coasts of Isla de la Mona went straight to the bottom of the ocean. A reef and shoals protected the rest of the island, running from the southeast around to the west. The landing strip was on the southwestern coast.

Pia hopped down from the third chair, leaned against the copilot's chair, and turned her phone back on. A hundred texts and emails waited for her, but she couldn't get to them because Mark, her soon-to-be former boyfriend, was sending her a current text that blocked everything. *We'll have dinner at 8. Capitol Grille.*

She texted back. Sorry, had to leave town. Back soon.

You need better org skills to be a top exec.

Pia gritted her teeth and stared into space. She counted to ten and thumbed out her reply. *Later. GTG.*

S. Kowalski looked at her. "You're getting a signal?"

"Ever heard of Sabel Satellite Systems?"

"Sure. They provide in-flight Internet connections for airlines." He looked over his shoulder. "You don't have a satellite phone. You have an Internet phone. Wow."

Pia didn't answer.

The flattop island was covered in dry scrub and cactus, while the thin beaches were thick with vegetation. Several cave systems were visible from the air. Kowalski told Pia of sinkholes with trees growing out of them and caves hundreds of yards long.

"Fly us past the base," Pia said. "I need to see the layout."

"Not happening. It's a no-fly zone. They'd shoot us down."

"Why? Aren't we bringing the supplies?"

"We've maintained radio silence since we left the standard flight path. I turned off the ID beacon two hundred miles ago. We're off the air controller's grid. There's no communications equipment at the base anyway. The men there shoot down anything approaching the western side. We fly in from the east and land. They hear us and call us on a handheld radio when they're ready to off-load."

On final approach, a thin ribbon of road, nothing more than two tire tracks, was visible running down the cliff, then out to the landing strip. On the other side of the strip, the road disappeared into thick vegetation.

The plane touched down, hopped up, stalled, then slammed down hard onto the runway. Pia lurched forward, holding the seat back to stay upright. The sleeping copilot bounced in his harness. The plane came to a stop and spun in a tight circle, ready for takeoff.

Pia said, "Pull it back to the middle of the runway."

Giving her a concerned look, the pilot pushed the throttles open and rolled the plane forward. He flipped switches and pulled levers until the engines stopped. The silence felt like a bad headache coming to a sudden end.

"How long before they get here?" Pia asked.

"Usually about thirty minutes, sometimes longer."

"Which one is the fuel dump switch?"

He stared at her, his head shaking.

She raised her gun. "Leave enough to get to Puerto Rico."

"You can control a fuel dump on Gulfstreams but not on this old bird. Once it starts, it's all or nothing."

She waved her gun. "Get on with it. I don't want anyone leaving until the authorities arrive and make some arrests."

After a resigned shrug, he flipped a switch labeled "boost pump," and then one labeled "cross feed valve." Then he hit more switches and valves. What sounded like a fire hose poured fuel from both wings. Within moments, the smell reached them.

She got up and went aft. A moment later, he caught up with her and lowered the cargo ramp.

They followed a narrow trail through thick vegetation that led to a beach. Salt and sea wafted in on the gentle breeze. The sand was smooth and white, the ocean a pale blue inside the reef and a deep blue beyond. The twilight air was soft and warm: perfect shirtsleeve weather. Under different circumstances, it would have been a romantic walk on the beach.

When the breeze changed, they smelled hibiscus and strolled back to the runway as the sunset glowed behind them. The strip had been cleared of vegetation for twenty yards on either side. Beyond that clearing, the jungle was thick with vines and bushes and palm trees. On one side, a cliff rose two hundred feet above them.

"The men come from that direction," Kowalski said, pointing behind them where the dirt track disappeared into the foliage.

"How many men are stationed here?"

"I've been doing this run for six months. I've seen three different groups swapped out on a revolving basis. Eight guys at a time. There could be twice or three times that many, for all I know. A few of them look like seasoned veterans. Most of them look like lazy kids."

She nodded. "So who's in charge of this place?"

"Caldwell's new," Kowalski said. "He yells at the Syrians the whole time he's here. There's a guy on-site named Nakdali, but I've never seen him. I think he's the head Syrian. Sometimes I hear the men talk about someone else they call TGW. I think he's over Nakdali."

"Ever hear of a guy named Hamoud?"

"No."

"What about Patterson?"

"Never seen him before."

Pia scanned the cliffs and the trees. "What about the guests? Who comes here besides Syrians and drugged children?"

"No one else flies." Kowalski blew out a breath. "But I've heard the men talking about meeting a boat."

"A boat is an easier way to smuggle passengers on and off the island. No airport security, no passports required. They can fly the captives in and out of the Dominican Republic or Haiti."

Kowalski nodded. "Turks and Caicos wouldn't be too far. Even Cuba." He paused. "I don't know why I'm helping you."

"Because you're helping the ones who escaped. So am I."

He stopped. "What are you talking about?"

"The toys."

He turned away, looking at a point of land covered in low palm trees and thick underbrush. "Don't know what you mean."

"You brought stuff for them," she said. "There are some of them out there, right?"

He kicked the sand and nodded.

A radio clipped to his belt squawked. He looked up and said, "What do you want me to tell them?"

"Come and get it."

He pulled up the radio and spoke. "Ready when you are. Out." He clicked off.

They walked back to the plane, where Pia rifled through the storage bins looking for anything useful. She found a flashlight and a knife. She slipped Caldwell's weapon, a Glock 19, into her holster. It weighed a lot more than her gun.

Kowalski watched her, chewing his fingernails.

When she was ready, she looked him over. "Coming with me?"

He didn't answer.

"Will it be better for you if they find you with the others?"

He nodded.

She walked him back to the flight deck and shot him.

CHAPTER 20

AN ANCIENT CHEVY'S HEADLIGHTS PRECEDED its arrival, a surreal glow rising above the brush in the dark. The light bounced and wound its way through the trees, heading for the airstrip, before popping into the open. Ten miles an hour, Pia guessed.

"They're here. I'm shutting down now," Pia said.

"OK. But don't do anything until we get there," the Major said. "Don't jump down any holes or dive into any rivers. Don't take any unnecessary risks—"

"Gotta go." Pia turned off her phone.

Slipping the phone back in her pack, she dropped from the tree branch and pushed through the bushes to the edge of the airstrip's clearing.

The truck looped around and backed toward the open ramp. It stopped suddenly, and Pia heard a shout, one of the newly arrived calling to the loadmaster. A rusty door creaked as it opened, and a flashlight swept over the ramp and into the hold. A second flashlight joined it. One of the flashlights disappeared into the hold and a voice called out names. The other stayed outside, his flashlight flowing over the fuel spill. Their words were too far away to hear, but the tone was easy to understand.

Finding a ghost plane had them rattled.

Pia smiled.

The men searched inside and out as best they could, then radioed for orders. All Pia could hear was the squawk of the radio over the gently breaking waves and the breeze. The men turned off their flashlights. Briefly illuminated by their vehicle's interior light, they retrieved weapons from the cab. Then they stepped away and slammed the doors.

Everything was dark again.

The moon was three days past full, still big and round and bright, but it had not yet crested the bluffs to the east. There was only enough light to make the shadows play tricks on the eye. Grayer than black, Pia could see the shadows of the men on the white limestone runway better than she could see the men themselves. She backed deeper into the branches and pulled her gun.

The men split up, one taking the road leading up the hill, the other hiking back the way they'd come.

Any noise—breaking a branch, bumping a bush, tripping—could get her killed. She moved slowly, testing each step.

She mirrored the second man's movements, staying a hundred yards behind him and ten yards into the vegetation. Feeling her way along until she dared go no farther, she crouched and eased closer to the clearing.

As she expected, the man began working his way back toward the beach. Pia waited, keeping a bead on him, willing him to come into range. With only one dart left, it would have to count.

His shape and posture became clear as he continued stepping closer and closer.

She ruled out running away. Too risky.

The waves rolled gently onto the beach, and the breeze swayed the leaves. Salt and fish and sand smells hung in the air.

The man kept working his way closer to her. He wore sport sandals, cargo shorts, and a loose-knit shirt. Leading with an FN MK 20, he swept five yards inside the bush perimeter, moving sideways. Every third step, he took a look behind him.

Pia glanced around to gauge visibility and decided he had a fifty-fifty chance of spotting her.

Shoot him, or hope he passed by without seeing her?

In the distance, the other man showed up for a fleeting second, just a shadow on a strip of dirt track far beyond the runway. Over a quarter mile up the road, he'd be two minutes away if he were a sprinter, but she would probably have three to five minutes. This was the best time to execute her plan.

The man near her pushed his pace, impatient with his progress, and shortened his procedure. Pia could see the whites of his eyes, strained and darting. He was half-afraid but fully alert and committed to killing anything that moved.

His weapon swung her way and stopped, aiming straight at her for what seemed like a lifetime, then moved on. He stepped directly in front of her, close enough to tackle in two strides. Close enough for him to fire before she could take those strides. He took another step, moving away from her. She coiled the springs in her powerful legs and readied herself to leap on him. But he froze in place, only slightly turned away. His weapon swung back toward her, brushing back a row of broad leaves that formed part of her cover.

She had a bead on his face, but she wanted his back. It was a larger target.

He turned toward her, looking straight into her eyes, his weapon trailing his gaze by a safe margin. Something had piqued his curiosity. They both froze for a breathless second. His head tilted for a better look, examining an undetermined shape. It was as if he knew something was out of place, but he wasn't quite getting it. He was looking for a thirty-year-old male commando in jungle fatigues and face paint.

The beach breeze shifted direction, stinging Pia's nose with the stench of aircraft fuel.

It burned the man's nose too, and his eyes shifted to the side.

Noises near the beach reached them, distracting him even more.

He rose to full height and looked for the source.

While Pia processed the sound, he tracked away from her. Still not presenting his back, he tried to do both jobs at once: hunting for an unknown enemy while investigating an unknown noise.

Pia replayed the brief sound in her head. What was it—footsteps on broad leaves? A held branch snapping back, maybe? An animal grunt? Were there wild boars on the island? She'd been so focused on her adversary, she'd missed the noise.

Then she heard another sound.

A muffled yelp, like a frightened child with a hand clamped over her mouth.

The man broke into a run.

Pia leapt from her hiding place and chased him down.

He heard her approach and twisted halfway around, his weapon spewing lead into the bushes. She threw herself into a roll, landing her torso at the side of his knees. His weapon fired again, this time into the night sky as he went down. Pia landed on her back and fired a dart into his chest as he fell.

Again, a child's cry floated on the breeze and was quickly muted.

Pushing off her attacker, Pia grabbed the Belgian assault rifle and his flashlight. Searching him, she found a pistol in his waistband—an HK45C if she remembered her training at all. Rolling him over, she found nothing. No wallet, no keys, no knife—nothing.

Peering into the darkness, she thought the voice came from the area where she'd left the children's box. She ran there, two hundred yards from the runway and deep in the brush, only to find the box missing.

Looking for the children would have to come later. She ran to the truck, found the keys in the ignition, fired it up, and floored it. At least it wasn't a motorcycle; this, she could drive. The back tires spun on the sandy runway before finding traction and pushing forward. She fumbled for the headlights, turned them on long enough to find the road, then switched them off again. The other man would be running full speed but would be at least a minute away. Would the truck be a target in the dark?

Following the track ten yards into the brush, she switched the lights on again in time to swerve away from a tree. She pushed her luck with the lights on for another two hundred yards, then cranked the wheel hard and pressed the gas, spinning the tires in the sandy track and sliding the truck sideways. When it stopped, she hopped out and pumped bullets into both tires on her side. After a moment's thought, she put another bullet through the radiator at an angle, hoping to do as much damage as possible.

She stepped into the brush, putting a few trees and thick shrubs between her and the road, and double-checked the guns. The Heckler & Koch pistol had never officially been adopted by the US Army but was available on the commercial market and favored by law enforcement. She could see why. It was lighter than her Glock and felt comfortable in her hand, yet the magazine held ten .45-caliber rounds. One quick glance confirmed what she'd thought after firing it. It was filled with hollow points, bullets meant to expand upon impact. There were seven left.

NATO chose the FN MK 20 for special ops teams, and the Navy SEALs had adopted it as one of their standard-issue weapons. It was not available commercially. It was a sniper support rifle, an odd choice for these men unless they never expected anyone to make it ashore. This one had the short magazine option: ten rounds. She pulled out the magazine and counted three left, plus the one in the chamber. With her limited experience working automatics and the weapon's high rate of fire, it would be good for one squeeze of the trigger.

These men were better armed than the ragged bunch of mercenaries in Mullaitivu.

She pushed through the underbrush back toward the runway. In the distance, she heard the sound of another truck. She picked up her pace, shoving the branches aside until something caught her eye.

She stopped.

Ahead, deep in the shadows between two small palm trees and behind a broad leaf, were two human eyes.

CHAPTER 21

PATTERSON UNSCREWED THE WIDE TOP and tossed it aside. He glanced inside to see ice floating in water. In a quick motion, he repositioned his grip, one hand on the bottom and the other on the open flange, and splashed the ice water in Caldwell's face.

"You even sat next to her," Patterson shouted, "so you could keep an eye on her. But you couldn't keep your eyes open. You idiot."

When Caldwell shook his head, water flew off him like a wet dog. He sputtered and frowned and tried to stand, but the flight harness held him in place. He wiped his face and shook himself once more, then looked at Patterson. "What the hell?"

"Tranquilizer darts." Patterson held up a spent dart. "You were supposed to keep her restrained. You failed."

Caldwell took a deep breath and looked around. Two men stood at the end of the empty cargo bay chuckling. He said, "What the fuck you looking at, assholes?"

The two men trotted down the ramp into headlight beams on the runway.

"What time is it?" Caldwell said.

Patterson looked at his watch. "Ten."

Caldwell nodded and tugged off his seat belt. "What happened?"

"You fell for her 'hand me my purse' routine."

"That damned loadmaster. Where is—"

"Don't blame someone else. You're supposed to be security here. Did it enter your pea-brain that she had a weapon in there?"

Caldwell stood up too quickly and flopped back into the seat, dizzy. He tried again, more slowly the second time, and grabbed Patterson's shoulder with a meaty hand.

"Gimme that." Caldwell grabbed the dart out of Patterson's hand and held it to the nearest light.

Patterson glared. "We need to find her."

Caldwell's eyes opened wide while he felt his empty holster. He pulled up the leg of his trouser, found his ankle gun, then kicked his pants back into place. He took another deep breath, shook his head, stared at the bulkhead, and blinked several times. "OK, fill me in. What happened?"

Patterson recounted what he knew. "Then she crashed the truck in the road and took off overland. It took the men an hour to clear the wreck and start the search. They can't find her, even with night vision goggles."

"She must know the island then. She knows her way around."

"No way. She'd have brought her army. No one knows about—"

"Shut up. Lemme think."

Caldwell went forward, opened an icebox, and grabbed a Red Bull. Popping it open, he slammed it back in one long gulp. He stalked down the cargo ramp into the headlight beams and accosted the two men waiting for him.

Patterson followed.

The waning moon lit the airstrip in light gray, leaving the tree line beyond it looking like a black curtain. To the north, clouds were building up, darkening the horizon. The wind gusted, and each wave broke harder than the last.

Caldwell stepped up to the shorter man. "What have you done so far?"

"Tracked her to the beach," the man replied with a thick accent. "Maybe she had a raft, or she went across the rocks. The waves are rolling in, so she did not go far."

As if verifying the statement, both Caldwell and the man cocked an ear to the sea and heard the waves crashing against the rocky shoreline to the west.

Caldwell said, "Any flashlights missing?"

"Two. One from the plane and one off Habib."

"Then she could have walked the rocks, maybe made it to the caves. D'ya check the caves?"

120

"Masri and Salih are out there now."

"That's it? Two guys?"

"That's all the Colonel wanted to spend on the problem, sir. He said—"

"Nakdali's not a colonel anymore. He's just another civilian working a contract." Caldwell stomped five steps away, looked out to sea, and came back fast, pointing his finger in the young man's face. "Take your damn groceries back to Nakdali, and tell him that woman and two of her bodyguards burned down Mullaitivu. If he doesn't get serious, he's going to be swimming for Puerto Rico by dawn."

The young man shrugged.

Caldwell said, "Since you're useless, give me your weapon and an extra mag." The man reluctantly complied, handing over his MK 20. "And the pistol, the NVGs, and a radio."

The young man handed over the gear. "The Colonel is on channel six, Salih on two. Base is four. What are you planning?"

"I'm planning to bring in our guest."

"The Colonel would not like that. You will complicate targeting, and we already have our best men out there."

"Best men? If your guys could find the moon, they'd be guessing."

The young man glanced over his shoulder at the gibbous orb, caught himself, and glared at Caldwell. The two Syrians turned and left, muttering Arabic insults as they went.

Patterson watched Caldwell stomp toward the beach, adjust his goggles, and look around. The big man turned up the path, while Patterson followed a smart distance back. They reached an open stretch of sand and began walking near the water, Caldwell's head swiveling from side to side.

"Make yourself useful for once," Caldwell said. "We're looking for a track in the sand. Three or four hours have gone by. It's going to be blown over, but there could be something. The giveaway will be a pattern heading in one direction."

Patterson stopped and looked out to sea. "Tide's going out. I don't have my charts, but I'd guess there's a one-foot sea on this shallow beach. That would put her up the sand farther."

"What d'you mean?"

"You're too close to the water. A couple hours ago, this would've been under. If there are tracks to be found, they'd be higher up the beach."

Caldwell nodded at him. "So, you're not just another pretty face."

Patterson pointed up the slight incline and trudged through the sand.

They strode a hundred yards and turned around. They'd reached the point where the coral met the beach. No tracks.

Caldwell pulled out the radio unit and set it on channel two. "Hey, search team, this is Caldwell. Where are you, and how much have you cleared?"

He picked up his pace as he waited for a response. None came, so he repeated himself. On his third try, his voice flared. A squawk came back, followed a few seconds later by a transmission.

"We needing radio silence, sir." The accent was thick and barely understandable. "We clear third cave now—open one on beach. No sign of entry."

"The third cave? That's all you've done in an hour?"

"Radio silence, sir. We believe she have unit."

Caldwell turned the unit off and stared at Patterson. "Those idiots."

Patterson waited for an explanation.

"Of course she has a radio. I thought they'd be smart enough to code their location. Now she knows where they are and where I am. She has weapons and a defensible position. We'll have to kill her."

CHAPTER 22

"FIVE OF THEM," PIA SAID. "The boy from Mullaitivu found me in the dark."

Pia paced as she waited and looked up into the night sky through the hole in the rock. She stood at the bottom of a twenty-foot vertical shaft that connected a labyrinth of caves to the surface. A serpentine tree rose from the muddy floor through the hole, obscuring some of the moonlight. Watching her signal strength meter, Pia found a straight line from her phone to the satellite a hundred miles above her, pushed her earbud in tight, and perched on a nearby rock.

The youngest girl sat next to her, leaning her back against Pia's side. Pia slipped her free arm around the girl and made soothing sounds. The girl clutched Pia's arm.

A minute later, a lyrical voice came on the line. "Ms. Sabel, I am Agent Dhanpal. The Major said you need my help."

Pia explained her problem: A girl and boy led her to the cave where three more children were hiding out. None of them spoke English. The eldest was the boy she'd seen kidnapped in Mumbai and tracked to Mullaitivu. The youngest was the cute young girl that gripped Pia's arm and wore a black hijab. Pulling an extra earbud from her pack, Pia linked the boy to Dhanpal as her remote translator.

His name was Khelemba and he told her that a boy at the compound had jumped off a cliff into the surging tide below, thinking he was committing suicide. Instead, he discovered an underwater cave entrance just below the water's surface. He snuck back into the compound and told the others. After several escapes, the guards sectioned off the cliff. For the first few days, the children stole food from the compound. One day, the pilot spotted the children from the air. From then on, they found stacks of meals-ready-to-eat, toys, and clothes after every flight.

Khelemba had arrived on the island a few days earlier and learned the story in rough translation from another boy. He immediately snuck through the barriers to make the leap.

He remembered Pia from Mullaitivu.

Dhanpal said, "He didn't understand what you were trying to do in Mullaitivu until too late. He was herded onto a boat and taken away. He hoped you would return."

She rubbed his dirty hair and smiled at him.

He looked up at her with big, brown eyes and smiled back. His arms slipped around her waist, and he hugged her as if he would never let go. She hugged him back and bit back tears, reminding herself not to give into emotions too soon.

After leaving Mullaitivu, Khelemba had been drugged and taken on a long trip with the tall man named Safwan and two other children. They'd stayed one night in a stone building. It had walls so thick that when he'd crawled into a windowsill to see outside, only his knees remained in the room. There were other children in the stone building, some from Mullaitivu and some he'd never seen before or since. It was cold and rainy in that place, and the children had huddled for warmth.

Of the children, Khelemba could communicate with two of them, and one of those could communicate with one more. The littlest girl, still leaning against Pia, was from Yemen but no one spoke her language. She cried a lot and wandered around all the time. It was her voice that had alerted the guard to their presence near the airstrip. Khelemba called her Bacci, or baby girl.

The little girl shrank behind Pia and squeezed Pia's arm harder, as if she sensed they were talking about her.

Dhanpal left Pia with a few basic Hindi words, then transferred the call back to the Major.

"Jacob is leading the team," the Major said. "Dhanpal is with him, so you'll have a translator when they arrive. A tropical storm is coming ashore on Puerto Rico's western coast. They've shut down Mayagüez and Arecibo. Jacob's trying to make San Juan before it closes, but it'll be a close call."

"Dominican Republic?" Pia asked.

"Not allowed to bring weapons into the country, and Jacob loaded the jet before he left. The Coast Guard won't send a chopper with the weather so rough. The team will try to find a ship's captain who'll take them to you, but that will be a longer route. You might be there twenty-four hours before we can get to you."

Khelemba gave Pia a tour of the cave system. From the sinkhole with its central tree, five arms radiated outward. One went back three hundred yards toward the island's center before narrowing to an impassable crack. Two more arms shrank to crawl spaces within a hundred yards, one of which the children used as a latrine. The fourth and largest arm served as their daytime space. Another cave branched from there to a cliff and another narrowed to a slot too thin for adults to pass through. The last one opened to a small dead-end room that the children slept in.

With Dhanpal translating, Pia sent the children to bed with orders to stay beyond the narrow passage until she had secured the island.

Dhanpal hesitated. "Children thrive on ritual, symbolism, acts that speak more than words. They believe you came to save them, and now you're going to leave them. They'll worry and come looking for you. Give them a sign that you'll return."

While Dhanpal sang *Nini baba nini, Sleep Baby Sleep,* on speakerphone, Pia held her hand to her heart, then pressed it to each child in turn and gave each a kiss on the forehead. She followed with a hug. Pia gave a longer hug to the Yemeni girl, Bacci. Dhanpal gave the children a password: *surakṣita*, Hindi for *safe.*

Closing the connection, Pia sent the children off and watched as the last blanket dragged through the narrow slot into the dead-end room. She waited and listened. They were quiet enough. She hoped.

Pia turned her attention to the caves. She tracked mud from the sinkhole to one of the short caves and fit a length of thread across a narrow point at ankle height. Back near the sinkhole, she took up an uncomfortable position behind a rock that afforded a protected view of the tree. She turned on her stolen radio and waited.

An hour went by. Then another. The sounds of rodents scurrying about and occasional static on the radio kept her alert.

Then the transmission came in: Caldwell checking with the search team.

She looked down the pitch-black cave that led to the beach. They were coming. The cave was defensible at the constriction near the beach, but that would leave the sinkhole vulnerable to a second team. Deciding it was better to confront the known enemy rather than wait one that might not exist, she moved through a dark terrain. In some places the rocks were boulders as big as cars, and in others they were jagged ankle-height chunks. Sometimes there were yards of smooth surface. Every few steps, she stopped, listening intently for any sounds. Occasionally, she risked turning on her flashlight for a dim view of the way ahead.

Eventually, she found scree leading to a constricted passage and crawled up the small mountain on her belly. When she reached the opening, she peered into the darkness beyond and listened. After hearing nothing, she risked a flash of light. Below her, the broken rock formed a ramp down into a larger room with smooth walls and a mud floor. To one side was a thin slot. She snapped off the light and waited.

After a long time, dim flickers of light flashed in the slot. They were closing in on her but were still a hundred difficult yards away.

NVGs required at least some starlight to work, so the searchers used their flashlights the same way she had used hers, but in their case, with a lot less care.

Using her phone for a dim light source, she surveyed her immediate surroundings. To the right, the limestone wall left no room to work, but the mound fell away abruptly on her left. She moved in that direction, her face just inches from the constriction, and worked herself into a vantage point with some limited range of motion. In one hand, she held the pistol, in the other, a ten-pound rock.

She stopped moving, held her breath, and listened.

Hushed voices came from beyond the constriction. Arabic. Neither was Caldwell or Patterson. These two would be easy enough if they tried to come through the opening, but that left a scary proposition.

Where was Caldwell?

CHAPTER 23

PATTERSON FOLLOWED TEN YARDS BEHIND Caldwell as they climbed the steep path at a rapid pace.

"Look," Caldwell said over his shoulder, "I don't mind you tagging along, but if you can't keep up, go back to the road and head for the compound."

"You never acknowledged me," Patterson said. "You cannot kill her. You are *not* authorized—"

Caldwell stopped and faced Patterson, his quad-optics NVGs giving him a comical appearance instead of the fierce look he intended. "TGW charged me with keeping this compound top secret. That order ranks higher than finding out who's on the guest list. I'll do anything to maintain the secrecy. If some rich punk has to die, what's it to you?"

"Scrutiny. If she dies here, there will be investigations, maybe even Senate hearings. This place would become a lot less than secret."

Caldwell's grin spread. "Her carcass will be found in Tampa Bay—on the *Seraphim*, the tender from her father's yacht. Quit worrying." Caldwell turned and released a branch he'd held behind him.

The branch slapped Patterson in the face. Patterson clenched his fists and fought an outburst while Caldwell strode twenty yards ahead of him. When he'd reined in his anger, Patterson caught up. "TGW never authorized deadly force. You cannot kill her."

Caldwell trudged up the trail.

In another twenty yards, they were above the tree tops with a great view of the ocean and southwestern beaches. There was less salt and more dust in the air. Behind him, Patterson could see the cargo plane shimmering in the moonlight. The shadow of a man ran from the plane, heading toward the bottom of the trail as if to catch up to them.

"I need you to acknowledge that TGW never authorized deadly force."

Caldwell shouted over his shoulder. "Did TGW tell you that? 'Cause he sure as hell never mentioned it to me. Deadly force is implied."

Caldwell stopped again, faced Patterson, and lifted his goggles. "What's the matter, Patterson? Never seen any action up close? All you navy boys do is press a button, and the cruise missile flies out of sight. Now you're all nervous about seeing a little blood, maybe a dead body or two. Well, don't sweat it. If you puke your guts out, I won't tell anyone you're a pussy. Now shut the fuck up. We're getting near the sinkhole."

Caldwell began to turn around but stopped mid move. He looked back at Patterson. "Do you even know how these operations work? Each member is independently empowered to do whatever's necessary. I'm doing what's necessary. You … what the hell are you? Are you even part of Snare Drum?"

"Let's get TGW to rule on your empowerment. I'm sure he'll agree—"

Caldwell stepped close to Patterson. "Can you get him on the phone?"

"Of course not," Patterson said. "As you so brilliantly pointed out earlier, the operational executive is classified. I don't even know what TGW stands for."

"The Grand Wazir," Caldwell said. "It had something to do with an old Broadway musical. The wazir was an advisor to the sultan, or so I've been told." Caldwell turned, tugged his goggles back into place, and marched on.

"Makes sense," Patterson said. "McCarty is the sultan in charge of the program, and the op exec is his advisor."

"Musicals are for fags, Patterson. Now shut up, or the authorities will find your body in the *Seraphim* next to hers."

"I have a sat phone and can get a question to McCarty and have an answer texted back in minutes."

"At this time of night?" Caldwell stopped and turned around. "TGW has to be a high ranking intelligence officer. You're going to wrench him out of bed right now?" Caldwell crossed his arms and leaned back. "Go for it."

Patterson did nothing.

"What I thought," Caldwell said. "You're full of shit, Patterson. You're used to having a ship full of grubs jumping over each other to bring you coffee. In covert field ops, rank doesn't matter. All that matters is results."

Caldwell turned and marched on.

Patterson kept a distance back while his mind ran through options for regaining control of his mission—or if he should even try. He heard a runner approaching and looked back to see the loadmaster running up the hill after them. The young man shouted.

Caldwell galloped back to meet him.

"Shut up, you idiot," Caldwell said as the two met where Patterson was standing.

Caldwell punctuated his statement with a slug in the loadmaster's stomach. While the punch was not as hard as it could have been, it was hard enough. The young man doubled over and dropped the rifle he was carrying. Caldwell picked it up and stuck the barrel in the boy's face.

"Copilot told me to help you," the young man said.

Caldwell scoffed. "You see any action?"

"I passed my weapons courses, sir."

"So no action. You mustered out and started delivering groceries?"

"They were downsizing the military, sir. No choice. But I know how to shoot. I was pretty good on the range and won some—"

Caldwell said, "You ever have a woman beat you on the range?"

"No, sir."

"You've got this. And you saved me from having to put Patterson down that sinkhole. He knows sextants, not weapons."

The two of them glanced at Patterson and laughed.

The three of them continued up the hill in the moonlight, the white limestone brightening the view. When they reached the plateau, the vegetation changed to cactus and scrub. More scrawny and sparse than the flora at the lower elevation, it was up to their shoulders in most places and higher in a few.

A hundred yards later, the radio chirped, and a voice spoke in a thick accent. "She hit Masri—main chamber, third cave."

Caldwell stopped in his tracks and stared skyward. He clenched his fist and clamped his jaw. After a long moment, he said, "Fucking morons."

He pulled out the radio and pressed the transmit button. "Salih, did you shoot her?"

"No."

"Why not?"

"He blocks passage in transom."

Caldwell nodded as if his man could see him. Then he spoke slowly, as if to a child. "Then pull his remains out of the way, stick your weapon over the transom, and pull the trigger—if that's not too complicated."

Caldwell let go of the transmit button, but Salih did not respond.

Caldwell pushed the transmit button. "Salih, are you standing in the main room with the radio volume up high enough for her to hear?"

No answer.

"Goddamn idiot," he said. He pressed the transmit button. "Salih, either you find a way to kill her, or I'm going to hunt you down and kill *you*. Now throw your radio as far away as you can."

Caldwell sent his over the cliff face and resumed his march. "TGW thought Syrians would make great PSCs. Plausible deniability, not even American citizens—perfect. Win-win, and all that idiotic management speak. Nobody stopped to think that they failed in their own civil war because they're a bunch of frickin' idiots. Heck, I watched one of them fire artillery point-blank at a wall. The shrapnel killed two of his own men."

Two hundred yards later, they stopped at the edge of a thirty-foot-wide hole in the ground. Rising from the sinkhole, a broadleaf tree stuck out above the surrounding bushes, leaning within four feet of their position.

Patterson looked around at the night sky. To the northeast, a line of black clouds grew larger by the minute. The moon rose ever higher, but the wall of clouds would catch up and overtake it within the hour. Within two, the island would be socked in. He considered his remaining time and the task ahead. He looked at Caldwell, who was finishing the same mental appraisals.

Caldwell got on his knees and crawled the last ten feet to the opening and put his chin over. After a long look, he rose and waved the loadmaster over. He said, "You shimmy down that tree trunk. Sabel's heavily armed, so shoot anything that moves, and clear at least the first three hundred feet in all directions. I want a safe landing zone when I get down there. Got that?"

With great difficulty, Caldwell levered himself back into a standing position and dusted his hands.

"Yes, sir," the loadmaster said. "Um. Could I have the NVGs?"

"Hell no. If she kills you, then she's got NVGs, and I don't. Christ, man, think for once in your life. Now get going." Caldwell kicked the boy in the butt, sending him over.

CHAPTER 24

PIA SILENTLY THANKED CALDWELL FOR the advice and shoved the rifle over Masri's inert shoulder. Using his body for a platform, she fired a three-round burst into the main room's ceiling. Salih's flashlight came on as he scrambled down the scree, found the exit, and fled without returning fire.

Masri moaned.

Pia gave him another thump with her rock. He stopped moaning.

His pockets were empty, but his backpack was full of goodies: NVGs, metal handcuffs and ankle cuffs, a length of chain, and a rope. Once she had his body pulled to her side of the narrow place, she propped her flashlight on a nearby rock. She cuffed his wrists and ankles, then connected the two together with the chain. She was unclear about how the restraints were supposed to work, but after a quick check, she was confident walking would be difficult, if not impossible, for him. She tossed the key into the dark.

If Salih and Masri were at this end, she could only guess Caldwell was headed for the sinkhole.

She had no choice but to defend the children.

Pia pulled the gun off Masri's shoulder. Then she pulled the pushpin that held her MK 20 together. The body swung open, exposing the chambering bolt, which she removed and put in her pack. She tossed the rest of her empty rifle into the dark. She slipped the new one, with a full magazine, over her shoulder and returned her .45 to her holster. She tried on the goggles and saw nothing until she turned on her flashlight. She took a breath and headed back up the tube.

Fifty yards short of the sinkhole, moonlight took over. She turned off the flashlight and felt her way along in the dark.

Something unnatural made a noise.

She stopped and listened.

Night vision worked well, but the contrast blocked her view of everything beyond the sinkhole's pool of moonlight. The other four arms of the cave were obscured by that bright center.

All she knew was that someone was in the sinkhole.

She strained to listen for some telltale sign of whom and where that person was. From the breathing, it couldn't be Caldwell. His cavernous chest would sound like a foghorn. The breathing she heard was fast and shallow: scared breathing.

Then she heard footsteps and the sucking noise boots make when slogging through mud. A slow suck followed by another slow suck. She raised her rifle and sighted down it.

Nothing.

She lowered it and stepped forward with caution. A flash of something in the moonlight caught her eye. She peered in that direction and caught another glimpse.

The loadmaster.

Blood pounded in her ears, nearly blocking out the sounds she needed to hear. The cave's darkness closed in around her. She tried to clear her head, to cool down, to think things through. She couldn't just kill the young man for having been conscripted into Caldwell's mission.

A car-sized block of stone resting against the cave's wall offered a protected vantage point. From there to the sinkhole was a wide-open space of over a hundred yards. She squeezed herself into the uncomfortably jagged corner where the rock met the wall and crawled up to a small v-shaped crevice. The boulder blocked her view to a third of the open space on her left, but the protection it offered was invaluable. Her only vulnerability was from the back should Salih show up. Bracing her elbows and the MK 20 in the crack, she listened and watched.

A crunch came from the left, just out of sight. She leaned into the crevice and saw a glimpse of a figure outlined in moonlight. His back was to her as he knelt, looking closely at something in front of him. After a moment, he clicked on a light, then clicked it off. He rose quickly and backpedaled five steps before turning and running to the tree trunk in the sinkhole.

The loadmaster shouted up to the surface, "Booby-trapped. She has it rigged. I'm coming up."

Pia wanted to celebrate. Her bluff—a simple piece of thread—had worked.

Caldwell's voice, low and steady, replied from above, "You do, I'll shoot you."

Pia bit her lip. So close.

The loadmaster stood with two hands and one foot on the trunk, desperate to climb. At Caldwell's words, he drooped and slid back into the darkness beyond the moonlight.

Pia saw a figure emerging from a dark cave: Bacci. She'd frozen in place at the sound of voices. Pia squeezed her eyes closed and prayed to keep the little Yemeni frozen solid.

The loadmaster sensed the girl's presence and stepped back into the pool of moonlight. His stare stabbed into the darkness, and he raised his rifle, aiming with nervous jerks left and right and center.

Pia raised her rifle and considered nonlethal options. Shoot the gun out of his hand? She was no marksman. Even if she pulled off the shot, Caldwell would know exactly where she was.

Her chest tightened.

A hint of light flashed in her goggles' peripheral vision.

She looked behind her. Salih was coming up, flicking on his light for a look before creeping forward. He was not in view, but the flicker of light could have come from only him. If she fired now, he would come running and shooting.

She turned back. The loadmaster was gone. Bacci was gone.

Clouds moved in, quickly fading the moonlight. The sinkhole turned dark.

The NVGs were much less effective. Pia turned one way then the other until she located the loadmaster. He stood back from the opening above, in the dark, his weapon still sweeping with tense, panicked moves.

She spotted Bacci, climbing over a rough pile of rock.

The loadmaster fired.

The little girl fell without a sound. Her body twisted and writhed for three seconds, then stopped.

Pia shrieked incoherently as her finger squeezed hard against the trigger.

All ten bullets left her weapon in less than a second. She threw the empty rifle away.

Behind her, Salih's weapon rattled off a single shot that ricocheted near her face. Splinters of rock smacked her skin. As long as he used the NVGs, he wouldn't see her against the rock, but if he turned on his flashlight, she would be an easy target.

But then, so would he.

Pia scrambled down the boulder as another shot cracked above her. She ran around the boulder, straight for Bacci.

Too late. Bacci's chest had a melon-sized hole in the middle.

Holding her pistol in front of her, she ran to the loadmaster, tears filling her eyes, and found his lifeless body. There were holes in his head, shoulder, and neck.

A bullet hit the ground by her foot.

"Don't move." Caldwell's voice came from above. "No one else has to die. Toss the—"

"You're wrong," Pia said and rolled out of his line of sight. "You have to die."

He cursed and fired three shots.

Her goggles flew off as she rolled. She twisted to reach them, snagging them a split second before another bullet chipped the rock floor near her elbow. Scrambling on her hands and knees, she went as far as she could from the tree. She looked around her, to the left and right, but saw no cover. With her NVGs back in place, she could see Salih approach the faint light of the sinkhole. She hoped his goggles were blinded as hers had been.

Caldwell fired off two shots.

"I am Salih," the soldier called out.

"I told you I'd kill you if you didn't kill her," Caldwell said.

"She no here."

"Don't give me that. Find her. Kill her."

Salih stepped back into the darkness as another cloud layer obscured the remnants of moonlight. She saw him adjust his goggles. The NVGs were quickly becoming useless for both of them.

She focused on hearing him. He stepped to the right, first one foot, then the other, each step carefully placed. He had only a general idea of her position. If he fired, the flash would give him away. The same was true for her. The first one to miss would die.

Her body shook with rage and fear and adrenaline and panic. With her forearm, she swept a wave of sweat from her brow. She tugged the neck of her shirt over her face and cleared her eyes. It pissed her off that Caldwell treated their deadly game like a sport, watching from above as two people fought to the death.

If she made it to the surface, Caldwell would die. She promised herself that much.

Repositioning herself, she felt her thumb touch a lever on her gun that moved. She tried to move it back but felt three positions. Her Glock had a double-trigger safety while the HK45 had several variants with different configurations for the control lever and slide release. Without light and time to examine it, she had no idea if it were ready to fire.

Her heart rate skyrocketed.

Salih stumbled and grunted. Fifteen degrees to her left.

Maybe.

She aimed by sound and pulled the trigger only to find it locked. Her thumb slid over the lever, and the second time the trigger pulled. She jumped up and sideways at the same time, ran three long strides, and ducked as she stopped in the dark.

Salih fired at her, missing.

She saw his muzzle flash, aimed at it, and listened intently for his footsteps. Like her, he'd moved immediately after firing, but his steps echoed off the walls, making it hard to pinpoint him. She heard his breathing and aimed her barrel at that place.

Salih fired again. This time, the flash showed him crouching and aiming away from her. He'd guessed she would keep moving. Bad guess. She pulled the trigger and rolled left.

This time, Salih didn't return fire. She heard him wheezing— breathing out excruciating pain. She approached him, circling wide to her right, stepping carefully.

Listening, she aimed at his noises.

"Please," he said with labored breath. "No."

She heard a weapon sliding across the ground followed by another.

"Surrender," he said. "I surrender. Please. Please."

She stepped closer, aiming at the sound of his words until she could just make out an outline of his form. He lay on the ground, his legs twisted beneath him, hands splayed out in front of him.

"Are you hurt?" she asked.

"Knee."

She pressed her gun to his head, flicked on a flashlight, and took a closer look. Blood stained his lower leg. His knee was a mangled mess of flesh and bone. She removed his NVGs and tossed them to the side. After patting him down and finding a knife, she said, "Handcuffs and shackles—put them on."

She slipped his knife into her sports bra. When Salih had shackled himself, she checked the locks, pulled the key, and tossed it into the dark. Taking his flashlight, she aimed it at the ceiling, collected his weapons, and helped him rest his back against a nearby stalagmite.

She checked out the ceiling around the sinkhole before shutting off the light. The opening was egg shaped with perfectly vertical sides, ten feet thick. She calculated how close she could get before Caldwell could shoot her and drew an imaginary circle on the floor. If he fell for her plan, she might be able to shoot him first.

"How many men are here?" Pia asked Salih.

"Eight."

She pressed her gun barrel to his forehead. "There was enough food on the plane for a lot more."

"Every person leave earlier."

Pia stepped back. "Children too?"

"Yes, every person."

Pia flicked the light onto the Yemeni girl's body. "Why didn't they take her?"

He gasped at seeing her. "I ... I was told she die. She fall at cliff."

Pia clicked off the light. If the other guards had believed the ruse, maybe the other four children would be safe.

She walked softly to the circle of light and tried to see the sky above. When she caught a glimpse of the sinkhole's rim, she squatted and examined it, trying to distinguish man from rock.

"Caldwell," she called out, "your man is bleeding. He needs medical attention. I'll give you safe passage to come get him."

"Shoot him. Put him out of his misery."

"Nice."

"Tell you what," Caldwell said. "You come up here, and I won't kill you. I'll take you to a place just down the road, clean you up, and send you home."

"OK. You swear you won't kill me?"

"He's not authorized to kill anyone," Patterson said.

"Oh, that's right," she said. "I forgot. You're here to make sure I don't die. Thanks, Patterson. You're doing a heck of a job."

She thought for a moment and realized Caldwell was up there because his knees were in too bad a shape to make the climb.

Pia grabbed Salih by the collar and dragged him backward into the short tunnel. He cried out at every scrape. Pulling him into a corner where he wouldn't see any more children who might venture to the latrine, she stood and took a look at him.

She said, "Salih, I can't help you right now. And Caldwell won't. I've got to run before he tosses a grenade down here, but I'll be back for you. Can you hold out for twenty-four hours?"

"He will kill me."

"I'll do what I can, but I don't feel guilty about leaving you behind."

She cut his shirt into strips and made a makeshift bandage for his knee. He grunted out of both appreciation and pain.

Pia put his canteen in his hand and squeezed his shoulder.

She turned on her flashlight and ran down the tunnel. At the sinkhole, she turned left toward the latrine, switched off the light, then backtracked into another tunnel. Leaving her noisy trail in a blind cave, she quietly retraced her steps toward the beach. When she felt enough distance would prevent anyone from seeing her light, she switched it on again and ran as best she could over the rough terrain.

With any luck, she could get to the beach before Caldwell got there.

CHAPTER 25

PATTERSON SHOOK HIS HEAD. NO.

"Get going," Caldwell said and pushed Patterson with one hand. "Don't be a coward. She's long gone—probably out at the beach, if she's as smart as you keep saying."

Patterson staggered back a step and snuck a peek behind him as the wind whipped his shirt. The smell of rain descended from the blackened sky, and sand thrown by the wind stung his skin. Years at sea had taught him how to read the weather by smell alone. Rain was ten minutes away, maybe twenty. The downpour would be torrential, the winds strong. A serious tropical storm was bearing down on them.

Patterson stepped up and shoved Caldwell with no effect. He felt like a five-year-old pushing an adult. "She's killed one of your guys and taken down two others. I told you to respect her. It's time *you* got to work. You're responsible for—"

An instant later, Patterson found himself hanging onto the tree trunk with one arm. His legs dangled into the open space below him. Curses streamed from his mouth before he swung his legs up to wrap them around the smooth trunk. Caldwell's laughter receded into the darkness above him. Patterson slipped himself lower until he figured he was close enough to the ground for a jump. When he dropped, his feet stung, and he fell on his butt.

He pulled his satellite phone out of his pocket and sent a text to his contact: *I'm taking Caldwell off the operation for insubordination. He's out of control.*

The phone couldn't connect. All he had needed was a good interrogator and they sent Torquemada.

He would have to suck it up, endure the monster's humiliations another hour or two. Then TGW would officially have the man replaced.

He picked himself up, wiped the seat of his pants, took one step, and stumbled over something soft. He reached for it without thinking. The loadmaster's dead body. Patterson cringed and rose to his feet.

For a long time, he listened. He tried hard to determine the presence of anyone nearby. After what seemed like an eternity, he decided his fall would have brought gunfire if Sabel were still in the area.

He called Salih's name and listened. In Arabic, he said, "Where are you? I've come to help."

A muffled reply echoed off the walls. Patterson worked his way through the cave, calling to Salih and following the weak voice as best he could. After several false turns, he found the man.

"We need to get you out of here," Patterson said, then tugged on the shackles. "Where's the key?"

"Leave me. She kills you."

"No, she won't." Patterson examined the makeshift bandage. "She didn't kill you when she had the chance."

"Salih not in charge."

Patterson paused to look at him before undoing a length of the shirt bandage. "Caldwell may be an asshole, but he'll take care of her."

Salih tugged on Patterson's arm and spoke an Arab proverb. Patterson had heard it before. "A wise man associating with the vicious becomes a devil."

Again Patterson paused. He huffed, then continued with his work, retying the bandage to make it tighter.

Salih leaned back. "Why Colonel take us? We work embassy—easy life in London, Beirut, Riyadh. America no good for us."

"Did she kill Masri?" Patterson asked.

"No, she beat him like dog. He is shackled. Key lost." Salih curled his arms around his head as if defending against unseen blows, then let them flop at his side. "We become devils in this place."

Patterson finished up the bandage and moved his light to inspect his work. "I'm not a medic, and it's not great, but I've slowed the bleeding."

"Thank you."

"Let's get you back to the compound."

"No. I wait. She returns."

Patterson stood up. "You're switching sides?"

"I tell you—she kills you. You see her eyes."

Patterson knew Pia's predatory gaze. He stood, shook his head and trudged back to the sinkhole.

Reaching the tree trunk, Patterson called out. "Caldwell, she's not here. I'm coming up."

No reply.

Patterson took off his dress shoes, tied the laces together, and carried them in his teeth. His socks gave him enough purchase to gingerly make it up the trunk, cursing every step until he landed on the surface.

"Caldwell!"

The wind, whipping the bushes hard, carried his words away. He bellowed several more times as he put his shoes back on. Still no reply.

Patterson donned the NVGs and looked around. With little moonlight penetrating the cloud layer, he could make out only scrub bushes and trees. No Caldwell. He looked at his pants, torn and dirty.

He heard footsteps—running footsteps.

Looking left and right, front and back, he found her.

She was in a dead run coming straight for him, twenty yards out.

The sensation he'd had in DC resurfaced—that of a tiger ready to pounce on him. He turned and ran as fast as he could go.

As if the first encounter had been a premonition, he felt her claws digging into his shoulders and her teeth crushing his neck as she leapt on him and pounded him into the ground. Only it wasn't her teeth that crushed him. It was a rock. The second blow hit his head. Black-and-white sparks closed in around his vision, and blood flowed from the back of his head.

Then he heard a different noise—like a charging bull. Sabel's weight lifted from him.

Patterson turned over and, peering through his tunnel vision, saw Caldwell, looking like a primeval monster, goggles protruding like horns from his head, towering over Pia Sabel. Caldwell blocked her first punch and landed a right cross that sent her tumbling over Patterson. She rolled twice, popping up on her feet at a safe distance. She reached for something in her belt.

Caldwell was on her before she could bring her gun around.

Patterson jumped to his feet and reached for Caldwell's arm, trying to stop the wild beast. He missed.

Caldwell landed a blow on Pia's face with enough force to snap her head to the side. Her NVGs flew off and sailed into the gaping sinkhole. The big man took her arm, steadied her, and landed four rapid punches in her belly. He finished with an uppercut.

She staggered backward, her eyes unfocused for a second. With a visible effort, she pulled herself together and stepped forward, her right arm cocked for an obvious haymaker.

Caldwell grinned and raised his hand to block it.

Instead, she kneed him in the crotch and followed with a lightning-fast hook that bloodied his eye. He staggered back, and she tried to kick him. He blocked her and pounded her jaw with a jab of his own. The force of the blow turned her sideways, and Caldwell slammed two punches into her lower back. As she fell forward, he grabbed her arm, swung her weight around, and landed a powerful uppercut that tossed her over backward.

Pia fell on the ground, her feet twitching.

"Holy shit, did you kill her?"

"Let's hope so." Caldwell dropped to his knees and checked her pulse. "Nope, the bitch's still ticking. Damn."

The big man pulled his weapon out and pressed it to her head.

Patterson kicked Caldwell in his ribs without doing any damage, but Caldwell stopped and looked up at him. The wind howled up another notch, and a small branch of leaves hit Patterson in the face. He brushed it away. "Goddamn it, Caldwell. We need her alive."

"She's caused enough trouble."

"TGW ordered you to get information out of her. I'm the one who decides when we're done. Without TGW's permission, anything you do would be murder. Not even McCarty could cover you on that."

"You don't know McCarty." Caldwell tried to stand but only rocked on his heels. He holstered his weapon and put out a hand. "Alright, asshole, your girlfriend lives til morning. Give me a hand up."

Patterson grabbed his hand and Caldwell rose to his feet with a groan. While Caldwell was busy finding his balance, Patterson grabbed Caldwell's weapon out of its holster.

Caldwell glared at him, but Patterson glared back, flashed his weapon, and stuck it in his belt. "Until I can trust you."

Caldwell scoffed. "You're just pissed because I used you for bait. Well, it worked. Results matter."

"Pick her up, and carry her," Patterson said.

Caldwell looked at the young woman's prone form. "Can't. The knees. Put her on my shoulder, or you carry her."

Patterson hesitated, then pulled Pia's dead weight up and maneuvered Pia onto Caldwell's shoulder. The big man jostled her body a couple times until he had her wrapped around his neck the way a hunter might carry game.

"Say, she feels good," Caldwell said. "She's not my type, but I like those tight muscles. I'll have a round with her before we start."

Patterson stepped in front of him, nose to nose. "Don't even think about it."

"What's the matter—you afraid of her? You should be. She could beat the living crap out of you anytime she wants." Caldwell laughed deeply.

"Shut up, and do your job. Interrogation—nothing else."

They started down the trail toward the airstrip, the wind buffeting them from all directions. Raindrops began to fall as they reached the cliff and started down the steeper part.

Patterson never studied interrogation techniques. He had no idea how to determine if a question asked was answered truthfully. He needed Caldwell for a few more hours. That meant he'd need to reboot their relationship, because right now, he was leaning toward shooting the monster in the leg just to slow him down. He took a deep breath and thought up a new conversation.

"Who chose you for Snare Drum?" Patterson asked, shouting above the wind.

Caldwell turned to glance at him, then turned back. "Been doing McCarty's laundry for a decade. You?"

CHAPTER 26

A GUNSHOT STARTLED PIA INTO consciousness. There might have been more than one. She wasn't shot, the sound had been too distant, but her anxiety rose. Neither her arms nor legs would move. Only her eyelids worked. She was bound with rope. As her mind cleared, her sense of immediate danger receded: they wouldn't have bound her if they'd planned to kill her. She took a personal inventory: nausea, a killer headache, dizzy. Concussion.

Pia struggled to understand her surroundings. She was in the flatbed of a truck and sensed three men near her. She looked over their silhouettes: Patterson's familiar form, a new man, and Caldwell joined them as the truck began moving. The passengers bounced through a stormy night. Heavy rain washed over her bruised face. Pia's captors had her in a seated position, facing the back. Taillights illuminated only a few feet of the dirt track behind them. Everything else was an endless darkness.

They stopped in a courtyard of sorts with a long, low brick building on one side and smaller wooden structures on the other. As Caldwell pulled her off the flatbed, she tried to inventory the compound. It seemed like a leftover from World War II. There was a bunkhouse in the distance and several other small houses. More men appeared from somewhere unseen, and five of them carried her between two buildings, down a long, concrete hall, and into what had once been a command center, a windowless, concrete cube.

Someone clanked open a steel door, and the men brought her inside. Gray and lifeless, the foot-thick concrete had never been painted. It smelled of decades of mildew. Harsh light sprang from bare bulbs fixed to the ceiling. A couple Syrians brought in a large gurney with a steel pivot point in the middle, and chained it next to a heavy table.

The Syrians strapped Pia's wrists down on the gurney. Her ankles were snapped into braces, and more straps anchored her knees, hips, and chest. A leather belt secured her head to the table. She couldn't move.

Caldwell checked Pia's bindings, tugging each one, then nodded to the guards. One man brought in two mop buckets of water and set them on the table next to the gurney.

The guards left, slamming the big steel door. The storm's incessant howl dropped fifty decibels but still drowned normal conversation.

Caldwell slapped Pia's face, then stroked her cheek. She refused to respond. He ran his hands over her breasts, past her belly button, and down farther.

"Hey," she yelled. "Get the … don't you dare."

"Wakey, wakey, little princess," Caldwell said with a growing snarl in his voice. "Your worst nightmares are about to come true because you came to my house and now, YOU'RE MY BITCH."

He punctuated his statement by grabbing her crotch and squeezing hard.

Pia strained against the bindings, kicking and pushing and twisting. Nothing budged. Her energy dissipated quickly, and she fell back against the table. Her mouth tightened. Her eyes narrowed. All her muscles strained.

Caldwell laughed and moved out of her line of sight. She could hear Caldwell moving around, picking up something up with a sloshing sound. Water.

Caldwell tossed a wet rag over her mouth, pulled a large lever, pushed the table until it reached a fifteen degree angle—head down, feet up—and picked up a bucket of water.

"Count off, Patterson," he said. "We'll start with thirty seconds."

Pia couldn't see Patterson, but for a long second, nothing happened.

"I said, count to thirty ya dumb fuck," Caldwell shouted.

Patterson moved into Pia's peripheral vision. His hand gripped a weapon aimed at Caldwell, his facial muscles flexed. The side of his face was scraped bloody where she'd pounded him into the ground. Dried blood stained the shoulder of his shirt.

Patterson took a deep breath and began counting.

Caldwell poured water onto the rag. At first, the sensation was frightening, but Pia held her breath.

A small amount of water began flowing into her nose. Then more. Holding her breath underwater was simple because no water entered the body. This was different. Water overran her nose and mouth, flooding her sinus cavities. The interior of her head rapidly filled with water—places meant for air only.

Alarm bells rang in her head, and panic began to overtake her as Patterson reached ten. She should have lasted at least thirty seconds. But the sensation of drowning was amplified a hundred times over by the water invading every space inside of her. Her mind screamed for a breath.

She kicked and bucked and writhed against the manacles. Her body thrashed against the restraints. She shook inside with uncontrollable terror. She tried to suck air through her mouth as the bulk of the water went into her nose. The soaked rag stuffed her mouth, and water filled her throat.

An involuntary gag reflex blew the water out but emptied her already oxygen-starved lungs.

I'm drowning.

Patterson reached twenty.

Horror filled her as she felt her ankle cut against the binding. The inside of her nasal cavity filled to overflowing. Still Caldwell poured.

Her need for air overruled her logic—her lungs expanded. Water rushed into her windpipe. She forced another gag and exhale. There wasn't an ounce of oxygen left in her. She had to breathe now, or she would die.

Inhaling involuntarily again, she felt the rag slip into her nose. The resulting sensation felt like a large hand suffocating her and drove her to the edge of madness. She had no idea whether she were breathing air or water, in or out. Her mind slowed and darkened.

Patterson said, "Thirty."

The water stopped.

Something metallic banged, and the gurney flipped upright. Gallons of water poured out of her. She threw up.

Caldwell loosened the straps around her forehead, allowing her head to tilt forward. More water came out.

But she could breathe air.

She wanted to scream at Caldwell, threaten him, bite him, but all she could do was breathe in giant gasps.

She looked at Patterson, who cowered against the wall with his hand on a gun tucked into his belt. He looked green and shrunken, as if he'd turned into a cowardly troll. She tried to say, "Shoot Caldwell." Nothing came out. Patterson's eyes met hers for an instant. Then he broke it off and turned away, like a child giving himself a time-out.

Caldwell pulled the straps back into place. Pia's head hit the board hard. The gurney tilted back to the previous position, Pia's head down. Caldwell said, "Hey, bitch, we having fun yet?"

She spat on him.

He backhanded her.

She heard the slosh of water and then Caldwell. "This time, to sixty."

Patterson said, "Aren't you going to ask her some questions?"

"Are you deaf?"

Patterson moved deeper into the corner of the room and started counting, his voice faltering.

Caldwell poured, and the spillage flushed her eyes. Patterson paused his counting to take a deep breath, then stepped up the speed of his count.

Pia held out until twenty-four seconds, then exhaled and gasped. Water filled her head and mouth and throat. Gurgling and choking and gulping became involuntary. She writhed and flailed helplessly against the restraints. Caldwell kept pouring.

Darkness closed in around her, and Pia lost consciousness.

As if in a dream, she heard Patterson's voice shout, "Sixty!"

There was a metallic bang again, and the gurney flipped upright. Once again, she threw up bile. Her body was exhausted, her muscles spent, her mind fast losing focus. All she wanted was to grab Patterson's gun and shoot Caldwell and Patterson both. She managed only a scream.

She gasped and gurgled and spit more water.

Caldwell tossed the rag into the corner and pulled a piece of plastic wrap from his pocket. He fixed it over her mouth, leaving her nostrils exposed, and duct-taped it in place. Once more, he tilted the table back and locked it in position.

"That's enough," Patterson said. "Let's ask—"

"I think you're missing the beauty of this little game," Caldwell said. "Waterboarding is slow-motion suffocation. It gives the brain enough time to contemplate death. The mind knows the inevitability of a blackout. A lot of times the person goes into hysterics on the board. I know it's hard to watch the first time, but don't worry. I did this to a guy down in Guantánamo 183 times, and he lived. But you can never tell. Sometimes, it can lead straight to what they call terminal hypoxia. That means zero oxygen in the blood cells. But when that happens, I figure— hey, Darwin was right—only the strong survive."

Caldwell laughed.

"My grandfather was an Australian commando who led the Double Tenth Incident," Patterson said. "Singapore, 1943. He and fifty-seven others were waterboarded by the Japanese Kempeitai. After the war, he went back to watch the men responsible hanged for war crim—"

"Shut up, you little faggot. This is nothing compared to what McCarty's got going on out there." Caldwell nodded at the door and stared at Patterson for a long time. "I'm supposed to keep this site from being exposed. But that's not what TGW's really worried about, is it? No, sir. He wants to know if this rich punk has any idea what she stumbled into. But then, why not just have McCarty and me take care of it? We could just skip the whole interrogation and toss her into the sea and everyone would be happy."

"There's a senator looking for her."

"McCarty knows how to handle those types. When politicians threaten him, he *always* out maneuvers them."

Patterson took a step back. "Just ... get on with it."

Caldwell stepped close to Patterson.

The smaller man lifted his weapon, holding it between them, and the big man pushed it away.

In a low voice Caldwell said, "Don't ever threaten me again."

Caldwell turned his back on Patterson and picked up his water bucket.

He looked over his shoulder at the navy man and said, "Now when you're ready, Tinker Bell, we're going for two minutes. Can you count all the way to 120?"

Patterson counted.

Caldwell poured.

Pia coughed and choked and gagged. She couldn't last as long the third time. Her body spasmed and strained so hard that it sounded as if the table were cracking. Her heels pounded, and her head shook in the restraint. Her arms flailed in place, and her back banged against the table. Her stomach muscles ached, and her arms felt as if they were breaking.

She faded to the edge of consciousness but heard Patterson speeding up his count. He passed ninety before the darkness overtook her.

When the light came back into her eyes, a blurred version of Caldwell stared at her from inches away. She sensed her condition. There were new injuries: her right eye was swelling, her cheek was bruised, and her jaw was scraped and bloody. He'd been hitting her to wake her up.

He slapped her. "Did ya hear me?"

She tried to spit on him but couldn't muster the energy.

"I said we'll start with something simple, to make sure you're telling me the truth."

Pia felt her head nod and realized the head restraints were loosened. She said, "I know about the third location. I'll destroy it too."

Caldwell stared at her blankly, checked Patterson for a second, then back to her. "What're you talking about? This is the only place where we waterboard punks like you."

She wanted to tell him to go to hell, but the thought of one more session made her throw up again. Unfortunately, Caldwell managed to get out of the way.

He stepped back with a sick, sadistic smile. "That's enough screwing around. Time for your first question. What was the name of the man who killed your mother?"

Pia glared at him, but her body wasn't helping. She was exhausted and hurt and barely conscious. She could lie to him about everything, and maybe she'd escape more torture. But his first question was a matter of public record—no big deal. She took a deep breath.

"Leroy … Johnson," she said, her voice barely above a whisper.

"And what became of Mr. Johnson?"

That wasn't part of the public record, but Pia didn't mind answering because she was proud of it. "I sliced the femoral artery in his right thigh. He bled out."

She felt a little strength return and concentrated on breathing away the fear and adrenaline.

"Were you ever tried for that crime?" he asked.

"I'll kill you too, Caldwell." She felt a little stronger.

"I asked you a question," Caldwell bellowed. "I said—were you tried for the murder of Leroy Johnson?"

Pia started coughing until she coughed up bile.

"No," Caldwell said, his voice rising above her cough. "You weren't because you were a minor. Do you know the name of Johnson's associate, the man who watched your father commit suicide?"

Pia stopped coughing. She stared at Caldwell, and everything else fell away.

"That's right," the big man said. "You heard me. Your father wasn't murdered. He committed suicide."

Patterson stepped forward. "What the hell is this—some kind of family therapy session? We need to start with Nakdali."

Caldwell broke off his staring contest to give Patterson a nasty look. He turned back to Pia. "Now we have something to trade."

Pia said, "You don't know anything about—"

"What did they tell you—that Leroy's associate killed your father?"

"How do you—"

"I'll make you a trade. I'll tell you the man's name. All you have to do is tell me what Nakdali looked like."

"I came here to find Khelemba," she said. "I know what happened to him. I'm going to find Safwan next."

"If I knew who they were, I'd tell you where to find them. Now answer my question."

Pia breathed hard through her nose, her face drawn tight. Her eyes stabbed into Caldwell's. Her hands clenched into fists in the clamps.

Caldwell said, "Or I can send Patterson out for more water."

"Doesn't matter. You're going to kill me anyway."

"Oh no," Caldwell spread his arms wide, palms up. "I'm going to rape you and dump you in the *Seraphim*. Dead or alive depends on how well you perform. Now, are you ready to answer the questions?"

CHAPTER 27

"JESUS, JACOB, YOU NEVER CHANGE," Agent Tania said. "The shooting's going to start any minute, and you think I'm going to jump in bed with you."

Guess those days were behind us.

"Just an idea," I said. I sat up on an elbow and watched her stagger back a step, then forward as the deck rolled under her feet. She grabbed the edge of a bookcase near the door, steadied herself a second, then let go. "Sabel Security paid a lot to rent this little boat; no need to waste it."

Truth was, I only wanted to know what the bed on a super yacht felt like. My sheets didn't have a thread count on the package. Mine had a 70% off sticker and crooked stitches. Tossing aside yards of silk, I stood up just as the ship lurched. Tania pitched over and landed in my arms.

Her eyes flashed with anger. "Don't touch me."

I shrugged and dropped her on the floor.

Apparently, that wasn't funny.

"Put some clothes on and get topside," she said. She pulled herself up, using the bookcase for support, and stalked out of the stateroom, sneaking a peek on her way out.

Maybe those days weren't so far behind us after all.

I kicked a pair of boxers into my hand, slipped them on with a T-shirt, and climbed to the *Inanna II's* bridge.

Captain Ashley Chamberlain stood with his feet planted wide and his hand gripping the First Officer's chair. He lifted his chin and gazed down his nose at me.

"We there yet?" I said, shouting above the winds raging outside.

"Hardly," he said. "The storm is worsening and has changed direction. Your National Hurricane Center's upgraded Dolly to a category one hurricane. They'll upgrade it again before long, I should think. We'd best turn back."

"Not happening."

I stepped forward between Chamberlain and his First Officer. Giant wipers swept across the windows, the bridge glowed from the scattered instrument screens. There was nothing to see in the darkness except rain smashing against the glass. I looked at the high-tech displays on the console. They could've been written in Greek for all I knew. "How far out are we?"

"An hour, at least." He hesitated, then looked me up and down. "I'm not keen on your bridge attire."

"I'm not keen on being late."

He pointed to a display with circles and arrows all over it. "We're fighting the seas. We're under full power, but the weather is against us, and we're making little headway. All our efforts are spent climbing up one wave and down the next."

As if to punctuate his statement, the bow climbed like a roller coaster going to the top. We hesitated for an unearthly second, as if the storm had suddenly stopped, then plunged down into the darkness. I grabbed the console in front of me and tried not to push any buttons. When we hit the trough, a million tons of white water hit the glass. For a second, I thought we'd gone under. I buckled over the console and had to push hard to get myself upright.

Captain Chamberlain watched me without so much as a flinch. "It's my duty to emphasize the danger should you press on. Whomever your client is, if you intend to save him," he paused as the ship crashed into another wave and the hull groaned, "making the attempt after the risk of drowning at sea has subsided could raise his chances of survival from nil to something more agreeable."

"Not happening."

Since our journey began, my stomach had been churning at the thought of leading my fellow agents on such a risky mission. The odds started out bad and were getting worse by the minute. And so was my digestion. But damned if I was going to let Chamberlain know.

He stared at me as if he could hear me thinking.

I said, "You know the Sabels have a mega yacht based in Tampa."

"*The Asteria*, yes, I know," he said. "I'm also aware it's captained by an impressive old salt scheduled to retire at year's end. That fact is the only reason we left port. Tell me, have you any influence in that part of the Sabel Empire?"

"Nope. But when I write my report, I will highlight people who risked everything to help. The Sabels rank bravery at the top of their list."

"I see. And where, pray tell, do they rank abject stupidity?"

"Uh…"

"I expected as much. There's no talking you out of this, then?"

"No."

"Very well." He motioned me to the grand saloon.

Everything small had been stowed somewhere, and the furniture was lashed to the deck. A sixty-inch display showed the Isla de la Mona from a satellite photo taken on a sunnier day. Chamberlain stood in front of it as his arm swept across the bottom half.

"We'll approach the southern coast," he said. "Dolly's tracking to the north, putting us in the navigable semicircle. Swells and storm surge will be lower but still extremely dangerous. Should she turn south, we'll be in the dangerous semicircle and I'll not faff about looking for you. But then, you'll be dead and won't care."

"Nice. The what semicircle?"

"Navigable and dangerous, or left hand and right hand, two sides of the hurricane. Dolly's moving at twenty-five knots west by southwest with winds rising over seventy-five knots. If you stand on the north of her, those winds hit you at one hundred knots, but on the south, only fifty."

I'm not much at math and science—I shoot people for a living—so I nodded as if I understood.

"Your drop-off—if we can launch our Zodiacs at all—will be here. Please note the coral reef." His hand motioned to a lighter area that hugged the coast. "The storm surge on this side will be low, perhaps four feet. The surf is lower as well, yet unpredictable. It might carry you over the rocks and straight onto the beach, or dash you headfirst into the coral."

"Roger that." I looked at the map.

A nasty wolf-whistle came from behind me. Carmen, Dhanpal, and Miguel stood at the entry, dressed in jungle fatigues and grinning at me. Miguel kept one hand pressed to the ceiling for balance, while his other hand held Carmen's upper arm. The broad-shouldered Navajo, who rarely spoke more than two words at a time, nodded at me. Carmen reminded me of a farm wife: sturdy, hard-working, late-thirties, and serious. Dhanpal was your typical former SEAL, mid-twenties, shorter than average, and ripped like a movie star with a pearly white grin to match.

A wave rolled the deck to what felt like forty-five degrees. In a rare act of charity, Chamberlain grabbed my arm in time to keep me from crashing out the window.

"This blurred area here," his hand swept the coastline again, "has been withdrawn by the cartographers, so we've no idea if there are any structures. Should you ride a wave onto the shore, it could easily carry you to certain death against the cliff here, or leave you nicely on the beach to be drowned under the next wave. With any luck, the currents will carry you out to sea where I won't be haunted by your screams."

I looked him over. "Let me guess—you used to be a motivational speaker."

"I'm trying to impress upon you Mother Nature's disdain for the barking mad."

"You're going to drop us a hundred yards offshore. That's not bad, right?"

He shook his head slowly and pursed his lips.

The ship pitched and rolled, tossed by the seas. Tania's multiracial beauty warmed up the room when she came in behind Miguel and gripped a couch for balance. Tony, our former FBI agent and my carousing buddy, came alongside her and held onto a table. Both of them looked green and sick.

"Understood," Miguel said. "Farther north?"

"No. That's a two-hundred-foot cliff of broken limestone. This is the only location where we can put you ashore, unless you're keen to have a go at the landing strip. Not that it matters much. Right, then. Which of you is the sailor?"

Miguel said, "Kayaked once."

"I have a little experience," I said. I'd been on the Mississippi during some nasty storms and I figured water is water.

Dhanpal said nothing.

The ship rolled with the Captain's eyes. "And you're all determined to go?"

No one spoke.

"Very well then, you've been warned," he said. "Will there be anything else?"

"Coffee," I said.

"No," he said, looking me up and down. "You'll vomit."

Couldn't argue that one. The only reason I hadn't yet was due to skipping a few meals.

We sat on the silk-covered couches, holding onto anything solid, and reviewed the intel gleaned from Ms. Sabel's last phone call. We still had nothing on TGW, the presumed mastermind behind Operation Snare Drum. Ms. Sabel's phone still transmitted its exact GPS coordinates, but she hadn't answered for over an hour. We talked about tactics and methods, about landing zones and weaponry.

Agent Tony gave us the latest update from DC.

When he finished, Tania said. "Talk to me about hardware, Jacob. What'd you bring?"

I pointed to the metal shipping crates secured to the walls. They ripped into them like kids opening birthday presents. I raised my voice. "Careful, there are thermal binoculars in there."

Tania held up a Heckler & Koch MP5-SD6 rifle. It had a three-round burst mode and a built-in sound suppressor.

I said, "We each get two sidearms: a Glock with Sabel Darts—to use when Ms. Sabel is watching—and a SIG Sauer with real hollow-points."

Miguel and Carmen laughed at my little joke, but Tania glared at me.

"What the hell's wrong with you people?" Tania said as she stood. "Pia says we use darts—we use darts."

"Against guys with .45s?" Dhanpal said. "No thanks."

"Body armor," Miguel said. "Darts bounce."

Tania shook her head. "Think for a minute. The kids Pia came to save are on that island. You can call her naive or whatever, but she wants us using darts 'cause she doesn't believe those kids are collateral. We'll do what we have to, but the children don't get hurt. No way."

No one argued.

She turned to me. "Sorry, Jacob, this is your op. I'm just telling you what she'd say."

I went over my plan with them. It was pretty basic: get on shore and wing it.

I went below and put on camouflage utilities and body armor. A minute later, I opened the watertight door marked 'Toys Bay' on the lower deck. It was the bay where they launched rich people's toys like jet skis and Zodiacs. Chamberlain and his crew had two of the small boats with outboard motors facing the rear bulkhead. My agents were crowding around them, waiting for my signal. The hydraulic system screeched and clanked and the entire back wall tilted outward.

It was solid darkness outside, but the storm roared in with savage fury.

I pulled on my fearless-leader face, and everyone turned to me a split second later. I radiated confidence. We were there to bring back Ms. Sabel—hurricanes be damned.

I left the captain with a Sabel Security satellite phone. Dhanpal took the helm of his boat, with Tania and Miguel riding along. Tony and Carmen went with me. We pulled life preservers over our gear, knowing they could do little to float the weight of our body armor, let alone the hardware we carried. But it was only a hundred yards.

We gave each other a thumbs-up. We were ready, determined, and focused.

The crew waited for the right part of the wave and pushed Dhanpal out first. He went right and disappeared immediately.

They pushed my boat off the deck and into the roiling sea. My boat went left—no matter what I did.

BRING IT

LEAVING A 150-FOOT YACHT IN a hurricane was the worst idea I'd had since I tried to simultaneously date the McDougal sisters. I couldn't see anything. Not the yacht, not Tania, not the coast, not even Tony at the bow. My bravado evaporated. I felt the doubts I'd repressed for the last hour whipping into absolute terror.

The waves were shocking. Even in complete darkness, their sheer mass was overwhelming. They loomed over us like monster-mountains intending to pile drive us to the ocean floor. The captain's warnings about taking a small boat out in a big storm began to make sense.

I cranked the throttle and powered up the backside of a wave, crested it, and we instantly shot downhill as if we'd skied off Mount Everest. Before we hit the trough, the sea rose up underneath us and hurled us into the air. Every joint in my body felt like it was being hit with a sledgehammer.

The wind howled in my ears as if undersea phantoms were screaming to claim our lives. We bounced off another wave. I fell forward and slammed into Carmen. In the next instant, I saw a palm tree just as we rammed it. Our little boat flipped over, centrifugal force pinning us in our seats. It landed right-side up and spun like a top until another wave hit us broadside. We flipped over too many times to count, all three of us flying in different directions.

I landed in sand on all fours, as the outboard motor bounced off my back and disappeared. The wave receded and I sprang to my feet before the pain of broken ribs shot through me, doubling me over. Forcing myself upright, I ran up the beach. Another wave chased me, carrying the empty boat, the motor still running and the propeller slicing everything in its path. It smashed into a wooden structure and popped like bubble wrap under a boot.

Carmen grabbed my arm and pulled me sideways to a wall as another wave crashed on the beach. When the wave went out, we backpedaled uphill until we were out of the surf.

She yelled above the shrieking wind. "Where the hell is Tony?"

CHAPTER 28

WE STOOD, BRACING OUR FEET wide apart, and leaned into the wind. Mud clogged my nose and salt water filled my mouth. We spluttered rain and sand every third breath. My ribs ached. My knees hurt and everything else groaned.

"You hurt?" Carmen asked.

"Fine. You?"

"Battered and bruised, but nothing permanent."

We stood in total darkness. No residual city lights, no street lights, no warmly lit windows. If I'd turned on a flashlight, the wind would've carried the beam away.

I could see enough of my GPS app to know Dhanpal was about a hundred yards from me. Whether he was on shore or at the bottom of the sea was anyone's guess.

Carmen shouted in my ear. "Should we wait for them?"

"No, they might not make it. Ms. Sabel's our top priority. But we have to find Tony."

Carmen tugged her thermal binoculars out of her pack and surveyed the area. I followed suit—no sign of Tony, much less Dhanpal and his crew. Between waves, we found a wooden beach cabana the size of a small mobile home. The front windows had blown out, leaving a tidal pool inside three inches deep. We stepped in and cleared both rooms.

Tony was outside, slumped against the back wall, writhing on the ground in serious pain. Carmen assessed him, concentrating on his collarbone and arm, while I kept watch. She shouted something to him, and he nodded.

A palm frond smacked my broken ribs like a baseball bat.

Carmen shouted in my ear. "Broken arm. I'm going to fix it. I'll need you to hold him real tight. I'm going to pull on his wrist. OK?"

I nodded and held his bicep against the ground.

She grabbed a broken branch, put it between his teeth, and pulled up on his wrist. His face told me all I needed to know about the pain. She tugged four times, feeling his forearm after each pull. She made him a splint from a tree branch and an Ace bandage.

Tony stood up, pushed the barrel of his weapon through his sling, and shook off the pain. After a long moment, he said, "I've got your six."

We sloshed forward fifty yards and heard three quick bangs. We knelt next to a palm tree with no idea where the shots came from. Another burst nearby proved they were firing blind into the storm. They must have found the Zodiac and were shooting at anything that moved.

Which was everything.

Someone smashed into me at a dead run. At first I thought it was Tony, but ruled that out when a weapon cracked three rounds in the air. Grabbing at the intruder's body, I snatched a leg and heaved myself upright. I heard a thud as Tony pounded a knee into the man. I slammed him, headfirst, onto the ground and heard his neck snap. We left him there and checked the thermal landscape.

Two of his friends continued shooting at the Zodiac. We took the opportunity to back out of the area before they found us. Within a few yards, we found another cabana and a large silhouette towering behind it.

Carmen and I shared a type of battlefield telepathy and knew our objectives with a nod. We separated, going wide toward the structure. Further uphill, surrounded by thick brush, we found the hulking shadow—a WWII-era watchtower. Thirty feet of iron lattice held up a square cab, fifteen feet wide. A set of stairs crisscrossed the tower. GPS showed Carmen in position opposite me and a hundred yards out. We began our spiral search for the bad guys.

I found mine right where I expected him, crouching behind a low palm, facing the watchtower entrance. He heard me, spun, and fired before he aimed. Rookie mistake. I put him down with a single shot. I scanned the area where I expected the other guard with my thermals and found Carmen stepping into the open. She waved an all clear.

Bullets ripped through a broad leaf near my head, and I hit the ground. From my backside, I heard the pphtt-pphtt of Tony's weapon.

"Got him," Tony said. "Think there's more?"

"A lot more than the Syrian told Ms. Sabel."

We left Tony under cover near the stairs and climbed. I slipped and banged a shin on the worn metal tread. Gripping the handrails for dear life, we made it to the base of the cab. A trapdoor led into the room. Opening it from below would be suicide. Carmen stood on the landing below it, aiming up.

I tapped on the door and used my favorite trick, yelling over the storm in Arabic. "Brother, let me in. I've been hit."

The trapdoor opened three inches. A muzzle poked through first, followed by a pair of anxious eyes. The man leaned into the opening at an awkward angle to examine me.

Carmen put a bullet through his forehead.

We scrambled inside. Tony followed as best he could.

We pulled the body into a corner and looked over his equipment. It was brand-new and expensive. He had night vision goggles—NVGs—in one hand but no thermal imaging. NVGs amplify light, but light was scarce, so the unit was little better than the naked eye.

Our thermal binoculars showed us warm bodies in contrast to their cold surroundings. We had a definite tactical advantage over the Syrians. That made us feel better about being outnumbered.

Each Syrian had a two-way radio with five channels—same kind they were using back in DC. No spread-spectrum, no encryption, which was odd considering the rest of their gear. We locked down the transmit button on four radios, closing down a different channel with each. If we could find another radio, we could listen in. That would give us a second tactical advantage.

I checked Dhanpal's team. GPS showed movement. After studying the display for a few seconds, I was relieved to see them heading in our direction. I took that to mean they'd landed and were working their way toward us.

Using our NVGs, we divvied up the landscape to count and map buildings over the twenty acre compound as best we could. Tony spotted a building that was his guess for the holding cell.

The hurricane cut off our communications with Sabel Satellite Systems, but we could still connect to each other locally. Carmen and I slumped below the windowsill just as Tania and Miguel arrived on the ladder.

"Where's Dhanpal?" I asked Tania.

"Good to see you too," she said.

"Securing the kids," Miguel said.

The cave system was the island's storm drain and would flood at some point. The kids needed Dhanpal. I pulled the team in close and outlined my plan. We would split into pairs: one to make a diversion and the other to take the bunker. Tania and I held out our fists and counted to three.

She had scissors. I had paper.

She chose her assignment, and we moved out.

We left Tony to report hostile movements from the watchtower via text messages and set our phones to read the texts in our earbuds.

A few yards out, relying on our thermals, we spotted three soldiers heading toward the tower. We fired on them and ran, hoping to draw them away from Tony. They dodged our bullets before chasing us. After a few yards, we lost sight of them.

We each took a tree to use as cover and searched the area.

"You see them?" Tania asked, scanning the area for any sign of them.

I texted Tony: *Hostiles?*

He texted back: Right flank, heading for bunker. Get moving.

We picked up our pace and crossed the road, evading two foot patrols. From there we circled around behind a large brick building and slipped past a sandbagged berm.

Close up, we could tell the bunker wouldn't be easy. It was set mostly underground, solid concrete, with no back door, no roof hatch, and no chimney. A thirty-foot ramp led to the entry about five feet below the surface. A concrete roof supported by columns covered the ramp. Between those spaces, we saw two men stationed at the entry.

I grabbed a nearby palm frond and pulled back one of the blades. Carmen and I took up positions, Carmen at the side of the ramp and me on the roof. We signaled our readiness to Tania and Miguel.

BRING IT

Sometimes Tania was brilliant, other times, totally insane. Her diversion consisted of a frontal assault on what looked like the CO's quarters. She threw a flashbang in a window while Miguel picked off anyone who showed up to investigate.

I crawled across the roof and dangled my palm frond over the opening. For the guards on duty, the obstruction had to be cleared. Just as my clever plan drew out one of the guards, the wind and rain nearly pushed me off the slick cement. My boot slipped over one side before I could get a grip. The guard started shooting, and Carmen popped the poor bastard in the back. I pointed my weapon into the opening and fired blindly until I heard a man cry out.

Carmen jumped into the ramp, and I flipped over the roof, landing on the ground. Bullets pinged off the concrete at my shoulder, forcing us to dive for cover. My thermals showed three Syrians approaching. I tossed a frag grenade at them while Carmen blew the door open with a breaching charge.

We barreled into the bunker, Carmen on the right, me on the left. The room was filled with concrete dust. A lone light bulb in the corner had survived the blast.

I saw only shapes at first. Then my eyes adjusted to the high-contrast, black-and-white world.

A muscle man stood behind a gurney with his hands in the air. Near us stood a man with a pistol aimed at the big guy. Between them, Ms. Sabel was strapped to a gurney.

All my training about controlling the situation fell by the wayside. I stared, my heart pounding in my throat, feeling something strange in my gut—a void, a coldness. Maybe it was my first true sensation of compassion. The proud, accomplished athlete of my dreams lay motionless on the table. Her body limp, her muscles lax.

Rage exploded deep inside me. Yet all I could get out was one choked question.

"Is she alive?"

CHAPTER 29

"DOWN! GET DOWN!" I YELLED in my command baritone when my logical brain came back online. "Hands in front of you! NOW!"

The big guy belly-flopped on the floor, his hands outstretched as ordered. From the descriptions we had, he had to be Caldwell and the other one Patterson.

Patterson shouted, "I've got him covered. You frisk him."

"GET ON THE GROUND!" Carmen yelled in Patterson's ear.

"He's armed!" Patterson repeated. "I've got him."

"Drop or I'll shoot you," Carmen said.

"We need them alive!" I said.

Patterson, just a silhouette with the light behind him, nodded at Carmen as if he were one of us.

A grenade rolled in the door and right to my foot. I swatted it back up the ramp with my rifle. Years in Little League finally paid off. The explosion was deafening. After a few seconds of stunned silence, the roof over the ramp collapsed on one side, leaving a triangular exit. While it narrowed the angle for them to shoot at us, it also meant a more dangerous departure.

"I know who he is," Caldwell said, his eyes locked on Patterson. "Don't shoot. I'll tell you—"

Patterson fired three quick shots into the big man's brain.

Carmen slammed her rifle's stock into Patterson's head. As he fell, I wrenched the pistol from his hand and tossed it aside. I held his wrist and slammed my boot into his shoulder. He howled.

"Stay down," I said. For emphasis, I placed the muzzle of my rifle at his ear.

He stopped struggling.

Carmen waved her phone around the room for a few long seconds.

"What the hell are you doing?" I said. "Secure the area."

"Evidence," Carmen said, putting her phone away.

She tugged at the straps holding Ms. Sabel. In seconds, she had the top half freed but had to work harder on the legs. Ms. Sabel didn't move. Carmen took the boss's pulse, checked her eyes, and looked at me. "Barely conscious."

My finger squeezed around the trigger as the rage in my head mounted.

I'd killed men for less, but never an immobilized prisoner.

Carmen said, "Don't. She wouldn't want that."

Carmen was right. I put my boot to Patterson's head and kicked his skull into the concrete. He exhaled like an unconscious man. I let go of his limp arm. I said, "One twitch and you're a dead man."

Unfortunately, he didn't twitch.

A noise outside caught my ear. Running to the door, I saw a figure trying to squeeze into the triangular opening and fired a couple bursts up the ramp. He fled before I could get a bead on him. The ramp was a tactical death trap for both sides. Stalemate for now.

I slapped plasticuffs on Patterson, stepped to Carmen's side, and looked at Ms. Sabel. Her right eye was black and swollen; her left cheek was scraped and bruised. Her eyes floated independently, one rolled back in her head, the other tried to focus.

"You motherf—" I turned to yell at Patterson but stopped, too angry to finish. I raised my rifle only to feel Carmen's tug again. I cursed and kicked the man a second time, harder.

"Jacob!" Carmen said. "Cool down. Focus on getting out of here."

"Yeah." I got to work, bagging Patterson's weapon and shoving it in my pack.

"Can you carry her?" Carmen asked.

Ms. Sabel stirred. Her eyes aligned, and she tried to sit up on her elbows. Carmen pressed her gently back down.

Ms. Sabel said, "Caldwell ... I need to talk. Caldwell."

I said, "He didn't make it, Ms. Sabel."

Carmen squatted next to Patterson and checked him out.

Ms. Sabel grabbed my arm and pulled herself up to a half-sitting position. "What … do you mean?"

I told her.

"No. No, he can't do that. I need Caldwell."

"I'm sorry."

She sat up fast and nearly passed out. I grabbed her arm and steadied her as she swayed back and forth on the gurney's edge.

"It's not a concussion," Carmen said about Ms. Sabel. "I think it's a brain problem of some kind. Looks like the bastards waterboarded her. She needs rest, which she's not going to get. I think the best thing we can do is take over her decision making, treat her like an eight-year-old."

"Roger that." I turned to Ms. Sabel. "Wait right there, and I'll carry you."

She stared blankly, sitting on the gurney's edge, holding on with both hands.

Patterson was also sitting up, not as woozy as Ms. Sabel and coming around quicker, but still in obvious pain.

I yanked him to his feet. "Why'd you kill Caldwell?"

His eyes focused on me. "Who are you?"

"Agent Jacob Stearne, Sabel Security."

He looked at his wrists. "He was going for his gun. Ankle holster."

Carmen checked the corpse, found the gun, looked at me, and shrugged. She went through his pockets, pulled a couple items, stuffed them in her pack, and rose. "Let's get out of here."

I patted down Patterson and shoved him forward. "You're Don Patterson, right?"

"I just saved your life." He looked me up and down. "I'm trying to help you."

"I never saw that guy so much as twitch, much less reach for a pistol."

Carmen stepped between us, her weapon jammed in Patterson's ribs. "I got this guy. You get Pia."

Facing the gurney, I put my shoulder under Ms. Sabel's arm and stood her up. She wobbled for a second, then slid a foot forward. She muttered something about walking on her own—always the proud athlete—then slipped and grabbed me. With one arm around her waist and my weapon cradled in the other, we started across the room. After a few steps, she let go of me and stood on her own.

Carmen looked up the ramp and ducked several incoming rounds. They'd gotten inside the opening. She jumped behind the door, stuck her weapon around the jamb, and fired a few shots blindly up the ramp. Tossing another grenade was out of the question. If the throw was short, it could roll back to us.

Carmen pressed her earbud. "Tania, Miguel, can you hear me? We need some help from outside. We're pinned down."

I looked around the room and traced the electrical conduit to where it disappeared behind a rack of shelves.

Tania's voice came back, barely audible above what sounded like a chain gun. "We're trapped in the CO's quarters, next building over. Can you make it here?"

I threw the rack to the floor and found a large piece of plywood nailed to the concrete wall, the conduit going through it. I fired a bullet into it to check my theory. No ricochet. I fired more rounds into the corners of the wood, then kicked it in. A mechanical crawlspace. Flashing a light down it, I could see no end, but plenty of seeping water and mud.

The electricity had to come from somewhere, and my guess was the CO's quarters.

We pushed Patterson in first, making him scoot forward on elbows and knees. Carmen followed with her rifle poking him in the ass. Ms. Sabel went next. I fired a few more rounds up the ramp and tossed a flashbang as far as I could.

I booby-trapped the space behind us with a remotely detonated explosive and clenched the trigger in my teeth. After inching through mud for five minutes, Patterson fell into a brick-lined basement. A generator hummed in one corner of the small space. With no grace at all, and covered in mud, the rest of us tumbled into the dim room. I blew the crawlspace mine and collapsed the tunnel at the bunker end.

The basement opened into a kitchen with a living room on one side and a hallway on the other. Tania and Miguel manned .50 cals barricaded with sandbags at opposite windows in the living room. Two dead Syrians lay in the middle of the room.

"Check the hallway," Tania said. "We tossed a grenade, but might be some Hajjis still back there."

Miguel brushed back attackers with a long burst and Tania added a shorter one of her own.

I gently guided Ms. Sabel to a recliner in what was left of the living room, then pushed Patterson against the wall in front of Miguel. "If he wiggles, shoot him."

Miguel stuck his sidearm in the man's mouth, keeping his other hand on the big gun. He turned back to the window and let off a burst.

Carmen and I checked the bedroom wing. We found one trembling guy cowering in the bathroom. Anyone who survived a firefight could feel his pain. I calmed him down a bit, disarmed him, and lashed him to the sink.

One door was still closed at the end of the hall. We blew it open with a breaching charge and found an officer knocked out by the flying door. No doubt about his rank: older, better-looking uniform, last room in the house, and the thickest door. A cache of new weapons lined the walls of his den. I gave the man a closer look—two stars and an eagle on his epaulet, the insignia of a Syrian colonel.

Carmen checked his vital signs while I took a look around.

Our fearless colonel had gathered a few essentials in a duffel bag on the bed: a couple power bars, a grooming kit, a phone, passport, and extra magazines of ammo. Ready to flee?

There was a bed, a bathroom, a wardrobe, and a laptop on the desk. On the laptop display was a map of the grounds with blinking lights. Several were moving. Several were not. They had ID beacons, same as ours, but a different frequency. I noted the positions and switched to the control panel. The username was Abdul Nakdali. He had encrypted e-mail, no internet connection, a military video conferencing tool, and little else. He was the administrator, so I changed his password and set the fingerprint reader to my index finger. I grabbed the laptop and three of the ten or so external hard drives lying next to it and stuffed them in my pack with his passport.

I grabbed a radio, set it to the only working channel, and shouted,

"Fall back," in Arabic. Probably wouldn't work, but worth a shot.

"How's he looking?" I asked Carmen.

"Minor head injury." She bound him with plasticuffs. "He'll be ready for questioning pretty soon."

When we dragged him into the living room, Ms. Sabel rose slowly from the easy chair, looking like she'd seen a ghost. "Colonel Nakdali?"

I pulled his passport out of my pack and handed it to her—Abdul Nakdali.

Her eyes jumped back and forth from the passport to the man. Her brow wrinkled, and her head tilted sideways. "But they killed Nakdali…"

Bullets raked the front door. Miguel answered with a long burst.

I shouted over the noise. "Some officers use doubles."

Dhanpal sent a text: Found pilots shot execution-style. Moved two Syrian prisoners. Have children safe. Water rising fast. Should we join you?

I responded: Negative. More hostiles than plan. Can you ride out storm?

Maybe, have 2-3 hours, but flooding – ???

We'll join you.

A couple hours in a cave was better than waiting for the Syrians to mount a full-scale assault. I'd seen the dots on Nakdali's laptop—we were outnumbered. There were four of us, and we were moving two prisoners and a foggy heiress. We scanned the windows for the best way out. None of us saw anything exciting.

Bullets were wearing down the thin sandbags, and the walls were beginning to look like Swiss cheese.

Over his shoulder, Miguel shouted, "They're massing for an attack over here."

I texted Tony: *Need an exit.*

He texted back: You're surrounded.

CHAPTER 30

WE PULLED A FRAG GRENADE each and took a window. After a short countdown, we threw them outside and used our thermal binoculars to count how many soldiers ran for cover before the blast. Tania's side had only two defenders. She chased them off with a long blast from the machine gun.

I jumped out the window first and took point. Miguel tied a rope around the necks of Nakdali and Patterson that would choke them both if either of them strayed. Tania pushed the pair ahead of her, with Carmen and Ms. Sabel right behind her. Miguel followed, covering our backs.

The wind pelted us with sand and pebbles and leaves as we snuck through the night. We cleared our route and rounded a brick building.

Tony texted an update: Syrians went for the bunker. They thought you doubled back.

We were deep in the trees before they figured out their mistake.

With Dhanpal's guidance, we followed a dirt track that switchbacked its way up the cliff face. From the high ground, we spotted the Syrians following us and used a grenade to discourage them. There were no more signs of them from there to the sinkhole.

After some difficulty, everyone made it down the tree into the sinkhole. Inside, Dhanpal led us up a rocky incline to a side cave where he had four children and two Syrians in a large chamber.

Dhanpal had set flashlights on end, reflecting off the domed ceiling, making a livable space. He'd set up perimeter intrusion alarms at the far reaches of the tunnel to give us fair warning if anyone approached.

Water from all the caves in the system led to a central tube that emptied on the beach. Unfortunately, it was filling up because of a restriction halfway through. The whole system would flood sooner or later, forcing us to the surface. Our side cave opened to the island's cliffs on the other end, but the Syrians would figure that out at some point.

Four children rushed to Ms. Sabel, their big brown eyes shining in the dim light. Three boys and a girl, almost as dirty as we were muddy, grabbed and held onto her. She still had a stagger in her step, and her speech was a little slower than usual, but she lit up when the children hugged her. She dropped to her knees, embraced them, dried their tear-streaked faces, and cooed.

Then something went wrong.

Maybe Ms. Sabel's injuries transferred to the children, because their attitudes changed from happy to worried. The girl's wavy locks swayed as she shook her head. One boy scowled and released her. Ms. Sabel was their heroine, and finding her beaten and exhausted shook their confidence.

Dhanpal, Carmen, and Tania joined in, trying to get the kids calmed and relaxed, but nothing worked.

One boy broke off from the group and walked away. I didn't recognize the language he spoke, but his tone was universal. He'd gotten his hopes up for a rescue, but his heroine turned out to be mortal.

The boy sat down at the edge of the light with his legs crossed. Dhanpal left him alone and told the other kids a story in Hindi.

I walked over to the lone boy and sat cross-legged near him. He turned away. I pulled out my muddy sidearm, dropped the magazine, and emptied the chamber. I pulled out a cleaning kit, laid a cloth on the stone, and disassembled the weapon. I began cleaning it with another cloth, amazed at how much mud had worked into the mechanism.

The boy looked over his shoulder and watched me.

All boys like weapons.

I tossed him a smile. He spun away, but a couple seconds later, he was watching me again. I kept wiping, and eventually he moved a little closer. I held the receiver, or grip, out to him and gave him a 'go ahead' look. After a moment's hesitation, he took it and examined it closely. I held out the slide next, which he took with his free hand. I wiped the recoil rod clean and held it out. He looked at it and then at the pieces in his hand. I nodded him over and he scooted closer to me. I pressed the recoil rod into the receiver in his hand, then pulled it out and handed it to him. He looked at me, a little apprehensive, then tried it himself. The spring got away from him, but he stuck his tongue between his teeth and concentrated for his second effort.

Ms. Sabel patted my shoulder and dropped to her knees next to me.

When the boy managed to assemble the slide and rod, we smiled at each other. Giving Ms. Sabel a peripheral glance, he thought through how the slide fit on the receiver. After a quick study, he lined it up and slid it back until he heard a click.

Pointing at the barrel, I pantomimed how to keep it pointed down and away, even when it was empty. As my instruction dawned on him, he nodded with a very serious look and kept it aimed away.

He pulled the slide all the way back and heard the distinct snap of a good fit. With a satisfied grin, he handed it back to me. I refused it, holding the magazine out. He took the mag, cleaned it, and slid it in until it clicked. Beaming with pride, he offered the weapon for inspection.

Dhanpal stepped behind me and held out a shiny Glock 33, the kind Ms. Sabel and Tania carried. They were smaller and lighter, a pound and a half fully loaded, and better suited for smaller hands. Ms. Sabel removed the magazine, cleared the chamber, then disassembled the unit onto my cloth.

"Khelemba," she said, "I need your help."

Dhanpal translated as she spoke. Khelemba watched her closely for a moment, then looked at the parts laid out on the cloth. He began reassembling the weapon.

She continued, pausing for Dhanpal to catch up. "I'm not going to tell you everything is good. It isn't. We're going to get out of here after the storm. If something happens to us, can you defend the others?"

Khelemba glanced over his shoulder at the other children. Two younger boys, Raju and Sithu, and a girl, Usha, played a wordless game with Tania and Carmen. He met Ms. Sabel's eyes again and shrugged as if to say, 'guess so,' and finished the weapon.

"I need a strong boy, Khelemba," she said. "I need someone who can look me in the eye and say he'll be brave for his friends. Can you do that?"

The boy spoke, and Dhanpal translated. "He wants to know if we're going to leave him on the island."

"No, Khelemba. I won't leave you. The men who kidnapped you are still out there. When the storm breaks, we're going to fight our way out. We'll do our best to win. But if they sneak in behind us, I need someone brave. I need someone who will shoot those bad men before he'll let them take the others. Can you do that, Khelemba?"

Khelemba looked at Nakdali and the other two Syrians held at the far end of our area, then over at the other children. He looked Ms. Sabel in the eye, his mouth closed down, his eyes narrowed, and he spat angry words.

Dhanpal said, "He's your man. He will kill them."

She squeezed his face in her hands, pulled him close, and planted a kiss on his forehead. To Dhanpal, she said, "Explain the darts to him. I don't want him killing anyone. And tell him to carry the Glock everywhere he goes—sleep with it in his hand."

When Dhanpal finished a long stream of Hindi, Ms. Sabel and I shook Khelemba's hand. He rose, stuck the weapon in his belt, and joined the others.

"Since you're in charge of this op," she stuck a finger in my chest, "I'm trusting you'll make damn sure he never needs that gun."

She sighed and watched the children for a moment. "What do you know about kids, Jacob? I want to make a happy ending, get them home. But I have to be honest, I don't know what to do. I don't know how to make them feel better when home is so far away."

Shocked that she would confide in me, I shot her a glance. Her admission unveiled one of her many mysterious facets. She was internalizing her hours of torture and looking for something to keep her mind off that topic.

In that split second, I felt exactly what she was feeling.

I felt it because I'd lived it.

But it wasn't just the torture. One of the worst secrets at Sabel Security was the boss's traumatic childhood. When she was a preschooler, Ms. Sabel had watched an intruder strangle her mother. Alan Sabel came to the rescue a minute too late and adopted her the next day. He did what he could, but a billion dollars won't repair a permanently scarred psyche.

I was no psychologist, but I had firsthand experience with permanently scarred psyches.

"The Army has a suicide problem," I said. "They offer counseling. I didn't have any warning signs, but I didn't want to end up like some guys I'd known, so I spent some time in therapy. It's a complex topic, and everybody's different, but I learned something about me. Being part of a war machine puts you face-to-face with how fragile human life really is. A squeeze of a trigger can kill a father or a daughter. People like me, who've been up close with death—faced it, caused it, witnessed it—we keep barriers between us and the people we love. Fear of intimacy. We don't want to love someone because they *will* die."

She nodded and turned away to keep me from seeing her eyes glistening.

"Those kids need some sleep," I said. "So do you. You'd be doing everyone a big favor if you could stop worrying about how fragile their lives are for a few hours. Lie down with those kids. Help them get a little sleep."

Ms. Sabel nearly had her back to me. Her shoulders trembled. I wanted to wrap my arms around her and tell her everything would be OK. That those fragile lives would be saved. But that was fantasy. We were hoping to get off the island towing four prisoners and four children. Liabilities that would most likely get us killed.

We all knew it.

Even the kids.

She sniffled a couple times and drew a slow, deep breath. Keeping her back to me, she wiped her face before turning around. "Thanks, you're right. These children need to sleep." She nodded to herself as she worked through her reluctance. "I can do that."

Ms. Sabel gave me a tired smile, took two steps, and stopped.

Over her shoulder she grinned. "Your little speech about intimacy— what does that say about your love life?"

CHAPTER 31

AFTER DOUBLE-CHECKING THE BOY'S WORK on my sidearm, I pulled Patterson away from the other prisoners.

"See that guy?" I said to Patterson, nodding in the direction of Nakdali. "He had a passport on him, Abdul Nakdali. Great news, right? Now you don't have to extradite Ms. Sabel."

He took a moment to answer, and when he did, his voice was halting. "That *is* good news. But they'll still have questions about the dead man."

I nodded. "You shot a prostrate man in the act of surrendering. Why would you murder a government official, Patterson?"

Patterson's eyes shifted, looking around me. He leaned in, conspiratorially close. "Did you see what he was doing to her?"

"You brought her here."

"I never thought he would do anything like that. My understanding was that we were meeting Sri Lankan investigators."

"In the middle of the Caribbean?" I said. "At a site that's blurred off the satellite maps?"

"You don't understand," Patterson said. "I can help you."

"Help me what?"

"You stormed a government facility. You'll be lucky if they call it treason instead of terrorism. I can help you. I can put in a good word for you."

"Syrians kidnapped Pia Sabel in Washington. My rescue team followed her GPS signals here. If this is a government facility, which department hired them to kidnap her? Yours or Caldwell's?"

Patterson moved back as if I'd slapped him. He pulled himself together and leaned back in. "I can help you. You don't know who you're dealing with."

"So clue me in," I said. "Who runs this place?"

Patterson shifted his weight. His eyes surveyed the ground around me. "That's classified."

Carmen stepped up to us.

"What do you think of this guy?" I thumbed over my shoulder at Patterson. "Did we rescue him or catch him?"

She shrugged and motioned me away. I walked a few steps with her.

Carmen said, "The water is rising. We need to move the group."

I looked down the slope, at the end of the circle of flashlights, and saw muddy water lapping at the edge. It was inching relentlessly up the incline. Connections to other caves were underwater. We had only one way out. The cliff.

Satellite and topographical maps are the lifeblood of soldiers. I'd been smart enough to save a few to my phone while I'd been online. One showed an old lighthouse on the northeast corner of the island and some fishing huts with a pier on the southeast. We were on the northwest, about five miles from the huts.

From the way Chamberlain described the storm's track and speed, we were in the worst of it now. If we could last another hour, conditions would steadily improve. That hour had a rising flood on one side and a platoon of Syrians on the other.

"Move everyone uphill," I said, "but leave Ms. Sabel and the kids for last. Let them get as much rest as possible."

I grabbed a flashlight and headed upstream with Tania. The cave narrowed to a slot twenty yards from our bivouac. We studied the darkness with thermals that told us we were alone, then switched on a flashlight for a brief look before moving forward. Twisting sideways in some places and crawling in others, we explored the opening.

In less than a hundred difficult yards, we came to the cave's mouth, an impressive opening that yawned into the storm's noise and darkness. The mouth was shaped like a cone, the narrow end being our cave exit. A flat floor had formed from sand caught in the bottom. Someone long ago had made a circle of stones for a fire pit. At some point even further back in time, the right-hand corner of the ceiling had fallen into the sea below, leaving a couple of jagged boulders behind. One formed a ledge to my right; the other stuck halfway out over the ocean, creating a defensible space behind it. Beyond the ledge, a trail ran from the fire circle, past the ledge, around the corner, and disappeared into the night.

Outside, daylight was getting through the cloud layer. Not enough to call it first light, but less than the total darkness when we landed. We could see rough shapes and distinguish between light and dark objects at short distances.

I inched to the left, and Tania crept to the right. I reached the boulder that stuck out over the edge and had a look around. Waves crashed against the rocks below, shooting foam and sea into my face. Wind and rain whipped around me like evil children trying to tug me to my death. On the opposite side of the opening was a good-sized trail that wandered away into the night.

I slipped behind the boulder and held my flashlight out over the cliff as far from my body as possible. With one quick flick, I illuminated a small section of the trail … and one pair of NVGs.

Three bullets whizzed past me.

I didn't stick around to count heads. Tania blew a few rounds at the first guy to come down the trail.

"What the hell you doing, Jacob?" she said. "Now they know all they have to do is seal the entrance."

"They just got here, or they would've done that already."

"So we should've left twenty minutes ago."

"And go where?"

She shrugged.

I reached in my pack and found a couple frag grenades. "Back in a flash."

Crossing to her side of the cave mouth, I reached the trailhead. A large, flat stone protected me from the hostiles on the trail as I heaved a grenade around it. The circle of death it created did little damage because it bounced away and off the cliff, exploding above the surf below.

Timing the delay a little better, my second attempt exploded in the air above the trail.

A little cautious inspection with the thermals showed me a clear path for at least twenty yards. I moved up it, Tania covering behind me, and discovered the trail ran along a jagged and treacherous cliff to the surface above. I could see Syrians taking cover twenty yards farther up.

We backed up to the drier and more defensible cave mouth.

"Can you hold here?" I asked.

"Does the pope sleep in the woods?" she said and crouched behind a boulder.

I made my way back down the narrow, twisting cave. Carmen stood at the edge of the rising water.

I stepped to her side. "How fast is it rising?"

"Faster every minute," she said. "I think the other caves are full or blocked, and this is the only empty space to fill. Twenty minutes from now, we're swimming."

A sharp shriek rang through the caves. Everyone turned to face Ms. Sabel, who was awake and looking embarrassed.

Most of us knew about the boss's nightmares. From the time her mother was strangled, she slept three hours and woke up with an ungodly screech. Word was, her mother's ghost visited every night and showed her an ugly future if she didn't do more, push faster, work harder.

Carmen and I stared the others down, even the children. Then we started moving out. Dhanpal and Carmen helped Ms. Sabel with the exhausted children while Tony and Miguel pushed our prisoners forward.

After snapping the plasticuffs off him, I put a shoulder under Salih and helped him limp forward. "You're the guy who told Ms. Sabel there were eight men on the island, right?"

"That's right," he said in Arabic. "The others took the boat and left with the children."

We lagged behind, his wrecked knee causing him pain with each step. He'd spilled his information easily, but I still didn't trust him.

"What boat?" I said.

"Colonel Nakdali contracted a passenger ferry."

Nakdali, a few yards ahead of us, flinched at the mention of his name. He glanced over his shoulder.

"How many children did they take?" I asked.

"Sixteen. All that were left." He waved at the children while his pal, Masri, tried to shut him up with icy glares. "We thought these children had drowned."

"There was a whole platoon out there when I landed. What happened?"

Salih stopped walking and squeezed my shoulder, a genuine look of surprise on his face. "I swear, I do not know."

They say the first thing to die in battle is the truth. I couldn't tell if I was getting it from him or not. He sounded sincere, but his information was way off.

Nakdali turned and faced us.

"I will help him," he said with a commanding tone. His accent was light, with deep vowels.

Whether he was genuinely concerned for his soldier or just wanted to shut the young man up was irrelevant. I let him take Salih's other shoulder.

Nakdali was a thin, wiry man, early fifties or a hard-used forty. His wrinkles were deep and plentiful, and gray hair ran in thick streaks through the base black.

"I hold you responsible for killing nine of my men," he said, leaning around our patient.

I admired him for taking the initiative, trying to take control.

I did some quick math in my head. "Eight, actually. One guy we tied up. They were trying to kill us, y'know."

"We do only what we are legally contracted to do—"

I held out a hand to stop. "Who contracted you?"

He clenched his teeth and glared.

Miguel had stopped in front of us, blocking the way. He motioned me to join him. "Too small a space." He waved a hand at the wider cave mouth. "When the water gets here, we have those ledges. Nothing else."

He was right. Once the water crested the last rise and began spilling out, all kinds of bad things would happen. You didn't have to be an engineer to see erosion would begin any minute and escalate quickly.

The ledge on the right was big enough for three or four adults. The boulder on the left, half of it hanging over the edge, could squeeze in a couple more. That meant I could save five or six of our fifteen lives.

"Jacob," Tony said from the back of the line, "water's coming faster.

Ten feet behind me."

"Miguel," I said, "take the machinegun and the two Syrian soldiers. Send them out on the trail ahead of you."

He nodded and pushed Salih and Masri ahead of him. Salih complained in Arabic, and I explained that they could give him the medical attention he needed. Which was true. But the hostiles on the trail would have to deal with their comrade's ravaged knee.

Pia and Dhanpal took the kids to the ledge, squeezed in, and held on tight. Carmen pushed Patterson and Nakdali to the cliff's edge just as water began pouring out of the cave. The stream went from a trickle to a hose to a fire hose in seconds. Tony and I were stuck in the middle, water hitting our legs hard. The fire circle stones washed away, nearly taking the two of us with it. Pulling him by his good arm, I got Tony to the trailhead seconds before a head-sized rock rolled through where we'd been standing. A moment later, a knee-high rock broke free, bowled through, and plunged over the cliff into the darkness.

Miguel made progress while Tania covered him. They advanced step-by-step as the trail edge eroded beneath them. With nowhere else to go, Tony and I followed them a few feet up the trail.

Salih called out in Arabic to his friends and waved a white cloth. After his third attempt at shouting into the tempest, a reply came back. They stepped out to help him.

Miguel hung back at the last bend, watching with his thermals. When our two prisoners were met and taken in, he and Tania reported back. "Three hostiles on the trail. Must be more topside."

"Agreed—" I was cut off by a crashing sound, followed by a child's scream.

In the cave's mouth, a man-sized chunk of limestone had fallen, forcing the water into two streams around it. One stream was hammering Carmen, Patterson, and Nakdali, forcing them nearer the cliff. They clung to each other and a piece of the boulder.

Tania kept watch on the trail as Miguel and I linked arms, planted our feet in the violent rapids, and reached out. My fingertips reached Carmen's, but the plume of water between us was too much. Ms. Sabel left the children and stepped through the charging water. She grabbed my shoulders and locked her arm in mine to lengthen our reach. Carmen grabbed her hand and pulled herself through the torrent.

Next came Nakdali, struggling with his bound wrists. He put his elbows around Ms. Sabel's head and wedged his foot behind mine before moving his arms to surround my head. As he made the last leap to Miguel, a taller and more difficult reach, his feet left him and he flew into the raging current.

Letting go of Miguel, I grabbed him by the collar and struggled with his weight in one hand. I was unwilling to lose my footing when Miguel grabbed him and tossed him like a rag doll to dry ground.

Patterson watched Nakdali's near-death experience in horror, then held his hands out to Ms. Sabel, begging her to release his plasticuffs. She shook her head. He came forward and encountered Nakdali's problem in the same place. As his feet swept out from under him, Miguel caught him and tossed him on top of Nakdali.

Ms. Sabel climbed back to the children while I pushed Patterson and Nakdali to the trailhead.

With sincere humility, Nakdali said, "Thank you for saving my life. And thank you for showing Salih a little mercy."

"You're welcome," I said. "I'd consider it a debt repaid if you told me where your men took the children."

"Children?"

"We're missing sixteen children. Salih told me you took them off the island. They had a window of about seven to ten hours, which means they transferred them to someone else in the Dominican Republic. Where are they?"

"They're coming," Tania called out.

Miguel and Tony scrambled to find defensible positions.

Nakdali's eyes searched mine for a long moment. "We will talk after the storm passes."

I stared at Nakdali, turning his words over in my head. There was a threat lurking somewhere in his phrasing.

Was he a step ahead of me?

CHAPTER 32

MIGUEL LOBBED A GRENADE AND moved up the trail, firing his machinegun in an endless arc. His aggressiveness took them by surprise, and they fell back toward the ridge. Tania and I moved up the trail behind him, taking ground and pushing for more.

They retreated with little provocation.

Halfway up, we saw why they were abandoning the trail. Erosion was crumbling chunks of it into the sea two hundred feet below. Miguel stopped at one section where only a three-inch foothold remained over a five-foot stretch of trail.

Tania leaned over me to check it out for herself as the wind and rain broke off fist-sized rocks above us and dropped them with relentless regularity. Twenty feet below us, a car-sized piece of the cliff broke free and crashed into the pounding surf.

"You put ropes in our packs, right?" Tania screamed above the wailing wind. "Tell me you put rope in our packs."

One day I will think of everything, and Tania will be happy.

I switched to NVGs and took a quick look over the side. More than a hundred feet below us, a roiling ocean crashed into solid rock, each wave shooting tons of water into the air. There was nothing out there—not a shred of beach, not a hint of another cave, no alternative trail. Making our way up the path before the rest of it washed away was our only option.

Miguel slid his feet along the slippery ledge until he reached the far side. Tania followed, losing her footing only once. Tony stepped up behind me and looked at the situation.

"May as well try," he said and stepped past me.

"Wait," I said.

He kept going without looking back. With only one good arm, it was a bad idea that quickly became our worst nightmare. The only large stone still sticking out from the cliff gave way. Tony tottered for a second while Miguel and I reached out for him from our respective sides. Tony's good arm swung my way twice but I only caught a piece of shirt, not enough to hold his weight. Miguel and I locked hands, but missed Tony. He fell away, disappearing with a shout.

Tania screamed while Miguel and I fell to our knees. In an instant, the fragile life of my best friend at Sabel Security was over.

Ms. Sabel came up behind me. "What happened?"

She didn't like my answer.

Dhanpal crowded in with us. "We brought the kids out. The roof was falling in on us."

We stared at each other for a silent moment.

An oven-sized rock broke loose above Dhanpal and bounced outward and away.

"Gotta move," Miguel shouted at us. "Mourn later."

I knelt on the trail and reached my hand out as far as I could. Miguel did the same until we locked our hands together, forming a backstop.

Ms. Sabel insisted on being next because her long arms could help pull the others across. She climbed over me, crossed the ledge with an athlete's balance, and took up a position behind Miguel.

The children came next, shepherded by Carmen and Dhanpal.

Usha, the little girl from New Delhi, cried hysterically while Dhanpal did his best to reassure her that she could make it.

We all thought of Tony, but no one said it out loud.

"Khelemba," Ms. Sabel called and motioned for him to go first. "Show the others."

The boy shook his head, the whites of his eyes shining. Dhanpal reassured him and patted him on the back. With a little more encouragement from Ms. Sabel, the boy took a deep breath and wedged a foot into the rock. Dhanpal held his hand until Ms. Sabel could reach his other. Because Miguel and I were in the way, there were two steps the boy had to make on his own. He did well, never looking down and only leaning back onto my arm once. I brushed his weight back toward the rock wall, and he continued on.

A loud noise caught our attention. A ten-foot section of cliff near the cave's mouth collapsed into the sea. The ocean's ruthless pounding at the base was weakening the entire wall. We had seconds.

Sithu, the boy from Myanmar, went next. Everything went fine until one foot slipped off just as Ms. Sabel caught his hand. He fell back onto Miguel's arm. I felt the boy's full weight straining our only safety mechanism and wondered if we could hold an adult. With a burst of strength, Ms. Sabel pulled the boy and swung him around to a soft landing. Everyone breathed a sigh of relief.

Having seen Sithu's fate, Usha and Raju refused to move. So we sent Carmen, who crossed without a problem.

Emboldened by Carmen's efforts, Usha went next. When she reached the middle, an extra stiff gust hit us hard, and she lost her confidence. She screamed in terror and went rigid with fright. Her body tumbled backward over our locked arms as if she'd pushed off the wall. Primal instincts took over. My hand flailed into the darkness driven by hope alone. What felt like eternity was actually a nanosecond. The instant I felt skin, my hand locked onto the girl's rain-slicked ankle.

At the same time, Miguel lost his balance and fell forward, staying on his narrow perch only by Ms. Sabel's lightning-fast grab for his belt.

Usha began slipping through my awkward hold. I swung the screaming girl like a pendulum, back toward the cave, then out toward Miguel, while I gripped half an inch of rock with my free hand. After three swings, my grip on the rock slipped. There was only one swing left before we went down together. I swung Usha harder. Miguel watched my progress, noting the cadence of my swings and caught her arm in one outstretched hand.

I wanted to shout for joy, but it wasn't over. The girl hung high above certain death, dangling from Miguel's arm. Miguel didn't have enough weight balanced behind him to pull himself and Usha upright.

Ms. Sabel planted her feet and tugged hard, her will to save them multiplying her strength, but the big guy's weight was too much. Carmen grabbed Ms. Sabel's waist and held her tight. With a second effort, they tugged and landed both Miguel and Usha back on the trail. All four fell in a single heap.

I turned to Dhanpal to say, '*holy crap did you see that,*' but instead I saw Nakdali standing with his cuffed hands over Raju's eyes. The boy never saw a thing. I gave the man a nod of appreciation for thinking ahead. He gave me a tight smile in return. Whatever his role in all this, he had retained some shred of decency.

Raju stepped up and climbed the wall like a spider, safely into Ms. Sabel's hand without any problems.

Patterson stepped to the edge next. "I need my hands free."

I shook my head.

"You're giving me a death sentence if you make me cross with bound hands."

"Better odds than you gave Caldwell," I said.

Another chunk of cliff behind us slid into the ocean.

Patterson made it across, double time. The group pushed him up the trail to clear space for the next person.

Nakdali and Dhanpal went next. Then I went without a safety net. Halfway across, I made the mistake of looking down. A big wave hit the rocks below; the resulting spray shot up, reaching for my face. Terror made me shiver. My foot slipped. I couldn't believe any of us had made it and found myself mumbling a prayer.

The ledge held fast until I took my second-to-last step. It fell away the same instant Miguel grabbed my bicep. My chest hit the rock he stood on. I scrambled over the edge and onto my feet in a flurry of arms and legs.

Miguel and I squeezed past everyone to take point at the head of the group. As I went, I counted heads. We were one short.

"Where's Patterson?" I asked anyone listening.

"Did he go over the side?" Dhanpal asked.

"No," Tania said. "He would've screamed louder than Usha."

Patterson didn't even show up on thermal.

"My bad," I said. "I didn't assign anyone."

"Not on you, brother," Miguel said, patting my shoulder. "We focused on other things."

We pushed up the cliff until we were ten feet below the top ridge.

Miguel and Dhanpal sent our last two frag grenades into the air over the cliff while Carmen, Tania, and I charged up the trail. We found two men running down a track before disappearing behind a curtain of bushes and low trees. We gave chase for a few seconds but stopped short of ambush range.

The vegetation at this elevation stood just above our heads and was relatively thick. A lot of it was flying through the air, stripped loose by the storm.

"Gotta be more," Tania said. "Wish they would step out where I can shoot 'em. Let's get this over with."

"Trap," I said and pointed to the only trail through the brush. "We forge our own way, zigzag."

Tania nodded, her eyes continually sweeping the area.

Carmen brought the others up the trail while Tania and I scouted ahead. Tania used thermal imaging while I tried NVGs. A hint of sunlight glowed in the clouds, enough to give me a gray-and-white view of the path ahead. I could make out shapes and could see Tania when she stood still. That meant our thermal binocular advantage was dropping by the minute. Worse, the rain was letting up, and the winds were down a notch. With the Syrian's superior numbers, we had a serious problem.

Twenty yards forward, Tania stopped and fired a few rounds. She pointed with her rifle barrel and said, "Did you see him?"

CHAPTER 33

THEY CAME AT US FROM two sides. Three men on each side of us.

We fired back. When Miguel opened up with the machinegun, they ran for it.

The whole affair lasted less than three seconds. Enough to terrify the children.

"Warning shots," Tania said.

"Or a lure," I said.

Miguel followed them into the bushes about twenty yards, sweeping his machinegun back and forth long enough to scatter them. I sent Miguel and Carmen to run wide on either side of us, and we began moving cautiously forward.

At our rate of travel, it would take hours to reach the island's eastern shore.

The rain continued to lighten up, if only a little at a time, and the sky marginally brightened. I could make out the clouds and distinguish one plant from another along the trail. White limestone rocks contrasted against the darker dirt surrounding them. While it still worked, our thermal advantage was effectively gone.

The Syrians shadowed us; we caught glimpses of them now and then. Miguel was pretty quick to scatter them with the machinegun, but the terrain didn't give us much room to end the standoff. Nakdali's odd statement about waiting for the storm to end still rang in my ears. Reinforcements? Only their respect for the machinegun kept them at bay. I positioned Tania next to Nakdali with a rifle pressed to the Syrian's chest for insurance.

We continued on our nerve-racking journey for two miles before the children became a problem. They did their best to keep up with the adults, but the journey was too much for them. Usha was in the worst shape. Her feet slowed and stumbled. Ms. Sabel tossed the little girl on her shoulders. The other children looked jealous until Dhanpal picked up Raju. I took Sithu. Khelemba refused a ride for another half mile, then gave in and let Carmen carry him. That solution made us more vulnerable; four weapons were offline, and the children were up high.

As we slogged on, the weather continued to improve. It was incremental at first, but increased with each mile. I tried connecting to a satellite every now and then before finally hooking in when we were a mile from the eastern shore.

My first call was to Chamberlain to get us off the rock. I dialed the phone I'd given him. He picked up after seven rings.

"Sorry, whoever you are," Chamberlain said. "This phone was left onboard a long time ago. I haven't time for further discussion. The US Coast Guard has boarded my ship with a warrant for the arrest of someone named Pia Sabel. Do you know this person?"

"Uh…"

"I thought not. Good day."

With that, the connection went dead.

"Bad news?" Ms. Sabel asked.

Based on the way she was looking at me, I realized my face was scrunched up, completely confused.

"Did you know there's a warrant out for your arrest?"

She made a face and dialed her father.

I made a few calls of my own, updating the Major and learning what little we knew about the arrest warrant. DC had issued a warrant for her arrest in the matter of two dead men back in Carver Langston. Something must have gone terribly wrong with the investigation since we left town.

Only a few minutes into my calls, Chamberlain called me back. He said, "Sorry about putting you off earlier, but your Ms. Sabel's in a world of trouble. The Coast Guard just left, unsatisfied with my passenger manifest. Bringing your party onboard might be hazardous to your liberty and mine."

"I understand," I said through clenched teeth.

For what I paid him, he should've helped me smuggle uranium into

Iran.

Chamberlain sensed my displeasure and cleared his throat. "I'm no smuggler, sir. I don't know much about giving the Coast Guard the slip, but if you can beat a hurricane, I'll not let you down. I'll send our tender and turn for port. With any luck, we can pick up your party along the way. Before you get too excited, the seas are still quite rough. Give me an hour."

"Did the Coasties have a chopper, by any chance?"

"Indeed they did, why?"

"I think I hear one approaching."

We clicked off and doubled our pace. The hostiles continued their pursuit at a distance. Still, their tactics bothered me. They were up to something.

In the distance, the rhythmic whumping of a helicopter came from the low clouds. Despite scanning the skies for a couple minutes, we couldn't spot them.

We trudged on until the dirt track wound its way down the cliff to the fishing huts. Looking over the edge, the huts were severely storm damaged. Only a few pilings remained of the pier.

Taking the track down was the only viable method of getting to the shore, but it would leave us wide open to a Syrian attack from above.

Dhanpal stepped next to me, reached into his pack, retrieved something, and handed it to me without a word.

A Claymore anti-personnel mine—a nasty piece of war material that could kill anyone fifty feet in front of it. Illegal for private ownership. I couldn't imagine Sabel Security had a corporate license for it, but I was *not* going to shake the rulebook at our vegetarian warrior.

"Thanks," I said. "Remote detonation?"

"Don't worry," Dhanpal said. "I'll make sure we aren't followed."

"Sorry, you're my only translator." I nodded toward the children.

He frowned. SEALs live for the chance to take all the risk and reap all the glory. He'd rather have been neutered than lose an opportunity to beat overwhelming odds.

Tania stepped up, took the hardware out of my hands, and headed up the track.

I'm old-fashioned when it comes to women on the battlefield. Something hardwired into my DNA tells me to protect women no matter how much I believe in equal rights. I wanted to call her back and send Miguel. But she would have ignored me anyway.

I watched her disappear into the brush.

Miguel gave me a look; I gave him a nod. He dropped to the back of our procession and faded away.

Carmen led us down the steep road to the beach. The tidal surge, receded by then, had leveled everything but one hut perched on a rise of rock. And it had a tree sticking out of the side. We corralled the group inside to wait for Chamberlain's boat.

The distant sound of war raged on the cliff above us. I never wanted to be an officer. Sending people to fight and die based on my tactical decision was more responsibility than I could stand. That thought was being driven home by the hammering of sporadic gunfire a quarter mile away. There was a shot, then another, followed by a burst of three, then silence. Then another burst. Then more silence. No calls, no announcements, no play-by-play updates.

Listening through wind and rain for a sign of Tania's success or failure ground my heart to dust. I realized that I'd done more than blow my relationship with Tania; I'd let the one woman I could grow old with slip through my fingers and out of my life. It was a mistake I'd understood superficially at the time. Now I realized how catastrophic losing Tania would be. She was still part of my professional life and losing that last thread of connection to her would kill a part of me, an even bigger part than died the day she slammed the door in my face.

There was another burst of gunfire.

The strain of hearing people you care about fighting for their lives etched the same lines in Ms. Sabel's face as mine.

The children clung to her like barnacles, their terror keeping them silent. Carmen and Dhanpal paced the small shack, peeking out the broken windows, assessing tactical alternatives should Tania fail to hold back the Syrians.

The distant rhythm of the helicopter grew louder, a little bit at a time.

More shots rang out, followed by return fire. They were single shots, indicating a running battle without clear targets. The worst kind of fight. Each soldier was taking cover, shaking with fear, shooting at any flicker of movement, then rolling away before an adversary could target his hiding place.

Then a voice, screaming obscenities, came through our earbuds. It was followed by a long burst from the machinegun.

I gave Ms. Sabel a thumbs-up. Everything was going to be fine.

Tania was screaming with all her might at Miguel's fleeing backside. "Goddamn it, Miguel! That was my fight. What the fuck did you think you're doing? Goddamn it, boy, get back here! I'm talking to you!"

She continued cursing him all the way to the hut where she burst in right behind him. She ran straight to me, jabbing her finger in my face. "You think I couldn't handle a bunch of sheep herders? You had to send Miguel? You think you're funny—"

I wrapped my arms around her and lifted her off the ground.

"Hey! Put me down, goddamn it!"

Everyone laughed until the helicopter grew louder. Dhanpal ran outside to sweep our footprints off the sand with a palm frond.

I drew my Glock and shot Nakdali.

CHAPTER 34

"DEAD WEIGHT'S THE WORST," MIGUEL said, hefting Nakdali onto his shoulder before climbing to the *Inanna II*'s deck. "Why dart the guy?"

"He would've waved down the Coasties," I said.

Once we were safely onboard the yacht, we gathered in the grand saloon, milling about without speaking. We glanced at each other nervously without realizing why we'd sought out each other's company.

Ms. Sabel knew. "Jacob, would you say a few words for Tony, please?"

Everyone bowed their heads and waited. I choked on my first breath. It was my op, but I'd never had to 'say a few words' before. Then I remembered the words Ms. Sabel had said when we lost Ezra back in Cameroon.

"Tony was a hero," I said. "The old-fashioned kind like Hercules and Theseus. The kind you see every day without knowing it. He was the kind of hero who when he saw something wrong, he tried to right it. When he saw suffering, tried to heal it. When he went to war, he went to stop it. That's what heroes do. Tony, we will get these children home and find the others. We will bring down those responsible for Snare Drum and stop their war."

Everyone muttered amen and wandered off to their duties, their mood improved at the prospect of going home.

I stared out the window and wondered. Through all my deployments, in all my missions, in every battle, I'd heard a voice that warned me just before something bad happened. I called that voice Mercury, the winged messenger of the Roman gods. He kept me, and those around me, alive through some serious shit. But you can't keep a secret in the Army. Eventually, officers became aware of my exceptional luck. Anytime the subject of gods comes up, there are those who believe, those who don't, and those who believe something different. The doctors believed in meds. Eventually, they made me believe in meds. But at that moment, saying goodbye to Tony, I wondered if Mercury would've said something. Would he have warned me? Maybe if I believed in something better than meds, Tony would still be alive.

There was work to be done. I quit wasting my time reliving the anguish.

We took turns catching showers and helping the children call their parents. Tania was angling for Agent-of-the-Year. She'd thought ahead and brought Ms. Sabel a new fitness outfit.

How come I never thought of bringing the boss clean clothes?

Once the children were napping, Ms. Sabel and Tania made calls in the grand saloon. I sat in the far corner and booted Nakdali's laptop. Nakdali's system was fairly simple: some management software for tracking employees, some contracts on file, some e-mails from home, and a separate e-mail account filled with cryptic notes from Caldwell.

A system search for *snare drum* narrowed down the stuff I needed. Everything came from Caldwell. Nothing mentioned the mysterious TGW. Several of Caldwell's e-mails included guest lists, including one with Ms. Sabel's portrait. That same e-mail also listed Patterson as a guest and featured a head shot. I ran another quick search for Patterson, but found him mentioned only in that one e-mail.

The other guest pictures were not what I expected. Some were dressed like Bedouins and others in shumagg and thoub, like Gulf Arabs. I copied one of the names and googled him.

An old article in *Al Bawaba*, a Yemeni news site, came up citing the man as a leader of something that sounded like Islamic boy scouts. Something just above the article in the website's banner caught my eye: *American Heiress Sought in Deadly Rampage.*

I gasped, drawing the attention of Ms. Sabel and Tania. Clicking on the headline, I scanned the article. It claimed she'd led a bold commando attack on a military base, killing several American security contractors.

TGW was running damage control quickly and effectively. He'd reached the press before we could expose the operation. Everything we said from now on would sound like a bad excuse.

Tania stood next to me, trying to decipher the screen.

Ms. Sabel dropped on the couch next to me, smelling of lavender after her shower, and pointed at her picture on the news site. "Read it."

After a short hesitation, I translated the whole article. A government source was calling it an act of terrorism and treason.

Tania turned to the flat screen at the end of the room and pulled up a news network. Over video clips from Ms. Sabel's soccer career, a reporter's voice said, "One source speculated that Sabel's attack could have been meant to drum up new security business by exposing her competition. An attack that my source claims backfired in the worst possible way."

Tania turned it off.

We stared, speechless for a full minute before anyone could speak.

"I know a woman at the *Post*," I said. "Maybe she can tell me what's going on."

"Call her," Ms. Sabel said. "I know someone at Channel Four. I'll call him. But I have to think it through first."

"No one should know where we are," Tania said, "or where we're going. Not even the Major or your dad. Right now, we're fugitives. The police will ask them, and we can't force anyone to lie for us."

We nodded slowly as the weight of the situation sank in.

Ms. Sabel stood up and walked out on the deck, the most wanted woman in the hemisphere. She watched the fast-moving gray clouds and the whitecaps and the birds swooping behind the yacht. Beyond her, right at the horizon, I saw a ship about the same size as ours following us.

I called my contact at the *Post*. "Emily, how are you?"

"You don't happen to be anywhere near Pia Sabel, do you?"

"I led the rescue."

"Rescue, nice spin," she said. "And you called me, a lowly travel writer, to apologize for leaving me at a coffee shop a hundred thirty-seven and a half days ago?"

"Uh. No." I cleared my throat.

"Cut the crap," she said. "We both know why you called me. You want your story out. I'll help you with that, but you better give me a big freakin' scoop. Tell me something no one else knows so I can forget about the weekend that never happened."

"Look, I apologized for that once," I said. "I was on a mission."

A mission to cure a lovesick cougar's loneliness, which is a very important mission in my book, but Emily would never see it from my point of view. I drew a blank for witty comebacks.

When I heard Emily's fed up sigh, I said, "Where is this crap about Ms. Sabel coming from?"

"It's a news storm; everyone's quoting anonymous sources that sound like the same source. Either it's one big circle jerk or someone in the administration is calling every reporter in town. Tell me the truth: did she really kill two guys here and twelve more in Puerto Rico?"

"No." I left a long silence as my exclamation point.

I heard her typing.

I said, "Did you know she was kidnapped in DC?"

"Can you verify that?"

"The store owners in Carver Langston, Douglas, Raissa, and Louisa can—"

"Douglas, the pawnshop guy? He's the one who claimed she killed the Syrian immigrants in the beginning."

Stunned, I fell back on the couch. That fat little weasel. Did the Syrians take his daughter again?

"Well," I said, "ask the other two then."

"Gone into hiding."

"When they come back," I said, "they'll back up my story. It's the truth."

She typed in the background. No doubt instant messaging an editor. "Where are you now?"

"No idea. Blown off course by a hurricane."

"I'll put that down as 'won't say.'"

"No, you quote what I tell you or I'm hanging up."

"OK. Don't have a cow, man." She blew a breath. "So tell me your side of it. Just the parts you were involved in."

I recounted the highlights about following Ms. Sabel's trail to the Caribbean. When I arrived at the part about finding her, I poured on the

204

graphic details. She slowed me several times and asked clarifying questions. I wrapped up by saying, "And everyone on my team will testify under oath."

"Any video?"

"What?"

"There are video cameras everywhere these days, Jacob. You took some footage on your phone, right?"

Two things popped into my head: all the USB drives on the island, and Carmen taking her phone out when she should have been watching Patterson.

I was quiet too long.

"Holy shit!" Emily said. "You have video. Oh boy, Jacob! You big handsome hunk of manliness, do you have a little video for your girlfriend?"

Girlfriend? That was a stretch. I tried to recall what she looked like.

"I'm sorry, Emily, you're breaking up. Can you repeat that? Emily? Are—" I clicked off.

When she called back, I sent her straight to voice mail, turned off my phone, ran downstairs, and burst into Carmen's cabin.

"Carmen, did you take a video of Pia tied up?"

She was naked, bent over, toweling off her legs. She scowled at me. "Can you give me a minute?"

"Uh. Sorry. Grand saloon, right away." I tried really hard not to look. She's married.

I ran back up, pulled out Nakdali's laptop, and ran a search for video files. Hundreds were reported as links that were no longer linked. The USB drives. I plugged in one of the drives I'd taken from Nakdali's office and searched it. It reported 83 hours of video in three hundred fifty-one files. All the file names were the same—some kind of six-letter code followed by a three-digit number. A quick copy and paste into the e-mail search box turned up an e-mailed guest list featuring one guest.

My heart stopped.

I knew him instantly from his photograph. Yusuf Farrah, the Somali warlord who'd killed three of my former comrades in Afghanistan. I opened another search window and copied another video code. The second search pointed to the same e-mail. Repeating the procedure three more times, everything came back to the same e-mail. Everything on that drive was related to Yusuf, a known terrorist and leader of al-Qaeda in Somalia.

With trepidation, I opened one of the files. Taken with a fish-eye lens from the corner of a small room, a uniformed young man entered, stripped sheets off the bed, piled them into a corner, put new sheets on, made the bed, grabbed the trash can, and left. The screen went blank. Motion-activated video. No wonder there were so many files of different lengths. I opened another random file.

Taken from the same camera in the same room, but early in the morning judging from the shadows. I watched as Yusuf dragged a young boy, naked and struggling, into the room and threw him on the bed. Shedding his clothes, Yusuf pulled out a condom.

I shut down the video and took a deep breath.

"What the hell happened to you?" Carmen said. She stood in front of me in a bathrobe. "You seasick or something?"

"Probably," I said and met her gaze. "Did you take a video in the bunker?"

"It was too dark, and all I ended up with is you trying to break Patterson's arm and Pia strapped to a table. Nothing definitive."

"Upload it to HQ right away. Have anything else?"

"Nope."

"Anyone else get anything?"

"Jesus, Jacob. There was a hurricane—"

I waved her off. "Just upload it. Thanks. And, uh, sorry about forgetting to knock."

"All in the family," she said, holding out two phones. "Oh, one other thing. When I frisked Patterson, he had two phones. I don't know if they were both his, but thought you should know."

There are plenty of reasons for two phones. What was Patterson's?

I stared at her extended hand for a moment. "Agent Marty decoded the phone Patterson used at his first meeting with Ms. Sabel—State Department, standard issue. Find out what's up with the other one."

She put the phones back in her robe and left.

Tania made calls from the far side of the room. Ms. Sabel still stared at the ocean.

I turned my phone back on and saw sixteen voice mails from Emily plus twelve other voice mails. Probably an escalating string of editors and vice presidents. I didn't bother looking at the many texts. Lesson learned: never tease a reporter with a big story until you're ready. No wonder Ms. Sabel was staring at the ocean. Think first, call later.

I needed advice, and the one person who always came through was the Major. She picked up right away. "You better have something."

"You know how Ms. Sabel thought this was about child traffickers?"

"Uh-oh."

"It's worse."

"Define 'worse.'"

"Snare Drum blackmails pedophile terrorists."

"What?"

"The operation kidnaps children and offers them to pedophiles inside al-Qaeda, then they video the guys having sex with children. I'm no expert on fundamentalist Islam, but I'm pretty sure that's frowned on, so they have these guys by the balls. The pedophile then has to give TGW the names of terrorist leaders, and TGW sends in drones. Notice how they've been picking off lots of terrorist leaders lately?"

"Holy mother of God. You sure this is a government operation?"

"Gotta be. They're using a decommissioned army base, and they hired Nakdali."

"Who hired Nakdali?" she asked.

"I don't know. TGW is the only name I have, and there were two State Department employees on the island. Who else could be involved?"

"The CIA. They got their wrist slapped for using torture. Maybe they resorted to the old ways, the honey trap. Only this time, they went way off the board." The Major's voice sounded distant, as if she were staring out her office window, trying to make sense of it all. "Who is this TGW guy? He has to be working for someone who can authorize C-130 flights and contractors." She paused a second. "Who the hell authorized kidnapping and molesting?"

"Major, this problem is way over my pay grade. I have a laptop full of kiddie porn. What am I supposed to do?"

"What do you mean? You bring it in; turn it over to the FBI."

"Begging your pardon, ma'am, but someone out there has the world believing Ms. Sabel committed an act of treason. We attacked a US military installation—supposedly. The kiddie porn becomes a problem. If TGW catches me with this crap in my hands, he'll claim it's mine. He'll say I'm using it as a cheap defense."

"I see what you mean." The Major took a deep breath. "TGW wanted you on that island so his people could repulse your attack, kill every Sabel employee who knows about Snare Drum, make you look like terrorists in the process, and still have a chance to get away. Only you were better than they expected and you got away—"

"—with enough evidence to bury him and his coconspirators."

The Major said, "They're going to terminate you with extreme prejudice."

Suddenly the answers to several questions crystallized in my mind. I understood why Caldwell threw up his hands and dropped to the floor without a complaint. And I knew why Nakdali put off answering questions until the storm passed. I rose and looked astern. The ship that had been on the horizon was larger. They were gaining on us.

CHAPTER 35

"CALDWELL SURRENDERED BECAUSE HE THOUGHT reinforcements would show up any minute," I said to the Major. "The Syrians didn't kill us during our retreat because they were waiting to attack in superior numbers. They didn't want to kill Nakdali in the crossfire. We arrived before the hurricane, the reinforcements rode it out somewhere else. Right now, those reinforcements are behind me and gaining. When they catch up, they'll send the yacht and everyone in it to the bottom of the Atlantic and the headlines will read, *Renegade Heiress Lost at Sea*."

"Yeah," the Major said, her voice distant again. "That's not good."

"The Syrians were carrying brand-new weapons," I said. "Still had Cosmoline on the barrels, and they had quad-barrel NVGs. Someone whipped out a checkbook in the last couple days. Odd thing about it though—they had cheap business-class radios. Nothing encrypted or secure."

"Encrypted channels have to be assigned," the Major said.

"Right, no paper trail for off-the-shelf radios. TGW kept everything untraceable."

"CIA, gotta be," the Major said. "State doesn't have the weapons or a black budget. We'll track down the connection from this end. Who else saw the video?"

"No one."

"I'll find someone we can trust at the FBI and have them set up a secure drop site in the cloud."

We clicked off.

Carmen stepped to me, back in drab clothes. "One of Patterson's phones is standard State Department issue. Last used just after he met with Pia in Carver Langston. The other phone is from the White House

SEELEY JAMES

Communications Agency. They handle comm encryption for more departments than just the Executive Office."

"Why would a mid-level appointee at State have one?"

"Beats me. And it'll take an act of Congress to find out."

I squeezed her shoulder as a thank-you and went to find the Captain.

The First Officer sent me to the galley, where I found Chamberlain eating a bowl of cereal. He stopped with a spoonful of Cheerios halfway to his mouth.

"Is that ship following us?" I said.

"I think so," he said. "We're in an unusual lane, and they've matched our course."

He munched his spoonful of cereal.

"I think they intend to sink the ship."

"Not very sporting of them." He scooped another spoon and again stopped halfway. He cocked his head to the side and waited for the punch line.

"Sorry to get you mixed up in all this, but it seems we've pissed off some powerful people, and, um ... uh ..."

His amused look began to melt. "They're going to kill us all?"

There was no denying the truth of it.

Chamberlain swallowed hard.

I said, "If I'd known who was holding Ms. Sabel, I'd never have involved you. But if they find us onboard, they'll assume you know everything, which means they'll kill you, and the crew, and sink the ship. Yeah. Well. That's the deal. Like I said, sorry."

He stared at me, frozen in time with the Cheerios still halfway to his mouth. A pearl-white drop of milk fell from the spoon and splashed in the bowl. His British reserve melted as his jaw dropped. "I find 'sorry' a bit lacking, don't you?"

"I have a plan," I said. "Knowing as little of it as possible is your best hope for survival."

"Now see here, Mr. Stearne. I agreed to this charter in the earnest hope of getting an interview for the *Asteria*. I expect you'll at least see to it that—" Chamberlain dropped his spoon in the bowl and pushed it away. His gaze turned out to sea.

I couldn't think of anything good to say. I had no clue about the *Asteria*, and I didn't really have a plan, so I shrugged and left.

Ms. Sabel had the children lined up in the dining room. She'd set up a video chat with Otis Blackwell from Channel 4, a translator, Senator Jeff Smith, and the children's parents courtesy TV stations in India and Myanmar. When she saw me, she excused herself and pointed me back to the grand saloon.

"We're very close to sending four children home," she said. "Sixteen more to go."

"You're wanted for terrorism," I said. "Isn't that our top priority—"

"The children are my top priority. The other children could be raped tonight. I can't let that happen."

Those piercing gray-green eyes stared right through me.

Ms. Sabel gave me a complex set of instructions for the next few days. I would take the children to DC, where Senator Smith had therapists and specialists standing by. The senator would see them home from there because I'd probably be arrested. She had attorneys standing by to bail me out and put me back on the trail of TGW.

I liked the executive side of her. She was thinking things through, consulting experts, and issuing orders. She'd grown up a lot in the last couple days. I went straight to work. First up: call Emily at the *Post*.

Emily picked up before it rang. "Start talking, 'cause my editors don't believe I was ever dumb enough to date a scumbag like you."

"Funny. You want an exclusive or not?"

"Excuse me if I find your use of the word 'exclusive' hard to swallow."

"I'm serious," I said. "You get my inside story. Ms. Sabel is giving hers to a TV guy named Otis Blackwell. That's it for press contacts—you for print, Otis for TV. I need your word that you'll follow my instructions for safety reasons."

"You don't get to dictate my story—"

"I'm not talking about spinning your story, Emily. The bad guys have already killed people." I let that sink in a second or two. "There are lives at stake here—not just mine, but yours, innocent children, and bystanders. Even the idiot editors who are listening in on this call are putting their lives at risk." I heard three lines drop off the call. "This is the last electronic communication of any kind. Emily, think about it carefully before you answer: Are you in?"

She choked. Ten seconds later, she said, "I'm in."

"Buy a prepaid phone and use it to call your mother in Springfield. She'll have a piece of the puzzle for you. Next, remember that coffee shop for our lost weekend? You need to be there at five in the morning. That's it for now."

"Wait! My mother doesn't live in Spring—"

I clicked off, hoping I remembered our pillow talk right. If I did, those clues would come to her, and she'd be in the right place at the right time. Unfortunately, I'm a roll-over-and-sleep guy.

Usha, the little girl from New Delhi, patted my knee. When I looked at her, she gave me a smile, her big brown eyes sparkled in the daylight. Dhanpal stood behind her and explained. "She's thanking everyone who rescued her."

I smiled and reached to pat her head, but she recoiled.

Clasping my palms together, elbows out, I bowed my head. "Namhast."

Dhanpal rolled his eyes. "It's pronounced Namaste."

I bowed and tried again.

Dhanpal said something to Usha, and she laughed. She patted my bowed head, then ran to Tania. Usha's gesture made me want to go back and pump another couple rounds into Caldwell's corpse.

Tania and Ms. Sabel were working on where the other sixteen were taken. We pieced together the bits and pieces we'd picked up along the way from the pilots and the children. Their captivity in Mullaitivu had been overseen by the tall man, Safwan. They stayed overnight in a stone building. Kowalski met them in the Azores and brought them to Isla de la Mona. But Safwan didn't make the trip.

"Where was the stone building?" Tania said.

"They stopped to refuel," I said. "They were using C-130s. That plane's range would make Sri Lanka to the Caribbean in three hops."

"Once at the stone building, and then in the Azores," Ms. Sabel said.

"If the CIA's involved, they have black sites all over the place. I'd draw a line from Sri Lanka to Azores and look for something near that line."

"Why switch planes?" Ms. Sabel said.

I shrugged. "Pilot fatigue, maybe?"

"I get McCarty and Caldwell," Ms. Sabel said. "They were running Nakdali. Where does Patterson fit in?"

"All three of them worked at the CIA then moved to State," I said. "But Patterson doesn't fit in Snare Drum as far as I can tell. He brought you here, witnessed your torture, and murdered Caldwell. There's no trace of his involvement until twenty-four hours ago. And now he's missing. The only clue we have is in the Azores. I can fly out there and have the info—"

"I need you in DC," Ms. Sabel said. "Tania and I are going to the Azores."

Disappointed, I left to work on my next job: interrogating Nakdali. For an interrogation room, I chose the outdoor dining deck. The air was fresh and clear after the storm and the view was stunning from the sunny upper deck. Behind us, the phantom boat continued to gain but was still a mile out. High speed chases in ships are a lot less dramatic than cars.

Nakdali was fed and awake when they brought him to me.

"I've opened and decrypted your laptop," I said. "I'm going to turn you over to the FBI and let them charge you with whatever they decide: kidnapping, pedophilia, murder. Probably all of them."

He studied the white tablecloth in front of him before slowly nodding.

I said, "Work with me, and I'll tell them you're a good guy caught up in a bad plan. Ignore me, and I'll say you were in deep."

He kept his eyes on the table as he thought. After a long moment, he looked up and shook his head.

"Let's start with Yusuf Farrah," I said. "How long was he a guest of yours?"

He flinched at the name. "I had a contract with your government. I will not talk to you until I have an attorney."

"You have rights during a police investigation. I'm just a citizen who's ready to throw you overboard for making kiddie porn starring Yusuf. Talk to me. How long was he a guest at your facility?"

Nakdali took a long deep breath, reclaiming his resolve while saying nothing.

"You said you'd help me after the storm passed," I said. "I figured it out. You were expecting reinforcements. Well, the storm passed, and they didn't show. They'll gun you down, just like you had your men killed in Washington."

His eyes snapped up to meet mine. "What are you talking about?"

"Ordering the drive-by shooting in Carver Langston was cold, Nakdali. How could you do that?"

He inched back, his eyes widening a fraction before he reined in his emotions. He sat perfectly still without speaking, his eyes pinned to mine.

"Pretending you haven't heard?" I said. "Hamoud executed one of your guys and barely missed Dakka."

His whole body shook with anger. He stiffened and took a breath. "Hamoud... Hamoud does not work for me."

"Who does he work for?"

"He used to work for me. He made bad choices." Only his eyeballs moved a fraction of an inch toward his right shoulder. He squared up and cleared his throat.

I'd served a decade in the military. The battle of Baghdad, a couple tours in Iraq, several more in Afghanistan. Of all the wretched jihadis and despicable Taliban I'd brought in, not one of them would have killed his own. Looking into Nakdali's weary eyes, I believed the guy.

Around us, the ship's crew set out linen tablecloths and shiny silver for an elegant luncheon. Nakdali and I watched them for a second.

"Tough deal, buddy," I said quietly. "Hamoud's gone rogue. So, what does that mean?"

He pulled himself together and straightened up in his chair, doing his best to look arrogant and unafraid. But his situation was obvious. TGW had labeled him expendable. A slight tremble in the looser parts of his skin gave him away. His posture slowly deteriorated until he'd slumped into the shape of someone who'd just been beaten with a hose.

He'd always known this day would come. I almost felt sorry for him.

With a shrug, Nakdali shut down. He stared at me, stone-faced through my follow-up questions. I continued asking questions until it was clearly useless, he was saving his important information for plea bargaining with the FBI.

Miguel led him back to his makeshift cell.

My fellow agents wound their way up to the luncheon deck and joined me. When Ms. Sabel strode onto the deck, I stared like a schoolboy with a crush on his teacher. She held her phone in front of her, talking to someone on her earbud.

"That's great, Mark," she said. "Tell your dad I really appreciate it. Any help I—" She stopped and looked over the railing while listening. "Yes, that's great. I'll be in town soon and I'll meet with them first—" She listened again.

Her boyfriend had interrupted her twice in a row. Jerk. She deserved better. I would never do that.

"I can't tell you that, Mark. People are trying to kill—" She paused. "If I tell you where and when I'm coming in, they might torture you to find out. We already know they like to torture—" She listened. "Yes, and I appreciate all the trouble they've gone through. I swear, I'll call you as soon—" She lost her patience. "Stop it. I will *not* tell you when or where. I have to go."

When she clicked off, she slipped into the seat next to me. "Mark's dad made arrangements so I can turn myself into the authorities. Isn't that nice?"

Sounded like a terrible idea to me, but not my call. I shrugged.

She said, "His father is a congressman."

My father grew corn and soybeans. No matter how much I admired her, she would never notice me among the unwashed peasants.

She leaned conspiratorially close and said, "His father wants to bring me in for the publicity. It never entered Mark's pea-sized brain that I'm innocent. He is *so* fucking dumped."

Chamberlain's crew served up a delicious lunch on fine china with sparkling crystal goblets. I tried to remember which fork to use first.

Ms. Sabel said, "Captain Chamberlain won't let me keep his tender. He wants someone to take me ashore and bring it—"

The words jumped out of my mouth. "I'll take you."

"Do you think Chamberlain's a good man?"

"He risked his life and his crew to get us ashore. He risked his career when he picked us up."

"He's not doing this just to earn the *Asteria*?"

"If he is, I'd say he's earned—"

Captain Chamberlain coughed, standing directly behind me. "Pardon the interruption, ma'am. The ship that was following us has turned around."

He nodded at me and left.

"That's good news," she said.

"Yes and no," I said. "Their ship wasn't fast enough. The bad news is, they're switching to defense."

She winced.

After lunch, Ms. Sabel called Otis Blackwell. She covered the same territory I'd covered with Emily. "You will get more instructions later. Keep your bags packed and your car full of gas. In the meantime, you can quote me on this: I am on the trail of pedophiles who have kidnapped sixteen children. As soon as I've freed them, I will return to DC."

She paused to listen to him. "Otis, the people who should be worried about my return are the people behind Operation Snare Drum."

CHAPTER 36

CHAMBERLAIN GAVE ME THE BASICS of navigating a tender. He went over the onboard systems and how to radio for help. Fortunately, the boat had a homing beacon built in, along with sonar to keep me off the rocks.

In much better spirits, he stopped mid-sentence and looked at me. "Thank you for standing for me earlier. She's asked me to submit my C.V. to her father. Is that a good sign?"

"You saved her life, rode out a hurricane, risked your career—works for me."

He grinned.

"But you should know her favorite quote," I said. "Never celebrate until the last whistle."

He nodded. "Good advice, that."

Ms. Sabel and Tania turned over their phones, credit cards, and passports to Miguel. They would travel off the grid. After saying their goodbyes, we boarded the tender.

Having traveled hours in the opposite direction from Hurricane Dolly, the seas were calm, the sun was strong, and our destination was little more than a dark line on the horizon. I followed Chamberlain's instructions, heading due south. Ms. Sabel sat up front in the open bow, staring out to sea.

Once we were underway, Ms. Sabel turned to me and raised her voice over the wind noise. "Do you still have those contacts at the DIA?"

"Yes. I owe Bridgette a dinner at L'Enfant Café in Adams Morgan."

"You can take her to the French Laundry on my jet if she comes through for me."

"French laundry?"

"It's a little bistro in Napa Valley."

A map of the US ran through my head until I found California and its wine country. All I could imagine were places and things I could never afford on my own. If there was a restaurant there, an appetizer would break my credit limit. But with Ms. Sabel paying the bills—yow. Bridgette would love that. I felt a huge grin spreading across my face and fought to get it under control.

I said, "I could get you the President's nuclear codes for that."

"Thanks just the same. What I'd like to know is, how did Sam Caldwell know undisclosed details about my parents' murders?"

With that, she turned back to the sea and stretched out on the bench. She seemed so melancholy, so depressed, that it hurt me. I liked talking to her. I wanted to keep the conversation alive. I said, "I still don't get why Patterson killed Caldwell."

"I figured it out," she said, her voice sad and distant. "I'm sure you will too."

Before I could ask her to elaborate, Tania stepped under the canopy and leaned against the helm, her back to Ms. Sabel. "You did OK, Jacob. You brought her back alive."

"Thanks," I said. "Hey, what's all this stuff about her parents?"

"She's had me research it for the last couple months," Tania said. "The original investigators did what cops always do when they get stumped, they claimed it was a drug deal, a home invasion at the wrong house or something. But last night a former CIA agent knew all about it and teased her with more information."

"What are the chances he'd done his homework and twisted some facts to make it sound like he had new intel?"

"Her parents were grad students living in a super nice townhouse in Georgetown."

I shrugged.

She sighed. "Drug dealers might do a home invasion in Anacostia. They don't do home invasions in Georgetown."

"You think the CIA guy might have been telling the truth? What does that mean? The CIA killed her parents and now they're going to kill her? Why wait twenty years?"

"That's what she wants you to find out from your DIA babe."

I looked over at Ms. Sabel, then back. "Don't worry, I'll find something. What about your mission?"

"She won't rest til she saves the children," Tania said.

"You'll be on their turf," I said. "And outnumbered."

"No problem," Tania said. "I was born to kill child molesters."

"What happened to your speech about darts?"

"Fuck darts. Did you see those kids? These guys get the instant death penalty."

"You need me with you."

"Forget it," she said. "You want to go 'cause you're hoping to save her life, and she'll hop in bed. All you ever think about is getting laid."

That wasn't my only reason, but I left it alone.

I glanced across the sea and thought about telling her how I felt about her. Then I thought of the fifty bad ways she might react. What the hell.

I said, "She's not the only one I worry about."

Tania gave me a sad smile and turned away.

Each of us stayed quiet the rest of the way, lost in our thoughts about the future.

We cruised until I saw land on my left. It was a good-sized island, not big enough for a city or a police force, but inhabited. Ten minutes later, I rounded a spit of land and crossed a pristine bay. Acres of white sand lined the pale blue water. Rows of expensive vacation homes sprawled along the beach. Several sailboats were anchored haphazardly offshore.

We made our way to where a twin-engine seaplane and a couple powerboats were tied to the private dock of a mansion.

I tied up next to the seaplane. A crusty old guy trotted out to meet us, his unbuttoned shirt flapping open to reveal a sea serpent tattoo that writhed from belt to neck. A trim white beard covered his weathered face, shaded by a Jenkins Pharmaceuticals cap. Ms. Sabel gave him a long hug that took ten years off his face.

Tania introduced herself to the man as Ms. Sabel turned and waved me off.

I couldn't leave. I stood there like an idiot, staring at her as the engine burbled and the bumpers squeaked against the wooden dock.

Her desperation to save the children clouded her judgment, and clouded judgment could get you killed.

I caught her eye and said, "If you don't mind, ma'am, I'd recommend going after TGW first."

"Thank you, Jacob," she said, stepping down the dock, closer to me. "In a military operation, that would make sense. Cut off the head and the war ends. But this is a criminal enterprise. What do criminals do when they feel trapped and the noose tightening?"

CHAPTER 37

DONALD F. PATTERSON STEEPLED HIS fingers and said, "Good lord, thank you for saving me from the storm on Isla de la Mona. And thank you for the Coast Guard who so gallantly brought me home to my wonderful family. Amen." Then he closed his eyes and prayed silently for the death of Pia Sabel.

Mrs. Patterson and his two middle-school daughters echoed *amen* and put their napkins in their laps.

"Is she really big like they say?" his younger daughter said.

"It's not nice to refer to a woman as 'big'," Mrs. Patterson said. "I believe Ms. Sabel is best described as athletic."

"She's taller than you'd think," he said. "And her shoulders are as big as mine."

Mrs. Patterson stifled a laugh. He picked up his fork and took a bite of fish.

A knock rattled the screen door in the kitchen. Puzzled, Patterson got up and motioned for his family to stay at the table. The visitor banged again with more intensity.

Patterson went through the narrow hallway and retrieved his sidearm from the coat closet. Leaning to one side, he opened the kitchen door an inch. Light from three windows cast yellow polygons on the broken cement driveway. A fat man in a suit and tie stood in the dark space between them, tapping his toe and looking around. Patterson left his pistol on the worn counter and stepped outside, pulling the door closed behind him.

"McCarty, what are you doing here?" he said.

"Why didn't you report as soon as you got back?" Under Secretary William McCarty said.

"I don't report to you."

"You were on a mission for me." McCarty's flabby jowls shook as he spoke. "And you failed. Not once but twice."

"I'll meet you in the office first thing tomorrow," Patterson said. "I'm in the middle of dinner with my family."

"No." McCarty looked away. "The Secretary ordered me to stay out—for now."

Patterson stepped down to McCarty's level, keeping the light at his back, his face in shadow. "Why?"

"That's what I want to know. What the hell happened back there?"

"Your moron, Caldwell, was going to kill Sabel after he tortured her."

"That was the plan. Where is he, anyway? I can't reach him."

Patterson paused, searching McCarty's eyes. "Killed in action."

"Those bastards," McCarty shouted. His gaze darted to the dark corners around them when his voice reverberated in the neighborhood. "TGW better find that bitch and solve the problem." McCarty stuck a finger in Patterson's chest. "Since you're incapable."

Four years of suffering McCarty's insults and ineptitude was enough. To allow the man one more day running Snare Drum would sink them all. The worst part was, McCarty and Caldwell were right. The only way to stop Sabel was to kill her.

"You can't be serious," Patterson said. "You can get away with killing a celebrity?"

"We've terminated plenty of traitors." McCarty looked around nervously.

"Why did the Secretary tell you to stay out of the office?"

McCarty shrugged.

The only person more dangerous than Sabel was McCarty. It was time to put the fat slob in his place. Patterson said, "Two months ago, Alan Sabel gave millions to the administration. Now Sabel's little princess has gone and attacked a US military installation. The Secretary doesn't know what's going on, but he knows you're involved. If she ends up dead—"

"Never connected to me," McCarty said. "What does that have to do with Snare Drum?"

"You and your boy Caldwell have something going on down there," Patterson said. "Something the administration doesn't want leaked to the press. Your idiot Syrians let her give an autograph to the guard at Andrews. If Caldwell *had* killed her, the evidence trail would have led straight to the Hunter Administration."

McCarty's face turned sour.

"Things are different from when we served at the Company," Patterson said. "Now, you're a political appointee like me. That sounds like a big deal until you realize it means we're nothing but ballast the president can cut loose anytime her balloon starts dropping."

"Bullshit. None of that matters. TGW set it up with total deniability. They can't trace anything back to me much less the administration."

Patterson took a moment before answering. "No? Who signed everything? At the CIA, signed requisitions never saw the light of day. At State, everything's an open book."

McCarty slumped and his gaze roamed the driveway. He stood still for a few awkward moments, then stiffened his backbone, took a deep breath, and glanced over his shoulder at Patterson.

"You used to be a good man," McCarty said. "Back at the Company, you made things happen. You followed orders. Now, you're insubordinate. You—"

"Don't report to you," Patterson said.

McCarty crossed his arms over his rumpled shirt. "You do for this job. What did you get out of her?"

"Nothing. Caldwell just tortured her until she passed out. All he asked her was some dumb questions about the death of her parents."

"What'd she say?"

"Nothing. He told her he knew who killed them, then she passed out." He watched McCarty turn pale. "Before the storm hit, Nakdali sent the children back to Sibiu. Most of his men were caught on the Dominican Republic when the hurricane hit. Sabel's people came ashore in spite of the storm. They freed Sabel and captured Nakdali. Now Sabel has him, a laptop, and four kids."

"A laptop? Shit. Where is she now?"

"Sabel's man, Jacob Stearne, has everything," Patterson said. "We think he's coming to DC. We presume Sabel will be going to the Azores, so we sent half Nakdali's men there to take her down."

"We?"

"I've been working with TGW," Patterson said.

The look on McCarty's face was worth all the trouble of the last few days. It was finally dawning on the fat, old jerk that the student was now the master.

"All the paperwork, the requisitions, the special clearances and passports—you and TGW set me up for this. From the beginning." McCarty backed up a few steps then trotted to his car. Before getting in, he jabbed a finger over the hood. "You think you can fuck with me?"

Patterson stepped out to the curb to watch McCarty's taillights disappear around the corner. Then he pulled his phone and looked up an old contact. A voice answered. Patterson said, "McCarty just told me not to fuck with him."

"So you finally came around, eh?" the old CIA colleague said. "You ready to tell me where he keeps all the recordings?"

"I'll text you the address. How soon can you be there?"

CHAPTER 38

WATCHING EMILY WALK INTO THE Café Carver reminded me of why I used to date her. She could swish better than any other travel writer at the *Post*.

She clicked off her call and dropped her phone in her purse. She said, "Jacob, my editors want you to sign a release."

"Release what?" I said.

"We posted all the information about the kids you rescued, posted Channel 4's video of you being arrested for it, had an article on how Sabel Security sent the kids home to India, and how Senator Smith provided counselors—all that stuff. But they have concerns about liability before they post that part about the pedophile compound run being by the government." She sighed as we walked. "They're writing up a release. They'll send it over in a few minutes."

"Have 'em send it to the Major. She'll run it by Legal then I'll sign it."

"Really?" she said. "You don't mind? I mean, that stuff is all classified. We can post it, but you could go to jail for releasing government secrets."

"They tried to send me to jail for attacking a US military installation and look how that turned out."

She stopped and made me look at her. She was worried. Not me. I mean, can they really do something illegal, classify it Top Secret, then lock up anyone who blows the whistle?

No way.

We stepped into the Café Carver, the place where Ms. Sabel met Patterson before some guys in trench coats tried to kill her and the whole mess began. I held the door while Emily swished across the sticky linoleum. Several people sat at tables inside.

The waiter recognized me at first glance and backed up a step. Last time I saw him, I'd found his pad, written in Arabic, in the enemy's den, aiding the bad guys. He switched sides, he said. Now, the spineless rat's shifting eyes told me all I needed to know. He elbowed his cook, and they watched us cross the small room.

Emily looked around and squeezed my arm. "Jacob, I'm not sure about this place. Those three in the corner look like they want to kill you."

"They do. I owe them money." We stopped a yard short of the table and I nodded to the leader. "Ishmael! What up, dog?"

"The Major has to pay." Ishmael's last vowel stretched out long and threatening.

I pulled out three crisp hundred-dollar bills and slapped them on the table. I offered a wire chair to Emily, who stared at me like I'd asked her to hold a scorpion. Grabbing a second chair from another table, I plunked down in front of Ishmael. After an eye-roll, Emily followed my lead.

"You need to turn him over," I said. "That was the deal."

Ishmael nodded at one of his associates. The associate rose and left. His third companion sat like a statue of Lincoln, motionless with his hands on his knees.

The scrawny waiter came up behind me and stopped a few feet back. "Weren't you arrested this morning?"

I turned slowly and looked him over once, then turned my back on him. In Arabic, I said, "How is it the only white guy in Carver Langston speaks Arabic?"

In English he said, "They told me you were going to jail."

"Did they also tell you a blond guy should never grow a goatee?" I rose and stepped into his personal space. "'Cause it looks like your face is dirty."

He backed up. "Omar, call the cops."

"Don't bother," I said. "The FBI did a preliminary investigation and discovered, hey, there is no military base on Isla de la Mona. There was one in WWII but it's been unoccupied ever since. No CIA, no secret facility, just an old leased area with an option to rebuild someday." I stuck a finger in his chest. "That means, whoever told you I was going to jail was the same dude who tried to kill Ms. Sabel."

The waiter stared at me with his pie hole wide open.

I said, "C'mon, sit down and tell us how you ended up on the Syrian payroll."

Beads of sweat broke out on his forehead when I pushed him into a chair. His nervous eyes bounced from me to Ishmael and back. With a sigh, he gave up and spilled his story. His journalism professor had convinced him that going to Syria would be like Hemingway in Spain. Reality was different. Instead of turning into a great writer, he'd lived the life of a scared rabbit, running from one hiding place to the next, in constant fear for his life. Colonel Nakdali plucked him out of an al Qaeda zone, gave him a swift kick in the ass, and sent him home to his mom in Bethesda.

I said, "And all Nakdali wanted in return was … what?"

"It's not Nakdali. I swear."

"That leaves Hamoud. So where can I find him?"

Ishmael leaned in, one ear cocked for the answer.

"Hamoud shot that guy." The waiter nodded out the window.

A leader who kills one of his own has minions who live in fear of him. Until they puff up some guts and do something.

In a low, gangster voice, Ishmael said, "Answer the question."

The waiter said, "Douglas is the problem."

He looked up at me, then looked away. I waited for him to speak again, but he stared out the window. As the silence stretched out, the pieces fell into place for me.

I said, "Raya."

Ishmael squinted at me. "Douglas's daughter? What's she got to do with it?"

"A kid with an Arabic name," I said. "Is Douglas a Shia Muslim?"

"Before you say something racially insensitive," Ishamael's quiet companion said, "I'm Muslim and so are a lot of black folk."

"Nothing for or against religion or African heritage; I'm interested in connecting the dots. If you're Nakdali, and you're stashing a bunch Syrians in the US, you don't just drop them off in any old neighborhood.

You drop them off where you have a local partner to keep an eye on them."

"And Douglas goes to Idara-e-Jaferia." Ishmael slammed a fist on the table. "The local Shia mosque. Lots of Syrians go there. I should've listened to Raissa—it's hard to hear her through all that Jesus crap—she never liked Douglas."

"You said Nakdali was a good man," I said to the waiter. "What happened?"

"You're right, Douglas was running things here," he said. "Nakdali brought in his guys as fast as he could get them out of Syria. Said he had this big contract, but he was gone all the time, setting things up. Without the boss around, Hamoud and Douglas started some deal on the side. At first they were cleaning up the neighborhood, doing good things."

"But the power went to their heads," I said. "Raissa and Louisa are missing. Did Douglas kill them?"

The waiter shook his head.

"And you're sure because you've seen them alive," I said. "Let me guess, you're delivering food."

He nodded. "Four women, a guy, and three children."

"Why did Douglas and Hamoud want all those people under wraps?"

"He wanted to keep Raissa and Louisa quiet about kidnapping your boss. The others, I don't know. They're married to pilots."

Caldwell killed the pilots because threatening their families had failed to keep them quiet.

Ishmael's man showed up with Dakka and put him in the chair next to me.

Dakka was done with Nakdali and Hamoud and all their promises of the good life. Without hesitation, he told me everything I wanted to know about Hamoud's hideout and defenses. According to Dakka, half of Hamoud's rank and file evaporated after the drive-by shooting. For some strange reason, they didn't like living in fear of their self-proclaimed CO. But it still left him with plenty of men. Dakka even coughed up Hamoud's phone number.

I called Special Agent Verges, the FBI agent on the case. He was the guy who reluctantly verified our story and got us out of jail. And he was the same agent who told every other agent in the Hoover Building that their former colleague, Tony, had lost his life on my watch. He was not happy to take my call. When I convinced him that he needed to do something, he gave me a tepid answer and clicked off.

I drummed my fingers on the table.

"No FBI?" Ishmael said. "Welcome to Carver Langston."

"I had only one get-out-of-jail card," I said. "He'll work on it—when he has time."

No one spoke. Dakka stared at me. Emily stared at me. The waiter stared at me. Ishmael and his boys stared at me.

"What?" I said, looking at each of them. "I'm the only guy who can free hostages in this town?"

Why do people think I'm dying to risk my life to save people I don't know from people I don't know for reasons that have nothing to do with me?

They kept staring.

"Shit." I stood up. "Emily, wait here with these guys."

"Whoa, brother," Ishmael said as he and his friends scrambled to their feet. "We're going with you. There used to be four of us. Rashad—"

"I don't have the manpower to protect you—"

"We don't need no protection."

I got in Ishmael's grill. "Drive-bys are one thing, capping a guy with a cheap .22 is another, but you've never gone up against a soldier. Hamoud and his boys kicked your ass up and down I Street." Ishmael leaned away from me. "Killing people is my business. I'm good at it. So is Hamoud. Don't kid yourself about getting revenge for Rashad, bro. If you follow me, you'll be the first to die."

I turned and left.

Outside, I snapped my fingers. Miguel and Carmen fell in with me. Miguel handed me an M4 with two magazines of darts and one of real bullets.

"Where we going?" Carmen said.

"Gonna check out Hamoud's crib. Word is we're only outnumbered five to one."

CHAPTER 39

PIA SABEL LEANED ACROSS JIMMY Jenkins, her white-haired pilot, and looked at the town of Praia da Vitória, five thousand feet below. A handsome, fifteenth-century town hugged the beach along the Azorean island of Terceira. The forecast called for a low of 69 and a high of 74 with plenty of sunshine and a gentle breeze. Red tile roofs topped whitewashed buildings. The streets were clean and had little traffic. A smattering of sailboats rocked in the sleepy marina. She decided it would be a nice place to die.

Tania leaned between them. "That's Lajes Field over there? Looks deserted."

"It was a Cold War asset," Jimmy said. He nodded at the airbase three miles up the coast. "Used to be a refueling station for bombers flying over the Soviet Union. Now they're just keeping the lights on by refueling short-range planes on long-range missions, like your C-130." He paused and held a hand to his headphones. "Hang on, he's giving me clearance."

A few minutes later, Jimmy splashed the Grumman Albatross flying boat into the water and docked as the setting sun turned the town's ubiquitous white stucco into warm gold. The shallow marina smelled of warm saltwater and old fish.

The marina's official met them at the dock and Jimmy handed over their passports. The harbormaster frowned, looking first at Tania then at Pia. After several awkward seconds, Jimmy shrugged and said, "*Adotado.*"

The harbormaster and Jimmy spoke in Portuguese for a while until Jimmy held up his hands in surrender. The harbormaster pocketed the passports and scolded Jimmy about something. After Jimmy agreed to terms, the harbormaster trotted off toward an official-looking building and disappeared inside.

Jimmy shrugged. "He thought our passports were suspicious. He's going to check them out and get back to us later."

"Could there be a problem?"

"He thought your picture looked scuffed up some, that's all."

Tania said, "Where'd you get our passports, anyway?"

"Don't ask."

Tania shot a questioning glance at Pia. She shrugged.

Jimmy said, "So you're hunting a molester named Safwan who refueled at Lajes a few days ago. What's the plan to find him?"

"Find the guys who refueled the plane."

They walked up the hill to the town and inquired at several shops about the bars where the US servicemen hung out. In the small town, it was a quick walk. They hit the first three bars in minutes and asked questions of the Americans. Within the hour, they'd narrowed things down and found the man they were looking for. Along the way, they acquired a follower. A shabby man with a swarthy complexion and unkempt hair left the first bar and beat them to the next.

The airman they were looking for was named Denton, and he was shooting pool with friends as heavy metal blared from speakers strapped to the wall. The airmen welcomed the tall woman in spandex and her exotic sidekick, breaking their circle only enough to let Jimmy slip them pitchers of beer.

Pia noticed Jimmy sneaking watchful glances at a drunk in the corner. "Something wrong?"

"Don't like MPs, or SPs, whatever the Air Force calls them," Jimmy said.

"Why not?" Tania asked.

"I take it you were an MP once?" Jimmy asked.

"Two years, but I got tired of wrestling clowns like you. What'd you do?"

"Don't ask." Jimmy gave her a smile.

Pia looked at the swarthy man, standing at the middle of the bar. He turned away and ducked outside.

Pia faced Denton. "I'm tracking down a child molester. A tall Arab guy, Syrian probably, flew in on a C-130 with a bunch of kids and changed planes. Someone said your crew might have worked on it."

"Yeah, I saw them," he said. "Strange bunch. Nothing right about them guys at all."

"Did you report them to anyone?" she asked.

"My CO. He made some calls, asked some questions, but the brass done shut him down."

"That's it?" Pia's voice hit a high note. "You see some grown men with kids and you and your CO wash your hands of it?"

"Done what I's supposed to, ma'am. Those was contractor planes, black ops. Can't do much there."

Tania touched Pia's arm and shook her head. Pia tamped down her outrage. "Any idea where the plane came from?"

"Yes and no. They said they was in from Rome, but the paperwork said Sibiu, Romania."

"What's in Romania?" Pia asked.

"Beats me. The paperwork come from a commercial airport."

"So the tall guy and the empty plane went back to Romania?" she said.

"No idea where the plane went. The Arab wouldn't leave. Fuckin' crazy bastard. He was carrying on about American war crimes and then he wants asylum. At least that's what we thought. None of my crew speaks much Arabic and he didn't speak no English. Didn't have a passport or nothing. I turned him over to the local guys. Don't know much else."

"What local guys?"

"I dropped him off on the marina dock. Hell, I didn't know what to do with him. He was babbling on in Arabic—I gotta work."

"And the kids?" Pia said.

"Sad-looking bunch. Air-sick patches on 'em. Those things makes 'em all drowsy. Had to carry them the first time."

Pia tensed up with anger, then took a moment to relax. It wasn't Denton's fault. "First time?"

"Yeah, we transferred them from one plane to the next, been a couple days now. But yesterday, no second plane. Nobody got out to stretch or nothing."

"Where were they going?"

"Sibiu, Romania," Denton said and chugged some beer.

"How do you know where—"

"Because they come back a couple hours ago. Same origination as last time. Hell, the plane's still on the apron. No kids this time. Just a bunch of those nasty-looking guys."

Pia's stomach flipped over, and her skin went cold and clammy. "Syrians?"

"Could be. Can't tell them hajjis apart." Denton slid off his barstool and headed to the men's room.

"Damn," Tania said. "We better get moving."

Jimmy bought another round for Denton and his pals while Pia and Tania went outside to wait for him.

Fish soup carrying hints of mint and dill scented the salt air. Thirty yards away, at the end of the block, sat a darkened cop car. On the cross street, a small car with a bad muffler started up and chugged away. The swarthy man who'd left the bar earlier, smoked and talked on a phone a few yards up the street.

Pia clenched and unclenched her fists. "I can't believe his CO would report abused children and no one would investigate."

"Whoever's running Snare Drum, the TGW-guy, classified it Top Secret," Tania said. "There's nothing they can do."

"Drugged kids transcend Top Secret. When you see something like that, you report it up the chain until someone does something."

"Get real, Pia. Everyone knows torture is ineffective and illegal, but generals watched the CIA do it in Guantanamo. And here we are, ten years later and they tortured you."

A man stepped out of the bar and stopped as if he were tethered in back. He staggered left, then right, then pointed in Pia's general direction. "You're that woman. Gotta be."

Pia and Tania glanced his way and recognized him as the man Jimmy thought was a military cop. They shrugged at each other.

At the end of the street, three figures left a different bar and headed for the cop car.

"Nah, really," the man shouted. He exhaled loudly. "You're the terrorist. She's the terrorist from Cuba. Nah. Puerto Rico terrorist. Rican. Puerto Rican terrorist."

The cops hesitated outside their car.

"Attacked a military base." The drunk's tether appeared to pull him backward. He fought it and made two steps forward as if fighting gale force winds. "Nah, nah, I got the bullet … bulletin in my roffice. Office."

The cops at the end of the street got in their car. The doors slammed. The engine kicked over and the headlights blasted light. Pia and Tania stared into the beam for a split second before turning away.

The drunk fell back against the bar door. "Yeah, yeah, I saw your picture on a bulletin from DHS. Fucking terrorist." He pulled away from the door, but couldn't cross the street.

Blue strobe lights strafed the lane. The cop car rolled nearer to them, the siren blipped once for attention, and a voice said something in Portuguese over the loudspeaker. The car doors opened on both sides. The cop on the passenger side walked toward them slowly. Dressed in all black, he was difficult to distinguish until he stepped into the headlight beams. The driver stayed in the open car door and spoke into a radio mic. A third man stepped out and into the light: the harbormaster with passports in his hand.

The bar's front door opened, spilling light and music as a small group of gawkers joined the drunk on the sidewalk. Pia caught a glimpse of Jimmy slipping between the curious patrons. He gave her a nod and vanished into the darkness behind the cop car.

The drunk's tether lengthened enough for him to stagger forward. He planted his feet and bent his knees as his torso swayed. "She's a fuckin' terriblist. Treblist." His voice rose in volume. "Terrorist."

The harbormaster spoke to the first cop in Portuguese with lowered voices. After some discussion, the harbormaster shrugged and held his hands out, palms up.

The cop turned to Pia and thumbed at the harbormaster. "He says there is a problem with your passport." He sniffed and shot a scowl at the drunken man. "Our harbormaster thinks your passport belongs to someone else. We will take you to the harbor cell and he can straighten you out in morning. *Uma noite*, ehm, one night only."

He grinned and shrugged at the same time.

The harbormaster said, "I, Paulo, keep the watch tonight." He nodded enthusiastically and motioned for them to follow. He stepped quickly ahead and walked away. "Follow me, yes?"

Pia shrugged and followed Paulo. Tania and both cops joined the procession. The drunk followed several yards back.

A few yards down the way, the harbormaster slowed and Pia came along side. "Why does this man call you the terrorist?"

"I was kidnapped by some Syrians and my friends attacked them. I guess there was a little misinformation about who attacked whom. Do you find him reliable?"

Paulo gave her a quick smile. "No. But then, are you reliable? Someone with your name, who once lived on Anguilla, died last year. Is that your passport—or hers?"

The group marched two blocks, around a corner, and into the harbormaster's office. A long, low building, they wound their way through desks to the modest police station at the back. Paulo flipped on lights as they entered and opened a heavy steel door in a solid block wall. He motioned them inside.

Behind the steel door were four flimsy jail cells. The cells opened to a central area where a steel picnic table was bolted to the floor. It was a holding area meant for occasional stowaways or drunken yachtsmen, not hardened criminals.

Against the back wall, a TV blared Al Jazeera news. In front of the set sat a tall, bewildered Arab who stared over his shoulder with an open mouth.

"Safwan?" Pia said.

The tall Arab leapt to his feet, tears filled his eyes, and he blathered in Arabic. He dropped to his knees and pulled the back of Pia's hand to his cheek.

The group stepped inside the jail, staring at the bizarre sight.

Paulo looked at Pia, then at the cop, then at the drunk who had followed them in, then at Safwan. He turned back to Pia. "You know this—"

A flash of blinding light burst into the room, followed by smoke and glass as an explosion ripped through the outer offices. The lights went out.

Paulo slammed the steel door behind them, locking them inside the cellblock.

His voice quaking with fear, Paulo said, "You *are* the terrorist!"

CHAPTER 40

PATTERSON TOOK HIS COFFEE OUTSIDE into Washington's late-summer heat near Dupont Circle. He chose the most secluded sidewalk table available. Snare Drum was sinking fast. Someone would have to go down with the operation. In the original plan, when failure seemed so remote, it was supposed to be TGW who fell on his sword. That would never happen. It came down to Patterson or McCarty.

Patterson pulled a USB hard drive out of his pocket. It was a copy of McCarty's original containing calls, videos, Instagrams, chat sessions, and emails between government officials and lobbyists. His friends from the CIA had verified the data, destroyed the drives and backups, and left the mess for McCarty to discover. This was Patterson's *insurance* drive. To survive, he would need the help of powerful people. And those people would need encouragement. He pulled his phone and made the first call.

"Damn it, Patterson," the Chief whisper-shouted into the phone, "I told you not to call me."

"Four children are on their way home to India," Don Patterson said.

"Well then, stop them. I can't talk right now."

"You saw the news. Alan Sabel choreographed the whole thing, we can't touch them."

"WHAT? Goddammit, give me a minute."

Background voices became muffled and echoed in marble hallways. Then a door slammed and the Chief asked someone to give him some privacy. There was a moment of silence. Then the Chief came back on the line. "No, I didn't see the news. What happened?"

"Sabel's jet landed out in Salisbury. They had *Channel 4* and the *Post* there, Senator Smith—"

"Jefferson Smith?" the Chief said. "He's one of Sabel's pets and running for president. What was that self-righteous bastard doing there?"

"Grabbing headlines, sir," Patterson said. "That's not the problem—"

"I thought TGW had it set to arrest them all, bring them in for attacking a top-secret facility."

"That's the problem." Patterson took a deep breath. "TGW had things set to intercept the Sabel Security jet at Dulles, where they usually land, but Alan Sabel met them out on the Eastern Shore with the FBI—"

"Damn it, the FBI Director's another one of Sabel's pets. Hell, the FBI's full of people who think they're holier than the goddamn Pope. They hear we're luring al Qaeda's pedophiles with children we snatched out of Mumbai, they'll tear us apart and make Pia Sabel look like an American hero in the process. We can't let the FBI investigate this. Tell TGW not to let them get anything on Snare Drum. Not a single thing."

"Sir, it's too late for that. They didn't buy the terrorist story. They already released the Sabel agents and they have Nakdali, a laptop, and three hard drives."

Patterson heard a distinct gasp from the Chief, followed by a long silence.

"Shit," the Chief said. "We have to do something. We have to cover our tracks right now. What does TGW have?"

"Nothing. We kicked around some ideas but the FBI has the evidence. We're screwed. The only thing we could think of was to hand them McCarty."

"OK. OK. That's good thinking. But think of something else."

"McCarty was our sacrificial lamb all along, sir," Patterson said. "It's time to sacrifice him." Patterson heard the Chief sigh twice in a long silence. "Sir?"

"Damn it, Patterson, why do you think McCarty was promoted after he was caught—red handed—in the middle of the CIA scandal? Think, man, think."

"You mean, the rumors are true? He has blackmail?" Patterson said and rolled his USB drive around in his fingers.

"You're smart, figure it out."

"What was McCarty planning to do?" Patterson asked. "Hand over emails to the *Post*?"

BRING IT

"Nothing you should worry about."

"Maybe I can help. I know some of his old cronies back at the CIA."

"Don't mess with him, Patterson. He has dirt on both parties and regularly threatens to release one side and not the other. That would turn this country into a single-party state."

"That's outrageous, sir. He should be stopped." Patterson let a moment of silence punctuate his indignation. "You know, back at the CIA, I was his property manager. I knew his hiding places. Off the top of my head, I would look at a chimney in Silver Spring, an old mattress in Alexandria, or an attic in Adams Morgan."

After a long silence, the Chief drew a long, slow breath.

Patterson decided to push. "I can deliver, sir."

"OK," the Chief said slowly and cautiously, as if he were talking to a snake. "Let's say you can pull off the stunt. What happens next?"

"Sabel didn't come home on her jet. That means she's headed for the Azores. TGW will send the Syrians there."

"So then, you're a problem solver. What do you want out of it?"

"It's not what I want that matters, sir. It's what I don't want." Patterson paused. "I don't want my business cards to have so much ink spent on them. I don't want *assistant* or *under* anywhere near *secretary*."

The Chief burst out laughing. "Yeah, no problem."

"I'm serious."

"Senate confirmation hearings are serious too, Patterson. You bring me McCarty's drives and we'll talk. Nothing is off the table if you deliver. But Sabel, what's your plan for her?"

Patterson hesitated.

"It's a secure line," the Chief said. "That's why we gave you an EOP phone."

Patterson said, "In your wildest dreams, what would be the best scenario for her?"

"She dies battling for her cause. The nation grieves for the heiress who gave her life to save children. We hold a vigil for her in the National Cathedral. President Hunter delivers the eulogy. And McCarty is exposed as the mastermind of her death."

"TGW and I will make that dream come true," Patterson said.

241

"What do you need to make it happen?"

"TGW may need some cabinet-level support. Who can we turn to? Is the Secretary of State aware of the situation?"

"If you raised his IQ fifty points you could teach him to fetch. The other Secretaries are loyal enough, but they're suspicious *and* cautious." The Chief thought in silence a moment. "You and TGW work it out, Patterson. *Aut viam inveniam aut faciam.*"

Find a way or make one.

Patterson clicked off, then played back the recorded call on his phone. It was crisp; the Chief's distinctive voice wouldn't have been any clearer if they'd been in a studio. Patterson let a smile turn up his mouth and he silently thanked McCarty for his mentoring. If I go down, you go down, Chief. So you better work your ass off to save mine.

Tapping his finger on the table, he looked around the sidewalk. Three patrons stepped into the midday heat and pulled out chairs at the table next to his. He glared at them until they decided to take a table farther away. Then he dialed.

"Bill McCarty," the voice answered.

"We need to meet," Patterson said.

"Patterson? Wait a minute. You're calling on a different line. This number is a—Hey. What the hell are you doing with an EOP phone?"

Patterson, who had a firm grasp on hundreds of acronyms, hadn't had the guts to ask the Chief what EOP stood for. "The what?"

"Executive Office of the President. Don't play dumb with me."

"Oh. Battery died, borrowed a phone. We need to meet."

"Bullshit," McCarty said. "I'm not going to stand on some street corner so your sniper can take me out. You want to talk, this's close enough."

"You need to get out to Base Two and clear it out. Dispose of everything and everyone. Your name is the only one Nakdali's people know. You need to get moving."

"I go there and you bomb the place. A nice neat package of dead bodies: the kids, the Syrians, me. You're probably going to lure Sabel there too, right? Everything wrapped up in a nice, neat package. Sounds great—for you."

"You have to go there. TGW's orders."

"Oh come on, Patterson. You think I don't know about TGW?"

Patterson clenched the phone and glanced around at the sidewalk tables. He said nothing.

"I'm no fool," McCarty said. "If TGW wants me somewhere, I'm taking your daughters with me."

Patterson clicked off. He tapped the phone on the table and looked around. More patrons filed out of the coffee shop and took the table next to him. He rose, walked down the sidewalk, and hailed a cab. He said, "Café Carver in Carver Langston."

CHAPTER 41

CARMEN, MIGUEL, AND I SQUATTED behind an A/C unit on the roof of the building next door and watched Hamoud's small warehouse for over an hour. Five sentries roamed inside, one of them occasionally visible through a broken window. Once in a while, one of them would poke his head out the office door and have a look. There could be extras bivouacked inside for all we knew. The dim hope that Agent Verges would bring a SWAT team withered in the heat.

"Jacob," Carmen said, "are you going to do something or what?"

That was another part of leadership I didn't like, people expected me to have a plan. Usually a good one that kept them alive. I had nothing.

But then one came to me. I sent my comrades to new positions and dialed Hamoud.

"Hamoud-Dude," I said in English. "I'll trade you Dakka for Raissa and Louisa."

"Who is this?" he said.

"Sabel Agent Jacob Stearne—the guy who's going to take you down."

He clicked off.

I took the opportunity to update my favorite FBI agent about the gunshots that would be coming from a warehouse in Carver Langston. "A smart agent would be assembling a heavily armed team just in case there really *are* kidnap victims inside."

"Agent Jacob," Special Agent Verges said with a sigh, "that kind of thinking is what killed Tony."

Ouch.

I clicked off and aimed my rifle where I expected action.

Seconds later, a man strode out of the office through a metal door and let it close behind him. His gaze roamed the pavement leading to the single-bay loading dock. Miguel stepped around the corner and darted him. The sentry fell to the ground and Miguel stepped back.

A few minutes went by before curiosity overtook our victim's pals and a second man came out. Behind him in the doorway, stood a short man with a goatee who I took for Hamoud. Hamoud stood with the stock of an AK47 resting on his hip while his man walked the hundred yards to the street.

I switched magazines from darts to bullets.

Miguel saw my signal and darted the sentry without exposing his position to Hamoud.

At the same time, I aimed at Hamoud's AK47, fired, and nailed it. The wooden stock exploded into shrapnel, the muzzle smacked Hamoud in the head. He fell back inside without his weapon as blood oozed out of a gash.

I love to gloat, so I called him.

He picked up on the fourth ring. This time I spoke in Arabic. "Hamoud, Dakka for Raissa. It's a good deal and you won't lose any more men."

"Who is this?"

"Pay attention," I said. "I'm Jacob Stearne—the guy who's going to take you down."

A curious face came to the open window. Carmen darted him.

"Third man down," she said on our comm link.

Charging down the stairwell from the roof, I ran to my position next to the loading dock door and signaled the others. As expected, the rolling metal door wouldn't slide up, so I banged on it instead.

At the same time, Miguel yanked open the office door, tossed in a brick, and closed it.

Explosives inside city limits would bring down a world of legal pain, so we scammed Hamoud with a plain old brick. All their eyes would be staring in horror at what they thought was a bomb for a couple seconds.

Carmen whipped her rifle into the broken window and ripped off three darts.

"Fourth man down," she reported. "Missed the short guy."

I ran to the office door, held up my fingers for a countdown. Miguel rolled his eyes and ripped the door open. I rolled in right while he stepped in left.

Inside was a dark and empty office space with two bodies on the floor. The office area was nothing more than flimsy waist-high cubicles that opened into a cavernous empty warehouse beyond. At the far end of the space was what looked like a construction trailer with the door just closing. Miguel and I exchanged glances.

"Hostages?" I called out in Arabic. "That's low. Even for a worm like you, Hamoud."

Nothing.

A child's wail started up, then was muffled, then a slap, followed by a woman's scream.

I switched my M4's magazine from bullets to darts to prevent collateral damage.

Carmen came in the office door as Miguel and I ran for the trailer. I yanked the door open. Miguel jumped in but didn't go far enough for me to follow. He froze a step inside.

Taking his move as a cue, I squeezed an eye into the corner to see inside.

The last desperado is always the most dangerous. He's cornered and outmanned. The crazy's will go down in a hail of bullets while cowards will leverage the innocent. Hamoud held a gun to a child's head.

Time was critical, as soon as Hamoud stated his demand he would know how impossible it was and might revert to the hail-of-bullets solution. We had a second or less.

I tapped my weapon against the back of Miguel's knee. He shifted his weight to the other leg, giving me a perfect angle on Hamoud from an inconspicuous hiding place.

In the same instant, Hamoud moved out of my line.

"You smug pig," Hamoud said, his voice strained. "Who is going to take me down? You back off now."

Moving quickly and quietly, I repositioned between Miguel's legs, trying to keep the muzzle hidden. Hamoud moved the child, a blond boy about eight, directly into my line of fire.

I found a third position and made the shot. Hamoud keeled over.

The women started screaming, half in horror and half in joy. Miguel cut them loose.

"Is anyone hurt?" I said.

Everyone shook their heads. Raissa and Jamal from the dry cleaners fell on their knees, crying. Louisa, the owner of the dollar store, wrapped her arms around me and thanked me endlessly. The other two women and children I'd never seen before but guessed they were the pilot's wives.

The hostages wanted fresh air and water, but we still had to secure the building.

"How many men does he have in the warehouse?" I asked the group.

Everyone shrugged. We went to work. Miguel took the right side with me covering him. Carmen cleared the offices after our original charge through. Once Miguel and I cleared a stack of shipping containers and abandoned junk, we went to work on five storerooms. A minute later, I heard Carmen's voice, distant and indistinct, her comm link on mute. She was arguing with someone. Miguel nodded in her direction and I left to give her cover.

I found her in the cubicles with her rifle lowered, talking to a figure silhouetted against the outside windows. As I approached I could tell she was scolding the man as a mother would a child.

A shadow slipped past the front door—or my imagination was working double time. I snuck quietly to the edge of the office area where an open, carpeted space met the warehouse floor. At the far end of the carpet, Carmen argued with the silhouette. To the left was the front door, where the shadow moved again.

"Identify yourself!" I said in my command voice.

No answer.

Carmen ducked next to a desk and pulled her friend down with her. I caught her eye and motioned in the direction I'd last seen the intruder.

The shadow darted from a side area, into the open warehouse but remained behind a set of steel shelving built to hold heavy objects. I fired three darts without hearing a body fall. Carmen duckwalked to the next desk. Her silhouetted friend stood up.

A shot echoed in the warehouse.

The silhouette fell.

I fired three more darts. One hit the shadow.

Miguel came running. When we'd cleared the remaining offices and the front reception area, we ran to the fallen silhouette.

Ishmael.

A phone-sized chunk of his head lay two feet away from the rest of him with brain matter scattered between.

"He wanted to help," Carmen said.

We stared until I turned away. "Who did it?"

Miguel nodded at the other body. "Douglas, the guy whose daughter you rescued."

I stepped the few yards to Douglas's darted form and checked his pulse. Carmen and Miguel joined me. We stood there contemplating who had lived and who had died.

Miguel grunted. "I have a magazine with bullets. You OK it, I'll terminate the rat."

Carmen and I looked at each other. Her mouth tightened and she gave me a long, slow nod. I looked at Ishmael's body, then at Douglas. He put on one hell of an act about his daughter being kidnapped. I recalled that earlier crime scene and realized little Raya had never been tied up. He'd used his own daughter as an actress.

"In the Army," I said, "in a war zone, I'd say yes in a heartbeat. But we work for Ms. Sabel now, she does things straight up."

"Soft," Miguel said. He put plasticuffs on Douglas.

As Carmen and I did the same for the Syrians, sirens screamed around us outside.

We surrendered our weapons to the first DC police on the scene and they secured the area. The hours and questions dragged by, and so did the parade of detectives.

Special Agent Verges showed up and took statements. When the police and FBI were done questioning me, I was given permission to check on the hostages. They were wrapping up meetings with the FBI psychologist. After a round of group hugs, Raissa praised Jesus a hundred times and made me pray for the souls of her captors. Jamal trembled.

Louisa took a different approach.

"My knight in shining Kevlar," she purred, fixing the collar on my shirt. "Do you have someone to cook for you?"

"Well, normally I just microwave an MRE," I lied.

I didn't mention my chef's certificate from the Culinary Institute. For a few months after leaving the Army I'd thought hacking the heads off trout would soothe my inner demons. I was pretty good at it too. Then the Major offered me a job at Sabel Security and I went back to a life of danger with the occasional chance to shoot someone.

A salacious smile curled in the corner of Louisa's mouth. "Come by my place later tonight and I'll heat up something for you. Besides, I might need my life saved again. And again."

God knows I love mature women—that's why he sends them my way—he just never sends them at the right time. She was definitely on my to-be-investigated list. But timing is key in life. She might have been feeling liberated and romantic, like the French after the liberation of Paris, but I was still in the middle of an operation with hours of important work ahead of me. There was no way I'd have time for a passion-moment. Absolutely no way.

I said, "I'll be there. Can I bring something?"

She stuck her finger in my belt loop and pulled it up while shaking her head slowly. "Everything you need will be waiting."

Louisa's lips were a paperclip away from mine when my phone rang. I could barely breathe, but I answered it anyway.

"Uh. Bridgette, how are you?" I said.

Louisa turned and sauntered away without looking back.

Confidence. The sexiest curve of all.

Bridgette, my new-best-friend inside the DIA, explained everything she had on Pia Sabel's parents: a sealed file was sequestered in the CIA vault. No one would see it without presidential approval. It had been sealed by William McCarty two decades ago. I was about to thank her when she started talking a mile a minute.

"So I checked the public records and found something interesting," she said. "Leroy Johnson was the man who murdered Pia's mother. He worked for McCarty at the CIA but resigned the day of the murders. I thought that was odd so I checked something else. Leroy Johnson resigned at 3:46 in the afternoon, but he died at 11:22 in the morning."

She ran on about something for a while—the woman knew how to talk—but my mind was spinning around this mythical McCarty. He had killed Ms. Sabel's parents decades ago and *now* he was trying to kill her? What was McCarty's problem?

"Yeah, so that'll work then?" she said.

"Sure. Wait. What'll work?"

She blew out an impatient breath. "I'll let you know tomorrow when I can get a few days off for the Napa Valley trip. Hey, are you listening to me?"

My mind went back to McCarty and his attempts to kill Pia Sabel. She'd stumbled into McCarty's plan to blackmail pedophiles and he decided to kill her because he missed his opportunity twenty years ago? How did that make sense?

"I mean, it is just the two of us, right?" Bridgette said.

"What?" I glanced at Bridgette's picture on my phone. Early twenties, pigtails, a face as innocent as a Mormon missionary. Louisa's polar opposite. Frankly, I favored women like Louisa who had neither fear nor insecurities. But Bridgette had come through for me. Showing her a good time was my duty. "There is no one else but you, babe."

"Good. Hey, you need anything else? Cause I've got to go."

"Yes, can you find all the CIA safe houses in the Washington Metro area?"

CHAPTER 42

VISIBILITY WAS ZERO INSIDE THE cellblock. The cops, the harbormaster, the drunk, Safwan all yelled in different languages. Outside, the sound of bullets raking the cinderblock obscured their words. After a long burst of gunfire, the cellblock fell silent.

"HEY!" Tania shouted and slammed the table. "How many weapons do we have?"

"I can take 'em down," the drunk said. "I got a Beretta."

"Anyone else?" Tania asked.

No one spoke.

"Great," Tania said. "That means all we have is shit-for-brain's peashooter?"

There was a loud smack and the sound of a body falling on the floor. The cop remembered his flashlight and flashed a beam on Tania. She held a Berretta. Sprawled at her feet was the drunk's body. She shrugged.

The cop turned his beam to the door.

Pia faced Tania. "How did the Syrians know we'd come to the Azores?"

"They knew you'd figure out the refueling thing sooner or later," Tania said. "The smoker on the phone must have been the lookout."

"Well, it's me they want," Pia said. "I'll negotiate something."

More bullets pinged off the metal door then stopped. An argument replaced the gunfire outside. Then Pia heard odd noises, as if someone were patting the door gently. Safwan stuck his arm in front of her and pushed Pia and the cop backwards, saying something in Arabic.

"He said, explosives," the harbormaster said.

Everyone scrambled backward in the dark.

The explosion reverberated with bone-crushing noise in the confined space. The cop's light cast about for the door and found it, bent but still intact. They listened to the now recognizable sound of someone placing another charge on the door. The group exchanged looks and backed up to the back wall.

Pia stepped back to the steel door.

"Hey, can you hear me?" she shouted through the steel. "Anyone?"

Bullets pinged off the other side. She flinched.

Behind her, the building's back wall crashed inward. Dim light filled the room. A sledgehammer batted away excess bricks, exposing the bent steel frame of a small flatbed truck. On the back, sledge in hand, stood Jimmy Jenkins. "Let's go, people! The good guys are coming."

Pia tugged the cop, while Tania guided Safwan and Paulo through the wreckage and onto the flatbed. Pia dragged the drunk's limp form into the pile of bricks and the cop gave her a hand. With a big heave, they landed the drunk on the flatbed. Jimmy stomped on the gas.

As they accelerated, a formation of police rounded the corner in full riot gear with weapons at the ready. Jimmy saluted them and one of them saluted back. He fishtailed into the marina and sped down a long dock between yachts bobbing in the water. Screeching to a halt near his plane, he jumped out and ran to untie it.

The cop stood still, shaking his head and staring at the developing gunfight three hundred yards up the hill. The PSP would win, but the cost would be high. He scowled at Pia, then trotted away to join his colleagues.

The plane's first engine coughed to life and the whine of the second began. Tania pushed Safwan onboard.

Paulo pointed to the plane. "Safwan is your friend?"

"No. He's a child molester. I'm going to make him show me where they keep the kids locked up."

Paulo looked confused. "He say same thing. American molests children. He says a tall woman comes but he does not understand at first. He asks me to find tall woman and she frees children. This is you, yes?"

"He wants to *free* the children?"

"Yes. Many days, this is all he says, over and over."

Gunfire from the harbormaster's building resumed at a fever pitch.

They watched for a moment. Then Paulo said, "I go now. You free the childrens. Safwan helps you. *Boa sorte, mocinha.*" *Good luck young lady.*

Paulo ran back up the dock.

Pia took a last look at the comatose drunk on the flatbed. She scrawled an IOU on the ruined truck's windshield and ran to the plane.

Jimmy flew them into the night sky.

In the cockpit, Tania shouted at Jimmy. "Why did you slink off when you should've been helping us with the passports?"

"Can't take the fingerprint risk," Jimmy shouted back.

"What's that supposed to mean—and don't give me that 'don't ask' again, 'cause I'm asking."

Jimmy shrugged.

"Hey. Why're you flying so low?" Tania said. "This is kinda scary."

"Radar," he said. "We don't want our whereabouts getting to Romania before we do."

"Where'd you learn to fly under the radar?" Tania said. Jimmy winked at her and she rolled her eyes. "Yeah, I know, don't ask. Hey, Pia, what's with this guy?"

"He used to be a drug runner," Pia said. "He flew tons of marijuana from Mexico to Texas and Florida."

Tania screeched "*WHAT?*" with such volume everyone jumped, even Safwan.

"You met Bobby Jenkins," Pia said.

"Your father's mentor, founder of Jenkins Pharmaceuticals, all that crap? What—are they related?"

"Jimmy is Bobby's big brother. He put Bobby through college and helped him raise startup capital. When the drug business changed from hippies having fun to cartels chopping off heads, he retired to Bobby's island house. The Feds have been after his money trail. He's still negotiating things. So, he doesn't want to drop anchor on American shores or tangle with American MPs."

Tania shook her head. "I can't believe you hang out with a drug dealer."

"When Dad told me about his past," Pia said, "I was shocked too. But

Dad said, 'you never know when a good smuggler might come in handy.'
And here we are."

Tania fell back in her seat. "Behind every successful businessman is a
gangster."

Jimmy gave her a big grin.

Pia turned to Safwan. "Do you speak any English?"

Safwan said something in Arabic.

From the front, Jimmy said, "In the cabinet, there's a laptop with a
Sabel Satellite connection. Try using one of those translator sites."

A few minutes later, Pia managed to get some basic questions
answered. Safwan had been hired to care for the children shortly before
her attack on Mullaitivu. They'd told him it was a camp for refugees. At
the time, he'd thought her attack was an act of retribution. He learned
about the abuse and kidnappings during the evacuation flight. Horrified,
he escaped the plane at Lajes and tried to get help. The harbormaster had
taken pity on him and let him camp out in the jail.

With a long flight ahead of them, Pia and Safwan started working on
the destination. Pia pictured the deep stone windows Khelemba had
described as a castle. She worked the satellite mapping software and
combed the Sibiu area for pictures of castles, but Safwan insisted they
look for a church. The hours ticked by, Pia methodically searching for
every picture of rural Romania. Finally, half an hour away from landing,
they found it.

"Valea Viilor," Pia told Tania. "A fortified church built in 707, it's a
small-scale castle. It's closed because of a special renovation being done
by an American-Syrian partnership."

Tania looked at the picture on the laptop.

"Can the two of us get the kids out of there?" Pia asked.

"We left our weapons behind, we have a smuggler for backup, and an
Arab who doesn't speak English. What d'you think?"

CHAPTER 43

PATTERSON STORMED INTO THE CAFÉ Carver and yanked the waiter's goatee, effectively throwing him across the café. "I said, who were the guys who just left?"

"Ow! Damn, man. They're just Ishmael's crew, local gangsters."

"Where are they going?"

"Who are you?" the waiter asked.

"I hired Nakdali and he hired you. That makes you my bitch. Where are they going?"

"Looking for Ishmael."

"Why?" Patterson asked.

"He went to warn the Sabel agents, he should've been back by now."

Patterson slammed a fist into the waiter's gut. "Don't make me drag it out of you. I don't have time for games. What's going down?"

An ambulance screamed past the window as the waiter brought him up to date. His story ended as a squad car flew by.

"Is all that noise for the Sabel Security crew?" Patterson asked with a nod outside.

"I doubt it," the waiter said. "Probably for Hamoud."

"Call him," Patterson said. The waiter stood motionless. "I said, call him."

The cook tossed the waiter a cellphone.

The waiter dialed with shaking hands. Patterson grabbed the phone from him and heard the ring tone. On the third ring a familiar voice answered.

"Who is this?" Patterson asked.

"Jacob Stearne, Sabel Security. Who are you?" After a short pause, Jacob said, "Hey, I remember that voice even without the howling wind.

Patterson, how are you?"

Donald F. Patterson, Assistant Secretary of State, Bureau of Political-Military Affairs, felt his heart stop and his insides grow cold as ice. "Why do you have Hamoud's phone?"

"Dude, I save your ass from a bunch of killer Syrians, we go through a hurricane together, you disappear off a cliff in a storm—and you never call, no flowers, nothing. Where does that leave our bromance?"

"You left me to die on that island. If the Coast Guard hadn't come, I'd be out there still. I've tracked the Syrians to a man named Hamoud. And you just answered his phone."

"Donny, if we're going to fix our relationship, don't you think we should base it on the truth—"

"I said, why do you have Hamoud's phone."

"And I heard you, but I thought we should catch up first. You know, some people try to be pleasant. Not you, though, huh? You're all business. OK. Here's the bad news: all your stooges are in FBI custody right now. I think they're going to follow Nakdali's lead and cut a deal with the Justice Department. Now for the good news, Donny old sport: you can turn yourself in to FBI Special Agent Verges over here at Hamoud's crib."

Patterson felt himself falling. Hamoud in police custody? His resources were dwindling fast. Only a few Syrians remained between him and the crusading Pia Sabel. It was McCarty's fault for trying to kill the woman at the outset. But now it seemed the only answer. No one could stop her.

"Kowalski's wife is pretty pissed off about Caldwell killing her husband," Jacob said. "Raissa and the rest put a hole in your story about Ms. Sabel's kidnapping. I'd say you're looking at a life sentence if they don't give you the death—"

Patterson threw the phone at the kitchen wall. It bounced into the deep fryer.

The waiter backed up behind the counter. "Get out. You guys are finished around here."

Patterson stormed out of the café and hiked up the street. He needed some good news. As he walked he pulled out his phone and made a call.

When the other end picked up, he spoke Arabic. "Was the mission successful? Did you neutralize her?"

Instead of Arabic, the answer came in Portuguese. Patterson's worst nightmare. "Quem é você?" *Who are you?*

CHAPTER 44

"THIS BETTER BE THE ONE, Jacob," Carmen hissed into the comm link. "I'm tired of breaking into empty houses all day. It's quitting time."

I ignored her and knocked again. No answer.

He was inside. This time I could feel him as if the door flexed with his breathing.

Miguel moved in behind me, crouching behind a bush and aiming his M4 at the nondescript townhouse in Alexandria. Carmen waited at the backdoor, tucked into a dark corner. My lock-punch took the tumbler out in one slam. I twisted the internal mechanism with the tool and heard it click.

Easing the door open, I stepped inside the foyer and stepped across the parquet floor. A man like McCarty would be ready to kill at any moment. If I were him, I'd have booby-trapped the entryway. Double-checking my thermal imaging, I found no threats.

Yet the sensation that he was nearby intensified. It felt like I could reach out and touch him. I made it to the living room and checked the thermal imaging. There was a man in front of me, sitting in the dark. Miguel slipped in behind me and closed the door.

The lights snapped on.

Under Secretary William McCarty sat in a wingback chair under a blanket. Peeking out from under it was a large-caliber barrel. Miguel moved left and I moved right, separating to present an impossible target.

McCarty looked amused. "I have a job for you, Jacob. Let's put the guns down and talk like civilized men, shall we?"

It bothered me that he knew my name. But then, he was an intelligence man. It made me both respectful and wary of him. As if I was chatting with a tame grizzly bear.

McCarty tossed the blanket aside, revealing a chrome-plated .50 caliber Desert Eagle pistol that he dropped carelessly in his lap before casually putting his hands halfway up. He wore a dark bathrobe and slippers.

Miguel glanced at me. I lowered my M4 while Miguel kept his aimed.

"No tricks," I said. "Or Miguel puts a hole in your forehead."

McCarty shrugged. "Save me the trouble." He picked up the Desert Eagle by the barrel and handed it to me. "I had that thing in my mouth when I heard your feeble scratches at the door."

I nodded at Miguel. He took the pistol and proceeded to clear the house.

"Your wife collects the life insurance if I pull the trigger?" I said.

"Crossed my mind."

"We could oblige you with that. Mind if I ask you some questions first?"

"If you agree to the little job I have for you, then no. Fire away."

"What's the job?"

"We'll get to that. What are the questions?"

I sat on the edge of a chair across from him, a couch and coffee table between us. "Why did you kill Pia Sabel's parents?"

"I don't know." He folded his hands in his lap. "I'm not being coy. I was young and ambitious, I received orders to terminate a young couple, I sent two men to do the job, I had no idea there was a child involved. I might have chosen a different day had they told me, but I still would've done my duty."

I stared at him, the way Ms. Sabel might.

"You can give me the evil eye all you want, boy. You can torture me or kill me, it won't change the fact that I didn't know anything then, and I don't know anything now. You know how these operations work—untraceable orders from code-named operatives. When the orders are unusual, like killing citizens on American soil, you verify with a separate operative on a different channel and, if the orders match, you go."

My special ops had always been in a war zone with clear-cut rules of engagement. McCarty came from a different type of service. His story sounded plausible.

He looked at me with sympathy in his eyes. "I imagine you're hoping to unravel the mysteries of her wretched youth so you can impress her. Maybe win some favors. But what do you know about her?"

"Don't try to duck responsibility by changing—"

"No, young man, I'm asking you a serious question. You know she killed Leroy Johnson. The question is when, where, and how."

McCarty leaned back with a smug look as he watched my face betray me. I didn't know Ms. Sabel had killed anyone. Bridgette's intelligence report left me with big questions, but killing someone?

"That's impossible. That guy died the day of the attack and she would've been four or something."

"Not only possible, my boy, but fact. Her mother had been chopping vegetables when my men went in. Leroy strangled the mother while my other operator took care of the father. Little Pia took her mother's sharp knife off the table and stabbed Leroy. They counted twenty-seven strikes, all but one of them superficial. Leroy probably paid her no attention, he didn't mind pain much. But then the girl hit his femoral artery. He bled out in minutes. Even with luck and a razor-sharp knife, that's a deep strike through dense muscle."

"You're lying."

"Ask her. You deserve to know what kind of woman you're working for." He laced his fingers across his paunch and looked to the ceiling. "Imagine the determination in that little girl. I find that kind of resolve inspiring, don't you? It never surprised me to open the *Post* and read how she'd set some new record or won another championship. Oh yes, I followed her career ever since. You know, I even thought about recruiting her for the Company." He burst out laughing. "That would've been a good one, eh?"

"You're a sick bastard. You killed a little girl's parents without asking why. Set a honey trap for pedophiles with innocent—"

"Life sucks, Jacob. I've done terrible things for my country and so have you."

"I never molested children."

"Really, Master Sergeant Stearne?" His voice boomed, incredulous. "You never called in an A-10 on a compound in Karbala during the war?

You don't think of those children as *molested*?"

A pang of guilt stabbed my chest, as it had many times since that day. My eyes squeezed themselves shut as I returned to April 6, 2003. A hundred Republican Guard fired on us from inside a walled compound. I called in an A-10 that strafed it with a 30mm Gatling cannon and reduced the building to rubble. In the wreckage were nineteen women and children—in sixty-seven pieces.

"War is hell," I said. "I don't like 'collateral damage' either. But the children you kidnapped were thousands of miles from a war zone. You have no excuse—"

"My excuse is the same as yours, Mr. Stearne!" McCarty roared. "I serve my country by unraveling an unseen enemy with the weapons at my disposal. Like you, I do what needs to be done and I don't question it."

"Then why the suicide attempt?" I asked.

He looked away and said nothing.

Miguel came back. "Clear."

McCarty said, "I've been screwed plenty of times. Part of the job. But this time ... damn it. This time that bastard has me cold."

"Who?"

"TGW. I verified the instructions. I made sure the operation was legitimate. But the confirmation and the originator were the same person. In other words—"

"Snare Drum was never officially authorized."

He blew out a long, soulful breath.

I said, "Why did Caldwell kill the pilots?"

"He killed anyone who betrayed the program. Kowalski reported the operation to me. I quashed it, but we knew he'd tell someone. You can't trust bastards like him—guys who only think in terms of right and wrong. You have to eliminate them, the sooner the better." McCarty's expression changed to curious. "Is that why you killed Caldwell?"

"Patterson killed Caldwell."

McCarty looked surprised then nodded as if that made sense in his tangled world. "Why?"

"Still can't figure that out," I said. "We tried to arrest them both, but

Patterson pulled the trigger, then handed me the gun."

"Pretending you were on the same side?" McCarty said and exhaled. "I thought he worked for me. The son-of-a-bitch set me up from the beginning."

McCarty pointed at a tray with a decanter and glasses on the coffee table. I pushed it closer to him, half thinking he'd throw it at me. Instead, he reached for a glass, poured himself three fingers of what looked like Scotch, and took a sip.

"Hamoud was your man?" I said.

"Yes. I never trusted TGW, so I kept the most unsavory little devil for my own purposes. Douglas smelled money and took them in a different direction. Clandestine operations are always susceptible to opportunists."

"What's the job you want me to do?"

"Kill TGW." McCarty took another sip of Scotch. "I'll tell you who he is, where he is, and you kill him. I'd do it myself, but you've rounded up all my resources."

"Whoa. I'm no hit man. If you think—"

"Of course, I have something to offer in return." He smiled a sick smile. "That is, I assume you want to know where and when Pia Sabel is going to die?"

CHAPTER 45

"THEY COULD BE KILLING THE children right now," Pia said. Her voice so loud it rattled the windows of Sibiu's Primar's Office, the mayor. "They could be burying them in the churchyard behind the fortified wall as we speak. They might have already—"

"Why the Syrians would kill them?" Primar Grigore asked with a halting accent.

"They tried to kill us last night," Pia said. The translator began to speak but stopped when Pia raised her voice another ten decibels. "The head guy, TGW, knows I'm going to find the place sooner or later. They're going to cover their tracks and get rid of the evidence because they know what will happen to them if they're caught. Kidnapping, molesting, and murder will not go unpunished."

The translator began translating her words

Exasperated, Pia stepped away from the group. Jimmy, Safwan, and the translator continued to argue the evidence. Primar Grigore considered the renovation project at the seventh-century fortified church a shining example of cooperation between Romania and America. It was not a relationship Grigore intended to upset based on the wild accusations of a foreign woman and an undocumented Arab.

Pia wandered around the office. Afternoon sunlight streamed into the spacious room. Rows of pictures lined the shelves: the primar with his family, at campaign rallies, with dignitaries. Behind the desk, the primar's official portrait hung symmetrically across from an official picture of the Romanian Prime Minister. Grigore's picture sparkled while the Prime Minister's portrait sported a thin layer of dust. On the credenza was a family snapshot.

A plaque was displayed on a bookshelf next to a framed newspaper headline. Thumbing the Romanian words into her phone's translator, she quickly discovered that Grigore headed the PNL, the loyal opposition party, and that the primar had been at political odds with Romania's Prime Minister for over a decade.

Pia snapped her fingers and all four men stopped speaking. She tapped her finger on the PNL plaque. "The project at Valea Viilor is the Prime Minister's project, right? He has a cozy relationship with the wrong people in the American government. If the primar should lead his people to Valea Viilor and expose the despicable things going on inside, he could topple the oligarchy and free Romania."

The translator and the primar discussed her statement. Grigore stared at Pia for a long time before speaking again.

"The primar wants a few moments with his advisors," the translator said and motioned toward the door.

"Is dangerous to challenge Prime Minister," Grigore said as they turned to leave.

"I put the children first," Pia said.

Grigore pursed his lips and nodded.

The translator ushered them into a waiting room, gestured for them to sit.

When he left, Pia dropped into a chair, put her elbows on her knees and her head in her hands. Everything she'd endured, the torture, the death of Agent Tony, the deaths of the pilots, everything, came down to the decision of one ambitious politician. Even if he agreed to send a few men along, their chance of success would be small. If the Primar refused, it would be the three of them, unarmed, against a squad of heavily armed Syrians. She would do it, no question. Tania was crazy enough to go with her. Jimmy might not be that crazy. Maybe it would be the two of them.

"You know Romania hosts a black site for the CIA," Jimmy said. "It's been in the *Times* and the *Post* plenty of times. The Prime Minister's relationship with the CIA is more than cozy. You're leaning out over a precarious chasm, young lady."

Pia's face tightened as much as her insides. "That framed newspaper article on his bookshelf says the primar spent several months in jail after he took a stand against Romanian involvement in Iraq."

"He's a rebel," Jimmy said. "I like that, but I'm not worried about him."

The translator stepped back in. "The primar wants to know if you would join him in leading the liberation of Valea Viilor."

POLICE OFFICERS RUSHED INTO THE *Piata Mare* or Great Square in front of the ornate Victorian *Primaria* building. With megaphone in hand, Grigore rallied his people with a speech that rose to a crescendo. Around her, the people watched him with rapt attention. When he finished, they were unified and energized. The crowd shouted their support to punctuate Grigore's speech.

Pia and Safwan ran to the primar's car with the translator. Behind them, Jimmy and Tania jumped in the local TV van.

At the car, Grigore said, "I take big risk on your words."

"I understand," Pia said.

He opened the car door for her. "If you are wrong, the Prime Minister will crush me."

"Let's save the children."

Grigore ran to the driver's seat. He belted himself in, looked at Pia, and let out a nervous laugh. "We save children *before* he crush me."

A train of Dacia police cars followed them as they sped down narrow lanes lined with sixteenth-century buildings. Turning on sirens and picking up speed, they flew through tight stone archways that formed the wall of the old city and out into the bustling newer streets. Minutes later they were streaming onto a highway that led to the countryside.

Someone had put the word out to the locals. People lined the road, waving and crowding onto trucks, ready to join the procession. On a long sweeping turn, Pia saw the convoy stretching all the way back to the city. They turned onto a smaller side road and headed up a valley. They slowed as they approached a village of medieval houses, some recently restored and others in original condition. When they rounded the last bend, the primar slowed and pointed. "Valea Viilor."

Half a mile in front of them, the road split around the ancient church, an impressive structure of dark red shingles and deep brown bricks. An outer wall twenty feet high protected a sixty-foot stone turret towering above the village. A series of arrow loops—windows set deep in the stone—stared down from the forty-foot level. Shadowy figures moved along the dark walkway at the top.

Syrians.

Pia's adrenaline ignited.

Grigore pulled to the side of the road a hundred yards short of the church, parked, and stepped into the deserted lane. The others followed his lead.

Pia strode toward the tower. Tania caught up to her on the right, Jimmy alongside her. After a short hesitation, Grigore jogged alongside, his bullhorn in one hand. Safwan followed them, a scowl etched deep on his face. A thousand people filled the street twenty yards behind them. Pia stopped below the tower, where she could see the shadowy faces— and the distinct shape of rifles—on the walkway.

Grigore aimed his bullhorn at the tower high above them and shouted a long statement. The translator joined them and explained to Pia the Primar's demands: the Syrians were to lay down their weapons and would be allowed to leave if the children were unharmed.

No one in the tower responded.

Grigore made a second, more impassioned plea. Again, the Syrians said nothing.

Safwan asked for the bullhorn and made a long statement of his own in Arabic. The translator told Pia it was similar to the primar's statement.

Someone in the tower replied in Arabic.

When he heard the answer, Safwan clenched his fists and turned red. He shouted something, the veins on his neck bulging and spittle spewing as he spoke. An angry reply from the tower followed, and Safwan responded in a nearly unintelligible scream. The translator looked shocked and tugged the bullhorn away. Safwan and the translator glared at each other, tense and ready to strike.

Pia tapped the translator and asked about Safwan's argument.

"He told them they are traitors to Islam, that they deserved to die, and that the crowd would kill them all. This is not good for hostage negotiations. It is not diplomatic."

Safwan grabbed the bullhorn back and ran forward to the tower, screaming in Arabic and shaking his fist.

Three bullets raked Safwan's torso. One came out near his waist. Another came out his shoulder. Both tore fist-sized holes in his back. The middle bullet went straight through his heart. He fell face-down.

Shrieks and shouts rose up from the crowd, half in anger and half in fear. The crowd surged forward to help Safwan. Pia and Grigore reached him first and turned him over. His eyes lolled in their sockets; the pool of blood beneath him quickly soaked into the loose asphalt. The crowd closed in for a look.

Safwan's eyes fluttered and closed. His body shuddered violently.

Grigore felt the Arab's pulse, then looked up at them and shook his head.

More shouts of anger rose from the group, not for the man they didn't know, but for the violence the foreigners brought to their streets. The civilians picked up rocks and hurled them at the structure. Most fell short of the outer wall; a few reached the tower far below the walkway. But three hit their targets.

The Syrians answered with bullets.

The crowd scattered for the safety of nearby walls and houses. Pia ran with them a few steps but heard a noise behind her. Twisting as she ran, she saw Grigore fall, clutching his ribs. She ran to him with two policemen close behind her. Bullets pinged off the roadway around them.

When she applied pressure to the wound, blood seeped through Grigore's suit and between her fingers. Grigore winced, stifled a yelp, and clenched his teeth. The policemen picked up his arms and drag-carried him to the safety of a strip of grass behind a garden wall. Paramedics came quickly but Grigore brushed them aside to look at Pia.

"You are right," Grigore said. "Children in terrible danger. You brought us here—you lead my people."

He collapsed and the paramedics swarmed over him.

The translator said something in the bullhorn but Pia paid him no attention. She looked up at the tower. It looked taller and darker and more fortified.

"We each take a group of police." Tania's voice came from behind her. "I'll take the main gate there. You and Jimmy breach the south door. Find something for a battering ram. Like a truck."

Tania tugged the translator and had him relay instructions to the crowd. People began moving in different directions. Some moved south. Others worked their way up the side street.

Pia felt a strange detachment. She'd led her agents into a fight but never civilians. In her head, she repeated Tania's instructions: *Breach the south door*. What did *that* mean?

Tania pushed her shoulder. "Snap out of it, Pia! You want to save the children, let's do it. First thing, we gotta take out those fucktard Syrians."

Tania sprinted away and three men fell in behind her. Then another four, then ten more, and then a flood.

Jimmy said, "I'll get a car. Work your way to the wall. Meet you in three."

Jimmy disappeared behind a group of expectant faces.

Pia tightened her stomach to keep everything down. Her heart pounded in a hollow ribcage. She turned to the quickly thinning crowd and waved. "This way!"

She darted across the street to an alley between houses. When she reached the far side, she looked over and saw a stream of people following her. Policemen in uniform were first. Then civilians.

The Syrians opened fire on her followers.

A policeman next to her shouted in Romanian and some people ran faster, while others went back.

"They will follow when they can," the policeman told Pia. He pointed down the short alley where twenty people waited. "Go!"

Pia ran ahead, turning behind the houses to run parallel to the road. The tower loomed above them, visible between rooftops. A few shots came at them but Pia's new policeman friend staggered the people in groups to lessen the risk.

Having taken a few casualties, Tania's team were close enough to the wall that the rifles above couldn't find the right angle to shoot at them. Tania's voice created a cadence above a loud pounding noise. The first attack on the main gate was underway.

Pia ran to the next opening between buildings and checked the church. From her new angle, she had a limited view of the tower and hoped it would keep her group safe.

She bolted across the street and plastered herself to the wall. The side door was ten feet away. A stream of policemen and a few civilians joined her. Just as her group reached critical mass, Jimmy roared down the street in a small truck.

He cranked the wheel over and accelerated straight into the door. The truck slammed violently into the small space, spraying dust and bits of stone outward. Despite his seatbelt, Jimmy's head bounced off the steering wheel. The targeted door disappeared along with a foot of wall on each side. The screech of metal on stone filled the street as Jimmy backed out of the wreckage two yards and stopped. He looked her way, his face pale under a sheet of blood that ran down his face, and gave her a thumbs-up.

Bodies pressed into Pia's backside. Against her better judgment, she instinctively held up her hand as if she were taking a corner kick then flew into the opening. Blood-curdling cries from her people followed her into the church yard.

It took the Syrians a few seconds to follow the noise and retrain their weapons. What seemed like sheets of bullets rained down on Pia's group. Two people crumpled, clutching bleeding wounds. The others dove for safe places, but the surge never stopped. More and more people poured through the broken entry.

Pia felt something burning her left hip but ignored it and headed for the main gate, where five inches of ancient oak had yet to yield under Tania's battering ram. Pia's policeman fired three shots at two Syrians guarding the gate. Both Syrians fell. The policeman disarmed them while Pia struggled to lift the bar and open the gate.

Tania's group flooded in, carrying Pia on a tidal wave of raw energy, into the church and up the tower steps. Pia felt woozy, her balance a bit off, as if she'd been drinking, but she ran to find the children.

In the dark, narrow passages, stone steps wound around until they reached a landing. Three Syrians waited with rifles ready. Two of Pia's policemen fired around the corner, killing one Syrian and sending the other two fleeing further upwards.

Behind the dead man was a thick wool curtain. Shaking off a lightheaded feeling, Pia pulled it back to reveal a mass of huddled children.

Sixteen faces, their eyes wide with fear, turned to her. She felt a warmth growing from her feet to her waist to her chest. Even though the battle was far from over, the children were alive. Nothing could be better than that. The good, warm feeling continued welling up to her face. It filled her eyes with tears of joy.

The children instinctively curled around her, hugging and squeezing her.

Pia's eyes clouded over and the dizziness intensified. She stroked a child's hair and smiled. One of the children pulled back and raised red hands into the air. Pia's vision turned gray and collapsed into tunnel vision. Then everything faded to black.

CHAPTER 46

THE BIGGEST THREAT TO THE United States of America was Pia Sabel. Patterson stared out the cab's window and watched the west side of Washington DC pass by. The Azores operation had failed, the Mona Island operation had failed, even McCarty's operation in Carver Langston had failed. One woman had dismantled it all. As he rode across town, her people were killing or questioning the last of his operatives.

He slammed his fist against the door. The cabbie spun around to give him a dirty look.

"Turn right on 18th Street," Patterson said. Three blocks later he spied what he was looking for, an old-fashioned bar in Adams Morgan called Bourbon.

He stepped in to the empty bar and plopped onto the nearest barstool. "Casa Noble, Añejo."

The bartender poured a shot from the large purple bottle and went back to washing glasses at the far end.

Patterson took a sip and savored the flavor.

Snare Drum's results were undeniable: intelligence had been gathered and terrorists had been stopped. What was it Pia Sabel observed about him at their first meeting? "You wanted to make a difference." That was exactly what he wanted, and that's exactly what he'd done. To outsiders, Snare Drum might look immoral or illegal, but the results saved American lives. He was making a difference in the world. It was Pia Sabel who was wrecking everything. She still had a pre-9/11 sense of morality.

He sat up suddenly; something in his peripheral vision set off an alarm in his head. The television above the bar caught his eye. It was Valea Viilor, close up and surrounded by throngs of people. That could not be good. Patterson snapped his fingers at the bartender and asked to have the volume turned up. The bartender slid him the remote.

"…news station of Romania reports the former soccer star and Washington philanthropist is leading an armed assault on an ancient Romanian landmark. More after these messages."

Patterson muted the TV and closed his eyes for a long time. He downed his tequila.

When the drink had burned its way down his throat, he checked that he and the bartender were still alone. He signaled for another drink and dialed the Chief.

"This better be the last call, Patterson," the Chief said. "What is it?"

Patterson said, "McCarty's files were successfully destroyed."

"Good news. Did you get the encryption key?"

Patterson thought for a moment. Technology had never been his strongest area but he'd made a duplicate, not a decrypted file-copy. He'd not asked the CIA tech for an encryption key.

The Chief snorted. "From your silence, I'm guessing that's a no. So any copies you made are useless. Good. Oh, and another thing, recordings on EOP phones are against policy and remotely wiped. The techs found three recordings on yours and wiped them. So tell me, why did you really call?"

As if punched in the gut, Patterson tried to breathe without anything entering his lungs.

The Chief said, "Patterson? You there?"

"Uh," Patterson coughed and gulped air. "Sir, Pia Sabel showed up at Valea Viilor with half the population of Sibiu. They're storming the church right now."

"How did that happen?"

"It doesn't matter," Patterson said. "They'll free the children; it's only a matter of time."

"Damn it. I thought TGW had that place nailed down—"

"It happened."

"Time for the defense phase then. Have TGW fall on his sword."

Patterson took another deep breath and slumped. "I say we stick with the plan to pin this on McCarty and Nakdali."

"Then why did you call me?"

"Anyone interviews her on TV, she'll name me. She was onto me from the beginning, I just know it."

"Patterson, pull yourself together. She couldn't know anyone beyond TGW. He was the last security link in case someone pierced McCarty. Don't worry—"

"Sir. There is no TGW."

The Chief shrieked "WHAT?" so loud, Patterson had to pull the phone from his ear. Patterson mumbled something to placate the most powerful man he'd ever dealt with in his career.

"You mean," the Chief said, "*you're* The Grand Wazir?"

"I approached three top people. None of them would take the job for any amount of money."

"You told people about Snare Drum and let them *turn it down?*" The Chief's voice rose twenty decibels. "You know none of this can blow back on the administration. TGW was supposed to die before letting it get out of control. Do you realize where that leaves you?"

Patterson said nothing. At that moment, he just wanted the whole thing to go away. Every second spent on Snare Drum—from initial discussions back at the CIA up to the conversation at hand—was a colossal mistake. Nonetheless, it was a mistake that had to be fixed if he wanted his daughters to have a father.

"I understand, sir," Patterson said. "I'm willing to die for my country. But I have an idea."

The Chief said nothing.

Patterson said, "I need an extraordinary rendition, sir."

"You've got to be kidding. Those take cabinet-level approval. Do you really think I'm going to take that kind of risk just to save your miserable—"

"Just hear me out, please, sir."

"Make it good."

"The nearest black site is in Bucharest. The CIA has a contractor there, Velox Deployment Services—"

"No way," the Chief said. "They're a huge liability. They were supposed to be banned for their work in Italy alone. They ran Abu Graib,

SEELEY JAMES

for Christ's sake. Are you telling me they still exist?"

"Not officially, sir. But yes, they're fully operational. The best part is, all their employees applied at Sabel and were turned down before going to Velox."

For a long time, the Chief said nothing. Patterson could sense the man pacing his cramped office. "You think they'll do what your Syrians failed to do in the Azores. You solve the problem by laying Snare Drum on McCarty gone rogue. I still have a problem—you, Patterson. Everything you've done with Sabel backfired."

"She presented a bigger problem than I expected. But I have taken care of McCarty."

"An hour ago, I thought McCarty was my biggest problem."

"Uh, well, yes," Patterson said. "I understand, sir."

"You're sure Velox will kill her?"

"No sir. I don't want them to. If word of their involvement got out, even in the clandestine community, things would blow up because they're Sabel's competitors. We'd lose Velox as a contractor for good this time. I just want them to deliver her to Washington."

"But she's still a credible witness."

"Sir, I no longer trust anyone else to do this. I'm going to kill her myself." Patterson spun around to make sure the bartender was out of hearing range.

After a long silence, the Chief drew a long breath. "Since you work for State, I'll get Secretary Highsmith to approve the rendition. His IQ comes in handy at times like these. But I require two things from you. Number one, McCarty dies with her."

"Understood, sir. And number two?"

"Falling on your sword is not an expression, Patterson."

278

CHAPTER 47

"DON'T ACT SO SUPERIOR, JACOB," McCarty said. "You're at war with a man who has endangered the country more than any foreign enemy. Killing him would save the nation."

I leapt to my feet. "There's no way in hell I'm going to murder a civilian just so you can escape—"

Miguel tapped my shoulder. He handed me his phone with a live video session in progress. The Major stared at me from the five-inch screen. She said, "Put me in front of McCarty."

"How long have you been listening in?" I asked.

"Lucky for you, Miguel had the good sense to hook me up. Now put him on."

Miguel shrugged when I looked up. He stepped around me and pointed the phone at our host. "Boss wants you."

"We'll neutralize Patterson for you," the Major said without introduction. "Under the circumstances, you can no longer trust your official security detail. You will hire Sabel Security for personal protection. You will authorize us to use deadly force in the event of a life-threatening situation."

McCarty's gaze moved from the screen to me and back again. "Now here's someone I can do business with. Agreed."

After the Major hammered out a bargain with the devil, McCarty went to get dressed. The Major had a few parting words for me.

"Agent Jacob, next time an intelligence officer offers information we need, don't be so damned high and mighty about getting it. Now go buddy up and find out what he knows. The sooner we find his source, the sooner we're done with him. Just make sure he makes it back here to the Ops Center. Alan wants to have a few words with him."

I mumbled my apology, but she'd already clicked off.

I found McCarty upstairs in the master bedroom. Even though his mood had improved, it seemed odd that he whistled while he sorted out his suit and collected his toiletries.

"Weren't you suicidal earlier?" I asked.

McCarty nodded at a pile of external hard drives on the bureau. "These guys were pros. I double-checked all those drives after the confirmation hearings, just to make sure the files were still there, then put them in two separate safe places. Sometime this afternoon, they destroyed everything."

Picking up a drive, I counted three holes drilled clean through. The thing would never spin again. The other devices were in the same state and an SD card lay in three pieces next to them. "Who're 'they'?"

He stepped out of the bathroom with his kit and a duffle. "Patterson, probably. It doesn't really matter, they cleaned me out."

McCarty grabbed a two-pound bag of Peanut M&Ms on the way out and shoved it in his suit pocket. He was humming when we jumped in the Porsche Panamera.

Miguel said, "Turn it off, McCarty."

"I can't help it," McCarty said. "I've not been in the field for, what, ten years? I feel alive, liberated. Besides, my archenemy, the architect of this wretched plan, is going to die."

I pulled into the narrow lane, intending to head for Sabel Security's Operations Center. Behind us, two cars pulled out of spaces.

It was the hour when most Alexandrians were coming home for dinner. I made three right-hand turns and parked right where we started. A two-car tag-team is pretty easy to work as long as you have the intellectual capacity of a gecko. The first car came around the corner and drove casually past us, while his friend saw the problem and drove away.

McCarty pulled out his M&Ms, tore the corner off and filled his fist. He popped them, one at a time, into his mouth. To look at him, you would have thought he was watching a mildly interesting TV show.

I pulled out and followed the man who had tried to follow me. Doing that really messed with his head. First, he acted like he had somewhere to go, but he knew nothing of the neighborhood and ended up in a cul-de-sac. My headlights illuminated his hand-to-ear move, a call to coordinate with the other car. He pulled into a grocery store and stopped. I stopped next to him.

Miguel jumped out and knocked on our pursuer's window. The flustered man dropped the window a notch. Miguel said, "Can I ride with you? There's no legroom in that thing."

The car jumped forward and sped through the lot, out to the street, and disappeared into traffic.

"How rude," Miguel said, folding his big frame into the back.

"He followed us here?" I said. "That's not good."

"We're driving one of Pia's cars, genius," Carmen said from behind me. "He probably asked Cousin Elmer for the tracking info. In case you didn't recognize him—that was Mark Fitzroy."

I swung my head around the headrest to face her. "Mark? As in *Mark*? The soon-to-be ex-boyfriend? He set up a two-car tail on *us*?"

Carmen shrugged. "You turned down a standard-issue company Passat for this bling-ride Porsche. What did you expect?"

Knowing Ms. Sabel's stables had row after row of exotic cars was too hard for this farm boy to resist. It had taken all my self-control not to grab one of the Rolls convertibles.

"OK, my bad, they found us. So why is Mark, the investment banker, following us?"

McCarty gave me a sideways glance as if I were dim, but he didn't speak. He popped another M&M.

Four blocks later, I dropped Carmen on the sidewalk and drove around the block six times.

"Three-car tail," she said when she got back in. "Mark was the weakest link. I'm betting they sent him home. We're down to a blue Ford and a silver Toyota. Catch the Jeff Davis and you can use this car for speed instead of posing."

McCarty kept munching and stayed silent, content to let us do our thing.

I pulled out and jumped on Highway 1, northbound. Though traffic was dying down, there was little room for ramping up speed. Using the airport access ramp, I accelerated into National Airport, then turned abruptly onto the George Washington Parkway.

The Ford made the last turn while the Toyota ended up snarled in airport traffic.

Using the engine's massive power, I was able to leapfrog a few cars by the time we reached the 14th Street Bridge. The Ford driver was no slouch and managed to catch up when we hit a wad of traffic. He found a lane on my left and pulled alongside.

There were two of them, one driving and the other holding a sawed-off shotgun. The Ford's passenger window came down and the barrel aimed at my head.

"Pia won't notice," Carmen said casually, "but the Major'll kill you if you let that clown scuff up this car."

"Would you mind taking a shot at him?" I asked. Nicely.

"Darts," she said.

Our boss's pacifist solution to collateral damage would bounce off the guy's window.

Timing it by the intent in my adversary's eyes, I slammed on the brakes as he squeezed the trigger. His buckshot flew across the front of our car, over the retaining wall, and landed in the Potomac.

Every car behind me slammed on their brakes. Tires smoked and horns honked and fenders bent. The locals weren't used to seeing live fire on the parkway. Several cars in front of us pulled to the shoulder, unsure what was happening in their rearview mirrors.

I stepped on the gas and flew by our attacker until we caught up with more traffic.

"You use darts?" McCarty said and poured himself another handful of M&Ms. Talking with his mouthful, he said, "We quit using those decades ago."

"Boss's orders," I said.

"Sore subject," Miguel said.

"Don't want to talk about it," Carmen said.

"Ah yes," McCarty said. "Your boss is a civilian. They never understand."

We all mumbled our agreement.

"Those guys work with you back at the Company?" I said.

"Didn't see him. I chose not to look at the barrel," he said. "But, shotguns on the Potomac—please. Only contractors would do something stupid like that." He glanced around sheepishly and shrugged. "Present company excluded, of course."

Weaving my way through northbound congestion, I pulled off at Theodore Roosevelt Island Park. With a U-turn entrance into a gooseneck lane, I had our pursuers trapped. I stopped in the lane, put it in reverse, and kept one toe on the brake, my other foot hovering over the gas pedal. Carmen and Miguel rolled out and took positions up the lane a few yards.

Our pursuer came around the corner in a four-wheel drift. Slipping my toe off the brake, I slammed the gas down and backed straight into his radiator.

Steam and water gushed from under his hood. The driver fought his airbag while Carmen and Miguel ran to the Ford. The passenger's window was still open and Carmen darted both occupants before she realized the passenger's shotgun had fired when the airbag blew. Half his head was splattered all over the headrest.

Carmen was shaking her head as McCarty and I approached. McCarty poured another handful of M&Ms and popped them while he examined the dead passenger.

"I know this guy," McCarty said with his mouth full. "Used to be in covert ops, went to a lobbyist."

"Lobbyists have hit men now?" I said.

"Inevitable, my boy. The stakes have gone up significantly since the Abramoff scandal."

"Why would lobbyists want to kill me?"

"Don't flatter yourself," McCarty said. "They're after me. If you had read Snowden's releases carefully, you would have noticed a solitary footnote about a CIA officer with full access at the NSA. I used it to keep a file on lobbyists and their corrupt politicians. My hard drives were full of fascinating phone calls and emails." He sniffed with self-pity and popped more candy in his mouth. "Saved my ass innumerable times. These guys don't know my cache has been destroyed."

McCarty gave a pensive glance at the dead man before he faced me with a faint smile. "But now that my leverage is lost, I find myself happy to be under the protection of the woman I've been trying to kill. Serendipity." He walked back to the Panamera, talking over his shoulder. "Good thing Caldwell wasn't successful killing your boss, or I'd be smeared all over the parkway right now."

"Who do these guys work for? TGW?"

"That's one of life's mysteries, young man. TGW must be running low on resources by now. All his assets, if he has any left, are deployed overseas."

The Toyota came around the corner, saw the carnage, made a hasty U-turn and fled.

When the cops finished with our statements, we continued our journey. Halfway there, McCarty took a call. He said little and listened a lot. When he clicked off, he said, "They're going to pick her up. I'm not sure who or how, but the Secretary of State just signed an extraordinary rendition order. They're bringing her here to DC later tonight."

"How do you know the Secretary signed something?"

"People tell me things."

"Where are they bringing her in?" I asked.

"I'm not 100% sure," McCarty said. "When the time comes, we'll follow someone who'll lead us to her."

"How do I know you're not leading me away from our target?"

He faced me with a thin smile. "Let's just say, my sources are quicker than your girlfriend, Bridgette Hargrove, at the Defense Intelligence Agency." He slowed his speech when he spelled out the DIA's full name just to drive home his point.

How much he knew about me gave me the willies.

"If you screw me on this, you're a dead man," I said as we pulled into the parking lot at the Ops Center.

"Then we'll be right back where we started." McCarty laughed. "Until then, I'd like to take a nap."

We walked into the Ops Center like four old friends. Intelligence people are like that, unassuming, helpful, with just the right degree of friendliness thrown in.

I asked Carmen to look up a few things about the Fitzroy dynasty, then reported to the Major. I gave her a quick run-down of the evening and McCarty.

"We don't have any assets in Romania," I said. "So it works out in our favor that they're bringing her here—as long as we intercept them. That means there's nothing we can do for the next few hours. So, we can just kick back."

She nodded cautiously, her eagle eyes stuck to me like glue.

"Yeah. So. I've got an errand to run," I said. I thumbed over my shoulder. "I'll be back in a couple."

The Major stared at me.

"Don't worry. Plenty of time for prep later." I walked backwards to the door and shrugged. "Besides. Really important stuff I gotta do. Personal."

She didn't stop me, so I turned and strode out to the Panamera. I felt her watching me the whole way.

My jaw dropped when Louisa opened the door in a chemise with matching stockings. She could've been Miss Africa with her fearless stage presence.

"Jacob, you look hungry," she said with a deep laugh.

An hour and forty-five minutes later, I walked back into the Ops Center. The Major, standing at a rack of Kevlar vests, looked over her shoulder and watched me as if she knew where I'd been. I don't know why I do things like that, run off at the slightest invitation. One day I'll screw up an operation and get us all killed. But Louisa was worth it. I could still smell her scent around me like a halo. I gave the Major my *so-fire-me* shrug.

"Ready to brief us, Jacob?" the Major asked.

We walked to the meeting room where Carmen hooked her laptop to a 90" screen.

I started the session. "McCarty thought Mark Fitzroy's men were lobbyists looking to shut him down. I don't. When we left Isla de la Mona, Fitzroy kept trying to figure out when and where Ms. Sabel was coming back. Ms. Sabel thought he wanted publicity. After the Fitzroy faction tried to kill us today, I asked Carmen to look up a few things. Turns out, Mark and his dad are big supporters of President Hunter's agenda. Mark's Facebook page has pictures bragging about White House connections."

Carmen displayed the pictures and took over. "Sometimes presidents make appointments based on merit and sometimes on campaign fundraising, but on rare occasion, loyalty. We figure the Fitzroy family is going for acts of loyalty. Mark's grandfather was in the marijuana business in Colorado before, during, and after legalization. When he was a cartel boss, he had killers working for him. Now that things are legal, he's been hiring covert ops guys with clean records to do the same work. We think the Fitzroy's are using that labor pool to help the administration keep this covered up."

"So we have two factions looking to kill Pia," the Major said. "TGW and Mark?"

"Not sure," I said. "The short version is TGW is facing the death penalty, he has nothing to lose by killing anyone. Logically, the same thing would go for anyone authorizing TGW or funding Snare Drum. Whoever authorized TGW is sending Mark as an insurance policy."

"How did you come to that conclusion?"

"They tried to kill us in the car with McCarty. Had they succeeded, you'd have three Sabel Security agents riding around with the architect of Snare Drum. That would shoot down any evidence Ms. Sabel might bring out later. She'd look like she's trying to cover up Sabel Security involvement."

The Major nodded. "How high up do you think it goes?"

"Too many resources deployed for a rogue operation out of the State Department. Either someone has a piece of the black budget, or they're cobbling what they need from several different departments. I'm no expert on funding authority, but that sounds like the White House."

Bridgette texted me: Black budget contractor scrambled out of Bucharest, landing stateside at 3:38AM.

I looked back to the Major. "We don't need McCarty anymore."

CHAPTER 48

WHEN PIA REGAINED CONSCIOUSNESS, SHE was strapped to a gurney. Even in the twilight, the tower loomed over her like a monster. Recalling the last thing she could remember, she spoke to anyone around her. "Are the children safe?"

"You're awake?" Tania asked from somewhere behind her.

Pia twisted around. A lightning bolt of pain shot through her. The gurney was tilted up slightly at her head. She could see people milling about, but heard no gunfire. There were no medics nearby that she could see. Braving the pain, she twisted farther and saw Tania behind her, pushing her gurney.

"What happened?" Pia said.

"You passed out. Blood loss," Tania said. "You have a bullet in your thigh. But don't worry, I won't say 'at least it didn't hit the bone' like you said to me back in Vienna. I'm not that kind of person."

"What happened to the children?"

"They're safe," Tania said. "The Syrians surrendered a few minutes after you passed out. The locals are all over the kids with food. Mostly candy."

The distinct whumping of helicopters grew in the distance.

Tania pushed her gurney across rough ground and stopped at the back of an open ambulance. Pia gave her gurney to an old woman with a head wound. Tania helped her onto the hood of a nearby car.

Primar Grigore hobbled toward her, a massive bandage around his torso and his coat draped over his shoulders.

"You do good thing," Grigore said in his halting accent. "You open Romanian eyes to Prime Minister's ethics."

"You were brave, Primar. But your people paid a high price."

"Price is yet to pay." Grigore pointed to the horizon where the helicopters' noises grew steadily louder. Four black dots swept low over the ridge, barely visible in the gathering twilight. "My people say, two American and two Romanian."

"The Americans are coming for me. Are the Romanians coming for you?"

Grigore nodded with a sad smile. "Whatever fate of you and me, it was the good fight."

CHAPTER 49

THE HOUSE WAS SILENT AFTER Secretary of State David Highsmith clicked off the TV. Then the chair squeaked and I heard his slippers padding through the downstairs rooms. I guessed he was turning off lights. He climbed the steps with a tired pace, rounded the hallway, and stepped into his bedroom. He snapped on the light—and screamed like a little girl.

I almost laughed as he gasped for air. Standing in the middle of the room, wearing my black-out gear with an M4 held across my chest, I would've scared Medusa. I said, "Wazzup dude?"

He began to shout but I put a finger to my lips, *shh.* "Do you want tomorrow's headlines to read, 'Highsmith, Secretary of Unsafe Homes'?"

"Who are you? How did you get in here? I'm calling security."

Funny, you'd think a cabinet secretary would know what happened to his security since I was standing in his bedroom.

"No need, I'm leaving." I slung the rifle, then snapped my fingers as if I'd remembered something. "Oh, I need a name."

He raised his voice. "You get out of here—"

"Dave ol' buddy, there's no need for rudeness. Just tell me the name and I'm gone."

He backed up, his hand searching the wall behind him for his panic button. I smiled. His fingers wrapped around the wires dangling from the missing pad. He said, "What do you want, money?"

"*Puhlease* tell me you pay more attention in cabinet meetings. I want a name." I stepped up to him, toe to toe. "Who told you to sign Pia Sabel's extraordinary rendition?"

His face trembled. He tried to step back but hit the wall.

"David," I dropped to a whisper, "I saw your signature with my own eyes. C'mon, buddy, everybody knows you were set up. Had to be. The FBI says you're so dumb you should come with a warning label. Now, just tell me who asked you to sign that document. Was it President Hunter?"

He was quivering so hard I almost felt sorry for him.

"I can't tell you. National security is—"

I grabbed his face and squeezed. "Even *you* know Ms. Sabel's not a threat to the country. She's a threat to Bill McCarty and Don Patterson. And someone else. I want to know who that someone else is."

"How do you know those names?"

"Bill McCarty is back at the Sabel Security offices, coughing up names and dates and directives so fast the FBI had to send a second agent. So. Quit stalling."

Highsmith stumbled to an armchair and fell into it. He dropped his head in his hands but he didn't say anything.

"You gotta understand my problem," I said. "If Patterson kills Ms. Sabel, she can't sign my paychecks. Do you have any idea how pissed off a former Army Ranger gets when he doesn't get paid?"

"FBI?" Highsmith asked. "I don't believe it."

"Believe it. Guy's name is Verges. He's planning to bring you in for questioning. But you'll want your lawyers, and they'll want to stall, and things will drag out. Dude, I don't have time for all that because I'm pretty sure Patterson plans to kill her tonight."

"That fucking bastard."

"Who? Verges or Patterson?"

"No, the guy you want. He promised 'no blowback'."

"Those FBI guys were right about you. Dumb as a post. Did this guy tell you the check's in the mail and he won't come in—"

The air density in the room changed a tiny fraction and an electrical tingle ran up the back of my neck.

I kicked Highsmith's chair over, slapped the light switch, and rolled.

From the open door, a silhouette fired off a three-round burst. The window behind me exploded into the street below.

I returned fire, but he fled before I could aim straight. My earbud filled with Emily's voice. "Jacob, are you all right? I didn't get anything incriminating from Highsmith. What just happened?"

"Emily, gotta go. Drop off the line."

Flying down the hallway, I leapt the first turn of stairs and stumbled onto the landing in time to see the hostile spin around. He stitched a bullet pattern in the wall that looked like a pointillist reproduction. With a quick scramble backwards up the steps, I managed to stay alive.

"But are you OK?" Emily asked.

The hostile's footsteps echoed through the house. From the changes in tone, I guessed he was running past the kitchen. Was he running away? He'd held the trigger down long enough to empty the magazine, but unlike movie-guns, real ones don't make a clicking noise when they're empty. There was no way to be sure without some ugly risks.

I took the stairs in three jumps and continued my chase to the living room, where the hostile tripped over something and tumbled behind a couch. His head popped up. I squeezed off a three-round burst only to see my darts stick in his balaclava. Instead of keeling over, he lifted his weapon and turned on me. I dove for cover in the kitchen.

I listened for any movement, any sound, that would tell me which direction he would take. He did the same thing. The house was so quiet the strain hurt my ears.

Emily's voice crackled in my ear. "Jacob? Was that gunfire? Omigod, omigod, omigod. Are you hurt?"

Lesson learned. Never let a *Post* reporter listen in live—no matter how pretty she is. She was supposed to report Highsmith's comments, but what seemed like a great idea when she'd batted her big brown eyes at me suddenly seemed like I-shoulda-known-better.

I tapped my earbud to end the call but it was too late. The other guy had heard the residual electronic squeak in the stillness. He fled. I heard the back door open. Either he was out of ammo, or he wanted me to think he was out of ammo. I ducked behind the breakfast bar, pulled my phone out, ended Emily's call, and clicked over to the open line with Carmen and Miguel.

"Jesus, Jacob," Carmen said. "If you'd kept the line open, we could've warned you."

"He went out back."

"Good. He's trapped back there, twenty-foot wall. He'll sneak around until he thinks we're gone. Want me to slash his tires?"

"No. I'll be out in a second. Did he come alone?"

"Yes," Carmen said. "He was in such a hurry he didn't see us. I put a tracker on his car when he went inside. Figured it was only fair since he put one on your Porsche."

I thanked god for Carmen.

I ran upstairs, flipped on the lights. The Secretary looked at me with glassy eyes. Blood ran out of his belly. Single entry wound, small caliber, through and through. I'd seen worse. I promised him some help and ran back downstairs, leaping over the two security guys I'd darted earlier. I gave my crew orders as I went. "Carmen, get the Secretary an ambulance. Miguel, jump in the Panamera and lead the hostile away."

Bursting into the street from the front door, I ran straight to Carmen's Passat and dove in while Miguel took off in my favorite bling ride, one of Ms. Sabel's many sports cars. Carmen and I shrank into the seats and waited with our thermal binoculars peeking above the windowsill.

After ten seconds, the hostile jumped the back gate and ran to a blue Chevy. He fired it up and took off after Miguel.

The hostile had planted a tracker under the Porsche's back bumper, an amateur move Carmen had undone while she waited. Carmen was the master of tracking devices. She'd glued her pencil-shaped tracker to the underside of his windshield wiper. She turned on her slate and waited for the tracking lights to register.

"How did he know we were here?" Carmen asked.

"What bothers me is the guy wore double layers to protect himself from our darts."

Per our unspoken plan, Miguel drove four blocks and tossed the tracker into some bushes. Carmen's slate showed the Chevy pulling to the curb seconds after Miguel was around the nearest corner. The shooter stopped to check his readings. After a few seconds, he drove up and down the street searching for us. It took him two whole minutes to figure out he'd been played. When he gave up and turned for home, Carmen fired up the VW and followed him.

Emily called. "Why did you hang up on me?"

"Because I wanted to live through the live-fire portion of the show," I said. "Emily, someone tried to kill the Secretary of State. You have a big scoop there, so write it. Your editor will go nuts. We're good here. I gotta go."

"Wait. Who are you chasing? Where are—"

I dropped her call and put her on auto-ignore.

Carmen smiled. "You should treat your women better, Jacob. She's going to write a nasty article about you some day."

"I can live through bad press. Bullet holes are little harder."

Carmen elbowed me.

We closed in on the would-be assassin.

"Why'd they shoot the Secretary?" Carmen asked. "That's bound to bring an investigation."

"None of these guys have trusted each other from the beginning. And they all have their own mercenaries. Douglas stabbed Nakdali in the back. McCarty stabbed Douglas in the back, now he wants *us* to stab Patterson in the back. And Patterson *shot* Caldwell in the back. When a bunch of ambitious guys turn desperate, anything can happen." I punched the dashboard. "It pisses me off that I knew that, planned for it, but they got away, and we still don't know who's responsible for Snare Drum."

"Hey, our guy pulled into a driveway up the street," Carmen said. "It looks familiar. Where are we, Tysons Corner?"

I examined her slate for a minute. "Whoa. Is that Fitzroy's house?"

CHAPTER 50

BY THE TIME MIGUEL CAUGHT up with us, Carmen had Fitzroy's guard hogtied. We dragged him behind the neighbor's hedge. I pounded my knee into his chest while she stuck her Glock up his nose. He held out for three seconds, then coughed up the tactical info we needed. Only one inside guard, and Mark never carried a gun. When we had what we needed, she darted him out of his misery.

We took our standard positions. Miguel covered my front door approach and Carmen covered the back.

The front door had two locks. Taking them apart would be too noisy. So I rang the doorbell.

The man who answered it had a balaclava in one hand that he'd just taken off, judging by his hair. One of my darts still dangled from it. His surprised reaction didn't include an exclamation because Miguel, ten yards behind me, put a dart in his eye. The man keeled over.

A yard deeper in the foyer stood Mark Fitzroy—looking like he'd just peed his pants.

"Have you prepared for the Second Coming of Christ?" I asked.

Mark turned to run. I jumped over his man's body and tackled him in the living room. Miguel was right behind me and shoved his muzzle in Mark's face. The three of us stayed motionless while Carmen came in the back door and cleared the kitchen. She moved on to clear the other rooms, calling them out as she went. I stood in front of Mark without saying a word until I heard the final all-clear from Carmen.

"Why did your man shoot the Secretary?" I asked.

He shook his head, then let it sag to his chest.

I stuck my finger under his chin and brought his head up. "I don't think you understand just how pissed off I am. Patterson's going to kill your ex-girlfriend. I'm trying to save her, but you took out the guy who could've named the head honcho in this deal. I'm running out of time." Punching him wouldn't solve anything, so I waited for him to look up at me.

Screw it. I pounded him with a right cross.

Carmen and Miguel formed an intimidating triangle with Mark at the center. Mark fell over like a loser giving up the fight. I dragged him to his feet. He glanced at me, then away.

He said, "The cops will be here any minute."

"I have nothing to hide," I said. "Your guy tried to kill the Secretary and I apprehended him. The cops are going to thank me. You and your attorneys can work your way through the slow wheels of justice later. But what I need to know—right now—is who you're working for."

"I'm not working for—"

Miguel slammed his rifle butt into the man's ribs.

"Every minute you lie to me Ms. Sabel comes closer to dying," I said. "Breaking a few ribs won't bother me in the least."

He glanced up again and made eye contact. He tried to stare me down but lost his nerve.

Several car doors closed outside.

We froze. Cops would come in with flashing lights, FBI would announce themselves; neither of those things was happening. That meant we had hostiles in the driveway. I reached in Mark's shirt pocket, pulled out his phone showing a live connection to 'Grampa' Fitzroy. Carmen and Miguel gave me a disappointed look that I deserved. But they're pros, the rebuke lasted a split second. With a glance and a nod at each other, we communicated our exit strategy.

Miguel zipped plasticuffs around Mark's ankles and tossed the guy over his shoulder. Carmen stood to the right of the front door and waited for my signal.

I yanked the door open and jumped behind it. From the front lawn, three weapons fired into the empty space where I'd stood a second earlier. Carmen reached her M4 around the doorframe and fired half her dart-magazine blindly into the street. I bolted into the dark with Miguel hot on our heels. Miguel fired three round bursts to the right, I fired to the left. Carmen ripped off a couple more as she brought up the rear.

Mark's head bounced off the C-pillar when Miguel tossed him in the back. I fired a few more bursts to keep the new arrivals pinned down as Carmen started the Passat. I still had one foot on the ground when she peeled out. The killers ran to their cars and came after us.

"Ready to talk, Mark?" I asked as we slid around the first turn. "Your guys don't stand a chance against us."

Sirens screamed a few blocks away. That was good news. The police would be our salvation if we could get back to them before Mark's people put rounds through our skulls. Carmen tried to find a route back to Mark's crib while driving too fast to check the map.

Mark turned to the side window. Miguel grabbed him and pounded his forehead into the seat in front of him. "Who do you work for?"

Washington's streets were laid out on a grid, but none of the suburbs were. Four right-hand turns in Tysons Corner was more likely to take you to West Virginia than around the block. Carmen swerved into, and back out of, a cul-de-sac, looking for a good route. Behind us, the killers' headlights gained ground. Carmen found a cross-over to get us halfway back and turned the corner on two wheels.

The first car chasing us blew the turn, but the second came around and picked up speed. A man leaned out the window.

"Down!" I yelled.

Our front and back windows exploded. Carmen's headrest spewed chunks of foam.

Miguel switched magazines to real bullets and popped back up. He fired three shots that hit their radiator and both headlights. They swerved into a parked car.

"What do you think of that, Mark?" I said over the wind-noise howling around us. "Your men are trying to kill you."

He looked at me with pathetic eyes. Then it dawned on me.

"Those guys don't work for you, do they?" I said. "Your grandfather has you running this operation—but he just ordered you killed when his men told him we were taking you to the cops. Wow. That's gotta be awkward."

"Hunter's Chief of Staff," Mark said.

SEELEY JAMES

I'm not the brightest guy in the world, it took me three seconds to process that one. "The President's Chief of Staff, Ron Bose, is behind all this? Does the President know?"

"I have no idea. All I know is, when Ron Bose calls, I send the guys out. No questions."

"They were going to kill the Secretary of State?"

"He was supposed to kill you both, make it look like a murder-suicide."

Miguel looked at me. "I don't get it. Why take such risks for a chief of staff?"

"Old Man Fitzroy's looking past Colorado," Carmen said. She glanced at Miguel in the mirror. "He wants the national franchise when the Feds legalize marijuana. Having the President in his pocket would land him some kind of sweet deal."

Mark dropped down as another set of headlights closed in on us. It was the car that had missed the first turn. They found us and opened fire. Back in the warzone, I never cared about stray bullets. Back home was different. Civilians slept in the houses lining the streets. I couldn't let a stray bullet from one of these assholes hurt an American. It was time to stop these clowns. I switched to a magazine of bullets, rose up and fired back, aiming for tires. We swept around a curve before I could hit anything significant. They came around the corner and opened up with weapons on full auto.

Real life is different from what you see on TV. When a bullet leaves the barrel of a gun, it's traveling at supersonic velocity. It will penetrate sheet metal and glass without much deflection from the original course. When Mark ducked, one of the bullets went right through the trunk, through the seatback, through the stuffing, and into his skull.

"Hey," Miguel said. "He's still breathing. Where's the nearest Emergency Room?"

CHAPTER 51

IT WAS JUST THE THREE of us in the ER waiting area: the detective, Carmen, and me. A nurse in blue scrubs came out from one room, glanced our way, and kept going. Like all hospitals, the place smelled of cleaning fluids and mechanically-filtered air. We waited in silence while the detective reviewed his notes, made tick marks, and muttered his disbelief.

Miguel joined us with a tray full of coffees and handed them out.

Carmen's phone buzzed, she turned away from us to read an incoming text.

"Thanks," the detective said. He raised his steaming cup and took a long, deep sniff. "Strong. I like that. So then, you tied up Fitzroy, but someone else shot him in the head. Now, why would I believe that one?"

I started to speak.

Carmen smacked my arm and headed for the exit. "Jacob, Patterson's on the move and has a twenty-mile head start."

"I've got to go," I said. "Call me tomorrow, after ballistics proves my story."

We ran to the parking lot, where a large sedan, an Audi S8, cut us off. Cousin Elmer, Mr. Sabel's car-wrangler, stepped out of the car. He tossed the keys to Miguel. "Since these guys wrecked the last two cars, you drive."

Cousin Elmer took the keys to the shot-up VW and the rear-ended Panamera and waved down a flatbed tow truck.

It was like being back in the Army, where the Taliban could blow a vehicle out from under you and the motor pool would bring you a replacement before you had your hearing back. The Army aimed to keep soldiers on duty, and in the line of fire, as efficiently as possible. Sabel

Security had the same agenda. The only difference was the new-car smell. Alan Sabel never kept a car long enough to lose the fragrance and the Army hadn't requisitioned a new vehicle since the late '80s.

I dialed up the Major, updated her, and joined her to a comm link with Carmen and Miguel.

"Bridgette called me directly with the latest," the Major said. "She identified the contractor who kidnapped Pia, Velox Deployment Services."

"Hell," Miguel said. "Those guys are doing black ops for State now?"

"She expects them to land in an hour," the Major said. "But she's still working on where."

"That's why we planted a tracker on Patterson," Carmen said.

"No need to brag, Carmen," the Major said. "I'm going on mute here; I'll continue to monitor you from the Ops Center."

From Tysons Corner, we hit the beltway and headed for Maryland.

Patterson's tracker showed him veering off I-495 onto Route 50 heading east toward the Chesapeake Bay. Miguel stepped up our speed as we crossed over the Potomac and into Maryland.

Carmen said, "We're being followed."

Miguel looked at me. "Who, Fitzroy's flunkies? They waited at the hospital?"

"Should've taken out their driver instead of the headlights," I said.

"What the hell, bro?" Miguel shot a glance my way. "You keep saying Pia doesn't want us killing people."

"Guys," Carmen said, "Patterson took the exit to Davidsonville, the 424."

She handed me her slate. I examined it and all the areas around it. Thirty miles east of Washington, the Chesapeake meanders through rural Maryland. Fingers of the brackish waters stretch between spits of land, throwing geography into a Mandelbrot set of infinite detail. Directionless roads break down into narrow feeder lanes that wander through wetlands, farm fields, and forests to waterfront homes or small docks. Patterson could be going anywhere in the warren of lanes around the hamlet of Davidsonville.

"Major, I need your help," I said on the comm link. She

acknowledged me. "Remember that list of CIA properties we used to find McCarty? I need to know any and all properties around Davidsonville."

"Agent Carter's on it now," she said. She had an offline discussion for a minute. "We found something. I'm sending the coordinates to Carmen's slate. What do you think?"

The display pinned a location about three miles southeast of Patterson. Zooming into street view, I checked out the location, a perfect open field of roughly thirty acres with four old sheds set back on a looping farm track. From any one of those sheds, a man could watch the approaches, direct his friends, and mislead his enemies as needed. I thanked the Ops Center team for their quick work.

"Give me a plan to shake the Fitzroys," Miguel said.

"Take the 301 south," I told Miguel. "A little short of four miles later, take Central Avenue."

Miguel floored the Audi. The big sedan growled and shot forward like it had a Lamborghini engine. Which it did. We came to the 301 exit in seconds. Only grabbing the dashboard with both hands stopped me from going through the windshield when he slammed on the brakes and took the exit ramp.

Behind us, the Chevy drifted across the gore point but made the turn. When we hit 110 mph, Miguel throttled back to let the Chevy catch up. They made the move to the left lane, attempting to pass. Miguel toyed with them, pushing the car's massive reserves just enough to keep them chasing. As we neared our second turn, they charged alongside. Miguel made his move, slamming on the brakes and diving into the cloverleaf exit from the 301 onto Central. The Chevy tried valiantly to make the turn behind us but slid sideways, drifting. It caught the rumble strips, tipped over, and rolled out of sight, slinging the sound of grinding steel-on-asphalt in every direction.

We followed Patuxent River Road at an alarming speed, then a series of winding farm lanes until we connected with the Mill Swamp Road. Carmen's tracking showed Patterson hanging around Davidsonville, at a Starbucks, about ten minutes away.

Just past our target site was a large horse stable. We parked there and hopped the fence into the CIA's farmyard.

We stood in the laurel bushes for a long time, listening. Silence echoed in our ears. Then an owl's hoot. Then silence again. The moon strained through high, thin clouds. Anyone with thermal or night-vision goggles would see us no matter what we did, so we took a quick pace across a field of recently mowed alfalfa. We stalked the nearest shed, spreading out as we neared. It was aluminum with a cement floor and a tripwire across the threshold that ran to a hand grenade. Quite the welcome mat. Otherwise, it was empty. Only the faint scent of diesel fuel—the constant residue of farm machinery—wafted through the space.

Across the way was another empty, booby-trapped shed. Closer to the woods, the third shed had nothing in it but boot prints tracking across the dirt floor and a great view of the first two. We had one shed left to clear. It was at the end of a single gravel track, two hundred yards away. Weathered wood, cracked in places, it was almost large enough to call a barn.

Carmen checked Patterson's location again. He was leaving the Starbucks and heading our way. We had five minutes to clear the last shed and set up our trap.

Miguel took the back, sneaking between maples and walnuts. Carmen took the left and hunkered down behind a wooden trough. The shed's big sliding door stood open and I slipped inside. My thermal binoculars scanned left. Nothing. Then right. Nothing. Then up.

He was in the loft, aiming an MK 20 at my nose.

For every thousand soldiers in the United States Army, there are nine hundred ninety-nine whose gallantry and bravery and dedication would bring tears of pride to any red-blooded American. The last one-in-a-thousand would make anyone cringe. If you lined up a thousand of those not-as-good soldiers, there'd be one of them who's so bad he'd turn the Dalai Lama into a death-penalty advocate. Looking down from the shed's loft was that worst-in-a-million-man: Shane Diabulus. I'd recognize him in any darkened building on any continent. He was a war exploiter, a racist, a mercenary, and a sexual predator with a lethal weapon in his hand.

Worst of all, he worked for Velox Deployment, a contractor so bad Halliburton canceled a merger with them.

Diabulus said, "Wazzup, Jacob?"

CHAPTER 52

STANDARD OPERATING PROCEDURE AT SABEL Security is to keep your earbud live at all times. Preferably with a teammate and not a reporter.

"You came alone?" I said. "You should know better."

"Aw, Jacob, you know better'n that," Diabulus said.

The shed smelled of straw and dirt and machinery. It also smelled of unwashed men. The kind of men who think bathing is what you do before you go to a whorehouse. Lights came on and a familiar face stepped out from behind a hay baler. A third man showed himself behind a combine that had tires as big as a car. From behind a big green tractor on my left came a noise, clothing against clothing, like someone struggling against someone else.

"They let you out of Fort Carson for good behavior?" I asked. "What have you been doing since, stealing cell phones from little kids?"

"I'd never trust a desk jockey to shake a tail," Diabulus said. "And now I've got you in my sights for the first time since you testified against me."

Carmen and Miguel would know it was Diabulus from that line and would do their own head count and threat assessment.

The guy with the familiar face on my right laughed. I knew that laugh, but it took me a second to remember who owned it. He was the man who once bragged about raping an Afghan woman. At the time, I'd lost my temper and cut him. I said, "Kasey, did your ear ever grow back?"

He sneered and turned his scar away from me.

Miguel's voice drifted quietly into my earbud. "On zero, make a loud noise."

"In case you're wondering—" I said looking up at Diabulus.

"Three… Two…" Miguel whispered.

"This thing is loaded." I rested the butt of my M4 on my hip as Miguel said the last positive integer. "See?"

Miguel didn't have to say "zero"; we fired at exactly the same time.

One of Diabulus's men fell to the floor. Diabulus couldn't see his man from the upper deck, but his tiny mind processed the sound of someone falling and he could see it wasn't me. Without waiting for him to figure it out, I dove to the right. Carmen stepped in the gap behind me. She fired a three round burst that sent Diabulus for cover.

Kasey opened fire. When a scum like him shoots, they tend to hold the trigger down and hope to hit something. He emptied a whole magazine blindly into the darkness outside while Diabulus shouted at him to stop.

Carmen fell to the ground with a pained shout.

Civilians think of Kevlar as a perfect shield against bullets. The truth is, it can stop a low-velocity bullet, and it can slow a high-velocity bullet, but the impact is significant either way. You'd be lucky to walk away with broken ribs from a direct hit.

Carmen had taken a direct hit. She'd had the wind knocked out of her and probably had a concussion from the fall. Broken ribs were a given. How many more injuries she had was something I'd have to check out later.

I put Kasey down with a dart and reported to Miguel. "Carmen's down. Second hostile down. Two still active."

The lights went out. Diabulus thought it gave him an advantage, but if there's one thing I know like the back of my hand, it's farm sheds. I lost my virginity in a farm shed. Several times.

Boots clambered down the loft's ladder in the dark.

Sheds never have a power switch in the loft. Nor would it be near the utility bay. That put Diabulus downstairs, on my right, and his man near the switch in the combine bay. I flipped my thermal into place and dropped to the ground. Beneath the combine on the far side of the shed were some feet. On the other side, behind the big green tractor, were four more feet. Rising to a crouch, I snuck behind the baler and took another look.

A pair of thermals looked back at me.

I spun back as the bullets shredded the baler's sheet metal. I kept the bulk of the machine's heavy internal workings between the shooter and me. For a moment, I listened to his feet shuffling along the ground. He was moving left.

Using the baler's tire as a ladder, I climbed to the top and squeezed into the small space between the baler and the loft above. The sheet metal buckled under my weight, shattering the quiet with an omnidirectional noise. He'd know I was moving without knowing where. My thermals showed a man below me, right where I expected. The tight space gave me an awkward firing position. I could point the gun but not sight down the barrel. I fired and missed.

Instead of shooting at me, my quarry fired at the opposite end of the shed where a couple boards had rotted out.

"Jesus Fucking Christ," Miguel shouted. He continued through a mix of deities and verbs long enough for me to drop the shooter. That left one guy with a hostage behind the tractor.

"Miguel, you hit?" I asked.

"Collarbone," he said. "Left arm."

He went back to his choice of expletives with a bit less volume.

I chanced a glance at Carmen. She was just regaining consciousness and tried to sit up. She made it to her elbows before the pain in her ribs put her back on the ground, writhing.

"Carmen, if you can hear me, stay down."

No response.

I slipped down as quietly as I could and dropped to the ground again. The four feet were still under the big green tractor. Two of the feet were moving to my right. I slid behind the combine's big tire and stood up. Calculating his speed and direction, I waited for the optimal surprise.

I spun from my hiding place and took a quick aim.

Diabulus stood stock still, holding a Beretta to someone's head. Thermal imaging won't deliver enough detail to see expressions, but I thought he was grinning.

"Put the gun down, Jacob," Diabulus said.

The Sabel trainers told me it took .25 seconds for the Inland Taipan snake venom in a Sabel Dart to produce flaccid paralysis. The Army taught me it takes .25 seconds to send a decision from the brain to the trigger finger. If he saw me pull the trigger, he had a good chance of responding by killing Ms. Sabel before the dart put him down. Very risky. But dropping my gun was not happening.

I pulled my trigger.

He pulled his.

CHAPTER 53

"GET AN AMBULANCE," I SAID and ran for the light switch.

"Did that when Carmen was hit," the Major said over the comm link. "You're in the middle of nowhere. Report."

Next to Diabulus was the body of a woman I'd never seen before with a hole in her head. She was older with thick black hair. A decoy hostage from Romania?

I ran to Carmen.

Her eyes were open. She reached up and grabbed my collar, pulled me close. "I heard them. That way." She flopped a hand outward, pointing at the shed down the lane. Her voice was weak but her mind was strong. "Go. We'll be OK."

I'd screwed up.

Diabulus set up a distraction to let someone else track back to the shed we'd already cleared. That meant they were handing off Ms. Sabel two hundred yards away. I hate it when someone beats me. Especially Diabulus.

Would Mercury, my long abandoned deity, have warned me about the trap? It was the kind of thing he whispered in my mind before I let chemistry wash him away.

I turned out the lights and checked my thermals. Heat signatures: two men struggled with a third person who was taller than either of them, and she was fighting as best she could with her hands cuffed behind her. As I watched, she head-butted one of them.

Only one woman in the world would fight like that.

I took off running.

Tracking through the brush as quickly as I could without making noise, I advanced from behind an oak. I scanned for other hostiles but could only find the two guys on my thermal system. They'd moved to the far side of a car outside the shed. She'd knocked down the one I figured was Patterson. She kicked the other guy in the balls.

They were lucky she had a bullet wound.

There was no clean shot so I peppered all three of them. One guy went down. Patterson ducked while wrestling Ms. Sabel into the back seat. He slammed the door and ducked again as I fired off a second burst of darts. With uncharacteristic courage, the weasel raised a gun above the trunk and fired off three rounds. I tried but couldn't get him in my sights and fired another burst out of frustration. Patterson duck walked behind the car and jumped in the driver's seat. At a dead run, I caught up in time to touch the truck but he was gone before I could jump on it.

The downed man must have been in charge. He had that craggy face and slight build of a twenty-year special ops soldier.

I sprinted back to Carmen and Miguel. Miguel had given up on European gods and was cursing in Navajo. He stopped when I was ten yards out and hurled the keys at me. "Bring her back, Jacob."

I ran to Carmen. She had her slate out of her pack and handed it to me without a word. They would have it no other way. My first priority was to save Ms. Sabel.

I sprinted across the alfalfa field for our car.

With Carmen's slate propped on the dashboard, I spewed gravel twenty yards behind me. By ignoring stoplights and other inconveniences, I hoped to catch Patterson before he made Davidsonville. But when I glanced at the slate, he wasn't going back the way he came. He was in Edgewater heading northeast across the bridge. I racked my brain to anticipate his destination. He was heading away from Washington toward Annapolis, the Severn River, Maryland's Eastern Shore, or maybe Baltimore, Delaware, or Philadelphia.

When I ripped around the corner onto Solomon's Island Road, it hit me. I pressed my earbud. "Major, did Patterson go to the Naval Academy?"

"Hang on," she said. In the background, her fingers clicked away on a keyboard. "Yes, and five years ago he taught a couple courses there."

"I think he's taking Ms. Sabel there. He knows the campus and must have some kind of plan. Can you get the county cops?"

"They set up a roadblock on the 50 at the Davidsonville exit," she said. "Half the squad cars on duty went out there, six miles west of you. The other half are heading for Diabulus. You're the closest one."

"How about Annapolis or Academy cops?"

"I'm calling," she said. "But it took me half an hour to convince the county, so don't wait for them."

Patterson had to be hitting 100 in his little Chevy. The tracker showed his dot veering north, several miles east of the roadblock. If I was right about his destination, he was taking the main entrance to the Academy, from the mall near the highway. The only way to cut him off was to fly through downtown Annapolis. That was a gamble. For all I knew, he could be heading to Baltimore.

I approached the decision point at 135 mph. At four in the morning, there was no one on the streets.

I went for the shortcut.

Crossing the bridge into Annapolis brought back warm memories and my mind began to wander. One of the best days of my life was the day I took Tania to see the Blue Angels at the Naval Academy Graduation. The jets screamed up the Severn River, roared over the spectators' heads at 700 mph, and flew in formation only eighteen inches apart. You line up to watch the show on the Academy's waterfront campus. No other airshow brings you as close to the jets as that one. But what made that day special was the time Tania and I spent together. We'd strolled Main Street and ate at the three-hundred-year-old Middleton Tavern. We knocked around the colonial town all day and into the evening. We were in love. It was the only time in my life I'd known what that meant. A few weeks after that wonderful day, I blew it.

I raced past darkened shops, resolved that if I lived to see the dawn, I'd do everything in my power to win Tania back.

Of course, if Ms. Sabel ever gave me a hint of encouragement, I'd have to go there instead. I mean, seriously, who could say no to an opportunity of her magnitude?

As my car howled down the narrow lanes, I wondered why I had such difficulty maintaining a serious relationship. Was it me?

A garbage truck backed into the street, forcing me onto the sidewalk where I clipped a newsstand and smacked a trash can. One day, just thinking about women was going to get me killed. I re-focused on more immediate problems.

I flew over the South River Bridge at criminal speeds and sluiced my way through a series of streets until I found Spa Road and turned toward the old part of town. I lost the passenger mirror to a parking meter with a startling *bang*. Two hundred years ago, the revolutionaries had paved the streets with bricks from Church Circle to the harbor. My wide tires sounded like a chainsaw as I buzzed over them. I screeched around the nation's oldest state capitol and tore down the last leg of my journey going the wrong way on a one-way street. At the bottom of the hill, I slammed on the brakes, threw it in a four-wheel drift, and turned a hard left up King George Street.

One pair of headlights headed toward me down the narrow road. Patterson. I floored it, entering the two-lane bridge before he got there.

Patterson charged toward me as if he were running for his life.

It made no sense. He showed no sign of slowing down. I realized he didn't know what car I was driving. He'd never seen the Audi's distinctive headlights. His paranoia must have overruled his logic, he feared I was behind him, bearing down with superior numbers and firepower.

I slid the big sedan sideways across the middle of the bridge. He accelerated, aiming for the gap between my front bumper and the bridge's outer barrier.

Leaping out, I jumped on the trunk of the car, my M4 in one hand and my Glock in the other. I slapped a mag of real bullets into my rifle. He was going too fast to kill him. If he lost control at that speed, he could flip the car into the Severn River and Ms. Sabel would drown if the impact didn't kill her first. I opted for Miguel's trick. A three-round burst blew out his radiator and one tire.

The space Patterson aimed for was narrower than the width of his car by a foot, but he was desperate enough to try anyway. The instant before the two cars collided, I jumped in the air and watched as the impact's momentum pushed both cars under and away from me.

A combined eight thousand pounds of American and German engineering assaulted each other like they were reenacting World War II. The front fenders touched first, condensing the crumple-zones and setting off airbags in both cars. Momentum carried them into the bridge's beautiful brickwork walkway where the Audi's front end merged with the Chevy's engine compartment. The windshield popped out and flew into the river.

Patterson's forward motion thrust the driver's seat into a rapidly collapsing space, a metal compactor formed by the Audi's midsection spinning into his car and crushing him against the bridge's low wall. When it stopped, the Chevy looked like a pie slice. The driver's seat was crushed between the Audi and the dashboard.

The steering wheel had decapitated Patterson. His head rolled slowly across the hood and fell into the river.

The smell of gasoline spilling from the wreckage hit my nose.

Ms. Sabel was still in there.

I bolted to the Chevy and climbed onto the trunk. The back window was shattered and spider-webbed but held together by the plastic sandwiched between the laminated layers of glass. I kicked out the safety glass, and hesitated before looking in the back seat.

I heard the ignition of gasoline at the other end of the wreck. Something had sparked the spreading fumes. I leaned in.

I could see Ms. Sabel folded in half and wedged between the two front seats.

CHAPTER 54

SHE MOVED A HAND AND a foot. Recalling a bit of battlefield medical training, I ran through the back-injury analysis. The last thing I wanted to do was cripple a world-class athlete.

An open flame lit up the night near the Audi's front end.

Crippling her was better than letting her burn alive. I could only grip one of her arms. I tugged hard enough to pull her shoulder to the window. Putting a foot on each side of the window frame, I wrapped my arms around her body and pulled with all my might. She came through enough to get a shoulder under her ribs.

The Audi exploded in a fireball at the same time I jumped off the Chevy's trunk. When I landed, the blast toppled me. I dropped Ms. Sabel and scrambled to get under her again.

She was not a small woman.

All that muscle was hard as steel and weighed as much. I staggered a few feet and felt her pushing with her good leg. That her leg worked was a relief. We staggered a few yards before I could get enough momentum to run. Light travels faster than heat or sound. I saw the light from the Chevy's explosion. The next nanosecond felt like an hour of anticipation, then the heat singed my back and the shock wave knocked us over. I pinned her beneath me.

The fireball rose in the air. We were peppered with searing chunks of broken glass and blistering bits of metal. Intense heat surrounded me for a split second before dissipating upward into the night sky. I stood her up and carried her close to a mid-bridge bench. Before sitting, she stopped, wrapped her arms around me, and squeezed me hard. It wasn't a love hug, it was a pain-passing-through-me hug. When the worst passed, she put out a hand and felt for the bench. She dropped onto it, unable to bend her wounded leg. She grabbed me, pulled me onto the bench and buried her face in my chest.

For a few minutes she sobbed, her fist clenching my chest, her other arm clamped around me.

I texted the Major our position and condition to avoid disrupting Ms. Sabel's privacy.

Sirens echoed around us.

She pulled herself together with a few sniffles and a long deep breath.

"Sorry. I've had a bad—" A wave of pain hit her again and she convulsed like someone was jolting her with a Taser. The athlete in her fought to maintain control and brought down her reactions to shudders after a few minutes. With a few more deep breaths, she pushed the nightmares she'd lived through out of her mind.

She started swearing using words that made Miguel sound like a five-year-old. But then, when a person has been shot in the thigh, kidnapped by government contractors, flown halfway across the globe, and tossed into the back seat of a car fleeing prosecution for all of the aforementioned crimes, some allowances can be granted for language.

Between curses, she told the first responders on the scene to leave her alone. The Major had an ambulance on the way to transport her to the Sabel Security Operations Center, where her personal physician waited in the company infirmary. The first cop on the scene and the paramedic talked up the benefits of the Anne Arundel Medical Center without changing her mind. They shook their heads and moved on to the wreckage. Then it was just the two of us again.

She pulled away with a self-conscious notice of our entwined arms and looked at me. Pain or no, the fire in those grey-green eyes never flickered. She was wide awake and ready to take on the world.

She said, "Why were you in the wrong barn?"

In seven words, she dashed my hope that Ms. Sabel's gratitude for saving her life might be expressed in the same way as Louisa's. I said, "Technically, it's a shed. A barn is where you keep valuables like soybeans, cattle, hay, that kind of thing. A shed is where you keep stuff out of the rain. They just *shed* the weather. Most often they don't have doors or—"

"Carmen and Miguel were wounded. I was nearly killed on that bridge. Why were my Sabel Security agents so far behind Vortex?"

"That's Velox Deployment Services. *Velox* is Latin for *rapid*, so it's like saying rapid deployment service—"

"Why did they kidnap an American citizen?"

"It's called 'extraordinary rendition' and is normally used to nab terrorists from—"

"You were supposed to make everyone understand I'm not a terrorist. What happened to that plan?"

I said, "We'd have to ask Ron Bose, the President's Chief of Staff."

"Snare Drum came from the White House?"

"That's what Mark Fitzroy told me." I savored the surprise on her face.

I brought her up to speed on her boyfriend's criminal career. As long as I was harping about Mark Fitzroy, I tossed in the man's Machiavellian grandfather and morally-challenged family just to make sure that even the second cousins were permanently off her dating list.

When I stopped talking, she was quiet and stared at a few Academy lights reflected in the water. She was about to say something nice, like *'good job, Jacob; guess you're not a total waste of humanity after all'*, when her ambulance arrived.

The crew pushed me aside and positioned her on their gurney. Aluminum tubes clicked into place and straps gently secured her. They rolled the gurney to the ambulance and snapped it into the back with precise movements.

The ambulance whisked us toward Gaithersburg in great time. They made me ride in front so the paramedic could sit with Ms. Sabel and relay her vital signs to the staff at the infirmary. That was probably a good thing since she was in a mood to blame me for everything.

Our intimate moment on the bridge was a beautiful, special moment for me. Not so much for her. Most women saw me as a weekend fling easily discarded on Monday. Ms. Sabel didn't even see the Friday night possibilities. There was a time when I found my disposability convenient, but those days were waning fast. I longed for a permanent relationship with someone special. Peering back into the ambulance at

Ms. Sabel, I realized it was time to give up on her as a fantasy relationship. How she felt about me was a mystery, but it sure wasn't romantic.

I went back to my earlier decision. Right after the Napa Valley trip with Bridgette, and after however many dinners I could get out of Louisa before she blew me off, I would do whatever it took to win Tania back. From then on, my world would revolve around Tania.

AT THE OPS CENTER, THE Major ushered me into our NSA-proof room. Half an acre of dark gray concrete made up the ceiling, floors, and walls. In the center of the sparse room was a glass table with four Aeron chairs on either side and one at each end. McCarty sat there alone, lit by three bare halogen bulbs dangling by single wires from the high ceiling.

Neither the Major nor McCarty spoke. They seemed to be waiting for something. I took one of the chairs opposite McCarty, put my forearms on the table, and looked around.

McCarty looked like a man who'd had his spleen removed with an oyster fork.

"Patterson's dead," I said.

McCarty nodded and leaned back, his hands flat on the table, his gaze on his hands.

"Where's Agent Verges?" I asked the Major.

She paced a small area behind me, her heels clicking on the bare concrete. "Pulled."

McCarty slipped me a sympathetic grin.

I twisted a glance over my shoulder at the Major. "Pulled?"

"FBI Counterintelligence took over the investigation."

"Counterintelligence," I said. "Where are they?"

"Investigating. I guess."

I looked at McCarty. "Does this mean you still have blackmail material?"

"No," McCarty said. "I've asked Jonelle for some help."

"Jonelle?" I said. "First name basis with the Major?"

"It's OK," she said. "If you have questions for him, now's your chance."

She stood with her back to us, arms folded tight across her chest. Her gray business skirt and jacket had twenty-four hours' worth of creases, but she still looked sharp and in-charge. A faint trace of her orange blossom perfume hung in the otherwise sterile air.

"Why were you and Patterson so intent on killing Ms. Sabel?" I asked.

"HVT," he said, exhaling slowly. "What's the first thing you do in battle?"

"Take out the high-value target. You knew she'd be relentless, you mentioned that. If that was the case, why try? Why not leave her alone?"

"We weren't baking cookies, Jacob. Snare Drum alone is a capital offense. But when she finds out I supervised her parents' murders—" He shuddered. "I'd rather not face that."

"What about Patterson? Where was he going?"

"Oddly enough, the Naval Academy teaches their students to sail. Annapolis is on the water. My guess, he was planning to dump her body in the Chesapeake using a boat with a thousand people's fingerprints on it."

"Why bother?" I said. "He was finished anyway."

"He was protecting someone higher up. Even though Snare Drum was a compromised operation and his career was over, he wanted to leave his bosses out of it and save the country the embarrassment. It would appear he succeeded."

"We already know Ron Bose masterminded the project."

"Bose?" McCarty said. "I'll be damned. That's higher up than I thought. No wonder Patterson was going to extraordinary lengths."

"You didn't know?"

"Like you, I'm a good soldier. Does it matter if an order came from the President or a lieutenant? Of course not. You execute your orders."

"Wait a second," I said. "Back up. You said Patterson succeeded? He's dead and we have Ron Bose cold."

"You have nothing."

"We have tons. We have Nakdali, the laptop, the hard drives, the testimony of the children. We have enough evidence to—"

"My boy, you have enough evidence to post a conspiracy theory on an obscure website and turn into one of those whack jobs no one listens to."

"What do you mean?" When he didn't answer, I looked at the Major. She kept her back to me.

Alan Sabel strode into the room. I'd met him twice in my career. He was built like a linebacker with a gregarious personality and an infectious charm. He exuded positive energy that filled the space around him everywhere he went. He commanded the room's attention the instant he entered. He had a quick, genuine smile and his eyes sparkled when he spoke to you. Everyone loved him. He left you no option.

At least, that was the case every other time I'd met him.

He marched straight to the table, his eyes hard on McCarty. His blue suit shimmered as he approached the light circle. In one hand he held a shiny Desert Eagle. He set the gun on the glass table and slid it to McCarty.

They looked at each other for a full second without saying a word. McCarty nodded and stared at the weapon, his hands still flat on the table.

Alan Sabel took the chair next to me and swiveled his back to McCarty. "Thank you for saving Pia's life, Jacob. I am deeply in your debt. I've asked the Major to give you a significant bonus. I trust you'll spend it well. Tell me something—did Patterson suffer?"

In order to speak to Mr. Sabel, I had to turn away from McCarty, but I kept the Desert Eagle in my peripheral vision. "Not in the physical sense, sir."

"What do you mean?"

"I'm sure his conscience was bothering him for a long time before he died."

The conversation made me uncomfortable. I'd spent a lot of time with my brothers-in-arms talking about combat killings and retribution and who deserved what, but I'd never heard a tone of voice quite as cold as Alan Sabel's. He sounded too comfortable with the concept of death and dying, as if it were another business transaction to be analyzed and considered. I turned to look at the Major. She still had her back to me.

Alan Sabel smiled weakly at her. As if she felt his gaze, she glanced at him over her shoulder. A muscle in her cheek twitched.

"You have a philosopher on staff," Alan said. His booming voice was at half its usual strength and yet echoed off the bare walls. It lightened the somber mood. He slapped my knee. "And a damn fine agent too."

I heard the scrape of metal on glass. McCarty picked up the pistol.

I didn't have time to scold myself for allowing Alan to put our lives in jeopardy by putting a loaded weapon into the hands of an unrepentant killer. Instead, I calculated the best way to save both the Major and Alan before the impending gunshot. In a quarter second, I ran six scenarios through my head. None of those scenarios saved both of them from certain death. I froze with indecision.

Then it came. Due to the nature of a concrete box, it was the loudest gunshot I'd heard since Patterson killed Caldwell.

CHAPTER 55

WHILE MY CENTRAL NERVOUS SYSTEM took a rapid inventory of my body, analyzing every nerve ending for bullet holes, Alan rose and tapped my shoulder. I stood with him, my eyes locked on his.

"I never liked this room," Alan's voice boomed with its normal energy and enthusiasm. "It's an overreaction to electronic snooping if you ask me. Let's go across the hall, shall we?"

He was a hard man to resist. I wanted to scream, but I tightened up and locked down any stray emotions. The Major didn't move.

Alan put a thoughtful hand on her back. "C'mon, Jonelle. Let the cops do their thing before the facilities people clean up."

The three of us walked out without looking back. The meeting room across the hall had a teak table, whiteboards, bright lights, a large video display, and carpeting that silenced the Major's clicking heels when she entered.

I slumped into the first chair I found. The exhaustion of the mission was taking its toll. There are only so many Provigils you can take before you need to sleep. And there are only so many suicides you can witness before you lose your mind. The Major paced the room, arms still wrapped around her ribs. Alan went to the credenza and poured a glass of water.

"Why did he do that?" I asked.

"How are Carmen and Miguel?" Alan asked. "They performed above and beyond the call of duty on this operation."

My preoccupied mind delayed my answer. "I don't know. But, McCarty—"

"Miguel is out of surgery and expected to recover in several weeks." The Major stopped pacing and looked at Alan. "Carmen is in better shape, a concussion, four broken ribs, and a broken clavicle."

"Well," Alan said. "Alive then. That's great news."

Some time ago I'd read the book, *The Psychopath Test*, which found that a small degree of psychopathy was evident in strong leaders, but Alan Sabel's reaction to McCarty's suicide had me rethinking my assessment of the man everyone loved.

"Why did you give him a loaded gun?" I asked.

The Major's face snapped my way, her eyes sharply focused on me.

"It was his gun," Alan said. "We don't steal a man's belongings."

"Jesus, the man committed suicide," I said. "Doesn't that deserve a comment at least?"

"The son-of-a-bitch was as good as dead anyway," Alan said hot and loud. "The list of felonies he committed was endless. He did the world a favor, saved the taxpayers the expense of putting him on trial. Besides, he was the one who ordered the execution of my friends, Pia's natural parents."

I felt a shiver run down my spine.

His answer didn't feel right at all. He studied me as I absorbed his words. His face strained red and the tendons on his neck pulsed. He was an inch from blowing up at me, an effective intimidation method. My mind raced through a tangle of questions that I couldn't straighten out, so I backed down for the moment.

"What did McCarty mean, we don't have anything?" I said.

Alan rose. He nodded at the Major, slipped a phone from his jacket, and made a call.

"Everything's been coded Top Secret by the Director of National Intelligence," the Major said. "All the evidence has been secured by FBI Counterintelligence."

We stared at each other for a full minute while I digested that information. "You mean they've buried the whole thing?"

She nodded.

"They can't cover up the children," I said. "They're safe back in India. We—"

"They only came into contact with Syrians."

"What about—" Then it dawned on me. "They sent in

Counterintelligence to make it look like they busted a Syrian spy ring. Anything that comes to light, they label as part of Nakdali's evil plan working on behalf of Assad or al Qaeda."

The Major touched her finger to her nose and returned to her pacing. The scowl on her face creased deeper.

"What about Diabulus? He kidnapped Ms. Sabel. That can't be legal no matter who signed it."

"They classified the rendition order along with everything else. Anne Arundel County cops went home when Counterintelligence showed up. We were lucky to get Carmen and Miguel to a hospital before they were mopped up by the cleaning crew. When our team went back later, the place was spotless. Patterson's accident was tragic—but just an accident. And, as I'm sure you noticed, McCarty didn't leave a note."

My elbows hit the table as my head fell into my hands. "Can this really happen?"

Beyond us, Alan Sabel finished his call in a terse voice. "Madam President, we will be there. But I'm bringing Agent Jacob and Pia anyway." When he clicked off, his face was red and his eyes bulged. "Goddamn that bitch. I paid good money to put her in the Oval Office and she put off meeting us for an hour. Unbelievable."

He sank into a chair, leaned forward, his elbows on his knees, and stared at the carpet.

"Why did you let our only witness commit suicide?" I asked.

Alan looked up quickly, the Major gasped.

"Watch yourself, Jacob," he said.

"With all due respect, sir, you handed him a loaded weapon. Why? Are you helping Counterintelligence sterilize the attempted murder of your daughter?"

"Jacob!" the Major shouted. "You have no right to accuse—"

"I put my life on the line for Pia Sabel, not either of you."

Alan held a hand up to the Major but never took his eyes off me. "It's OK, Jonelle. He earned the right to ask some questions." He paused. "The way I saw it, he had it coming. Frankly, I didn't consider the witness angle."

Executives of his caliber consider all the angles as far as I knew.

Either he had missed it, or he was ten angles ahead of me.

"Did he ask you for his gun?" I asked.

"The only time I saw the man was with you."

Cute answer, but there were many ways to communicate with someone besides speaking to them. I looked at the Major. She paced with her eyes sweeping the floor.

I turned back to Alan. "Sir, could I ask you a question about Ms. Sabel's parents?"

He looked up at me as if I were the guy who'd murdered them.

I said, "McCarty told me he had orders to execute Ms. Sabel's parents twenty years ago."

Alan didn't say anything.

"He also said Ms. Sabel killed one of the attackers."

He continued to stare at me with a blank, unreadable face.

"You aren't shocked," I said. "You knew that."

He didn't say anything, but then I hadn't asked anything.

I said, "Do you know why they were killed?"

He leaned back in his chair, stretched out one hand and tapped his index finger on the tabletop. I let the question hang there, prepared to wait until hell froze over for his answer. From across the room, the Major stopped pacing and watched Alan, with an occasional glance my way.

Finally he spoke. "If they knew something that got them killed, would you want to know what they knew?"

"Do *you* know what it was?"

"No." He never broke eye contact. He didn't even blink. "The killers weren't trying to find or take something. They destroyed a hard drive and killed her parents for having it. They didn't take the drive. I've pondered that for years. It means either they didn't want to get caught with incriminating evidence or they knew what was on it. I don't know what was on it."

"You have some ideas."

"I was working on my MBA at Georgetown. They were neighbors, a nice, unmarried couple with a love child. She was an athlete, a shoo-in for gold in the 400 meters. He was a physicist working toward his PhD in electrochemistry. I babysat for them once in a while to get away from the noisy group home I lived in." He looked at the Major, then checked his finger tapping on the table, and sat up straight. "After twenty years of wondering about it, the only thing I've figured out is that I don't know a thing about electrochemistry."

Doc Günter, the Sabels' personal physician, stuck his head in the room. "Alan, I have her ambulatory, but she could tear out the stitches, or damage her leg, or—"

"I can't stop Pia," Alan laughed.

The Major shot him an angry look. He went quiet and looked up at the door behind me.

Ms. Sabel hobbled into the room on one crutch while finishing a conversation with a police officer across the hall. Gingerly, she sat in the chair next to me and put a hand on mine. She said, "I'm sorry for snapping at you earlier."

Her face had a soft, sweet look. Genuine remorse is nothing you can fake.

"I'm the one who put everyone in danger," she said. "Safwan was killed, the Primar was wounded. The pilots. Tony. Several innocent people in the Azores were shot by the Syrians." Her voice trailed off and so did her gaze. She stared into space, thinking about something with her eyes narrowed and her cheeks hard. "But I can't feel guilty because the real blame lies in the White House."

Her muscles flexed under her spandex. Tension oozed from her pores. She wasn't happy about missing McCarty, but at least she wasn't blaming me.

"You did the right thing," I said. "Those children are home with their parents."

She patted my knee and gave me a forced smile.

She glanced over her shoulder at the Major. "McCarty, Patterson, and Caldwell are all dead. Is Nakdali still safe?"

"He was stabbed by an inmate this morning," the Major said.

Ms. Sabel nodded with heavy, sad eyes and rose with pain in her expression, and found her balance with the crutch. She faced her father. "Did you do it?"

CHAPTER 56

OUR LIMO TURNED INTO THE Eisenhower Executive Office Building from Pennsylvania Avenue and waited while the dogs sniffed for bombs. When we parked, I hopped out and held the door for Ms. Sabel.

Alan Sabel came out first.

"Why here and not the White House?" I asked.

Alan said, "President Hunter doesn't want the press to see Pia arriving on crutches. They'd ask too many questions."

Ms. Sabel stepped out and looked around. Considering we only had fifteen minutes to clean up and change before the meeting, she looked great. Her thick, wavy hair flowed as she walked. Her tastefully short skirt suit showed off one muscular leg and one large bandage.

I wore slacks and a polo shirt. An outfit far too casual for a presidential meeting but I hadn't been home for laundry in a while.

After clearing the metal detectors, Ms. Sabel led us through the building, expertly hobbling on her crutch. Mr. Sabel came next. I hung back, uncertain why I was there and barely keeping up. I'd never met a president before. I wasn't intimidated, I just didn't know things. Like how to address her, or if I *should* address her, or if I was allowed to shake hands, or why my palms were sweaty.

I offered Ms. Sabel my arm to help her up the stairs but earned a glare.

"Listen, Jacob," Alan said. "I invited you as a material witness to identify Pia's kidnappers. I will let you know when to speak."

"That's not accurate," Ms. Sabel said. "I asked the Major to make sure Dad included you. I want you here for moral support as well as your testimony." She gave me a smile that made my heart race. Then she scowled at her father. "Sometimes Dad forgets it's my company."

A Secret Service agent greeted us when we reached the upper floor and opened the double doors to the Indian Treaty Room. Inside was an immense space with the most amazing panels, moldings, ceiling, and tiled floor I've ever seen. A balcony overlooked the main room with an incredible wrought iron railing. A gilded Greek god looked down from the cornice above the entrance.

The only thing the room didn't have was a president.

After a long wait in which Alan Sabel reminded his daughter to behave herself, two Secret Service agents appeared and double checked the room. One of them said something into an invisible comm link.

The doors flew open. President Veronica Lodge Hunter strode straight toward Alan Sabel with a big fake smile and an extended hand. "Alan, how good to see you again. I wish it were under happier circumstances."

"Drop the fake pleasantries." Ms. Sabel intercepted the President three steps before reaching Alan. "We know what you did. I uncovered your whole operation. You're responsible for child molesting on an unimaginable scale—"

"I understand you're upset, Pia." The President sounded like a kindergarten teacher calming a child. "But don't pen your own version of *J'accuse* until all the facts are in."

"I've been wounded, tortured, beaten, and kidnapped, accused of terrorism—"

"It must've been dreadful, I'm sure—"

"And all those people worked for you."

"My dear, four and a half *million* people work for me. Statistically speaking, some of them are bound to be misguided on a rare occasion. But don't destroy the hard work of so many patriots who protect this country just because of one isolated incident that unfortunately involved you. When you make such rash accusations, you discolor the great sacrifices our veterans make every day. Take your, um, friend Jacob as an example. Don't destroy his exemplary service record by making unfounded claims about the government he so proudly served."

Destroy *my* record? Unfounded claims? Alan gripped my arm as I started forward, ready to leap on Hunter. Deferring to him for the moment, I kept quiet.

"You're right," Alan said and stepped forward with a sharp glance at his daughter. "Pia's veered off script here. We came here to find those responsible for Pia's ordeal and bring them to justice."

Pia wheeled on him. "We know damn well who—"

He cut her off with the same stern look my father often used.

Ms. Sabel's muscles rippled and twitched but she said nothing.

"Pia, you should be proud of your accomplishments," the President said. "You've done a great thing for your country. You've exposed a despicable Syrian group and dismantled their whole operation. Now that I think about it, we should give you the Medal of Freedom. Yes. I'll look into it right—"

"Your Chief of Staff orchestrated the whole thing," Ms. Sabel said. "Right from your office. Are you saying Ron Bose made those decisions without talking to you?"

"Impossible. Ron would never touch such a thing. At worst, we had a couple men who went rogue—"

"I have McCarty's phone," Ms. Sabel said. "He had several conversations with Don Patterson. If you dig out the records for Patterson's phone, you'll find it ties directly to Ron Bose."

"Fine. Turn over the evidence and I'll see that it's fully investigated." Veronica Hunter slowed her cadence. "Can I assume McCarty will testify to this?"

Ms. Sabel leaned back. "Uh. No."

"Oh?"

"He committed suicide this morning."

"How awful. Where did this happen?"

Ms. Sabel said nothing.

"At Sabel Security Ops Center," Alan said.

I snapped a look at the man. His face was blank.

"Your main witness killed himself in your custody?" The President shook her head. "How awkward."

Ms. Sabel rubbed her furrowed brow. "Look. It's not like—"

The President stepped around Ms. Sabel and extended her hand again. "Alan, as I said, it is good to see you. How are my agencies treating you?

Are your companies getting the proper federal contracts allotted to them? Do I need to call someone?"

Alan grinned, took her hand, and patted her shoulder. "It's good to see you too, Veronica. Sorry I couldn't make it to the State dinner last week. I hear Queen Elizabeth had a few too many drinks. Now that must've been something to see."

Ms. Sabel stepped to the President. "Don Patterson tried to kill me."

The President said, "Who?"

"Donald F. Patterson. One of your appointees. He stood by while Sam Caldwell tortured me, then he tried to kill me himself. Ron Bose connected with him several times. He was also in contact with Velox Deployment, the people who kidnapped me in front of half the population of Romania. I have a ton of evidence stacked against you."

Veronica Hunter's face grew red. "An incoming president has many people eager to get noticed. If Mr. Patterson did the terrible things you say, I'm sorry to hear it. But if he did anything, he did it on his own."

Ms. Sabel stepped close and towered over President Hunter. "Is that how you remember Kipling's poem? *If you can keep your head by blaming all those around you?*"

"Pia!" Alan said. "You're addressing the leader of the free world. Show—"

"Respect? She had me tortured and—"

"We don't know that for sure." Alan motioned for her to calm down. "We only have Fitzroy's word that Patterson was working for Bose." He turned to Hunter. "Veronica, I apologize for Pia's outburst. This ordeal's been very stressful—"

Pia faced the President. "You and I both know who did this."

This was no cat fight, it was a tiger fight. The President looked ready to claw through Ms. Sabel. Two women cut from the same cloth, separated by three decades and miles of morality.

"You don't have any witnesses and you don't have any evidence because your accusations simply are not true."

"Wait a minute," I said. "What about the Fitzroys shooting your Secretary of State?"

Alan glared at me. I ignored him. I had just as much right to be pissed off as any billionaire in the room.

"Secretary Highsmith is recuperating from testicular surgery." President Hunter looked genuinely puzzled by my outburst. If it was an act, she could've put Meryl Streep to shame. "Have the decency to allow the man some privacy for his medical condition."

I considered explaining what I'd witnessed but decided the details might incriminate me. What was I doing at Highsmith's place? Oh, just a little breaking and entering, intimidating a federal employee, drugging security guards. Stuff like that.

"I apologize, Veronica," Alan said. "We've gone pretty far off track here. We're taking up too much of your time."

The President stepped back. "The government has to do many things to keep the country safe, Pia. There are many departments within the government, and they're all doing what they think best. If one of them went too far, they will be reprimanded. But the results are undeniable. My administration keeps the country safe. There have been no attacks since I took office. Those are the results the voters expected when they voted for me, and I have delivered."

"Then tell them *how* you deliver those results."

"I'm not the first president to make tough choices, Pia. Years ago, the voters didn't just elect a president who allowed torture, they re-elected him." Hunter gestured toward the door. "There is nothing in this to concern you. We're done here."

With the tension mounting, Ms. Sabel looked ready to punch out the President. Just beyond me, one of the two Secret Service agents tensed. He was planning to shoot first. Not a good thing for my job security. I made a mental plan to tackle the boss in case she lost her temper.

Alan Sabel put a hand on his daughter's shoulder and gave her a gentle tug. She shook him off, gave Hunter a look that said, *this ain't over*, and stormed toward the exit as best she could on a crutch.

The President asked, "Alan, did Sabel Satellite ever get the radio spectrum you wanted?"

Alan gave Hunter a glare of his own. "You're overdue on that score."

He turned and followed Pia.

After a moment's hesitation, I realized I was alone with President

Hunter. She looked me up and down. I patted my thighs, shrugged, and took off after the Sabels.

The instant the limo door closed on us, Alan gave me the same glare he'd given the President. "If I ever invite you to a meeting again, don't speak until spoken to. Got it?"

"Dad, he works for me." Ms. Sabel faced me. "Anytime you have something to say, speak your mind. You asked a good question back there and now we have an answer."

I mulled that one as the limo eased into traffic. What answer we had was beyond me, but damned if I was going to make a fool of myself by asking.

Ms. Sabel read the confusion on my face. "First, she didn't ask who the Fitzroys are. And second, she didn't know Ron Bose ordered the Fitzroys to kill Highsmith."

After an uncomfortable mile, Ms. Sabel spoke in a quiet voice. "She tried to have me killed, Dad. That doesn't bother you?"

"Of course. But, she was unsuccessful. You know the adage, keep your friends close and your enemies closer. Pia, to be effective in business, shake off the setbacks and keep focused. Like a shark, always move forward, never waste cycles on retribution."

Ms. Sabel looked at him until he shrugged.

Alan Sabel turned on his famous charm that lit up the limo like he'd brought in a New Year's Eve party. "Let's look at the positives. You saved a whole lot of children from exploitation and fired a warning shot across Veronica's bow. You've done more to clean up her administration in the last three weeks than anyone has in years. You can count this whole affair as a win, Pia."

"She's guilty."

"Let it go. Revenge is a waste of time. And a waste of time is bad for—"

"Business. I'll take care of it."

Alan looked her over while she watched Dupont Circle pass by outside. "Does that mean you'll let it go?"

Ms. Sabel stared at her father until he looked at his cufflinks and tugged them straight. They were silent for a long time. She turned back to the window.

A mile later, she said, "What was that President Hunter said about spectrum?"

"If the government allocates more radio spectrum to Sabel Satellite," Alan said, "we could provide high-speed internet to the entire country, urban and rural. Our application's been held up for a decade in favor of the cable companies. When Veronica asked me to support her campaign, she and I had a clear understanding about those allocations. Damn clear."

My eyebrows rose to my hairline.

Alan shot me a disdainful look. "Jacob, don't look so surprised that your government's for sale. What should shock you is how cheap it is." He huffed and straightened the crease in his slacks. "Twenty million for a candidate is nothing—hell, the revenue potential is north of fifteen billion."

Business and politics are complicated worlds. I like the Army. You shoot the bad guys. Then you go home.

No compromises with people who want to kill your daughter.

In the glass, I saw Ms. Sabel's reflection. Tendons in her jaw flexed as she thought. She looked like a wild animal poised for a deadly fight of slashing claws and snapping teeth. Part of me wanted to run away and part of me felt the urge to get in close.

As I watched her reflection, I knew I had a decision to make. I could re-enlist and take down the next wave of Hajjis in some god-forsaken part of Central Asia. Or I could dig out that culinary degree and sauté up some trout. On the other hand, I could stay on Ms. Sabel's right flank, duck the incoming rounds, and fire back at will.

Ms. Sabel dialed the Major. "Do we have any government contracts? Then get out of them as soon as possible. I need to be clear of President Hunter's reach. Tomorrow."

That did it for me. I was in. All the way in.

The End

A note from your author

I hope you enjoyed the story and will join my VIP Readers by signing up at SeeleyJames.com/VIP. I hold a drawing every month for things like Kindles and coffee mugs, plus I give you the inside scoop on things like how certain characters were named; which Shakespeare soliloquies I ~~plagiarized~~ drew from; what I'm working on next, etc. If you didn't enjoy it, don't let the door hit you ... I mean, that's OK, sometimes the magic works and sometimes it doesn't.

If you found any errors, or just want to chat, please email me at seeley@ seeleyjames.com or join me on Facbook, SeeleyJamesAuth.

EXCERPTS FROM SABEL SECURITY SERIES:

ELEMENT 42, SABEL SECURITY #1

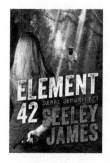

The voice in my head returned when I stopped taking my meds. My caseworker said the voice was part of my condition—PTSD-induced schizophrenia—but I call him Mercury, the winged messenger of the gods, and a damn good friend. For years, he was my biggest ally in combat and helped me predict the future. I'm not talking about very far into the future. Sometimes minutes, sometimes seconds, and sometimes just enough to see it coming. Mercury would draw my attention to small changes in air density, the faint sounds of rustling cloth, or the weak electrical charge of someone lurking nearby.

He saved my ass more than once and, as is always the case with gods, there were those who believed and those who didn't. Believers fought and lived and died beside me without ever disrespecting Mercury. Non-believers sent me in for evaluations. My docs didn't believe in gods, they believed in meds. They told me they were smarter than my abandoned deity, so I took their advice until one day everything went wrong and good people died.

I was resting in a dark jungle when I reaffirmed my faith in that ancient divinity. Prama, the hotel owner, was drawing lazy circles on my chest with her finger when Mercury spoke to me in a voice loud and clear and slightly panicked.

Mercury said, *Dude, you better think about your future real fast cuz it's coming. Can you hear it?*

I raised my ear off the sweaty pillow and listened to the noises coming from a ways down the road. Tin doors squeaked open, truck springs creaked, boots hit the ground, voices issued commands. It wasn't hard to predict the future. Sixty seconds from now at the hotel up the lane, soldiers would throw doors open, drag sleepy eco-tourists from warm beds, shove them against the wall, push a photo in front of them, and bark in whatever tribal dialect they speak in that corner of Borneo, "Have you seen this American?"

They were searching for the perpetrator of something.

I hadn't perpetrated anything, but I was pretty sure I knew who had.

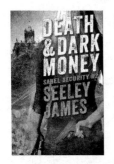

DEATH AND DARK MONEY, SABEL SECURITY #2

Sixteen minutes before David Gottleib died, I was alarmed that a nearly-naked black man leaned against my refrigerator with a casual grin. It wasn't because he was tall with supernaturally chiseled muscles. Nor was it the lone fig leaf he sported over his substantial manhood. It wasn't the leather sandals or the bronze helmet with small bronze wings either. What alarmed me was that I could see him at all.

No one can see a god.

At least, no one with a shred of sanity left.

The baking sheet in my hand fell to the stove top.

I closed my eyes and wished he would go away.

Behind me, Bianca kept talking. "So, I appreciate that you invited me over for dinner, Jacob. I'm flattered, actually. Um. But there's something I think we should discuss before you open that bottle of wine. You know what I mean? Like. We should have a clear understanding of … expectations. You know? Right? Jacob?"

I couldn't take my eyes off him. He looked like Will Smith from his Fresh Prince days. My brain dialed up an instant replay of my last session with my psychiatrist. He told me, "Remember, you're only in trouble if you hear more than two voices talking at the same time or if you see someone who's not there. Either of those things happens, restart your medication and call me right away."

"Jacob?" Bianca's voice drifted to my ears from a million miles away even though she was sitting at my in-kitchen table. "Are you OK?"

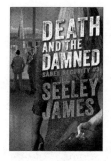

DEATH AND THE DAMNED, SABEL SECURITY #3

Who to trust is the scariest decision we make in life. I grabbed him by the hair, pulled his head back, and, cheek-to-cheek, we contemplated the sparkling stars dotting the moonless Syrian sky. I sensed his eyeballs strain all the way to the right to look at me. His fingernails dug into my forearm. Anxiety caused him to miss the grandeur of the moment. Too bad. It was stunningly beautiful. You don't see that many stars from over-lit American cities. But I tired of our two-second relationship and drew my blade across his throat, severing his carotid artery and larynx before he could scream a warning to the others. I dropped his carcass on the other jihadi at my feet. He trusted me because I speak Arabic. Bad idea.

I stared at the dead fighters and thought about how ISIL's perversion of Islam wasted so many lives.

But then, I'm hardly the guy to judge other people's religious beliefs.

Mercury, winged messenger of the Roman gods, waved to me from the narrow, dusty village lane. *Earth to Jacob. Ain't the time for contemplative yoga, dawg. That monster raped three women yesterday. C'mon now. Get your head in the game. You need to find that cowboy.*

After a decade guiding me through battles as a disembodied voice in my head, Mercury decided to make himself manifest. Some people would consider meeting god in person as a divine miracle. Others would encourage me to go back on my meds. Maybe I had taken a swan dive off the sanity cliff, but when I ponder how lucky I am to have god on my side—even if he's been surviving on unemployment benefits since the late fourth century—I count my blessings. And when he tells me to keep my eyes open for a cowboy in an ISIL-held Syrian town, I listen.

I clicked my comm link open and queried my mission teammates, scattered around the houses we were about to invade. "Anyone see a cowboy?"

The president, a billionaire, and a disgraced FBI agent were talking about disrupting democracy with the casual air you and I might use to pick a movie. It made my blood boil. Back when I was an overconfident, pimply-faced teenager, I joined the Rangers and swore to protect the Constitution from all enemies, foreign and domestic. That commitment still anchors my soul. My outrage nearly caused me to miss the conspirators' after-thought scheme to kill my boss, Pia Sabel.

I could hardly do anything about it since I was eavesdropping on them through a hidden mic I'd planted in the billionaire's library.

I'd been walking my puppy in Central Park on a beautiful summer day while live-streaming the conspirators' chat over my Bluetooth earbud. We'd had a tip that the refinery king, Chuck Roche, was plotting something. Roche had been conniving with his personal goon, the hastily-retired FBI man, David Watson when President Veronica Hunter unexpectedly joined them.

The bug was totally illegal to begin with—but eavesdropping on the POTUS could earn me an extra-death-penalty. I checked my surroundings for Secret Service agents tracking me down.

A second later, those were the least of my problems.

Mercury, winged messenger of the Roman gods—my friend and personal deity—snapped his fingers in front of my nose. *Yo dude, you see what I see?*

Walking toward me were two mothers with baby strollers, side by side. Their mouths were wide open in horror, their eyes focused on something behind me.

I spun around.

Kasey Earl, an old nemesis from my Ranger days, charged me brandishing an eight-inch knife.

Mercury grinned. *You got this, right?*

Yeah. Yeah. Yeah.

OK. I know what you're thinking: *Mercury? You should go back on your meds, pal. Everyone knows it's all Jesus versus Allah these days with the smart money on the Prince of Peace because of His advantage in nuclear warheads.*

I get that a lot. My first Army-issued psychologist told me Mercury was a manifestation of my PTSD-induced schizophrenia. What did he know? The soldiers who lived and fought and died beside me knew that Mercury's divine guidance made me the beast of the battlefield. Under his celestial direction, I rampaged through Afghanistan and Iraq and several other places that I'm not allowed to discuss until 2058. But the Army, in all its infinite glory and wisdom, put me on meds. My life went downhill fast. A godless life is no good at all. Besides, he's the only god who talks to me. Just because he's been living on the kindness of strangers for fifteen hundred years is no reason to make fun. He's not much, but he's mine. Before you get all high and mighty, where's yours, huh? Does your savior appear before your very eyes complete with period costume?

Yeah. What I thought.

So. Are we over it?

About the Author

His near-death experiences range from talking a jealous husband into putting the gun down to spinning out on an icy freeway in heavy traffic without touching anything. His resume ranges from washing dishes to global technology management. His personal life stretches from homeless at 17, adopting a 3-year-old at 19, getting married at 37, fathering his last child at 43, hiking the Grand Canyon Rim-to-Rim at 59, and taking the occasional nap.

His writing career ranges from humble beginnings with short stories in The Battered Suitcase, to being awarded a Medallion from the Book Readers Appreciation Group. Seeley is best known for his Sabel Security series of thrillers featuring athlete and heiress Pia Sabel and her bodyguard, unhinged veteran Jacob Stearne. One of them kicks ass and the other talks to the wrong god.

His love of creativity began at an early age, growing up at Frank Lloyd Wright's School of Architecture in Arizona and Wisconsin. He carried his imagination first into a successful career in sales and marketing, and then to his real love: fiction.

For more books featuring Pia Sabel and Jacob Stearne, visit SeeleyJames.com

Contact Seeley James:

Email: Seeley@seeleyjames.com
Website: SeeleyJames.com
Facebook: SeeleyJamesAuth
BookBub: Seeley James

Made in the USA
San Bernardino, CA
21 November 2017